I0738748

Enclave

Written by Brandon Blake Varnell
Edited by Dominique Goodall
Illustrated by Lawrence Mann

Enclave – The Executioner Series
Copyright © 2018 Brandon Varnell
Illustration Copyright © 2018 Lawrence Mann

To see Brandon Varnell's other works, or to ask for permission to use his works, visit him at www.varnell-brandon.com, facebook at www.facebook.com/AmericanKitsune, twitter at www.twitter.com/BrandonbVarnell, https://www.patreon.com/BrandonVarnell, and instagram at www.instagram.com/brandonbvarnell.

ISBN: 978-0-9989942-9-1 (paperback)
ISBN: 978-0-9989942-8-4 (ebook)

CONTENT

Chapter 1

Tristin jerked awake as the rattling of chains reverberated around the room. His head shooting up, he surveyed the room with weary eyes, half-lidded and blinking. When he found nothing near him, he let out a deep breath and brought his hands to his face, rubbing his eyes.

God, he was tired. Tired and hungry. Tired and hungry and anxious and sex depraved. Not a good combination. What did he do to deserve this? Oh, right. He'd betrayed the Catholic Church on Samantha's orders and discovered something he really shouldn't have. In hindsight, that probably hadn't been the best idea ever conceived. However, the thought of going up against the Church, and possibly reuniting with his best friend, or at least keeping him alive, had overridden all of his common sense.

Which was funny, because Christian and Samantha always told Tristin that he didn't have much common sense to begin with.

Gotta keep what he had left, then, right?

Pulling his hands from his face, Tristin tried to ignore his surroundings. He tried to pretend he wasn't sitting in a dank, dark cell that had the sickly-sweet smell of rotting corpses. He tried to ignore the cold, hard stone floor with its several layers of grime beneath him. He tried to ignore the bars to his left that kept him from leaving the tiny, ten square foot space. He'd seen it all before, and he'd had more than enough of this gloomy place to last a lifetime.

Tristin could still remember what happened after the Church had taken him into custody. During the ride to this lovely cell, they had beaten him, bruising his face and battering his ribs. He hurt everywhere. There wasn't a single part of his body that wasn't in pain. The only consolation, if it could be called that, was that they had not broken any of his bones.

Not that it mattered anyway. Broken bones or not, he wasn't going anywhere.

How long had he been in this jail cell anyway? Days? Weeks? He'd lost count after the first few minutes. Ugh, he wished he had his computer. Then he would have been able to tell the time and how many days had passed easily. Damn those fanatics! Couldn't they have at least let him keep his Apad? Jerks.

A loud rumbling caused Tristin to look up again. Some dust shook from ceiling, landing on his head and causing him to cough as he inhaled a lungful of the crap. As he hacked and coughed, several louder noises echoed down to him, and while Tristin could not be sure, he had the distinct feeling those noises sounded a lot like explosions. Explosions and gunfire.

The noises got much closer. Tristin was soon able to pick out individual sounds. Gunfire. Shouting. Explosions. The sound of weapons clanging, steel on steel. There were many different sounds intermixed together to create a cacophonous symphony of violence. A threnody of voices soon went up. The shouting and sounds of battle came closer. Tristin almost thought he recognized one of the people barking out what sounded like orders, but it was impossible to tell within that dissonance of chaotic pandemonium.

Another explosion occurred, this one actually blowing up the door that led into the prison. Tristin had a front row seat as he watched the metal door get blow right off its hinges and blasted into the room. It tumbled along the floor, banging and clanging and booming against the stone, a piece of warped metal crashing against the ground repeatedly. It didn't stop until it struck the far wall, slamming against it with enough noise that Tristin was sure every two-bit guard and their mother had heard it.

Booted feet echoed unusually loudly against the backdrop of explosions, yells, and cries of pain. They walked, a slow, steady gait, getting louder and louder with each tap. Those boots. They definitely belonged to a woman. Tristin could tell. The "click" of sharp heels tapping the stone followed by the lighter "thud" of a sole hitting the floor gave it away.

Getting to his feet, Tristin stumbled over to the bars, whereupon reaching them, he grasped them to keep himself from falling over. His legs shook from a lack of proper sleep and nutrition. He was hungry and tired and hurt. Just keeping himself upright was a chore.

It was just as he reached the bars that he saw her enter the room.

Long, raven hair with curled tips whipped this way and that as she strode into the room. Intelligent blue eyes pierced the darkness, while small, thin lips were set into a stern frown filled with determination. Crisp blue pants ruffled only slightly with each step she took, with each sway of her hips. A light blue cape was set over her shoulders, rustling as she swung her arms forward in light motions. The dark blue, long sleeved shirt underneath, held together with several straps, looked as pristine as ever, as if this woman had not just fought her way into this prison. Her heeled boots clicked and clacked as she strode toward his prison cell with confidence.

"Samantha?" Tristin looked at the woman, his jaw nearly dropping to the floor. He managed to pick it up, albeit, it took a while. After the surprise wore off, however, he gave the woman a rather boyish grin. "Well, hello there, boss lady! It's a pleasure to see you. May I ask why you've come? What can this humble prisoner do for you?"

He would never say this but seeing the commander for the Executioners of the entire western hemisphere gave him strength.

"This isn't the time for sarcasm." Samantha's voice was harder than steel as she stopped in front of his cell. She flicked the sword in her left hand, cleansing it of blood by sending the crimson liquid spraying across the floor. She then re-sheathed the sword, her right hand resting on the hilt, her left hand going to the sheath on her belt. "If you do not want to be sliced in half, I suggest you move away from the bars."

Not needing to be told twice, Tristin scrambled out of the way. He moved far enough that he wouldn't get caught up in whatever Samantha was going to do, but close that he could see everything she did clearly. This was, after all, a once in a lifetime opportunity. How many people could say they got to see this woman in action?

A deep breath was taken as Samantha slid into a sword stance that Tristin had only heard about from Christian—on the rare occasion Christian was in a talkative mood. She was leading with her left foot, which had bent at a forty-five-degree angle. She shifted her right leg behind her, also bent, but not as much. There was a second's pause, a building of incredible tension, before, without even a hint of warning, the blade was no longer in its sheath but instead being held hyper extended and above Samantha's head at a diagonal angle with the blade pointed at the ceiling. The blade was then brought back down in a single, smooth, controlled motion, and re-sheathed. A soft click echoed around them as the metal of the blade met the material of the sheath. A second later, the bars that had once held Tristin inside of his cell fell apart, sliced diagonally across.

So that was iaido? The art of drawing the blade. Christian had told him about it once before. He was not a practitioner, as his swords were sheathed across his back instead of his hip, and he used two, but he'd told Tristin about how it was supposedly one of the deadliest sword styles in the world. He had said that a master of iaido could kill someone before they even realized someone had drawn a sword against them. Tristin hadn't believed his friend back then, had played it off as a joke.

He believed now.

And he only had one thing to say about it.

"Holy shit, that was awesome."

"Thank you."

Smack!

"Owch!" Tristin rubbed what was going to be a nasty bump tomorrow morning, wincing. "What was that for?"

"For swearing," Samantha answered in a mild voice, as if she had not just smacked Tristin on the head with the hilt of her sword. "Do so in my presence again and I'll hit you much harder next time."

"Ah, ahahaha!" Tristin rubbed the back of his head, a feeling of nervous tension settling over him like a thick, smothering blanket. Samantha was rescuing him, so he really didn't want to be on her bad side right now. "Erm, right. I gotcha. No more swearing."

"Good. Now take this and follow me."

Tristin fumbled and very nearly dropped the gun that Samantha threw at him. It was a standard Smith & Wesson 9mm pistol. The M&P model. All Executioner members of the Intelligence Division had one.

"Uh." Tristin stared at the weapon, and then looked up to find that Samantha was already walking away from him. He ran out of the room, stumbling a bit as his legs buckled. Catching up to the woman, he said, "Why are you giving this to me? You know I've never been that good with guns."

"I am perfectly aware that you are a horrible shot," Samantha said without a hint of compassion or understanding. Ouch. "But we are in enemy territory, and you're going to need something to protect yourself with, just in case myself and the others cannot protect you."

"Oh. Yes, I guess that makes sense." He looked at the gun for a moment, then undid the safety. Tristin could only pray he wouldn't have to use it. He didn't want to shoot off his own foot, or Samantha's. That would be really bad. "So, if you're rescuing me, I'm guessing you got my USB and managed to read the files I had compiled?"

"Yes." Samantha scowled. She was, quite obviously, not happy at the mention of the USB that he'd hidden just before being taken into custody. Not that Tristin blamed her. The information contained in those files could flip the entire world on its head, and it had very likely pulled the metaphorical rug out from underneath her feet. Not a pleasant experience. "We will talk about that later. For now, I need you to keep up."

Puffing a bit, out of breath, Tristin tried to keep pace with Samantha as her long strides carried her out of the prison and up a set of stairs. He made a quick vow to himself that after this was all over, he would start exercising to get back in shape—at least, until he could start using his unique abilities without fear of reprisal. Fortunately for him, it looked like that might be happening sooner rather than later.

"You mentioned... there are others," Tristin said as they entered a pristine hallway made of white tiles and stone walls. The explosions and gunfire were getting louder now, and Tristin thought he heard laughter.

"Of course. You didn't think I'd come all this way to rescue you alone, did you?"

"Um, well, no, I guess not."

"I have got two others with me."

"Just two?"

"These two are more than enough for a small vanguard of minor demons."

Tristin would have asked what Samantha meant, but he soon found out when they entered a large entrance hall. The once beautiful and clean room was now desecrated with pock marks, scorch marks, cracked marble tiles, and corpses. Some of the corpses looked like Wolverine had gone to town on them, but there were also quite a few that had been squashed flat, or had their heads crushed. Several of the Corinthian columns, once proud monoliths standing in neat rows, had been reduced to rubble, nothing more than large piles of granite.

In the center of this room were two people fighting off nearly a dozen of these strange figures with long, black jackets. The figures were lanky. Their skin, what could be seen of it, was a blistering red. What's more, glowing red eyes, clearly demonic in nature, glared out from underneath a hood that covered their heads.

One of the people fighting against this small horde was a tall man. Built like a brick shit house, the guy was a monster. He had muscles on his muscles. They bulged and flexed, veins popping up all along his arms as he swung an equally ginormous warhammer around like it was made of papier mache. His sleeveless, skin tight white shirt stretched to the point of breaking as he smashed his hammer down on one of the guards trying to shoot at him, crushing the demonic warrior like a grape and sending splatters of blood, bone, and brain matter flying everywhere. The man laughed a joyful, child-like laugh filled with a lust for battle.

As a point of contrast, the other figure combating the demonic warriors in cloaks was not large at all. In fact, she was quite tiny.

Standing no more than maybe four feet ten, the other figure was lithe and graceful, weaving between demonic warriors and slicing them apart with her obsidian-colored Orichalcum claws. The bottom of her pure white duster flapped about her legs as she danced across the battlefield, while the upper half was drawn taught across her bust, held together by a zipper and adorned with several straps that were fastened so tightly they squashed her breasts. Unlike Samantha, this girl wore boots with steel-toes instead of heels.

"Come on, you fools!" The man, his warhammer twirling in his gargantuan hands, growled as he swung the weapon horizontally, smacking several enemies and sending them crashing into a wall a good few yards away. "Is this all you are capable of?! Have the demonic armies of the Underworld truly grown so complacent!? Give me a challenge!"

Several demonic warriors tried to fire at him with automatic rifles, but the man blocked the projectiles from hitting him by hiding behind his ridiculously oversized warhammer. When the hailstorm of bullets ended, the hammer was swung up from its place on the ground, crashing into the chin of one enemy and tearing its head clean off. The giant of a man then spun around, his left fist catching another demon warrior in the temple and sending them to the ground, their neck twisted at an awkward angle.

Darting around the giant man, taking out the enemies that he missed, the lithe figure in the duster spun about with the grace of a dancer. Her short, boyish brown hair fluttered as she twisted her body a full 360 degrees. Extending her left hand, she let the four long claws of her gauntlet tear apart the face of one enemy that got too close for their own good.

Blood sprayed from the four lines that ran from the left side of their face all the way to the right, deep furrows that had gone halfway through the demon's skull. The attack had cut apart the hood. This allowed everyone to see the red skinned face of their opponent, an almost stereotypical-looking demon with horns, eyes that were all white, and fangs jutting from the mouth. The attack had also slashed open the demon warrior's eyes, causing them to burst like overripe fruit when they were shot by a pistol.

She swung her other hand and sliced apart a steel knife that had been set to stab her. Finishing her spin, she pulled her left hand back in, which she thrust forward at impressive speeds—for a human. Four sharp claws penetrated the warrior's chest. Then, in an incredible display of acrobatics, the woman flipped onto the figure's shoulders, her claws pulling out of the now gushing chest wound. She locked her feet against the demon's head and, with a sharp twist, snapped the neck. The warrior was sent face first to the ground while the woman flipped off the dead creature's shoulders and landed back on her feet.

Darting forward, Samantha was quick to join the fray, and, for the first time since joining the Executioners, Tristin got to see why Christian admired the woman so much. She moved with the speed, grace, and power of a jungle predator. Her sword flashed out of its sheath at light speeds, creating nearly a hundred blinding flashes of silver, an untraceable number of cuts, and then went back into its sheath. The demons surrounding her comrades fell apart into segmented pieces of bleeding flesh.

It was damn impressive. Not to mention scary.

Tristin was not a fighter. He'd said it plenty of times before, and it really was true. He was terrible at combat. He had a few skills that could allow him to fight back, but at the moment, he was not able to use them. A lack of sex would do that to a guy like him. He just didn't have any energy left to use his skills.

So he stood there, looking like an idiot, watching as the three demolished what was left of the demonic horde guarding him, the 9mm pistol held loosely in his hand.

When the trio of fighters were done, the Goliath of the group clicked his tongue in discontent. "Well, that was boring. I was expecting a bit more of a challenge."

"You cannot expect every group of demons we run across to be strong, Leon," the woman said in a light, almost airy tone of voice, sounding just a tad dry. "You also have to remember that it is unlikely they expected anyone to find this place. This location is rather off the map. I doubt they would send anyone stronger than minor demons to guard a single individual."

Leon laughed, his shaggy lion's mane of hair shaking. "I guess." The large man then turned to look at Tristin, squinting his light green eyes at the much smaller figure. "So, this is the person we've come for? Kind of a shrimp, ain't he?"

Tristin bristled a bit, but instead of responding like he was annoyed, he gave the man a massive smile. "That's an awfully mean thing to say. I prefer the term gracefully lithe myself. It sounds so much more pleasing to the ear, don't you think?"

"Ha ha!" The man's booming laugh reverberated around the room, making Tristin's body rumble. "You've got spunk! I think I like you!"

"You don't know how pleased I am to hear that," Tristin said in a voice laden with sarcasm. He then looked at the much larger, towering figure with an inquiring gaze. "So, you're Leon Tréan? The fifth member of The XIII and the one called Lionheart."

"That's right." The man grinned, bright white teeth gleaming in the light of the room. Tristin could swear he saw the man's teeth actually sparkles. What the hell kind of toothpaste did this man brush with to make them shine like that? "I'm pleased to see that my reputation precedes me. Hahaha! It's good to be well-known."

While the man laughed, Tristin looked at the other figure, the female with the claws. Now that he was getting a better look at her, he had to say that she was definitely his type. Granted, he didn't really have a type. If someone was hot and female, he was more than willing to bed them, but that was exactly why this girl was his type. She was hot, and she was female. Sure, she might be a little on the short side, but she had the most awesome legs he'd ever seen on a woman. They were the kind of muscular legs found mainly on gymnasts and female martial artists. She had legs like fucking Chun Li. Her eyes were bright sapphires, though they lacked much in the way of emotions. Not that he cared. Her eyes might be twin pools of emotionless epicenters, but her face was gorgeous, soft and feminine, with delicate cheeks, luscious lips, and a rounded chin with a cute little cleft.

He wondered if he could seduce her to his bed. She could probably give him a lot of vitality.

"If you keep staring at me, I am going to stab you."

And she apparently didn't like people staring at her.

"Sorry," Tristin said, not quite staring anymore but still glancing her way. "I was just wondering how long it would take to get you into bed with me."

While Leon laughed like a loon, the scowling young woman turned her head to look at Samantha. "You did not tell me that the person we were rescuing was such a lecherous man."

"Because I knew you would not help me rescue him if I told you," Samantha said, her voice even. She ignored the way the other woman glared at her. "Tristin is the best intelligence operative I have. It was he who discovered the insidious nature of the new Pope and Bishop Vertrou."

The woman, unable to say anything, looked away from the raven-haired commander. Tristin found that amusing, even as he finally managed to identify who this woman was. "You're Sif, aren't you? The one called the Destroyer of Men."

Sif didn't answer him, simply choosing to glare at him instead. Tristin scratched at the back of his neck. He could totally see why this woman was called that now. It seemed her absolute hatred of all things male and perversion rang true. Like Leon, she was also a member of the XIII, the Seventh, if he was not mistaken.

"You know, if you keep glaring at me, you're going to get wrinkles all over that beautiful face," Tristin commented, matching the woman's glare with an obnoxiously bright smile. If this woman thought he would back down because of her glare, then she had another thing coming. He messed with Christian for shits and giggles, and screwing with that man was like poking a sleeping dragon.

Sif just glared harder.

"Hahaha! He makes a good point, Sif. You should stop glaring so much and start smiling a little more."

Sif shifted her glare from Tristin to Leon.

"We don't have time for this," Samantha declared. "We need to leave before the Church realizes what's happened here. Come on, you three."

"Yes, ma'am!" Leon said, his massive, booted feet rumbling as he began to move, following Samantha as she marched from the room. Sif tossed one last glare at Tristin before she, too, stalked forward in the raven-haired woman's wake.

Tristin took one last look around the room, sighed, and then hurried to catch up with them.

"I really hope the next place I'm taken too is a big city. City girls are so easy, and I could really use a good, hard fucking."

***

Christian woke up on something soft. As he stirred back to the land of the living, that was the first thing he noticed. The object underneath him, a bed, he guessed, was like heaven against his back. It managed to somehow conform to his body, like a mold almost, but far softer. Several other soft things rested under his head. Pillows, most likely. There must have been a lot of them, or maybe just one really large, really fluffy pillow. He imagined this must be what it would feel like to lay on a cloud—if clouds had solid mass and weren't just gathered precipitation.

After a while, Christian's mind started to finally become a little more coherent, allowing him to think about something other than cloud pillows and how nice the bed felt. He noticed that his body was warm. There was a thick blanket of some kind covering him.

Questions popped into his mind. Where was he? How had he gotten there? What happened to Asmodeus? Was Catherine still alive? And what about Lilith?

Lilith...

Recalling the name of the young woman he'd fallen for, Christian opened his eyes. He needed to find Lilith, to find out if she was alright. But before that, he needed to know where he was.

You can't start looking for someone if you have no idea where you are yourself.

Everything was blurry when he first opened his eyes. It was all just an indistinct mass of color. He blinked once, then again, his eyes adjusting, his vision sharpening, regaining focus, allowing him to see what was in front of him. A ceiling. At least, he suspected it was ceiling. It looked different from every other ceiling he had ever come across.

Much of the ceiling was made of varnished planks of wood and granite—all except one spot directly over the bed, which was a tiny square of space that was made of glass. The crystal-clear material allowed plenty of what he assumed was natural sunlight to filter in through the room. It was probably the sun shining in through the glass that generated the warmth he was feeling. That said, it was quite odd. While that space was made of glass, he couldn't see a sun or sky. It was just a uniform shade of yellow.

Wanting to know more about the room he found himself, Christian sat up. The covers, a thick, soft blanket, slid down his frame, the cool air of the room hitting his body and bringing goosebumps to his skin. He ignored the chill and scanned the room's interior, surveying everything with a keen eye.

Wooden walls made up most of the room. Only one wall was not made of wood but white plaster instead. There was a door located on the wall on the opposite side of the bed, which Christian assumed led to the outside. Another door was on his left. A restroom, maybe? Other amenities were arranged neatly around the room: a desk and a chair, a small coffee table made of lacquered wood, two dressers, a closet, and two potted plants near the door that added color to the room.

As he studied his unfamiliar surroundings, a slight shifting of the bed alerted him to the fact that he wasn't alone. Someone else was in the bed. Shock running rampant through his system, Christian looked to his left and down.

It was Lilith.

Relief washed through Christian, sweeping away the worry he'd been feeling in the back of his mind. Lilith was here, with him, safe. While there were a few more issues to deal with, the biggest one had been solved. He still had a lot of questions, such as how they had gotten to... wherever they were, who took him and Lilith to this place, what happened to Asmodeus, and where was Catherine, but at least he could now rest easy knowing that Lilith was safe.

He continued looking down at Lilith. The young woman was sleeping with him in the bed, lying on her back. Golden hair spread around her like a halo and shone with a brilliance and luster that made her feel like she was not of this world. Her chest rose and feel with each breath, which caused her two prominent twins to jiggle enticingly. Slightly parted lips whistled a soft melody as air passed through them. It was captivating and enchanting in ways that shouldn't have been possible.

Christian found himself mesmerized by Lilith's incomprehensible beauty, from the sway of her chest to the elegant splendor of her lovely hips that tapered off into a thin waist and her spectacular legs with their awe-inspiring flawlessness.

As he continued to stare down at the woman he'd fallen for, his eyes were invariably drawn to her lips. Shifting positions so that he was lying on his side, his left arm propping him up, Christian raised his right and reached over to Lilith's face. Calloused fingers trailed across unblemished skin, from her cheek up to her forehead. He touched a strand of golden thread before slowly tucking it behind her small ear. He then cupped her face and used his thumb to caress her delicate cheek.

While he continued his actions, his thoughts began to drift. He really should figure out where they were. Christian didn't even know how they got here, and that was a problem. What if they'd been taken hostage? Were they in danger? But then, if they were in danger, wouldn't they be tied up and in separate rooms? Why put them in a comfortable bed together? Why go through all this trouble?

After several seconds of vicious, circular thinking, Christian shook his head. The only people after him were the Catholic Church, and they had a kill on sight order for him. It couldn't be them. And he didn't know anyone else who was after him. Samantha? No. she'd been taken off the case. Say what you will about her, but Samantha wasn't the kind of woman to disobey direct orders no matter how much she disagreed with them.

"Christian?"

Startled by a soft voice that flowed through his ear with the soothing sound of a wind chime, Christian looked down to see Lilith, her eyes fluttering open. Bright, baby blue eyes stared at him from behind a half-lidded gaze. They moved about the room, slowly, before landing back on him.

"Christian," she said again, her voice a little firmer.

"Hey," he greeted. "I'm glad to see you're awake. How are you feeling?"

"I'll feel better after you give me a good morning kiss."

A blink was the only sign Christian gave that he'd heard her. One second passed, then another, before, finally, the young man shook his head, his raven hair swaying. "Somehow, I feel like I should have expected that response."

Lilith couldn't help but nod. "Yes. You should have." She then looked at him with an imploring gaze. "Kiss?"

Perhaps it was because of the way she phrased the question, or the tone in her voice, so childish and carefree despite their strange situation, but Christian couldn't help the laugh that escaped him. Lilith puffed up her cheeks, eyes narrowed ever so slightly at the sight of him laughing, but he spoke through his chuckles, saying, "Sorry. I didn't mean to laugh. I just couldn't help it for some reason."

Before Lilith could complain about his insensitivity, he leaned in and planted a small kiss on her lips. Lilith sighed into his mouth, content little noises escaping her parted lips. The kiss, soft and ephemeral, lasted no more than a few seconds. When they broke off, neither of them were very satisfied, but Christian knew they couldn't afford to let their actions become too passionate.

Now that she was awake, Lilith sat up in the bed to get a look around the room. The covers pooling about her waist to reveal a light pink, spaghetti strap shirt hugging her feminine figure. One of the straps slid down her shoulder. Lilith absently brought the strap back up, her brows furrowing as she took a gander at their new surroundings.

"Christian? Where are we?"

"I wish I knew," Christian said with a helpless shrug. Running a hand through his hair, he released a deep sigh. "I just woke up a while ago myself." He paused, considering something. "I might not know where we are, but I don't think we're in any danger. I have no clue how long we've been here, but the fact that we aren't bound or locked away in a cell tells me whoever brought us here means no harm."

"I wonder how we got here," Lilith spoke her thoughts out loud. She looked over at Christian, her eyes questioning, but he shook his head.

"Don't look at me. I have no clue either."

"What about that... that demon we fought?"

"You mean Asmodeus?" Lilith gave a nod. "I'm not sure." Pressing a hand to his face, Christian closed his eyes and tried to recall all he could about the battle against the Demon King of Lust. "I don't remember a whole lot. Asmodeus and I fought, I lost, but then something strange happened." While much of the battle was a blur, there were two things about it that stood out to Christian the most. The first was when Asmodeus had dropped him after he'd already been beaten. The second was the strange red dot on the demon's back. "I think I remember stabbing Asmodeus in the back, something powerful washing over me, and then nothing."

"So, to sum things up, we have no clue where we are, how we got here, who brought us here, or anything else," Lilith said.

"Pretty much."

Lilith didn't seem to know how to take that, so she kept talking. "What do you think we should do, then? I mean, we can't stay in this room forever."

"True enough." Christian slid out of the bed, bare feet touching incredibly soft carpet, the kind that must have cost a fortune. He wasn't wearing much, just a pair of black pajama pants and nothing else, but Lilith didn't seem to mind as she gazed at his broad back and shoulders. "I suppose we could just go out and do some surveillance or something, provided the door isn't locked. Since no one's come to get us and it doesn't look like we're prisoners, I think it'll be alright if we leave the room."

He turned to her and extended his hands. Lilith took them, allowing him to pull her out of the bed. Her little toes flexed as they touched the velvety floor.

"You sure this is a good idea?" asked Lilith. She didn't look very convinced. "Just because it doesn't look like we're prisoners doesn't mean whoever brought us here will appreciate us wandering around their place."

"It's not like we have much of a choice, though," Christian said. "I mean, I suppose we could stay in here, but who knows how long it'll be before whoever lives here comes to check up on us. We also don't know who brought us here to begin with, and then there's Catherine to consider. She was with us when we fought Asmodeus. She's given us a lot of help in the past, so I want to find out what happened to her."

"I guess you're right." Lilith worried her lower lip. "I had completely forgotten about Catherine, but now that you've mentioned her, I am a little worried. She had been pretty badly injured when our car was tossed around by that explosion."

"Right, so we should find her as quickly as possible. After that, we can find out where we are and who brought us here."

Their decision made, Christian and Lilith took a quick moment to look around them room for their clothes. They didn't find them, each guessing that their clothing had been ruined by the battle, but they did find a pair of sandals to put on. After slipping the footwear onto their feet, they went toward the door. It was unlocked, which both did and didn't surprise the two. It showed a complete lack of security, but it also supported their belief that whoever owned this place wasn't keeping them as prisoners.

Upon exiting the room, the two found themselves standing in a long hallway. The soft carpet had gone from a light, off-white color to a deep amethyst. The walls, made from varnished wood, had several pieces of artwork hanging off them as decoration. Most of them were landscapes, a prairie with waist high grass and a clear blue sky, a savanna featuring a large tree in the center surrounded by a pride of lions, a cityscape set ablaze by a beautiful sunset. Each painting was beautifully done. Someone must have put in a lot of effort to paint those landscapes.

Lacing his fingers with Lilith's more delicate digits, Christian began walking down the hall. He had no clue where they were going, but if they wanted to get even a basic feel for the place, it probably didn't matter where they went. They had to start somewhere.

As they padded along the hall, the pair saw that there were several doors in this hall. All of them were on the same side as the door they had just come out of. Several of the doors were locked, but the few that weren't revealed fully furnished bedrooms that looked almost identical to their own.

"I wonder," Lilith murmured with a contemplative expression as she gestured at the doors. "Do you think this is some kind of hotel or something? It sort of looks like one. A long hallway filled with doors. Identical bedrooms. Maybe this is some kind inn and the person who owns it is the one who brought us here?"

"It's possible," Christian began, "But I don't think so. While most of the rooms are nearly identical, there are several differences. I noticed a few personalized touches to each room, posters, televisions and the like. Some of them look like they've been lived in for a long time."

"A dorm room, then?" Lilith theorized.

"Also possible, and more likely than a hotel or an inn." Christian frowned as he looked at the wall with the paintings. They were passing one called "Descendancy." In it, there were dozens of statuesque women, all tall and possessing a dignified bearing, and all containing a regal beauty that reminded Christian of a queen. "It might also be some kind of boarding house, though how we could possibly end up in such a place is beyond me."

That was the real mystery. It was clear to them both that someone had taken them from the sight of the battle, healed their wounds, and brought them here. But who had done so? And why? Not knowing the answer to these questions was truly beginning to bother Christian, even more so than usual.

By this point in time, his danger senses should have been blaring warnings at him left and right. He was in an unknown place and had been brought there by an unknown person. They had also clearly stripped both him and Lilith, which disturbed him greatly, more than he was willing to admit. And yet, despite the fact that he literally knew nothing about their current circumstances, he'd not felt so much as a blip of warning from his normally sharp instincts.

Was something dulling his senses? Maybe. He couldn't say for sure, though one part of him hoped that was the case as much as the other part of him didn't.

The hallway, which up until this point seemed to go on forever, finally came to an end. Situated before them stood a very large, very ornate looking double door with golden handles. Christian and Lilith stared at the extravagant door with its artistic rose motifs painted in silver and gold. In the center of the door, surrounded by more silver and gold rose motifs, was the image of a beautiful woman with long legs, slender shoulders, and a perfect hourglass figure. She was naked, her breast visible for all to see, as well as her crotch. Behind her were a pair of large, reptilian wings.

They looked at each other.

"I don't think this is a boarding house," Lilith said at last.

"It could be, you know. Maybe these people are religious fanatics who worship women with... with wings."

"Maybe," the way she said that made it clear to Christian that she did not believe his words. "I guess there's really only one way to find out."

Their decision made, the two stepped up to the door and pushed it open.

On the other side of the doorway was a massive bathhouse. Built in a style of architecture that was reminiscent of the buildings found in Greece, the bathhouse had several dozen large, Corinthian columns, six across the width and twelve going down the length on either side. The floors used a more modern tile, tiny squares with rounded edges that were beige in color. In the center of the bathhouse was a gigantic pool that took up at least ninety percent of the available space.

Steam rose from the water's surface. White, wispy, cloud-like moats that swirled about the air, forming lazy patterns that took no shape but were constantly shifting into different forms. The water was obviously heated. It was also recycled. Situated in six different locations—one in the center of the wall with the door, another on the opposite side, and two more on the walls that ran lengthwise to make a total of four—were several waterfalls. There was a shallow canal that went underneath a small bridge and let water flow out of the pool. Christian could only assume the water went out through the canal, was recycled somehow, and then came back out through the waterfalls.

Situated in and around this pool were a bunch of women. Some were inside the pool itself, lounging around or splashing water at each other in playful fun. Others were sitting on the edge with just their feet in the water, and still others were standing off to the side in small groups. Each woman was just as gorgeous as the one before them, each possessing the same inhuman perfection found in Lilith.

Each one of them was also very, *very* naked.

And every single one of those women had stopped what they were doing and were now staring at him.

Under the gaze of so many women, all of whom were gawking with wide-eyed, open-mouthed surprise, Christian very nearly found himself paralyzed. He was so shocked and numb to everything except the stares that he didn't even feel it when Lilith tightened her grip on his hand.

"Um." he tried to think of something, anything, to say. "Y-yo. Sorry for, um, intruding?"

Christian winced.

Truly, his oratory skills could use some work.

Chapter 2

In a darkened chamber with very little in the way of light, seven figures sat around a table.

"So, Asmodeus has been defeated, eh?"

"It would appear so."

"What's more, the Executioners managed to break the incubus out of prison."

"It seems we did not put enough guards over the penitentiary."

"Understatement of the millennia. I heard the people who broke in and rescued the incubus were members of the XIII."

"And how do you know that? All of the demons we had guarding the penitentiary were killed."

Bishop Vertrou sat at the table, listening as the others discussed the recent string of failures. There had been a lot of troubles happening on his side of the world. The failure to kill Samantha Gale, the disappearance of Christian Crux and his little succubus, not to mention the death of Asmodeus. It was bad enough that the Executioner commander in charge of the western hemisphere of the USA had managed to escape death, but for one of the Seven Demon Kings to have their soul severed from this world was a disaster.

And then there was Christian Crux. The very idea of that man having escaped death caused Vertrou to feel a deep, burning anger within him. How he despised that boy, that stupid child with his high moral fibers despite his origins. He wanted nothing more than to kill that fraud with his own hands, to watch as the life faded from his eyes.

Taking a calming breath, he studied his surroundings. The room was dark, almost pitch black. There was just the barest trace of light coming in from several blue lines that ran along the wall and ceiling like veins. And yet, even with that small trace of luminescence, Vertrou still couldn't see anything, nothing but the black silhouettes of those who were in charge of the Catholic Church—the ones who ruled from the shadows.

"What of the Quatra?"

"You mean the killer of Abaddon? He is still missing, or so I hear."

"According to the reports, he and the succubus went missing in Las Vegas, Nevada, after defeating Asmodeus in combat."

"What of the humans who saw the battle?"

"There is no need to worry about them. Mephisto is controlling what the media hears and has taken care to silence those who saw the battle between the Quatra and Asmodeus."

"I still find it hard to believe that a mere human could defeat one of us."

"Asmodeus likely underestimated him. You know how he loves to play with his food."

"That, or he was distracted by the succubus. It's well-known that Asmodeus tends to let his lust get the better of him."

Bishop Vertrou nearly clicked his tongue at the mention of Asmodeus's insatiable lust, remembering the number of times he had been forced to cover for the demon king when the urge struck him. How many times had he entered Asmodeus's room to discover the place littered with the naked corpses of those he had bedded? It must have been in the hundreds by now.

He was glad Asmodeus was gone. Now he wouldn't have to cover up the numerous crimes that demon committed.

"Bishop Vetrtou," a deep, dark, and rumbling bass voice spoke his name, startling the bishop from his reverie.

"Yes, my lord?"

"Do we know where the former Executioner known as Christian Crux has disappeared to?"

"Our hordes are still searching," the bishop admitted with just a bit of reluctance. His master was not known for his kindness. Reporting failure could easily result in his death. "However, we have heard rumors that he and the succubus were last seen being driven off in an ambulance. According to the reports, the person driving it was a very beautiful woman with olive skin and dark hair. Another succubus, I'd wager."

"So, another one of those wretched women has put a damper on our plans. I want you to find this woman, Bishop. Find this woman, kill her, and bring Christian and his little whore to me."

Bishop Vertrou nodded his head at the darkened figure of his master. "It will be as you command, my lord."

"Remember, we cannot have the one who carries the title Quatra know of his origins. He is the most dangerous enemy we have right now."

"What of the Executioners?" asked Vertrou.

"The Executioners are irrelevant. Mere ants who scurry underneath those whose powers they cannot begin to comprehend. They are to be ignored unless they decide to reveal themselves. However, should they choose to reveal themselves, crush them."

Bishop Vertrou wasn't sure he agreed about the Executioners not being a threat, but he didn't voice his opinions, not wanting to find himself prematurely killed for disagreeing.

"Of course, my lord," he said, bowing his head to the dark silhouette.

***

Lilith turned to look at Christian, an expression that was both amused and perturbed, probably due to the situation. "Yo? Really, Christian? You're standing in a bathhouse filled with naked women, and that's the first thing you say?"

Christian had the decency to look sheepish. "It was the only thing I could think of to say."

The twitching of Lilith's lips showed that she was trying to hide a smile, while a small vein pulsed on her forehead, denoting her irritation. She didn't know what to feel. Amused by the first words that came out of Christian's mouth since entering this room, angry that there were a bunch of naked women for him to potentially stare at, or perturbed, because she had no idea why there were a bunch of naked women all congregating together in the first place. Was this some kind of women's bathing convention or something? And how come she and Christian were in the same area as them if that was the case?

Lilith looked out at the sea of feminine flesh. There was a lot of it. Just by counting heads, she could see that there were at least over four dozen women in this room. Most of them were lounging in the pool, sitting on the staircase that led into it, leaning back, their chests thrust forward in an unconscious show of their bountiful assets. There were more in the center of the pool, younger women who looked to be in their teens. They were playing with a beach ball, tossing it back and forth, or they had been. Now they were staring at Christian in undisguised curiosity and maybe an odd hint of apprehension.

Huh. Looking at them now, the younger ones' sort of reminded Lilith of how she used to be, only not quite as fearful of men as she had been. That was... weird.

There were more women, too. A good deal were simply standing around by the columns, forming groups. They looked like they had been discussing something, though Lilith would likely never know what they had been talking about. They weren't conversing now, that was for sure.

One thing Lilith noticed about the women lounging in what had to be some kind of massive, communal bathhouse was that all of them were exceedingly beautiful. Not just beautiful. Stunning. There wasn't a single female in the entire group that could be considered even just mildly attractive. All of them, regardless of their height, their skin color, their eye color, the size of their breasts and hips and waists, were resplendent and otherworldly. Perfect. That was what they were. Perfect in every way possible.

Having learned about her own origins, Lilith knew.

There was no way these girls could be human.

They were succubus.

The prolonged sense of tension, thicker than even the foggiest day in Los Angeles, that had descended upon the room was finally broken when a young woman walked over to them. Her olive skin shone and glistened in the dim light. Perspiration clung to her skin as she walked forward with slow, sensual movements that drew the eyes to her amazing legs and hips. Bare feet padded lightly along the stone surface, barely making a noise, other than the soft "pitter patter" that could just barely be heard above the sounds of rushing water. With each step she took, her breasts swayed. Her looks, this sensual grace and elegance, this hypnotic rhythm of motion, was enough to intoxicate any man.

It was a good thing, Lilith mused, that Christian was not any man.

"It's you!" He pointed at the woman, his eyes widening in surprise. "You were the one who took our order at that Mexican restaurant!"

The woman paused, her eyes turning to look at him.

Lilith, upon hearing this, gave the woman a more scrutinizing look. "You're right," she said, surprised. She then looked over at Christian, her eyes narrowed just slightly. "And just how long were you staring at her to be able to recognize her on sight?"

"You mean you couldn't?" Christian looked at her, his head tilted, the glimmer in his eyes visibly confused. "I mean, isn't it kind of hard *not* to recognize someone like her? She's pretty memorable."

"Why? Because she's pretty?"

"No, well, partly, but mostly because you don't see many people who look like her." Christian, still seemingly confused, looked out over the crowd of women, all of whom were still staring at him. "At least, you don't usually see women like her."

Lilith frowned at Christian, but before she could think of saying anything, the woman finally spoke up. "I am pleased to see you two are finally awake." Her voice was just as light and airy as it had been when she'd been taking their order at the Mexican restaurant. "We had not been expecting either of you to awaken for a long time. Your wounds were rather... extensive."

"Our wounds?" Lilith furrowed her brow for a moment.

"She's talking about the injuries we received during the battle," Christian said, keeping his narrowed eyes on the olive-skinned woman. "Right?"

"Indeed, the wounds you received during your battle with Asmodeus were substantial. Even with our comprehensive knowledge of the human body, healing your injuries was almost impossible. The most we could do was bandage you and cleanse your bodies in our springs."

"How badly were we injured?" asked Lilith. She did not remember how the fight against Asmodeus had ended. Actually, the last thing she remembered was seeing Christian get speared through the shoulder and lifted off the ground. Everything after that was blank, and no matter how much she tried to recall what happened, her mind continued coming up with nothing. It was frustrating, especially because she could almost swear the memories were there, hiding just a little beyond her perception.

"This is not the place to discuss something like that," the woman said. She then began walking over to a small side room, but she paused long enough to gesture them over to her. "Follow me. I shall do my best to explain what you wish to know."

The two shared a look, a silent conversation. As Lilith stared into Christian's eyes, she saw that he was thinking the exact same thoughts that she was. They didn't know this woman, and neither were sure they could trust her. At the same time, it seemed as if they didn't have much choice. There wasn't anyone else they could rely on right now, except maybe one of the other nude women in the room, which wasn't anymore appealing.

They followed her, doing their best to ignore the eyes on them. Christian, in particular, seemed to be getting the most stares, and Lilith felt a small stirring of anger at these women. Didn't they have anything better to do than stare at her man? The nerve of them.

The side door they went through led into a small changing room. White walls. White tiled floor. White ceiling. Aligned along one wall was a large rack made of wood. Within each of the small, square cubby holes was a hamper filled with clothes.

Walking up to one of them, the woman began to get dressed. She picked up her panties, a rather racy black thong and, after stepping through it, slid it up her long legs. She then grabbed a black dress. As she put it on, Lilith had to admit that it was a lovely gown, shimmering and sparkling as it moved, like thousands of stars had been imprinted into the dress and were designed to shine as the light hit them. She also saw that it was sleeveless, had a plunging V-neckline that showed off ample amounts of chest, and went down all the way to her feet.

Now that she was dressed, the woman gestured for them to follow her again. She led them back to the large bathhouse, and then out of the door they had first entered through to get there.

As they began walking back down the hall, the woman started talking. "Before I begin explaining what I can, allow me to at least introduce myself. My name is Clarissa Farland, and I am the current leader of this enclave."

"Enclave?"

Lilith and Christian both shared another look. Seeing this, Clarissa gave a small nod of affirmation.

"I am sure you're already coming to this conclusion, but this is a succubus enclave, one of the last remaining bastions of our kind." Clarissa turned her eyes toward Christian, narrowing them just a bit. "Your Catholic Church has done much to destroy my people. In the last thirty years, the number of succubus enclaves has gone from sixty-five to just five. Mine is one of the smaller ones."

"I wouldn't know anything about that," Christian told her. "Men are not usually assigned to take down succubi due to your allure. Lilith was the first one I've ever met."

"Yet it does not change the fact that you were, at one point, a member of the Executioners." Clarissa's voice was not harsh, but it held a reprimand in it, one that made Christian wince. "But we are not here to talk about that. The past cannot be changed, and all we can do now is continue to look forward and try to build a better future."

Lilith bristled a bit at the insult Clarissa tossed Christian's way. That had been completely uncalled for—Christian was no longer an Executioner, and she knew he was beginning to regret everything he'd done under their orders. She didn't say anything, though, as this was neither the time nor the place. She also didn't want to get on the bad side of the woman who had rescued them.

The walk became silent after that. The woman, Clarissa, didn't seem to mind this, almost like she was giving the two time to absorb what she'd said. By this point in time, the three of them had reached the end of the hall on the opposite side, which led to a T-junction. Clarissa went left, beckoning the two to follow her.

By this point in time, the area around them had changed. They had been led out to a sidewalk, allowing the two their first glimpse of where they were. The first thing either of them noticed was that they were in an enclosed space. The sky was invisible, hidden behind a massive wall of stone that stretched over head into an almost dome shaped ceiling. Craggy stalagmites and stalactites hung from the ceiling and jutted up from the ground, each one bigger than several humans combined—one even looked to be the size of a house. These giants, standing silent like mute colossi, glistened and shone as water ran down their surface. Several stalactites rose up from the surface of a giant lake in the center of the cavern, like claws grasping at the ceiling, trying to claw their way up from the retched waters that kept them submerged.

The waters were steaming. Wafts of heated moisture rose in the air like mist, creating lazy motes that gathered and swirled, coalescing into odd shapes and patterns that did not follow any known forms of geometry.

At least now they knew where all the hot water for the bathhouse was coming from.

The place they found themselves in looked almost like a city. There were buildings and sidewalks. The roads were made of stone and not pavement, but were easily recognizable for what they were. Just from where they were standing the two could see at least twenty buildings, square-shaped yet somehow elegant in their simplicity. They looked similar to boarding houses, made from a combination of wood and stone. There were no windows, probably because there was nothing to see.

Overhead, light poured down. Christian and Lilith both looked up to see the reason. Hundreds of thousands of crystals embedded into the dome shaped roof were refracting light that somehow managed to come down through gaps in the stone surface, creating a strange multitude of colors.

"In case you two are wondering, you are currently underneath Yellowstone Lake in Wyoming. This village you see before you is one that was built here as a safe house for young succubi long before humanity turned the wilderness above ground into a park for human amusement."

So they were no longer in Nevada, then. That was good. Actually, that was really good, as it meant that whoever might have tried to pursue them would be thrown off their trail. Perhaps they would even be safe in this place.

"Come." Clarissa motioned for the two again when she noticed they had stopped to admire the scenery. Christian and Lilith made to follow her some more, picking up the pace of their walk in order to catch up.

They moved along one of the many sidewalks. Their feet made dull thuds against the cement. There were a number of people walking about, all of them women, all of them exceedingly stunning. Everyone they passed stared at the trio like they were some kind of oddity. No. Lilith realized they were not staring at all three of them. Just Christian. They looked upon the young man in shock, and in some cases, fear.

"Impressive, is it not?"

Lilith looked up, startled. Clarissa was staring at her from the corner of her eye, a single brow raised in question. The young woman, her blond hair swaying slight, gave a slow nod.

"It is," she agreed. "I've never seen anything quite like it."

"This enclave is one of the most secure we have ever built." There was a definite note of pride in her voice. "My mother and several hundred other succubi built this place with their own hands. What you see before you is the result of two-hundred years of hard work and toil."

Now that was impressive, Lilith had to admit. She couldn't imagine how much effort must have been put into building this place. The cave itself was natural, she assumed, as she doubted anyone could have created it three centuries ago, not with the level of technology that had been at their disposal. But it was certainly possible they had built the buildings and the walkways. If the Egyptians could build those large, ridiculous looking triangles, then surely a group of succubi could build an underground safe house.

"You mentioned something about our injuries," Lilith pressed at some point during their walk, when it became clear that Christian was not going to say anything. The young man did not appear comfortable around Clarissa anymore, probably due to the woman's words earlier.

"I did," Clarissa said. "You two suffered greatly in your battle. Your mate lost a lot of blood, and several of his bones had been broken. The tendons in his left leg were severed, and there was a large hole in his shoulder." The woman turned to Lilith. "You had less wounds, and they were nowhere near as bad. Much of the damage you suffered was simply exhaustion. I imagine you wore yourself out by using your powers too much."

"My powers?" Lilith furrowed her brow. "What powers are you talking about?" As far as she was aware, she did not have any powers beyond her allure. Then again, the only reason she even knew that she was not human was because Christian had told her. It was back when they had just started to run, when they had boarded the train to leave Seal Beach.

Christian sadly wasn't as knowledgeable about succubus because they were supposedly outside his jurisdiction, but he knew enough. He'd told her that the reason men flocked to her, stared at her, and tried to commit despicable acts on her was because she was a succubus. All succubus had an Aura of Allure, which tempted men and made them lose the ability to think rationally.

Could there be more to being a succubus than what she had been told?

"Indeed." The woman looked at her in understanding. "Though you appear to not be aware of them. That is something I will have to rectify while you and your mate are here."

"Mate?" Christian brought a hand up to his face, rubbing his jaw, his eyes reflective and his face pensive. "I've heard several other people call me that."

"Mate is simply the term we give to those select few who have become the partner of a succubus," Clarissa told him. "Later on, I shall educate you on just what it means to be the mate of a succubus, as well as why it is so important, for both you and Lilith."

As Christian went silent, Lilith found herself growing curious.

"How do you know my name?" she asked, her voice a hushed whisper. She was sure that she had never given this woman her name, and she was equally sure that Christian had not spoken her name the one time they had bumped into Clarissa.

"Because I was there at your birth," Clarissa admitted.

Lilith nearly stumbled as she misstepped, tripping over her own two feet. Christian managed to catch her, thankfully, wrapping his arms around her waist and pulling her back up. She looked at the older succubus, her eyes wide and disbelieving.

"But... how could you know who I am just from that? I changed my name."

Her name had originally been Eve, but she had changed it to Lilith after Damien killed her foster mother.

"Hmph. Do you really think Eve was your original name?" asked Clarissa.

"Well, I..." The words made her pause. Eve wasn't her original name? How could that be? Shaking her head, Lilith decided to focus on a matter that was more pressing to her. "If you were there when I was born, does that mean you knew my mother?"

"I did." Clarissa paused in their walk for just a second, flashing Lilith a quick smile. "I was good friends with her, until we had a falling out." She paused, her lips turning downwards, her eyes glazing over in remembrance. After a second or two, she shook her head and continued speaking. "If you would like, I can tell you what I know about her later, perhaps after we have had a chance to discuss the recent developments that led you all here."

Lilith had to bite her tongue to keep from demanding to know more about her mother. She had never known her birth mother. While that had never really bothered her when she was younger, it did once she learned that she was a succubus. She had so many questions, about her mother, about the circumstances that led to her being abandoned. There was a lot that she wanted to know, that she needed to know.

She held her tongue, however, not only because there were more important things to discuss, but also because Clarissa had promised to tell her later. So long as this woman was willing to tell her about her mother at some point, then Lilith could find it within herself to wait a little while longer.

Patience is a virtue, or so it has been said.

She hated being patient.

Christian and Lilith were eventually led into another building, which turned out to be a large cafeteria. As their sandals clicked along the tiled floor, which was mostly one uniform gray color except for several large, reddish brown hexagonal shaped tiles that randomly dotted the floor, Lilith turned her head left and right, taking in the sights. It looked almost like a school cafeteria. There were upwards of two dozen round tables, each of which had a dozen padded chairs with curved backs. They were black, while the table tops were white. A number of square support pillars stood arrayed around the room, close to the walls. Over on the side opposite of where they entered was a combination of buffet and restaurant. There were several long, square tables with tin dishware filled with food, but there was also a place behind the buffet tables that looked like a kitchen.

The room was mostly empty. In fact, it pretty much *was* empty, save for one table where, surprisingly enough, a man was sitting down and inhaling the pile of food in front of him.

"Andrew," Clarissa called out as she walked closer to the man. The man stopped eating. As he looked up from his plate of food, Lilith could make out glowing yellow eyes peering out from underneath a fierce-looking mane of dark brown hair. He peered at the group, his eyes going from her to Christian to Clarissa. He then set the fork down, scooted his chair back, and turned to face them more fully. Lilith noticed immediately that he was missing his entire right arm up to the shoulder.

"I see they finally woke up."

"They did." Clarissa nodded as she walked over to him, her hips swaying with a sensual elegance that somehow managed to look completely casual, as if walking like that was as natural as breathing. And perhaps it was, Lilith realized. This woman as a succubus, and an old one, if her words were to be believed. "And I see you're using the time my girls are in the bath as an opportunity to eat as much as you can."

"Eh, what can I say?" The man shrugged. "I was hungry. And sitting around, doing nothing but waiting isn't my thing."

Clarissa's lips curved into a delightfully amused smile. "Yes, so you've told me. Half a dozen times, I might add."

"Heh."

"Um, excuse me," Lilith interrupted the pair, feeling just a little bit annoyed. Couldn't these two do their flirting some other time? Like, when she and Christian weren't looking for answers? "Not to be rude, but who are you?" she asked, pointing at Andrew.

"That's right." The man's face took an expression that made Lilith think of the word "Eruka!" It was as if he'd just now realized they hadn't been formally introduced. "Even though I was part of the team that fought against the No Life King, we never actually got a chance to talk, did we? My name is—"

"Andrew James Fortis," Christian interrupted, finally coming out of his own reverie. He walked forward until he was standing shoulder to shoulder with Lilith, looking down at the massive man as he sat at the table. "You were not only at the battle against Damien, but you were also the one following us when we were in Las Vegas, and you're the reason Catherine was able to find us."

"So you did know I was following you." While Lilith looked at her mate in surprise, Andrew scratched the back of his neck, a bit of a sheepish grin splaying across his face. "I knew you had sensed my presence, but I hadn't realized you managed to spot me too. You're pretty good."

"You were very hard to miss." Christian shook his head, black bangs swaying in front of his face. "Despite trying to remain hidden, you're a rather conspicuous person. Very easy to spot in a crowd."

"Yeah, I guess that's true. I always told Catherine I was no good at sleuthing, but she never listens to me." Andrew devolved into degenerate grumbling. Lilith thought she heard words like "smell" and "just because" and "can't believe she would" but couldn't really make out anything else.

"Speaking of Catherine, where is she?" asked Lilith, breaking the man away from his discontent.

"She's here," Andrew said.

"The one you call Catherine is currently in the hospital ward," Clarissa added. "Unlike you two, she doesn't have any supernatural healing abilities. She's just a human and is still unconscious. I suspect she won't wake up for at least another week."

"What do you mean by 'doesn't have any supernatural healing abilities?' And how much time has passed?" asked Christian.

"I mean just what I said." Clarissa turned her head to look at him. "You two have healing far above those of a normal human's. I suspect it has something to do with you, young man."

"Me?" Christian blinked to convey his surprise and confusion. "But I'm just a normal human?"

"Are you? Are you really?" Clarissa raised an eyebrow. "Are you so sure that you're human?"

"Of course I am," Christian muttered, sounding just a tad annoyed. "What else would I be?"

"I couldn't say for sure," Clarissa said, and something about the way she said it made Lilith think the woman wasn't being entirely truthful. "But I can tell you right now that the eye you have, that red eye in your right socket, is not human eye."

"My eye?" Christian raised a hand to touch the skin just underneath his red eye. "What do you mean? I've always had this eye."

"Then that just proves my point."

Lilith could almost feel Christian's confusion and anger. Looking at him, she could see it, too. His eyes were just a little more stormy, his mouth set into a thin line, brows furrowed into a mild glare. He really did seem upset at someone telling him that he was not human.

She was about to comfort him, perhaps offer him a hug or even just hold his hand, when several loud alarms blared to life. The obnoxious, nail-grating shriek had Andrew raise his one remaining hand to his ear, while both Lilith and Christian winced.

As one, they turned to Clarissa, who looked startled, resigned, and more than just a tad fearful.

"That's the proximity alarm," she said to their unspoken question. "We have set up several alarm systems to alert us whenever the goblins are trying to invade our sanctuary."

"G-goblins!?" Lilith gasped, startled. Even Christian looked surprised, for his eyes had gone wide and his mouth actually dropped a bit. "There are goblins down here?"

"Of course." Clarissa's smile was both grim and humorless. "You didn't think we were the only ones trying to find a safe haven underneath the earth, did you?"

Chapter 3

With the alarm sounding loudly in their ears, letting everyone know that the time for conversation and pleasantries had passed, Clarissa led Andrew and Christian to the armory.

"You have an armory?" Christian asked.

"Of course." Clarissa's pointed look stated that it should have been obvious. "There are many dangers in this world. In the event that we are attacked, we need a way to defend ourselves."

"Yeah. Good point." Christian could not help but agree.

Lilith, much to her disappointment, had been directed to the hospital, where Catherine was still resting, comatose and unable to commune with the rest of the world.

"I'll see you when I get back," Christian told Lilith as Clarissa beckoned a young woman over and asked her to lead Lilith to hospital wing.

"Right." Lilith gave Christian a strained smile as she leaned on her toes and kissed him. "Be careful, please."

"I will. I promise."

Lilith split ways with Christian, Clarissa, and Andrew. Meanwhile, the leader of the enclave led the two men over to a walkway that crossed the large body of heated water. There were quite a few of them. The many walkways crissed and crossed. Large support beams dove into the water's surface. Christian didn't know how deep this heated lake was, but even if it was just ten or twenty feet, he'd be impressed by the construction of these bridges.

The steam that rose from the surface of the slightly bluish green liquid was stifling, or maybe it was just the coming battle that had caused sweat to break out on Christian's forehead. He would not deny that the idea of facing a horde of who knows how many goblins was not a pleasant one.

"This way," Clarissa, acting as their guide, said as they took a turn at one of the intersecting walkways.

They crossed the lake and she brought them to another building, this one smaller. The building was situated near what Christian thought of as the back of the enclave. It was a squat little thing, nowhere near as big as the other buildings and not nearly as decorative. Plain and boring were the words he'd use to describe it.

It appeared to have been partially built into the cavern wall, with about a third of it sticking out. Because it was made from the same gray stone as the cave, most people probably wouldn't have even realized there was a building there at all.

The inside was not as ordinary as the outside. Stepping into the room, Christian and Andrew were greeted to the sight of weapons. A lot of weapons. Everything from swords and staves and spears, to guns and explosives were there, hanging on racks that were set against the walls. Christian recognized a few of the weapons there; 9mm pistols, magnums, sub-machine guns, glocks, automatic rifles, dirks, daggers, bastard swords, flails, and spears. There was even a naginata, ornately decorated to look a dragon was curving around a red pole with the curved blade sticking out of its mouth, resting on a rack separate from the other weapons. A number of lockers sat to one side, looking almost out of place.

Andrew whistled. "You've got some serious firepower here, little lady. Damn, this is impressive."

"Language," Christian muttered, annoyed, but too focused on the weapons arrayed around him to really care about the other man's foul mouth.

"Hahaha! What a straight-laced guy!"

Andrew slapped Christian on the back. His large hand smacked the much younger man so hard that Christian was almost sent face first to the ground. He stumbled forward, almost tripping, but managed to right himself before suffering a meeting of the face on rock kind. Ignoring the stinging sensation in his back, he straightened, then directed a mild glare at Andrew.

"What a scary look," the wild man said, chuckling. "You could probably kill demons with that glare."

"I would like to ask that you not do that again," Christian said, grumbling about inconsiderate buffoons under his breath.

"Alright, alright. Yeesh. What crawled up your ass and died?"

"Nothing." Christian scowled, both at the language and the blasé attitude. This man almost reminded him of Tristin, a bigger, badder, and much fiercer version of Tristin, but still reminiscent of the annoying intelligence agent. And that was not a good thing in his book. "I just don't like being touched."

"You seem to enjoy it when Lilith touches you," Andrew teased.

Christian's scowl deepened. "That's Lilith. You are not her."

"Ouch."

"We do not have time for bickering, you two," Clarissa said, her voice hard and her eyes cut from diamonds. "The sirens have been going off for at least five minutes now. We need to get ready and get dressed. I have prepared outfits for both of you, just in case this day would come, and Christian, I have your weapons stored in this locker with your clothes." She gestured to one of the many identical, plane wooden lockers. Then she looked at Andrew. "This is your locker. Get dressed please."

"Will do," Andrew said, moving over to a locker that Clarissa indicated was for him. He opened it up and grabbed the only article of clothing inside, which he began putting on.

Christian ignored the other man in favor of Clarissa. "Where are the others? Surely we're not the only ones who are going to defend the enclave?"

"Of course not." Clarissa looked like she wanted to roll her eyes and just barely managed to restrain herself from doing so. "This is not the only armory we have. There are seven more, one at each of the four cardinal points, and four more located in between them. This one is a bit farther from the others, and just happens to be where I had stored your weapons and outfits. Had I known we would be attacked so soon after you arrived, I would have stored them somewhere else."

Nodding at her answer, Christian opened the locker, undressed, and then stepped into his new clothes. The clothing she had decided to give him was not something he was used to wearing. The pants were skin tight and stretched around his thighs and calves. They weren't uncomfortable, but they looked outlandish. Likewise, the shirt was pure white and conformed to his body with the same tightness as the pants. He was also given a set of gloves that were missing both the middle and index fingers, socks, and a pair of black combat boots that had both a zipper and straps to keep them closed.

Just like Clarissa had said, all his equipment was also stored inside with the clothing. His swords, Michael and Rafael, sat in their sheaths, waiting to be put to use. Gabriel and Phaneul, his two pistols, were likewise sitting there within their holsters, their grips gleaming in the low light. When he finished getting dressed, strapping on all his weapons and attaching several clips of ammunition to the straps around his thighs, he checked himself over in the mirror to make sure each article was placed on properly.

Christian had to admit that, abnormal clothing or not, he didn't look too bad.

Now if only he had a cloak.

"I apologize for the lack of all but the most basic of equipment, but my smiths have not been able to make any form of protection for you."

Christian turned to Clarissa to see the woman looking at them both. She was no longer dressed in her bathrobe—thank God—and was now wearing a black, skin-tight body suit, equally black combat boots, and black leather gloves. Several throwing knives were strapped across her thighs, and Christian could see two sub-machine guns attached to her back. In her hand was a naginata, a Japanese spear with a curved blade.

"Do you know how to use that thing?" he asked, nodding at the pole-like weapon in her hand.

"Do you know how to those swords?"

"Touché." Christian then turned to Andrew. The older man was wearing clothing similar to his own but much larger so as to fit his bulkier frame. "Where's your weapon?" He furrowed his brow, not seeing anything for the muscular man to use to help fight off the coming horde of goblins, though he couldn't imagine what the man could wield, what with his missing arm and everything.

"Don't need one," Andrew's gruff voice was accompanied by a grin. "I am a weapon."

Christian stared at Andrew for several seconds, and then dismissed him, much to the older man's consternation.

"Come, you two," Clarissa said, twirling her naginata around until the pole was running parallel against her left arm, the rounded end sticking into the air, blade pointed down. "Let us make haste."

The two males looked at each other, and then moved to catch up with Clarissa.

As they walked down another walkway, Christian took a deep breath.

He had only just woken up and was already knee-deep in trouble.

***

Lilith found herself sitting in a sterilized room with white walls, a white tile floor, and an equally white ceiling. A hospital ward, a fairly large one, too. At least, it was when one took the fact that it was built inside of an underground cavern into consideration.

The room was large enough to fit a grand total of twelve beds. Over near the door was a long table that acted as a desk. Cupboards hung over the table, suspended from the ceiling and set into the wall. She didn't know what they contained, but she imagined they held medical supplies. Another cabinet, this one large and made of glass and metal, stood next to the table. It held within it jars, bottles and containers, all of which had either pills of some sort, or liquids of varying color. Medicine, she guessed.

There were a couple of nurses in the room, four of them. They were over by the table, sitting on stools that looked much more comfortable than her own chair, conversing about something. She didn't know what they were talking about, but they kept looking over at her, making Lilith assume that she was their topic of conversation.

The chair she sat on, which she had pulled up to Catherine's bed, was blue, made of plastic, and uncomfortable. It was one of those standard chairs you see in every doctor's office. She'd only been sitting in it for a few minutes, and her butt was already beginning to grow sore.

Trying to take her mind off her thoughts and discomfort, or at least hoping to, she looked at Catherine. The older woman was lying on the bed, her blond hair no longer in a tight bun but instead spread across the pillow and sheets. She had longer hair than Lilith had suspected, almost as long as her own. It wasn't as shiny, or as smooth, but that was to be expected. Humans didn't have perfect hair. Catherine was only wearing a basic white medical gown, along with the covers, which had been pulled up to her chest. Deep, slow, and even breaths caused her lungs to expand and contract. She appeared to be sleeping peacefully.

I feel so useless.

Despite not wanting to, Lilith's thoughts turned toward her current quandary. Here she was, sitting in a hospital, twiddling her thumbs and waiting patiently. Meanwhile, Christian, her mate, was going out to fight against a horde of monsters, goblins, who were trying to invade the enclave. She hadn't tried to stop him, nor had she attempted to go with him, because she knew that she wouldn't be much help.

She'd hardly done anything when he battled Damien. When the Executioners had come aboard the train, she'd been useless. And when Nicholas Cruor—who they found out later on was actually Asmodeus the Demon King of Lust—had come to kill them, all she'd been able to do was let Caspian protect her.

Why can't I do anything to help Christian?

Every time when something came up that required protecting, it was Christian who saved her, not the other way around. When she was in danger, he would come in with guns blazing and swords flashing. She was the damsel in distress, and he the gallant knight coming to her rescue.

I don't want to be so useless anymore.

But she didn't want that. She didn't want to be the one who was always in need of saving. She didn't want to have Christian shoulder all the burdens himself. She wanted to help, to be useful, to prove that she could stand by his side. She wanted to show him that when chaos was upon them and the forces that be were threatening to overrun them, she could be just as strong as he was.

"I imagine you simply wore yourself out by using your powers too much."

Her powers. Clarissa said something about her using her powers. Did that mean that she had special abilities not even she knew about? Lilith didn't remember ever showing any powers other than her allure, which she could never actively control. It had just always sort of been there, like a hose whose knob had been broken and, unable to be shut off, simply flowed out of her body, out of control and impossible to stop.

But what if she really did have powers? Abilities that she could use to help Christian? Could they be taught? Would Clarissa be willing to teach her? She hoped so.

I'll ask her when she gets back, Lilith decided, then and there, that she would not be useless anymore. The next time battle was upon them, Christian was not going to leave her behind.

***

The cavern walls were the same dull gray as everything else. The difference lay not in the color but in the light. Near the enclave, over that body of water and with those strange crystals that glowed with an unusual luminescence, it was bright, almost cheery, if a tad stifling. But here, inside of this long, winding passage made of rock and stone, it was dark, dank, and cold.

Water dripped down from the ceiling, splashing against the floor. There were several puddles littering the ground.

The sounds of almost two dozen boots walking along granite was accompanied by the resonance of soft breathing and the clinking of weapons. In the distance came strange noises, croaks and warbles and low, hissing grunts. While it was impossible to see them, everyone knew what they were.

Goblins.

When Clarissa, Christian, and Andrew had met up with the rest of those who would be defending the enclave, the reaction to the presence of two males had been surprise, astonishment, uncertainty, as well as resentment and even outright hate in the case of two young women there. While a few had simply appeared curious, it was clear that most of these women did not approve of having two men with them.

Most succubus apparently did not like men. Who knew?

Clarissa had explained to the others what he and Andrew were doing with them, that Christian was mated to a succubus and Andrew was immune thanks to a medallion he wore around his neck. That had garnered a bit more attention and a little less hostility—at least for Christian. They still seemed suspicious of Andrew. However, it appeared that being the mate of a succubus was something worthy of respect among them.

Christian was beginning to realize that there was a lot he didn't know about succubi and their culture. Go figure.

While they walked along the spacious cavern, with only the light from a couple of battery-powered lamps to let them see where they were going, Christian looked at the man next to him. Andrew strode beside him, his steps lumbering and loud. A medallion made of gold and silver danced and jingled along his neck. Carved onto its surface were symbols, letters to a foreign language that Christian did not know.

According to Clarissa, it was that little medallion that kept Andrew from being affected by the allure of all the succubus surrounding them.

At the front of the group and just ahead and him and Andrew, Clarissa stopped and raised her hand, causing all the others to halt as well. The woman looked around, her eyes glowing with the light of the lamp in her hand. Her nagitana was in the other. She was coiled, her body tense and ready to spring, like a rattlesnake just before it struck.

Christian had the feeling that this woman's bite was more poisonous than any rattlesnake.

Clarissa made a gesture with her hand. Several women reached into their clothes, pulling out a small, cylindrical object. They were flares, Christian realized. They used the flares to light up the area in a bright red glow, dropping them all over the ground to further illuminate the area that was to be their battlefield.

Another hand gesture caused a number of succubus to move to the front. Each one was carrying a long-range weapon of some kind, mostly pistols, but a few had auto and semi-automatic rifles. So they were going to attack at range first? Mow the enemy down before they reached them and then close the distance and destroy the few that were left with close combat?

He nodded. That was sound plan.

Moving up to the front as well, Christian pulled Gabrielle and Phaneul from their holsters. He knelt next to one of the women, a young girl who couldn't have been much older than him with shoulder length red hair and green eyes. Like every member of her race, she was pretty, not as pretty as Lilith but still gorgeous. He looked at her, if only for a second, to give her a nod of acknowledgement, noting her shock, and then he turned to face the long passage of the cave.

He took a deep breath.

He closed his green eye.

And he began to see.

The darkness of the cave began to brighten as his eye's sensitivity to sunlight was increased by tenfold. Everything around him became clear, the bumpiness of the floor snapped into sharp focus. He could see the stalactites sticking up from the ceiling and count the number of cracks each one had. He could see the moisture coalescing on the walls and ceiling, running down in tiny trails across gray stone and then dripping onto the ground below. Anything and everything within his line of vision was now visible.

Including the goblin army.

Christian nearly swore as he saw the overwhelming number of goblins coming at them. He could not even begin to guess at their numbers. There had to be hundreds at least, all packed into the wide cavern in lines that extended far beyond even his vision.

Their ugly green skin was covered in filth. Sparse amount of straggly hair sat upon their heads, not covering it nearly enough as the flesh of their cranium was still plenty visible. They were all gangly legs and thin arms attached to a body that made holocaust victims look fit. Looking closely, he could see the ribcages of the ones up front, protruding and repulsive, with the skin peeled back and looking more like leather with a bad dye job than actual flesh.

Most of the goblins wore nothing but a loincloth, but he could see that a few actually had armor; chainmail skirts and shirts, gauntlets and grieves, some with a breast plate, others without. The armor was all worn and ragged, scuffed, with several pock marks and dents. Their armor was obviously used, probably old too. Judging from the number of goblins who wore some—about one for every dozen or so—it was likely a symbol of status. The goblins wearing armor were probably the best warriors, the ones who had proven themselves and shown their superiority in combat.

They were also the ones that Christian would want to take out first.

There were many legends about goblins. Most of the stories Caspian heard classified them as annoying creatures no larger than waist height, and possessing of various magical abilities and a love of money. In modern fiction, there were two branches in which goblins were associated with in popular fantasy; evil and amoral. Some people likened them to evil beings, creatures born of darkness who would steal your children, feast on their flesh, and use their bones to pick their teeth clean, or something like that. The amoral kind were often associated with bankers, a somewhat accurate description as Christian had met a few bankers and they certainly reminded him of goblins, though it was not wholly accurate either.

Goblins were creatures whose lives were run by greed. Everything they did was to gain more; more money, more land, more interesting and unique items, more, more, more, more, always trying to acquire more than what they truly needed. They would lie, steal, and kill anyone who got in their way to get more of what they wanted.

They were also nasty little fighters. Christian had slaughtered a number of them and they always fought dirty, throwing dirt in your eyes, biting your legs, playing dead and coming up to stab you in the back when you turned away. When fighting a goblin, you could never turn your back until you were sure they were dead.

Christian found the best way to know when a goblin was alive or not was through decapitation. If they were headless, you knew they were dead.

Several harsh, labored breaths echoed in his ears. The girl he'd been standing next to, the one that couldn't have been much older than him—possibly even younger—looked to be on the verge of panicking.

"Easy," Christian murmured, loud enough for the young woman to hear. "Don't get worked up. Take deep, slow breaths. Keep yourself calm and collected. Take in a breath, hold it. Now release."

The young woman did exactly as told, taking in slow breaths and releasing them after several seconds. Christian kept an eye on both the approaching horde and the girl. The goblins were getting closer. He estimated them to be about no less than one-hundred meters now. In the darkness, the succubi wouldn't be able to see them yet, which explained why they were not firing.

"Thank you," the young succubus muttered, her cheeks turning a little pink. She must not have been used to someone helping her, or maybe she was embarrassed because he was a guy. It was something to think on at any rate.

"You're welcome. Now get your gun ready. They'll be coming in a few seconds."

True to Christian's prediction, the first line of goblins soon became visible. Clarissa, who'd been holding her hand above her head, gave the command to let loose with a loud bark of "fire!" while bringing her arm down in a swift chopping motion.

All around Christian, lights blazed as guns went off. The loud thunderclap of heavy guns like magnums banged against his eardrums. The steady buzzing of submachine guns sounded out like a swarm of bumble bees. Christian's own twin handguns went off with several loud, violent bursts, the tips lighting up like short-lived stars in the night.

The first round of fire mowed down the first line of goblins, about a dozen or so, as well as the second dozen. Goblin bodies were struck with bullets. They jerked and spasmed before crumbling to the ground. Blood splattered from their wounds, spurting out like tiny fountains and splashing across the ground in small droplets that grew larger as more crimson liquid gathered.

Bodies fell, tumbling to the ground where they lay still. Several goblins in the back would trip over their dead comrades in their haste to advance. Others simply kicked the bloody corpses out of the way. They were rushing now, hurrying to reach them before another salvo was unleashed. Christian was determined to get at least another two rounds in before it became a close quarters battle.

With the click of a button, the now empty cartridges fell to the ground with a clatter. In a single, smooth motion, Christian brought his guns down butt first to the ammo clips attached to his belt, smoothly sliding them into their respective slots. He then brought the guns up, hit their butts together to lock the cartridges in place, and then proceeded to unleash another salvo.

With his enhanced eyesight, Christian had far better aim than usual. Thirty-four bullets were launched from Gabrielle and Phaneul, each metal shell finding and penetrating the head of a goblin, killing them instantly and causing their limp bodies to roll along the ground.

Two more empty cartridges clattered to the ground. Another two were loaded.

Christian fired again. By now, the goblins were close enough that he could make out all their distinctive features.

While all goblins had a very generic appearance: green skin, long, pointy faces, and pointed ears, scraggly matted down hair on their nearly bald heads, and gangly arms and legs, that did not mean there were no variations. Some had thicker brow ridges, others an extra row of sharp, rotting teeth. A few had missing body parts, an ear, a part of their lip, an eye, even patches of skin. Streaks of mud, or maybe some kind of dark brown war paint, covered their bodies in an array of patterns, like tattoos. Christian could see one tattoo that looked almost like a wolf, but it was all smudged and blurred out.

Goblins were notoriously horrible artists.

The last salvo was fired. Christian managed to kill another thirty-two goblins. Then the horde was upon them.

Rising to his feet, Christian raised Gabrielle, blocking an overhand strike from a rusty sword. He holstered Phaneul, the motion smooth as silk, and then he raised his hand behind his back, gripping Rafael and sliding it out of the sheath with a hiss that was lost in the din of battle. The blade came down, its black surface strangely reflective in the darkness. It cut straight through the goblin's arm and head, taking the arm off entirely and splitting the head down the center. The arm dropped to the floor with a wet thump. It twitched several times before going still. The body fell after it, tilting backwards before crashing into another goblin that was directly behind it.

He slid Gabrielle into its holster and pulled Michael free from its sheath. Christian sidestepped to the left, dodging a thrust knife aimed at his throat. He swung his arm. Michael came down, whistling. The sword sliced straight through the hand bearing the knife. While the goblin screamed as it held the now bleeding stump, Christian spun around, his hair whipping around him fiercely as he brought Rafael up into a diagonal swing that carved a trench into the goblin's flesh from the left hip to the right shoulder.

The creature was dead before it hit the ground.

With such a large horde battling against him, Christian began to expand his awareness of the battlefield. He could feel the vibrations of feet pounding on stone. Feel the shifts in atmospheric pressure as swords were swung and spears were thrust. The clinking of chains let him know that one of the goblin he had dubbed a commander was coming up to him from his blind spot, the sword in its grip aimed at his kidney.

Christian moved. Using some fancy footwork, he sidestepped the attack meant to take his life. His left hand came up, Rafael whistling as it battered against the steel blade in a clash of sparks and shrieking metal. At the same time, he thrust Michael at the goblin's face with incredible speed and power. The green-skinned creature was so surprised that it had no time to move out of the way as the tip of Christian's blade penetrated its head right through its left eye socket.

With a single, swift, and violent jerk, Christian yanked Michael out of the head in a spray of gore, its silvery surface now slick with dark crimson. Christian spun, turning a full circle as he felt another attack, aimed at his head. He swung his left hand, Rafael singing as it clanged against the mace trying to bash his skull in. Rather than allow himself to take the full brunt of the attack, however, Christian used the heavy weapons own momentum to direct the skull-crushing attack into a goblin trying to stab him with a dirk from behind. As that goblin's skull was crushed, blood and brain matter oozing from its destroyed cranium, Christian lashed out with Michael in a sweeping diagonal slash that cut through flesh, bone, and muscle with ease.

The mace-wielding goblin spun about, its body rotating a full one-hundred and eighty degrees before it hit the ground, consequently tripping up another goblin and allowing the red-haired succubus who'd been fighting alongside Christian to kill it with a knife she had pulled from her waistband. Yet while she was stabbing the creature with wide, almost unseeing eyes, she didn't even notice the one coming up behind her.

Christian sheathed Rafael and pulled out Phaneul, loading another clip and then shooting two bullets at the goblin. The first shot the hand holding the weapon—a pick ax—taking out three fingers in the process and launching the weapon into the air, where it would find itself buried in the head of another goblin. The second shot fired pierced its right eye, killing it instantly and sending it stumbling backwards into two more goblins that were trying to gang up on one of the other succubi.

A flash of surprise followed by one of gratitude entered the redhead's eyes. Christian didn't have time to acknowledge her feelings of gratefulness because another six goblins had decided to bum rush him.

And so, he began to dance.

He moved right, dancing across the bumpy ground with impossible to predict movements. A club, thick, large, and made of metal instead of wood, crashed down on where he had been standing. He pulled up Phaneul in a smooth motion, there was a flash of light and the bang of gunfire, followed by a loud gurgling as the goblin who'd tried to squash him flat was shot through the throat.

Christian then spun on the balls of his left. Michael sang a song of death, whistling loudly as he swung the blade so fast it was nothing but a silver streak. The horizontal swing struck hard steel as an armored goblin blocked it. Christian pointed Phaneul at it and the gun rang out loud and clear, the small shell it launched out penetrating the monster's flesh right between the eyes.

The feeling of air shifting to his left had the young man ducking, his messy locks flowing down with him. There was a shriek of outrage from the goblin who missed. Christian decided to return fire by kicking the thing's legs out from underneath it. Before the goblin hit the ground, he slid Phaneul into its holster and pulled Rafael out with a hiss.

Christian spun, bringing Michael up to decapitate the falling goblin while the reflective black sword blocked a swift yet strong blow from another blade, a falchion. He shifted to the left, allowing the blade to move past him as he used Rafael to redirect the enemy weapon's motion and flow of energy. He also transferred all his own kinetic energy into his left foot, bending it. Christian then lashed out with a powerful heel kick that struck the knee of the goblin with the falchion, a loud crunching sound echoing around him as the knee shattered.

Just before the goblin could squeal in pain, Christian mercifully ended its life with a swing of Michael. The creature's head slid off in a disgustingly smooth motion, small traces of blood squirting from the stump and trailing down its flesh as the headless body tumbled to the ground.

The battle progressed from there. Christian lost himself in the moment, feeling rather than thinking, allowing instincts and reflexes honed from years of intense training to take control of his body. The human mind was incapable of reacting quickly enough to survive a combat situation when a person was surrounded by enemies. It just wasn't possible to account for that many variables at once and come up with an appropriate course of action for each one. And so Christian did not think, did not plan, and did not allow anything to clutter his mind.

He simply moved.

It was on this battlefield where Christian proved why he was one of the Catholic Church's most powerful Warriors—former most powerful. He danced around his opponents, skirting the edge of disaster. Weapons came at him, set to strike at all the openings in his stance, openings that Christian himself had made. With knowledge of where all the holes in his stance were, he was able to accurately determine where each attack was coming from. It was almost as easy as breathing.

A swing aimed at taking out his legs was dodged. Gabrielle came in and sliced off the offending hand while Michael parried and redirected a spear aimed at his back when he spun a full three-hundred and sixty degrees. That same goblin whose hand was cut off soon had its throat pierced by the spear that had been previously aimed at Christian's back. The young man used the moment of shock that the goblin felt from having his own spear thrust into one of its brethren to remove that creature's head.

Time on the battlefield was interminable. Knowing how much time had passed was impossible when you were fighting for your life.

Christian did not know how long he'd been fighting, but it must have been a long time. The endless of horde of goblins came at him and the succubi that he was fighting alongside, scrabbling over the bodies of their fallen brethren. He must have killed over one-hundred of the monsters by now, but there were still so many.

His breathing was getting heavy by this point. Each breath came out as a loud, ragged gasp for air. Sweat had long since broken out on his forehead, dripping into his eyes, stinging and distracting. He tried to ignore it. Distractions in the midst of battle could prove fatal—had proven fatal. Many of the greener Executioners had gotten themselves killed while on the job due to their attention being diverted.

Yet the more Christian tried to block out the feeling of his eyes burning, the more of a problem they became. He was forced to shut his left eye, the one he had been relying on, when a slick stream of blood from a wound that had been opened on his forehead due to him not being fast enough to dodge poured over his eye.

That proved to be a mistake.

In that single split second where his left eye was closed, Christian didn't see the goblin coming in on his left until it was already halfway through swinging its club. He tried to dodge, throwing his body to the left, but the large, wooden weapon still smashed into his shoulder.

Pain exploded in his shoulder, a white-hot flash of agony that made his body almost seize up. Nerveless fingers loosened, dropping Michael in the process. He could feel his shoulder give under the attack, feel the acromion bone break as it was struck, while his humerus bone was pulled out of its socket. He wasn't sure what hurt worse: his bone breaking or getting his arm dislocated?

Doing his best to ignore the pain, Christian moved with the stumble, letting it take him past another attack meant to take off his head. He came back up, lashing out with Rafael, and felt satisfaction when he tore open the goblin's stomach.

As the now dying creature fell to the ground, ichor and innards spilling out of the gaping wound in its belly, Christian turned around, only to find himself staring at a sword descending toward his head. A jolt raced through him as he tried to move, but he found himself to do so. Hands grasping at his legs let him know that a goblin had decided to play dead and was now grabbing his feet, keeping him from dancing around the incoming attack. He couldn't dodge if he couldn't move. He tried to swing Rafael up to intercept the attack, but another goblin had latched onto his right arm.

So, he was helpless then?

Is... is this how I'm going to die?

It was said that when someone knew they were about to die, their entire life flashed before their eyes, moving at speeds not even the greatest super computer could hope to match.

Is this really the end? Dying on the battlefield in the middle of a cave surrounded by goblins and succubi?

Christian did not see his life flash before his eyes. Having accepted the possibility of dying long ago, the idea of death did not cause him fear like it would others. Instead of watching his life play in front of him like some kind of cheesy flashback, Christian's vision was filled with an image of silken blond hair, blue eyes, and a dazzling smile. He was really going to miss Lilith.

What an ignoble ending.

He did not close his eyes as the sword descended. Christian was not going to let his fear cow him. If this was the end, then he would meet it head on.

A loud howl rang in his ears. In the instant before the sword descended, the goblin was swatted away by a large, clawed, and furry hand. Christian stared at the hand in shock, then followed the large digits up to a thick wrist covered in black fur. He continued moving up and up, following the wrist to the arm, then up the shoulder to the clavicles, before finally reaching the face; a streamlined muzzle with a row of sharp, jagged teeth, and piercing yellow orbs.

A werewolf.

A really big werewolf.

More like a massive werewolf.

Did that thing have giants blood or something?

Towering over everyone there, the massive, furry, and hugely muscled bipedal monster was easily two or three feet taller than he was. It also had a lot more mass. Hulking muscles covered its frame, flexing and twitching as it moved. The two pointed ears on its head swiveled as it zeroed in on certain noises. Strong legs and a single, muscular arm trembled, as if in anticipation of the blood bath to come. And as Christian stared at the beast looking over him, only one thought came to his mind.

How the hell did I miss that?

The werewolf's eyes landed on him. It let out a loud howl, causing Christian's eyes to widen as a powerful shockwave smacked into him with incredible force. His eyes watered and his hair was blown out of his face. He even stumbled backwards for several steps, such was the power behind the howl.

However, the howling served another purpose. The goblins that had been latched onto him let go and fled, freeing him from their grip.

"You alright, kid?" the werewolf growled out in a deep, bass rumble.

"Uh..." Christian's mind blanked. All he could do was stare in shock at the dominating mass of muscle and fur. Had he ever seen a werewolf that was so big?

"Oi! Kid! I'm asking if you're alright!"

"Um, ah, yes!" Christian eyed the werewolf more closely now that the shock was wearing down. "You're... Andrew, right?"

"Who else would I be? Now get your head back in the game, Executioner. There are still plenty of goblins left that need to be slain."

Christian shook his head, snapping himself back into the game. "Right. You're right."

His grip on Rafael's handle tightened. Without waiting for a reply from the werewolf, Christian spun around to block the mace coming toward his head. He moved his sword in a circular motion, forcing the mace to the side, and then thrust the tip of his sword into the goblin's lower jaw, piercing its mouth and going straight into its brain.

The creature didn't even get a chance to squeal in pain as it was killed. Blood spurted out of the wound as Christian yanked Rafael free. The goblin crumbled to the ground, but he was already on the move.

Out of the corner of his eye, Christian saw the redhead he'd been standing beside by struggling. Blood seeped out of several wounds. Her clothes were still there, but it had a good deal of tears in them. She was on the ground, her hands pressed against a rather nasty-looking gash on her thigh, crimson leaking from beneath her fingers to trail down milky flesh. Her tear-filled eyes were wide as she stared at the goblin standing over her, his hands raised to bring an ax down on her head.

Phaneul was whipped out before Christian even realized what he was doing. Three shots were fired, one hitting the ax's head and knocking it off course, another hitting the goblin's right shoulder, and the last piercing its temple. The dead body was thrown toward its left, falling to the ground like a marionette with its strings cut.

Christian sensed another attack coming in from behind. He moved to counter, but he saw that Andrew the werewolf already had things well in hand. One large clawed hand was clamped down over the goblin's head, various types of liquids oozing from between massive clawed fingers as the skull was slowly crushed. The goblin struggled, kicking its feet as it was lifted off the ground, hands clawing and trying to pry the muscled fingers off its head. The struggling soon ceased. The kicking grew weak. The creature's arms and legs twitched a few more times before they went limp.

Christian turned away, not bothering to watch anymore. He looked around the battlefield. Scores of bodies lay strewn across the cavern floor, green skin glistening with crimson ichor. What little he could see of the ground amidst the piles of corpses was stained with blood, the craggy surfaces filling up with dark puddles, the scent of copper permeating the air.

All around the area, spread out amongst the bodies of dead goblins were succubi. He was pleased to note that he could not see a single succubus among the dead. All of them were moving, albeit, some were groaning in pain and a few seemed unable to stand without aid. Injured was still better than dead, and he was more than willing to count their blessings.

There didn't appear to be anymore enemies left to fight, which was pleasing because he was tired. His legs were shaking, his right arm was weighed down and leaden, and his left shoulder throbbed with a dull ache. It was only now, after the battle had ended, that Christian realized just how long the fight had lasted for.

"I want everyone who did not suffer an injury or are only lightly injured to help carry the wounded to the hospital!"

He turned toward the source of the voice that shouted out into the now nearly silent cave, strong, proud, and commanding. It was Clarissa. She looked every bit the beautiful and terrifying warrior, standing within a ring of corpses, her nagitana gripped in her hand, its butt end planted firmly on the ground, the blade stained red with the blood of her foes. Her clothing was ripped and torn. Christian could see several cuts marring her skin, some deeper than others. She ignored them, however, in favor of acting like the leader she was.

"We've done well to survive the battle, but the fight has not truly been won until everyone here is back at the enclave, safe and out of danger! Let us leave swiftly!"

As the group of succubi headed the commands Clarissa had given them, Christian released a gusty sigh. The battle had been won, but the thought did not bring him any solace. Maybe it was because he was tired, and his mind was playing tricks on him, but he had the very distinct feeling that this would not be the last time he and the group of succubi tangled with the goblins.

Chapter 4

The walk back to the enclave was slow. With so many succubi injured, moving any faster than a snail's pace was difficult, if not impossible. The steady pounding of feet resounded all around them, echoing along the walls and bouncing down the cavern, the noise sounding much louder than it should have. The few lamps that had survived the battle and not gotten crushed lit the path in front of them.

Despite having helped the group of women quite a bit, Andrew and Christian were relegated to the back. It seemed that, despite what they had done, there were many in the group who did not trust them. That was fine, though. Faith in others was not something that could be built in a day. He understood that, which was why, rather than feeling surely and self-righteous about how he was getting the cold shoulder, Christian vowed to earn their trust through his hard work and dedication.

This enclave might be the only place that he and Lilith would be safe from harm—relatively speaking, because those goblins were seriously harmful. He couldn't afford to jeopardize their standing within this group of unnaturally beautiful women. Not if he wanted to have a place for Lilith to stay.

By that point in time, most of Christian's wounds had already healed. Even his shoulder was feeling a lot better. He'd always had a fast recovery rate, but he was still shocked by how quickly his injuries were healing these days.

"You two have healing far above those of a normal human. I suspect it has something to do with you, young man."

Christian almost stumbled when the words of Clarissa swam through his mind, haunting and clear. He shook his head. There was no way she could be right. He was human. He knew he was…

Wasn't he?

"Are you? Are you really? Are you so sure that you're human?"

Doubts floated through his mind. What if he wasn't human? If he wasn't human, then what was he?

Not wanting to think about that anymore, nor let anyone know how shaken those words made him, Christian looked at the figure walking beside him. Harsh shadows were cast upon Andrew's angled and square face. His shaggy main of hair swayed back and forth as he walked, his heavy, ponderous footfalls rumbling like the sound of distant thunder.

"So you're a werewolf?"

"Figured that on your own, did you?"

Christian winced at the snarky tone in the older man's voice. "Sorry. I didn't mean to sound like that. I'm just surprised. I hadn't realized you were a werewolf."

"That's to be expected," Andrew said, cracking his neck back and forth, loud, ghastly noises issuing with each swift movement. "We never spoke back in Seal Beach, back when that No Life King kidnapped your girl. Hell, we haven't even really met face to face until today, or tonight, as the case may be. It would only make sense that you didn't know what I am?" Andrew looked over at him, his raised eyebrow just barely visible in the low lighting. "You got any problems about me being a werewolf?"

"Had you asked me that several months ago, my answer would have probably been yes." Christian frowned as he thought back to when he was still an Executioner. Everything had been so black and white back then, so easy. The Executioners were the good guys, the monsters the bad guys, and the good guys killed the bad guys. Simple. Or it had been. Things weren't so simple anymore.

"And now?" asked Andrew.

"Now? Now the most important person in my entire life is a succubus, so I would have to say that, no, I don't really care whether you're a werewolf or not." Christian furrowed his brows, thinking. "I'm beginning to realize more and more that it's not what you are that's important, but who you are and what you do with your life that really counts." His hair shifting as he turned his head, shadowing his eyes ever so slightly, the young man looked at his older compatriot. "You seem to be an alright guy, so I don't think we'll have any issues."

"Good to know," Andrew grunted, "and surprising."

"Why is that?"

"Kid, I've been around for a long time, long enough to have had more than my fair share of run ins with trouble. Before I even became a cop, I knew about the Executioners, and I saw what they could do. I saw what they did."

Andrew's eyes glazed over slightly as he spoke. Christian imagined the man was remembering something from a long time ago. He also wondered what kind of trouble the man was talking about.

"I wasn't always a werewolf," he said softly. "I was cursed with lycanthropy when I was young, about sixteen or so, I'd say. Like all those who started off human, I was bitten by a werewolf on the night of the full moon, when I had gone out into the forest to gather some firewood. We didn't have air conditioning back then. Homes were heated by lighting fires in the fireplace."

No air conditioning? The first air conditioning unit had been built in 1902 by Willis Carrier. That meant Andrew must have been born sometime in the eighteen hundreds. That meant he was, at the very least, over 125 years old.

He was startled. No wonder the man's werewolf form was so large. Werewolves grew bigger and more powerful with age.

"I didn't think much of it back then, and neither did my parents. We thought I had just been bitten by a regular wolf. They'd been known to come out on occasion. My old man often had to chase them off the property. It wasn't until the night of the next full moon that I realized something was wrong with me. I remember waking up that night, hurt and aching and hungry. I remember feeling a strong desire to hunt. The urge grew so overwhelming that every thought I had was consumed by this simple desire, until I was nothing but a beast." The man shuddered, like he was reliving the memory of that night. "I don't remember anything after that—I must have passed out, but I do remember waking up in the middle of a destroyed cabin, the torn apart bodies of my mom, dad, and little sister laying scattered around me, and myself lying naked on the ground, the lingering taste of blood in my mouth."

"So you... you killed them, then? Your family?" Christian asked, his throat dry. He tried to work some moisture back into his mouth, but nothing seemed to help.

"I must have," Andrew said dryly. "There was no one else around who could have done it. My family and I lived in a small cottage deep within the forests of Pennsylvania. The nearest town was almost half a day on foot."

"What did you do after that?"

"I did what anyone else would have done. I ran. I ran as far and as long and as hard as I could. I kept running until I couldn't run anymore. After that, I had two options: Find someplace quiet and kill myself, or try to live with what I'd done." He paused long enough to scratch his chin. "I didn't have the courage to kill myself, so I decided to live instead. I got a job working as a carpenter. Life moved on, and I more or less got over what I had done, but then another full moon came. I bet you can guess what happened."

Christian could indeed guess what happened. A shudder ran from the crown of his head all the way to his tailbone. Despite how he pretty much already knew how the story would go, Andrew told him anyway.

"I transformed again. I hadn't really been aware of the transformation. The first few times you change from a human to a werewolf is strange. Your mind, the logical thinking human part of your mind, is sent somewhere deep and dark, a place where no light shines, and you feel and see nothing. You're not really aware of what's happening. It's almost like you're asleep."

Andrew shivered as if a cold chill was sweeping through him.

"I ended up killing in my transformed state again, only this time I was in a town and people saw me. The townsfolk began to suspect that a monster was lurking in the woods, perhaps a beast that had been summoned by a witch to destroy the town or something equally outlandish. Not that it mattered. The people soon created a large mob to go after the beast. I was invited to join, but I think a part of me already knew what had happened. I knew that I was the one who had killed those people, just like I killed my family. And so, I ran again."

Christian didn't speak, but he certainly imagined how Andrew must have been feeling at the time. He could almost picture the scenario this man presented play out before him like a movie. It was suitably horrifying.

"After that, I realized that the only thing I could do was stay as far away from civilization as possible. I lived out in the forest, hunting for a living, and occasionally making small runs into the nearest town to sell animal pelts in exchange for things like blankets and quilts."

By now, they had made it all the way to the entrance to the succubus enclave. It was just a small door embedded into a wall that was disguised as a dead end. A curtain hung over the door to make it blend in with the rocks, but anyone who was observant enough would be able to distinguish the difference between curtain and granite.

Andrew paused, took a deep breath, and continued.

"I found myself a small cave to live in, and I lived in it for about a year before someone found me, a woman named Elanor. She was a werewolf like me, but unlike me, she had complete control over her ability to transform. She and a small group of four others called themselves Lycanthropes. I guess they wanted to differentiate themselves from normal werewolves."

Finally, the dismal expression on Andrew's face broke. Like clouds breaking apart to let the world bathe in sunlight, a smile appeared on his face.

"I traveled with them after that, moving from one place to another. The group played themselves off as a traveling band of street performers. They would do small shows on the streets. During that time, Elanor taught me how to control my transformation." From the small light shining in Andrew's eyes, Christian could see the man was clearly drawing upon some good memories. "Those were some of the best days of my life. I learned how to master my power, met others like me, and fell in love with an incredible woman."

"You and Elanor, I'm guessing?" asked Christian.

"Yeah, me and Elanor. We ended up getting married about fifteen years after she found me. By that point, I had pretty much mastered the art of transforming from a human to my werewolf form, and I no longer suffered the need to hunt while under the effects of the full moon." His countenance, which had been pleasant and happy while talking about Elanor, began to darken. "Of course, good things like that are not made to last."

Andrew grew silent. Christian watched as several of the succubi who'd been injured during the battle were carried by their friends. They disappeared through the flap, the sound of their footsteps slowly fading as they entered the enclave.

He turned back to look at Andrew, who still looked moody. While some part of him felt horrible for letting his curious get the better of him, the other part couldn't help but ask, "What happened?"

"The Executioners happened." Andrew scowled. "They found us and tried to kill us. I managed to survive, barely, but my friends, my wife, and our unborn child were all slaughtered that night."

Christian turned away from the man, unable to look at Andrew anymore as guilt ate away at him. He didn't know why he was feeling guilty. It wasn't like he had killed Andrew's friends and family. And yet, his conscience still felt stricken and remorseful. He couldn't help but question himself. Had any of the supernatural beings he killed been like Andrew? People who had been forced to live a cursed existence through no desire of their own. Had they tried to find a place in this world? Tried to blend in? Did they have friends? Spouses? Husbands, mothers, brothers and sisters? How many families had he torn apart in his quest to protect humanity? He didn't know, couldn't know, and that made him feel even more ashamed.

The rest of his time standing guard as the succubi were led into the enclave was silent.

***

Lilith was aware that something was wrong almost as soon as the first group of injured succubi entered the hospital wing. She watched as they walked through the door. Sometimes it would be one person supporting another, but there were occasions where two people would be carrying one person between them, the injured person's arms slung over their shoulders.

All of them were injured to some degree. A few had scrapes and large, black bruises forming somewhere on their body—one girl looked like the entire left side of her chest and stomach had turned black. Others had cuts ranging from small nicks on their skin that had stopped bleeding some time ago to large gashes of torn flesh that were bleeding copious amounts of ichor. Large wads of fabric were being held to those injuries to stymie the flow of blood, but the cloths were already soaked through.

One of them, a young redhead who couldn't be more than a year older than Lilith, had a stab wound on her leg. And she knew it was a stab wound. She'd seen Christian get stabbed enough times to know what one looked like on sight. The enchanting female was being supported by none other than Clarissa, who had one arm wrapped around the girl's waist. The other was making sure the redhead had her arm around Clarissa's shoulder. The older, more mature succubus brought the young female to one of the beds, setting her down.

The nurses that had been on standby until now all came over to help the injured. It was startling to see how fast they shifted from gossipy females to serious nurses, like some kind of switch had been flipped. They walked over to the beds, which were now completely occupied by injured succubi, and began tending to the numerous injuries.

Lilith watched the whole process take place, watched as the nurses would diagnose their patients, then turn to the ones who brought the injured succubus in and ask them for something. Those women would go over to the cabinets or the cupboards, grab whatever was asked for, and then return to the bed. Seeing such unity and teamwork was impressive. Lilith didn't think she'd ever seen a group of people so focused on a single purpose like that before.

The sound of rumbling footsteps had Lilith turning her head just as Andrew walked through the door. Because he was so big, he had to bend over to walk in. He looked around for just a second, taking in the scene. Then his eyes strayed toward her, or to be more specific, they were locked onto the comatose figure lying on the medical bed next to Lilith.

"Andrew," Lilith said when the muscular man lumbered up to her. She looked around again, frowning as a pit of worry settled into her gut, and then looked back up at him. "Where's Christian?"

"He split off from us when we got to the enclave," Andrew said, rubbing the nape of his neck and looking a little uncomfortable. "I don't know where he is."

Lilith released a breath she hadn't known she'd been holding. When Christian had not entered the hospital with Andrew, for a moment, she had feared that something might have happened to him during the battle. Knowing that he was not injured lifted the weight that had settled onto her shoulders ever since Christian had gone off with Clarissa to fight.

She then felt worry settle into her stomach again. Why had Christian split off after the battle ended? Where was he? Was he okay?

"If you are worried about your mate, Lilith, then you should find him," Clarissa said, stepping over to them. There was a nurse surrounding the redhead, working on cleaning the wound with anesthetic. It looked like they were getting ready to stitch the injury back up. She could see the needle and thread sitting on the table.

"But I don't know where he is?"

"I suspect you do," Clarissa refuted, "but even if you do not, there is no need to worry. You can still find him. All you need to do is search for the place within yourself that belongs to Christian. Think of this as your first lesson."

"Search for the place within myself?" Lilith parroted as she blinked several times, confusion spreading. "What does that mean? H-hey! Don't walk away! What does that mean?"

"I am sorry," Clarissa said, moving over to one of the other beds and holding the hand of the woman lying on it. The woman had a stab wound in her shoulder. It was being cleaned right now with disinfectant, causing her to whimper and moan. "That is all the information I can give you. You must figure out the rest."

Lilith frowned at Clarissa, who was now completely ignoring her. Andrew moved past her, grabbing a chair and setting it down next to Catherine's prone form. He plopped himself in the chair and slouched over as if bearing the weight of the world on his shoulders.

It took her a few seconds, but Lilith eventually realized that she would not be getting any answers inside of the hospital. Clarissa wasn't talking, and Andrew didn't know anything about succubus, so it wasn't like he could answer her. One of the others might know what Clarissa meant, but she had no idea who they were, having never talked to any of them. What if they acted just like every other girl she'd ever met? What if they were rude to her? What if they felt like they were too good to answer her question?

Lilith decided to take her leave of the hospital. She didn't want to stay there anymore.

She walked out of the door and into a hallway, followed the hallway to door at the end, and made her exit.

Lilith moved along the walkway, her sandaled feet tapping a light, staccato rhythm against the ground. As she walked to nowhere in particular, her mind went back to Clarissa's words: search for the place within yourself that belongs to Christian. What did that mean? How could she "search for a place within herself?" Was there someplace inside of her that would help her find Christian? Like a metaphysical place? And how could she find this place? How could she look within herself when she didn't even know what that meant?

Stopping with a sudden abruptness, Lilith turned to face the railing. She placed her hands it and leaned forward, taking in the sights of the cavern. It really was very pretty, the lights from overhead crystals reflecting off the pool, steam rising from the surface of the water, and several walkways and buildings resting on top of the lake while more buildings sat along the shore, presenting a strange yet placid picture.

While she admired the scenery around her, Lilith tried to puzzle out Clarissa's words.

Search within myself. Search within myself. I don't get it. Does that mean I'm supposed to meditate or something?

Lilith had never done any kind of meditation. Was that what those old Yoga masters did? Sit with their legs and bodies crossed in strange pretzel shapes with their eyes closed while humming soft hymns? That didn't sound like something she could do. Lilith wasn't flexible enough to bend herself into a pretzel.

But then, maybe she didn't need to contort herself into strange shapes. Maybe all she needed to do was close her eyes and try to... feel out Christian's presence? Something like that. She had nothing to lose by trying.

And so, Lilith closed her eyes and tried to search inside of herself. She didn't know if she was doing it right—she didn't even know what she was doing, but she tried anyway. With her sense of sight shut off, her other senses became enhanced. She could smell a strange, almost acidic scent, sulfur maybe? From the lake? She shook her head, willing those sort of extraneous thoughts away. Her others senses also seemed to have picked up more than they normally would: the feel of cold stone underneath her palms, the heat from the steam that wafted off the lake in plumes, the sound of falling water. There must have been a waterfall somewhere inside the cavern.

After a time, even her five senses seemed to disappear. Lilith was about to panic and open her eyes again when she felt something strange, something foreign. She didn't know what it was, but it felt like it was a part of her yet at the same time not. This anomalous sensation, a strange swelling inside of her chest, felt familiar, but it was also an alien feeling, known yet unknown. What was it?

She began to walk, and the sensation got stronger. Deciding to follow it, she moved along the walkways and buildings, turning when the sensation intensified and moving backwards when it grew weaker. As she continued to follow the feeling, Lilith eventually came to a stop in a familiar hallway, in front of a familiar door. This was the door to the room where she and Christian had woken up in.

She paused, just for a moment, and then opened the door and walked in.

Christian was there, sitting on one of the chairs in front of the coffee table. His eyes were sightless, unseeing as they stared at nothing. There was a glazed over quality to them, the kind he had when his eyes were open but not being used. He was thinking about something, perhaps an issue that had come up during the battle against the goblins, or maybe an old problem that cropped up and needed a new solution.

Blond locks shimmered as Lilith shook her head. Whatever his problem was, it would not be solved by simply standing there, looking like an idiot.

She walked over to him, stopping right in front of his chair.

"Christian?"

He didn't answer. He didn't even blink. Whatever he was thinking about must have been deep if he didn't even hear her.

"Christian?"

Lilith tried calling his name a few more times, even speaking up a little louder each time. No matter how much she called, she couldn't seem to reach him.

She felt her cheeks swelling with air. If he was going to ignore her, then it looked like it was time to take more drastic measures.

Moving up to the chair, Lilith sat herself right on Christian's lap, sitting so that she was facing him, her legs straddling his thighs, her arms wrapping around his neck. This finally seemed to get a reaction out of the young man. He blinked several times, his red and green eyes snapping back into focus before they landed on her.

"Lilith..." he murmured, his voice sounding weak.

"Hey." Lilith smiled at him, pulling one of her hands back to cup his face. "Are you okay?"

"Maybe. I'm not sure."

"You're not sure?" The smile turned into a frown. "Did something happen?"

Christian sighed. "I was just talking to Andrew about something, and it made me think. Did you know that he's a werewolf?"

"I did not," Lilith said, not bothering to contain her surprise? She didn't know much about Andrew, but he didn't strike her as the type to get all furry and violent when the full moon was out. Then again, that was sort of the point, wasn't it? If you could tell someone wasn't human just by looking at them, then the Executioners wouldn't have such a hard time finding targets to kill. It would also make blending in with humans impossible.

It would also bring a whole lot of problems that she didn't want to think about. The term "opening up a can of worms" felt too clichéd, overrated, and not even close to describing the problems that would be unleashed if humans could tell when someone was not human at a glance. She could only imagine the panic that would spread.

"So what's bothering you about that?" Lilith asked, getting the conversation back on track. "I know you were an Executioner, and that you sort of killed people like Andrew... and me, but..."

"That's exactly the problem," Christian said, his shoulders slumping and his eyes losing a bit of their spark. "I used to be an Executioner. I spent years slaying all manner of supernatural beings: demons, vampires, werewolves, trolls, ogres, goblins, and mythological creatures of all kinds. I can no longer count the number of lives I've taken. And now I can't help but wonder if any of the people I killed truly deserved to die. How many innocent lives did I claim during my time as an Executioner?"

Lilith remained silent as Christian began to unload his troubles and worries. Her mother had once said that it was better to talk about the things that bother you, get them out into the open where someone you trust could help you get through them, instead of locking them away. Bottling things up only ensured that your emotions would explode when there was too much negative energy inside to be contained anymore. Christian needed this.

"Andrew told me about his past, about how he, his friends, and the woman he loved had gained control over their werewolf transformation and tried to make a living as street performers. They never harmed anyone, well, never harmed anyone on purpose. I imagine they had all killed a few people before gaining mastery over their transformation. Andrew did, at least." Christian paused, then sighed. "Either way, none of them harmed another living soul after that. They just wanted to live their lives the way they saw fit, and they had been until the Executioners found them."

Lilith sucked in a breath. She still didn't know much about the Executioners, but Christian had told her enough about them to know that nothing good was going to come from this story.

Christian must have sensed this because he gave her a sardonic smile laden with self-loathing. "I don't really think I need to tell you how this ends, do I?"

"No," Lilith whispered, shaking her head. "You don't."

"All this time, I thought I was doing the right thing, but Andrew's story made me think, really think about what I had done. And now I find myself asking questions I never thought to ask before. Did any of those people I killed deserve to die? How many of them had truly been evil? How many had families? How many people lost fathers, brothers, sons, mothers, daughters, and sisters because of me?" Christian gritted his teeth, and for the second time since she had known him, Lilith saw true conflict in his eyes. "I keep thinking about this and I... I realize that I've become the very thing I swore to destroy; a monster."

As the first tear fell from Christian's eyes, Lilith found herself frozen in shock. Christian a monster? What kind of nonsense was that? The very idea that he could be a monster, or even a person with evil in his heart, was utterly ridiculous.

It was only after taking a second to think about it that she understood how he must be feeling. Christian was a young man who lived by a strict code of morals. Every action he committed was because he thought it was the best thing to do. When he joined the Executioners and began slaying supernatural beings, he had only done so because he believed it was the right course of action, because he thought that by doing so, he was protecting humanity from the threat of creatures that far surpassed them in power.

And now he was finding out that he had been wrong. That even if there were some beings out there that would gladly harm humans, not every werewolf or vampire or whatever that he came across was going to be like that. It was a revelation that had started with her, but it was only now truly hitting home.

She suspected that the reason for this was due to Andrew not being someone he was intimately familiar with. It was probably easy for Christian to forget that she was a succubus. Lilith doubted the young man saw her as anything other than the woman he had fallen in love with. Now he was confronted with someone else who wasn't human but who also wasn't evil, and he was being forced to reevaluate everything he'd ever done.

"Come here," Lilith whispered, her voice soft, gentle, and filled with all the compassion and love she had for him. She wrapped her arms around Christian's head and pulled it down to rest lightly against her chest. She reached up with one hand and began to stroke his head like her foster mother had done for her so many times.

Christian didn't resist. Like a child seeking comfort from a strong adult, the young man buried her face into her chest. He wrapped his arms around her back and pulled her body as close to him as humanly possible.

The front of Lilith's shirt soon became soaked. The wetness near her chest began to spread across to the rest of the fabric. She ignored the chilling cold that came with it, as well as the way her shirt clung to her body. Every bit of her attention was focused on helping Christian.

"Don't worry, Christian," she said in a voice that was reminiscent of wind chimes. "You are not a monster, and you never will be. It's thanks to you that I'm still alive. You saved me. Those are not the actions of a monster. You have been here for me ever since we first met. Now it's my turn to be here for you."

Alone in the room, Lilith continued to hold Christian as he wept.

***

It was later in the evening, and Lilith found herself lying in bed, spooning against Christian's larger frame. The young man had used up a lot of energy upon releasing all of his pent-up thoughts and emotions. Having drained himself dry, Christian had fallen asleep almost before Lilith even managed to get him in the bed.

He'd been asleep before his head even hit the pillow.

Unlike her mate, Lilith had not fallen asleep. Oh, she was a bit tired. Watching the love of her live shed tears like he'd done exhausted her emotions, too. Maybe it had something to do with being a succubus, but she could have sworn she was able to feel his emotions as he cried; his sorrow, his sense of self-loathing, the rage he felt at being used to take innocent lives. There was a lot of repressed negativity inside of him, like a storm that had been building for years without anyone even noticing.

Lilith wondered if that storm had disappeared, or if it had merely subsided and was just waiting for the time it could come back with vengeance.

She hoped it was the former.

Lying on her side, her front pressed up against Christian's back, Lilith buried her nose into messy raven locks.

Christian had not taken a shower before going to bed. He smelled of sweat, metal, and blood, a coppery tang that was rather unpleasant all things considered. For some reason, the scent didn't bother Lilith very much, or at all. It was repugnant and disgusting, yet she didn't care. Beneath the odor that came from someone who'd shed the blood of others in combat was the fragrance of the man she had come to love. Nothing else mattered.

Yet Lilith knew she could not stay there. Now that Christian was asleep, there was something she had to do. It wasn't something she intended to hide from him, nor something she planned on keeping a secret, but it was, nevertheless, important that she make this choice on her own.

Unwinding both her arms and legs from Christian's body, Lilith carefully crawled out of bed. She paused when her bare feet hit the carpet, her toes clenching at the feathery soft feel as the strands of fabric wove between her toes. It felt so nice...

Lilith shook her head. Honestly, getting distracted by carpet of all things!

She grabbed her sandals and put them on, then exited the room.

Lilith was not exactly sure where she was going, or even where she wanted to go. She wandered the halls and down the walkways, searching. The night was late. Even though she could not see the sky, the lack of light being refracted off the cavern walls gave the late hour away. According to Clarissa, those crystals reflected sunlight that streamed in through small cracks in the ground.

She eventually arrived at the hospital, having not found anywhere else she could think to go.

Fortunately, the person she was looking for was there.

"Lilith," Clarissa greeted the younger woman with a nod. "I somehow get the feeling you're not here to visit the patients. I take it there is a reason for you to be seeking me out at this late hour? Do you wish to learn more about your mother, per chance?"

Clarissa was sitting on a chair next to the young, red-haired woman Lilith had seen her helping before. The other women was asleep, and she was tenderly stroking her hair like a mother would do for a daughter.

Lilith paused. "Yes," she admitted after a moment's hesitation. "But not right this minute."

"I see." Clarissa stopped her tender ministrations to the young woman, who released a mild whimper of complaint. Hearing this, the oldest among them shook her head, and then resumed her hair petting. The redhead sighed and relaxed. "If you are not here to learn more about your mother, then I am going to go out on a limb and say you wish to learn about the powers we succubi have at our disposal?"

"Yes."

"May I ask why?" Lilith stared at the woman, confused. Clarissa must have seen this, because a second later, she spoke again. "What I mean is, why do you wish to learn how to use your powers? What is your reason for wanting to learn them?"

"I..." Lilith started, then stopped. After another moment, she began again, choosing each word slowly, as if afraid of saying the wrong thing. "From the moment Christian and I met, it has always been him who had to save me. When a No Life King I once made contact with years ago came to claim me against my will, it was Christian who rescued me and fought against Damien. Even then, he almost died. And when we ran to try and escape pursuit from the Executioners, it was Christian who protected me, fighting them off and nearly dying several times in the process."

Lilith clenched her hands so hard that her arms shook.

"So far, every single time we have been confronted by something dangerous, it was Christian who was in the lead, taking me by the hand and guiding me along, shielding me from harm. I didn't question it at first. I think a part of me was just too happy to have someone who cared about me so much. But, as the danger we found ourselves in began to escalate, I found myself growing more and more worried for his safety, and I... I can't help but feel useless. Day after day, he risks his life for mine, but I can never do anything to help him."

Shuddering from her head to her toes, Lilith tried to center herself.

"I don't want to be that person anymore. I don't want to be the girl who constantly needs to be rescued. I want to be able to stand side by side with Christian, not behind him, staring at his back as he braves the dangers that threaten to consume us." Lilith looked at Clarissa, her eyes narrowed in determination and her feelings laid bare. "I want to protect Christian just as much as he protects me."

Clarissa stared at her for a long moment. The woman's eyes contained within them a wisdom that Lilith had never seen before. It was only now, as she gazed into this succubus's dark eyes that Lilith realized just how old this woman truly was. She may look like she hadn't aged past twenty-one, but she was likely three or four times the age of Lilith herself, maybe even older than that.

"Your intentions are pure," Clarissa said after several moments of silence had passed. "I can see that your only desire is to keep your mate safe, to stand at his side instead of standing behind him and letting him protect you. That is good. Had you come to me wanting to learn how to wield the powers of a succubus for any reason other than the one you just stated, I would have turned you down."

It took Lilith a moment to process Clarissa's words, but when she did, her eyes widened. "You mean...?"

"Yes, starting tomorrow I will begin training you in how to use the power granted to us succubus."

"Thank you very much." Lilith bowed to the woman, partially in gratitude but also to hide her relieved tears. She was finally going to become useful to Christian. No more would she have to hide behind him, helplessly watching him bleed for her. This time, she would be the one protecting him. "I won't let you down. I—wait." Lilith paused in her celebration, her exuberance dying down. She looked at the woman, frowning. "Why tomorrow?"

"You want to start now?"

"Uh," Lilith suddenly looked unsure of herself. "Yes?"

"Lilith," Clarissa's tone was patient, but held a touch of exasperation. "You do know what time it is, don't you?"

"Um..."

"It's 9:54pm. Everyone else is asleep."

"Oh..." Lilith felt heat rise to her cheeks. She looked down at the floor, her hair shifting to frame her in a curtain of blond. It did a decent job of masking the redness in her cheeks. "I was just hoping, you know, that I could get a head start on learning to control my powers."

"Lilith. Go to bed. Get some sleep. Tomorrow, we will begin your training, not tonight."

"...Yes ma'am," Lilith said in a quiet tone before she shuffled outside.

Chapter 5

Having rescued Tristin, Samantha and the other two members of the Executioners, Leon and Sif, escaped from the prison that had been holding the ex-intelligence operative and made their way into the nearest city. It might not have been the best option, being so close to the place that they had just managed to break into and out of, but the next closest city was several hours away, and it was already late.

Cedar City was a tiny, quaint little town in Utah. Built along the I-15, Veteran's Memorial Highway, the city was one of those stopping points where people usually stayed to rest before traveling through it on the way to their true destination. It was more or less a tourism gateway to attractions such as Bryce Canyon National Park, Zion National Park, and Dixie National Forest.

The place they had chosen to stay in was a cheap little motel called Supercedes Motel. Like a good deal of motels of its kind, Supercedes was a tiny one-story building. Its red bricks looked a little dull, worn down and baked from being in the sun for so long without refurbishing, and the brown roof was more than just a little rickety. The building was shaped to look like a U, with the parking lot located in the center. It was the kind of place truckers and other people who just wanted a really cheap place to stay the night got a room in before moving on.

Samantha looked out the window of the small room she and Sif were sharing. Their room was basic, bare bones even. It had two twin-sized beds with a nightstand in between them, and a small, beaten up dresser. Near the front, next the entrance, was a door that led to a basic shower/tub bathroom combination with a toilet and a tiny sink. Even her previous office had more decoration than this.

As she stared at the cars passing by, their lights the only way she could see in the darkness, the young woman tucked a strand of her long hair behind her left ear, wondering where Christian was and if he was safe.

She then thought about the succubus he was with and scowled.

It was dark outside. Night had long since fallen, and the stars had come out. The moon, shaped in a crescent, was casting its pale glow upon the earth. From where she was standing, Samantha could easily spot the mass twinkling of celestial bodies in the velvet-colored sky.

Samantha used to love the night. Back when she was a kid living in a small town just off the border of San Diego, she would always go out at night, lay on top of her mother's trailer, and stargaze. She'd been a fan of the time when the sky was dark, and the moon was out. She used to love it when millions of stars twinkled with an incredible luster, as if God had taken a paintbrush and given the world a masterpiece the likes of which no one would ever be able to replicate.

That was before she had learned about the horrors this world had to offer, before her mother was killed by a vampire, her blood drained and her body turned into a withered husk, a ghoul, a soulless shadow of her former self. After that, Samantha had no longer enjoyed nighttime. How could she? Ever since that moment, whenever the world descended into darkness, all Samantha could think about was how this was the time when mothers, brothers, sisters, fathers—when family members were stolen away by the insatiable hunger of monsters that most humans could never contend with.

Pressing a hand against the glass, her fingers splayed, Samantha stared at her reflection in the mirror. Long raven hair. Blue eyes. Her face was a little long, her chin a little pointed. She had pale skin and dark lips.

She'd never considered herself particularly attractive, though some of the people she corresponded with outside of the Executioners seemed to think otherwise—she'd even caught some people within the Executioners staring at her as she walked by. But to Samantha, when she looked at herself in the mirror, all she saw was a woman with, maybe, slightly above average looks and an athletic build.

Was that why Christian had never taken notice of her? Other than the obvious "Executioners aren't allowed to fall in love" law, of course.

She sighed. The law about Executioners not being allowed to fall in love was an old law dating back to the middle ages. It had never been changed or removed, but very few members followed the law anymore, which had become obsolete. Christian was the only person she knew aside from one or two others who followed it.

"Commander, I'm done with the shower."

The voice of Sif intruded upon her thoughts. Samantha turned, taking in the much shorter woman as she walked in. She was wearing nothing more than a simple towel wrapped around her short body, showing so much leg Samantha was sure that if the fabric were any shorter it would reveal much, *much* more than just her tanned thighs. Another towel was being used to dry her hair. She didn't appear too concerned about being covered in nothing but a towel in Samantha's presence.

Modesty was not something most people in the Executioners had, at least when dealing with the same sex. Much like Sif, Samantha had once lived in the barracks where all female Executioners lived. When you don't have your own facilities and are forced to share a shower with a bunch of other women, things like modesty get shoved down the garbage disposal and then ground into a fine paste.

Objectively speaking, Samantha thought Sif was much more attractive than she was. The younger woman was short, to be sure, but her features were a lot more feminine than her own, soft, gentle, and not nearly as sharp. Except for her eyes. Those two orbs were so sharp they could probably slice through Orichalcum with ease.

"I'm not your commander anymore, Sif," Samantha said, shaking her head to get rid of her errant thoughts. Maybe it was due to Christian suddenly running off with a woman, but Samantha had found herself checking out other females more and more, wondering what it was that he saw in Lilith that she didn't have.

She wanted to blame it on the girl being a succubus but found that she really couldn't. She didn't know why.

"You will always be my commander, regardless of whether we are still with the Executioners or not," the other woman replied. Sif set the towel she'd been rubbing her hair dry with on the table, then unwrapped the one around her torso, revealing her full glory to

Samantha. When she'd set that on the table as well, she began getting dressed.

Unlike her normal clothing, Sif had chosen to wear basic blue jeans that road a tad low on her hips and a white shirt that stretched across her surprisingly large chest. She was still wearing her duster since it looked at least halfway normal. There was also the fact that the woman couldn't bear to part with it ("It's a symbol of everything I've been through up to this point," had been her excuse). On her feet were her normal black boots with a slight elevation. Sif looked down at herself after she finished, clicking her tongue a bit as she pulled at her shirt.

"Still uncomfortable without breast bindings?" asked Samantha.

"I just don't see why I can't wear them," she muttered, huffing a bit as she moved to sit down on her bed. The small bed was the definition of quintessential cheap motel beds. Stiff mattress. White comforter. A basic red quilted blanket folded up and laying at the foot of the bed. Exactly four white, stiff, and uncomfortable pillows. Samantha and Sif had only slept in those for a day—the day before they had gone to rescue Tristin, and they already didn't like them.

Even Executioners lived in more comfort than this.

"You'll have to get used to it," Samantha informed her, moving away from the window and sitting on the chair next to a small table. "Because you've always worn those bindings, no one realizes how big your, well, how large your chest is. That means when they come searching for you, they'll be looking for someone who has a small, almost nonexistent chest. So long as they don't give you a closer inspection, they won't even notice it's you."

"That's true, I guess."

The sense of sight was an unusual thing. Most people never really noticed the smaller details. If someone were to look at a person's face, they would only be able to pick out the most obvious details: the color of their eyes, the shape of their nose and face, and whether or not they had any identifying marks. Smaller details tended to get lost during observation.

While certain supernatural races saw the world differently (vampires saw the world in shades of heat, for example), every race still saw people by their physical traits. If the demons were looking for "a short woman with a small chest," they would completely dismiss "a short woman with a large chest who just happened to have a similar face."

Sif accepted this, though she still didn't appear too happy by the prospect of not having her breast bindings. Samantha knew what the problem was. The short woman had always felt uncomfortable with her bust size due to her small stature. She was absolutely tiny, the same size as most middle school girls, but her breasts were huge, bigger even than Samantha's. When combined with her diminutive stature, her chest stood out, and not in a good way.

Those two things on her chest received more attention than anything else.

"Having these large... *things* on my chest makes it hard for me to fight. They're always getting in the way, bouncing around and causing me nothing but trouble. I don't know why so many women want them. They're such an inconvenience."

Of course, she made up the excuse that having them made it harder to fight, which they did, but Samantha knew the real problem.

"I know, but there isn't much we can do." Samantha tilted her head just a bit, thinking. "If you really want to, you can still wear the bindings. That will make it easier for them to recognize you, but we might still be able to avoid detection if we're careful."

Sif paused before saying anything, her face scrunching just slightly. She appeared to be in deep thought.

"No," she decided at last, sighing. "Your choice was the correct one. Very few people will recognize me like this. Only those who shared a barracks with me know about my chest, and they're all dead. We'll be safer if I just tough it out." Even though she apparently agreed with Samantha's decision, she still looked at her chest like it was something disgusting.

A knock at the door sounded out. Samantha and Sif both looked over at the door, then at each other.

"It's probably the boys," Sif said, referring to Leon and Tristin. They had their own room, which was across the hall and two doors down.

Sif stood to her feet and walked to the door. Opening it, she looked at the two figures standing outside. From her place near the table, Samantha could see that one of them was massive, easily overshadowing Sif and casting her in slight darkness as the light from the hallway was blocked out by the person's bulky frame. It was likely Leon. There was no one else she knew who was that large. Her thoughts were confirmed when Sif moved out of the way, opening the door wider, allowing Leon and Tristin to enter.

The two swept into the room, Tristin flouncing onto Samantha's bed, bouncing several times, a grin like that of a child's plastered on his face. Leon, on the other hand, walked into the room and took to leaning against the wall near the door, his arms crossed and an uncomfortable look on his face.

"Get off my bed, Tristin! You're soiling it!"

"Aw! Come on, boss lady!" Tristin modulated his voice into a pitched whine, his blue eyes growing large. "There's no other place for me to sit. Let me enjoy the lovely strawberry scent of your hair—I mean, your pillows."

"Tristin," Samantha hissed in a low, poisonous voice, her eyes narrowed into twin daggers. "You will get off that bed right now or so help me God, I will shove Zaphkiel down your throat!"

Maybe it was the threat of impalement through the mouth, or maybe it was her glare, but Tristin jumped off the bed with a girlish squeak. "Eek! I-I mean, hahaha, yo-you drive a hard bargain, boss lad—I mean Samantha. I'll just, eh, um, sit over here on the floor. Eh, eh hehe."

Despite Tristin getting off her bed and sitting on the floor, Samantha continued to glare at the blond-haired pretty boy, prompting him to gulp. She kept this up, watching him squirm underneath her fierce stare, until she was sure he was properly cowed. And then, once she was positive he wouldn't do or say something stupid, she turned to look at the other male in the group.

"Problem, Leon?" asked Samantha.

"Nah, it's just..." The large, muscular man paused, then shrugged his shoulders, his face looking put out. "I just feel a bit naked without my hammer, ya know? This is the first time Sandalphon and I have been apart since I became a member of the XIII."

Samantha nodded, absently rubbing a hand down the long, black case sitting on her table. "I understand how you feel."

And she did. For members of the XIII like herself, Leon, Sif, and Christian, the bond between wielder and weapon was indispensable. The weapons they possessed were more than just mere weapons. They were an extension of the self, as much a part of them as an arm or leg. To be away from your weapon was similar to having a piece of your body cut off. It was a truly discomfiting feeling.

"But you know we had to leave it in the van. That thing is far too large and conspicuous to be carrying around in public. And it's too heavy to place in a case."

"I know, I know." Leon sighed, scratching at his head. "Doesn't make me feel any better about it."

Samantha stared between Sif and Leon before shaking her head. "You two really are birds of a feather, you know that? Sif was saying something very similar just a little while ago." It might have been about something completely different, but the semblance between their words paralleled each other too much to simply ignore.

It was almost amusing, watching the way Sif and Leon looked over at each other, turned red, and then looked away. Samantha almost snorted. The Executioners really were an inept group when it came to matters of the heart. Not that she could say she was any better.

Coughing into her hand, Samantha decided that it was time she started explaining everything. "Tristin, I know you don't know about anything what's happened recently, so before I get into what our next course of action is, I figured I'd tell you what's been going on while you were imprisoned."

"That would be nice," Tristin admitted, shrugging his shoulders, his smile shining and bright. "I feel like I missed out on a lot of stuff. The guards weren't very talkative, so I never heard any news from the outside."

"I thought low-level demons like those marionettes couldn't talk?" Leon said, frowning.

"They can't." Sif snorted, crossing her arms under her chest. "Tristin was just being sarcastic."

"Ah."

"I figured you would appreciate that," Samantha started again before anyone could interrupt her. "You should—are you listening to me?"

"Hm?" Tristin didn't respond when Samantha asked her question.

Narrowing her eyes, the young woman looked over to see what Tristin was staring at. Less than a second later, she was trying to burn a hole through the obnoxious man's head.

"Tristin, if you don't stop staring at Sif's chest right now, I am going to let you experience what it feels like to have three feet of steel shoved through your hindquarters."

The threatening proclamation prompted a response from everyone in the room. Sif moved her hands to cover her chest and tossed Tristin a ferocious glare. Leon growled, sounding like an angry lion whose pack was just threatened. He, too, gave the most perverse member of their group a stare that contained enough vitriol to fill a pool. On the other hand, Tristin squeaked like a scared mouse, then began searching the room wildly, as if he were looking for a place to hide or trying to judge the distance between him and the nearest exit. When he realized that he was in the center of the room, surrounded, his frantic eyes turned toward his former boss.

"I'm sorry! I'm sorry!" He apologized, clapping his hands over his head and holding them up in a prayer sign. "I couldn't help it. This is the first time I've gone so long without sex, and it's really getting to me."

It was most unorthodox, how the rules regarding romance within the Executioners worked. Relationships were forbidden. The act of falling in love was seen as a sign that your loyalties were being split and you were no longer capable of bearing the burden of protecting humanity. At the same time, sex was not forbidden, and there were a number of Executioners, both male and female, who took advantage of this loophole to partake in the act.

Samantha knew the reason for the loophole. Very few Executioners had been religious. Only about ten percent of them had actually been Catholic. The rest were mercenaries hired off the streets. Forcing such harsh restrictions on people like that was akin to lighting a stick of dynamite and then tossing it into a box full of TNT. The Catholic Church had therefore decided to be lenient. The laws that had been established for over one-thousand years, when the Executioners had only numbered in the thousands, were changed as more and more members were needed to help fight off the growing number of supernatural creatures.

She knew this, and she knew that Tristin was one of those people who abused that law every chance he got.

That didn't mean she had to like it.

"Why would a lack of sex—" Samantha started, but quickly shook her head. "You know what, I don't want to know. I really don't. And I don't care what your problem is either. Stop ogling Sif and start focusing."

"Right. Got it. No more ogling Sif. Just let me write this down in my notepad."

Samantha rolled her eyes, aware that the young man was trying to play off his anxiety and fear of the two former XIII members. Idiot. "Now that Tristin's moment of stupid has passed, I should start by telling you that it's been exactly three weeks and one day since your incarceration."

"Three whole weeks, huh?" Tristin looked amazed to know that so much time had passed while he'd been imprisoned. "I hadn't realized it had been that long." Which made sense. Keeping track of time when you were in a place that offered no sunlight and no news from the outside world meant knowing how much time had passed was nearly impossible. Even someone like Samantha would have been hard pressed to track the passage of time in that situation.

"Yes, well, a lot has happened since you were arrested for treason," Samantha said, looking to continue. She took a deep breath and, upon blowing it out, began to tell Tristin about what he'd missed. "This may come as a shock to you, but about one week after you were arrested, every single Executioner stronghold in the entire world was attacked by several hundred low and middle-class demons—"

"What!?"

"Don't interrupt me!"

"Sorry." Tristin rubbed the back of his head as Samantha scowled at him. "I just didn't, I mean, I did sort of expect something like this to happen, just not so soon. It's a bit of a shock."

"I imagine it would be," Samantha allowed, calming down so that she could continue her story. "I believe they acted more swiftly than you had anticipated because of the information you managed to find on their network. I don't think they realized you had actually downloaded it onto a USB drive," she added after a moment's thought. "But I'm positive that they were acting in haste on the off-chance that you did have a way of getting that information to me."

Undoubtedly, their enemies knew that if Samantha had managed to acquire the information that detailed their plans, then she would have alerted the other Executioner strongholds and bases. That would have meant the Executioners would have had time to either prepare for imminent attack or abandon their base before an attack could take place, thereby nullifying the plan to destroy the Executioners before they knew what hit them.

"I was fortunate enough to survive the attack on the base in Los Angeles, and I managed to get out with a few other Executioners. Thanks to the information you provided, I was also able to learn about their plans. That said, most of the other bases were not so lucky." Samantha paused for a moment, pensive as she worried her lower lip. "I had tried to get out a warning to the other strongholds, but I was too late. Many of our bases were attacked and destroyed before I even managed to send the message."

"Do we know if anyone managed to survive?"

Samantha shook her head. "We do not, but I doubt there were any survivors. Demons are nothing if not thorough when it comes to killing those around them. They do not stop until everybody in their vicinity is dead." Demons were a relentless species, one of the few who could be classified as truly evil. Their entire purpose was nothing less than the subjugation or eradication of all mankind. "Only Leon and Sif managed to survive the attacks and escape, taking a mere handful of Executioners with them. But by the time I had managed to find them, all the others were dead or dying."

She still remembered how she'd found Sif and Leon, surrounded by a horde of middle-class demons, bleeding and battered and bruised, with dead bodies lying all around them in varying states of dismemberment. There had been a swathe of destruction leading from where they'd fled, showing that they had been fighting a running battle in their attempt to escape. Had Samantha been a few minutes late in finding them, it was incontrovertible that they would have died that day.

Tristin raised a hand up to the back of his neck, giving it a strong rub as he closed his eyes and sighed. "So out of all the Executioners, only Leon, Sif, and a small handful of Executioners from our Headquarters managed to survive?"

The three powerful warriors all shared a look before turning back to Tristin.

"We're unsure," Samantha admitted. "We have no way of knowing how many truly survived. All communication between the Executioner strongholds has been cut off. We were unable to get word out to the others, which leads me to believe no one else escaped. Even Sif and Leon only managed to escape because of their own prowess on the battlefield and luck."

Leon and Sif were both exceptionally powerful warriors, renowned for their great strength and ability. Alone, they were more than capable of taking care of just about any threat they faced short of the higher-class demons and monsters like No Life Kings, Ancestors, and those few supernatural beings that managed to claw through the ranks of their respective species. They hadn't earned their titles and rank for no reason.

"It is possible that others survived," Sif decided to add her own input. "Especially if there was a member of the XIII with them at the time. That being said, I doubt anyone who did not have one of us with them is still alive. When the demons invaded our stronghold, they were teleported directly inside, past our defenses. They were like a swarm. They just kept pouring out of these red portals, running over everyone, tearing people apart with hands, swords, and teeth. I've never seen anything so horrible in my entire life."

Sif shivered, the act causing Leon to walk over to her and place a hand on her shoulder. She looked up at him, so small and vulnerable in that moment. No longer was she Sif, The Destroyer of Men. Instead she simply looked like a helpless little girl. Seeing people you had literally grown up with get torn apart did that to a person.

"Sif and I were lucky," Leon added. "We weren't in the area where the portals were opened, and we heard the screaming well before the first demon reached us. I think that might be part of the reason we were able to escape. We must have gone through at least two hundred demons before managing to make our way out with the few other Executioners we were able to save. And yet even then," Leon clenched his free hand into a fist, "even then, they followed us. The rest of our group were all killed, and we were the only ones left. We might have very well died that day, were it not for Samantha's timely arrival."

All eyes turned toward Samantha. Tristin was grinning.

"That's my boss lady. Smart, strong, and super sexy," he said, giving the ravenette an exaggerated wink.

Samantha's right eye twitched. "Prison must have rid you of any sense of tact, Tristin. You were never this bold, or this stupid, back when you were working for me."

"Um, yeah, let's go with that explanation," Tristin said, nodding. "It sounds better than any explanation I've got."

"So what do we do now?" Sif stared at Samantha, her eyes once more those of a hardened warrior.

"The first thing we need to do is get back to base," Samantha said, "I want to make sure the Executioners I managed to bring with me have everything set up at the safe house. After that, we need to start gathering allies."

"I doubt there are many allies left to be gathered," Tristin commented, sounding at least a little more serious now that they were talking about their plans. "If what you all said is true, then there's likely less than a dozen Executioners who managed to escape when the demons attacked. And none of them will be in North America. Aside from you, Sif, and Leon, the only other XIII member on this continent is Christian."

"Speaking of Christian, just where is the little guy?" asked Leon. "I would have expected him to be right by your side."

Samantha shifted, uncomfortable as Leon and Sif stared at her, expectant looks in their eyes. "Christian is... gone."

"You mean...?"

"He's not dead," Samantha said when she saw the looks of disbelief directed her way. "However, he will not be able to help us here."

"But why?" Sif looked honestly confused, even if it was hard to tell because of the generally cold facade she often put up. "Was he injured?"

"No. He wasn't injured, at least to the best of my knowledge."

"Then why can't he help us? I'm not sure I understand. Christian has always been one of our most loyal and powerful members. Ever since he started working as an Executioner, he's always done his best for the cause. It's how he managed to climb through the ranks in such a short amount of time. I can't see him just dropping out of contact and leaving you high and dry."

"That's because you don't know the whole story behind his departure from the Executioners," Tristin said, gleeful, his eyes twinkling with amused merriment and his mouth stretched into a Cheshire grin.

"Tristin," Samantha said, a hint of warning in her voice.

It was a warning that Tristin ignored. "Christian found himself a girlfriend."

"Tristin!"

"A girlfriend?!" Eyes widening, Sif and Leon looked between the now glowering Samantha and Tristin with his sunny disposition. Of the two people whose mouths were agape with astonishment, it was Leon who managed to find his voice and actually ask the question that was burning in their minds. "You're telling me that Christian, straight-laced, morally incorruptible Christian Crux, found himself a woman?"

"And not just any woman," Tristin added, his ever-present grin widening to the point where it split his face in half. "He's got a—"

"That's quite enough out of you, Tristin Baluf!" Samantha hissed, her tone sibilant, poisonous, and angry. "You need to learn when to keep your mouth shut!"

Under that glare, which was harsh enough to burn just about anything in its path, Tristin found himself shrinking back. She watched as he quivered, eyes wide in fright. Samantha wondered If the young man even realized he'd gone too far, or if he was just afraid of being on the receiving end of her sword.

Knowing Tristin, it was probably the latter.

"Now hold on, Samantha." Leon held up a massive hand, forestalling her glare at Tristin. The other male sent him a thankful look, which he ignored. "I think we've got a right to know what Tristin's talking about. A lot of rumors about Christian had been circulating before the demons attacked. All of them were far-fetched and unbelievable. This would go a long way towards clearing that up."

"What's it matter if we clear this up now?" asked Samantha. "Christian Crux is irrelevant to our survival. He is no longer one of us, and I doubt we'll be seeing him any time soon. If he's not already dead, then he'll have gone into hiding, and with Bishop Vertrou chasing after him, I doubt he'll show himself."

"But if the Catholic Church is after him, then wouldn't he make a good ally?" Leon argued his case. "I'm a damn good fighter, and you and Sif are unbelievably strong and capable warriors, but Christian is the only one among us who's defeated a high-class demon in single combat. Having him on our side could prove to be invaluable. If nothing else, his presence would raise our morale."

Samantha struggled with herself, debating whether or not she should inform them of Christian's betrayal. It was not something she liked to think about. Out of all the people in the world, she had never imagined he would betray her, especially in the way he'd done it, by running off with an inhuman creature.

And yet despite her anger toward him, Samantha still desired to protect his reputation. If Leon and Sif learned that Christian had run away with a succubus, his standing would be sullied in the eyes of his former companions. She didn't want that. Even though he had betrayed her and the Executioners, she had no desire to see the reputation of the young man she respected get run through the mud.

Then again, was what he did really a betrayal? With everything that Samantha had learned these past three weeks, could she truly, honestly say that Christian had betrayed them? Yes, he had run away with a creature they had sworn to kill, but it was beginning to look like the Executioners had been played for fools long before she or Christian had ever joined the secret branch—former secret branch—of the Catholic Church.

Samantha pressed a hand to her face, her eyes clenched shut and her teeth grit in irritation. She was no longer sure of anything anymore. She was no longer convinced that she could say with absolute honesty what was right and what was wrong. Her faith had been shaken, her beliefs cast in the mud. Everything she knew, or thought she knew, appeared to have been lies passed through the lips of a man—a monster—whose silken words were like a poison, slowly eroding everything that was good and just and righteous in this world.

"Samantha?"

A hand on her shoulder caused Samantha to look up. Tristin stood before her, looking mildly worried. His blue eyes, holding slight bags underneath them, a sign that he'd not gotten a good night's sleep in a while, stared down at her in concern.

"I'm fine," she said, waving off his hand and standing up. Tristin stepped back, allowing the woman to get back to her feet. Upon rising from her chair, Samantha, her raven hair falling about her body like a wreath, gazed upon her two compatriots. "I suppose you do have a right to know why Christian is no longer with us. He is your—was—your companion as well. I just..." Samantha bit her lip, hesitating. "I simply do not want either of you to think any less of him when you learn about his reasons for leaving."

Leon and Sif shared a long, powerful look at each other. They both seemed to realize that what Samantha had to say was big. Maybe it was not as significant as several hordes of demons simultaneously attacking and ransacking every Executioner base in the world, but it was big enough that it could fundamentally change the way they thought about someone, a person they both knew well enough to consider a respected comrade, if not a friend.

"Samantha, me and Sif just had our base overrun with demons that were summoned by another demon disguised as a Clergyman. I doubt there is anything you could tell us about Christian that would make us feel anymore betrayed or confused than we already are."

"He is right," Sif added, her voice solemn. "Christian was never one to do something without a good reason. If he left the Executioners, then it must have been something he felt needed to be done."

"I wouldn't be so sure of that," Samantha muttered, then sighed. Maybe her own perception of Christian was being colored by her own personal betrayal. She knew that, realistically speaking, she and Christian would have never worked out. She was older than him by several years, his superior officer, and before she'd become the commander of the western US hemisphere, she'd been a former Warrior much like himself. That justification didn't really help her feelings on the matter, but it might explain why she felt so jaded by the experience.

She shook her head. When had things gotten so complicated?

"The reason Christian is no longer with us is because—"

Samantha's words were cut off mid-sentence as an intense feeling, a wave of vile, repulsive energy, washed over them. A thrill ran down her spine. Her skin crawled. The feeling of her heart quickening pumped adrenaline into her veins.

Everyone went wide-eyed as the feeling of being covered in a layer of tainted power overcame their senses and left them reeling.

Leon's startles eyes were wide and unfocused. "That's—"

"—Demonic energy," Sif finished, her expression grim.

Demonic energy, often known by many different names depending on the country a person was born in, was the energy utilized by demons, denizens of the underworld. Most people were not sensitive to the energy because it was foreign to the Earth. It was a power that did not manifest itself in a form that could normally be felt by humans. Only those who had been trained to sense it, like Samantha, Sif, and Leon—or those who were naturally sensitive to such energies like Tristin—could detect when the energy was being used.

Samantha ran over to the window and looked out. It did not take her very long—less than a second, in fact—to discover the source of the taint, or at least discover what the repugnant feeling that surged over them was for.

Everything looked almost exactly the same as it had. The streets were still there, the cars were still there, there were still people walking along the sidewalks, but that was where the similarities ended. The images were blurry and unfocused. Crimson seeped across her vision, obscuring everything around her. It was similar to looking at a roll of film before it developed.

Turning around, a grim feeling settling on her shoulders, Samantha looked at Leon, Tristin, and Sif. All of them were wearing the same expression as her.

"Something just set up a barrier," she said, though it didn't really need to be. "They've found us."

Chapter 6

Barriers were a unique ability that only certain types of demons possessed. These demons, once having been believed to be the resurrected souls of sorcerers and sorceresses, were a type of upper-class demon. They were not on par with beings such as the Demon Knight Abaddon the Destroyer, but they were infinitely more powerful than a middle-class demon.

Executioners ranked them as A-ranked threats.

This particular barrier that had been cast was one that separated a specific area of the human world and placed it within another dimension: limbo. Once the barrier was put in place, it was impossible to break free unless the demon who cast the spell was killed.

"This really, really sucks," Tristin bemoaned, holding his hands to his face. "I just managed to escape from prison, and not even a day later, those stupid marionettes are coming after me."

"Don't forget they're coming after us as well," Leon said.

Tristin ignored him. "What did I do to deserve this?"

"Shut up, Tristin!" Samantha snapped. She turned away from the window and looked at the three people in her room. "Sif, put your gauntlets on." Sif nodded and moved over to her bed, pulling a case from underneath it. Samantha then turned to the pretty boy of the group. "Tristin, do you have your gun?"

"No. I left it in the car. But it wouldn't matter even if I had it with me. You know how bad of a shot I am. I'm more liable to shoot one of you guys in the head than I am my enemies."

"Dang it," Samantha swore, but did not dispute Tristin's claim. The man was a horrible shot, and everybody knew it. The last test he had taken had been given the grand score of -10 because he almost shot the person administering the test. "In that case, Sif and I will have to protect you and Leon on our way to the car."

Samantha opened the latches to the long, black case on table, revealing her sword, Zaphkiel, residing in its sheath. Both blade and sheath were unique weapons. The blade was shaped like a standard Japanese katana, but the hilt and guard were designed more along the lines of a fencer's sword. The guard was made from a series of long, interweaving metal strings that came together and curved around the handle, protecting Samantha's hand and fingers. The sheath was red and black, inlaid with golden crosses. Much like her sword, it, too, was made of Orichalcum.

"Are we going to try driving out of the barrier?" asked Leon, frowning. "That doesn't seem like the smartest idea. We'll be sitting ducks in a vehicle."

"We're not going to be driving out," Samantha said, grabbing her weapon by the sheath. "You can't drive out of a barrier anyway. However, your Sandalphon is in the car. We need to grab it so that you have a weapon to defend yourself with."

"Ah. Gotcha."

"I'm ready," Sif said, standing up and holding up her hands to reveal her clawed gauntlets attached. The gauntlets were actually small, only covering her hand and a bit of her wrist. Four long, thick blades extended outwards from the gloves' fronts. The clawed extensions were at least half a foot in length and looked more than capable of tearing any known material to shreds. Known as Daniel and Gladreel, the gauntlets were made from Orichalcum just like every other weapon used by the XIII. Tristin shivered, no doubt remembering what she'd done to the marionettes with those claws.

Samantha nodded at the other woman. "Good. Let's go then."

The group of four left the room and hurried down the hall. There were a few people walking around the hall, but their forms were indistinct, blurry and smoky, like they weren't really there, like they were some type of hologram that kept flickering in and out.

Which made sense. Limbo was not a place that could generally sustain human life. It was a border world, the dimension in between earth and hell. Only those who were dead, or those who had taken a special vaccination created by the Science Division of the Executioners, could enter limbo and retain physical form.

Samantha turned to look at Tristin as they ran. "Tristin, how is it that you have managed to retain physical form? I know you have not taken the vaccination, as you are not one of those who deal with slaying demons or slaying anything."

"Oh, you know me." Tristin grinned at her as he panted for breath. "I'm just awesome like that."

"Tristin..."

"Urk!" Tristin looked away. "I-Is now really the time for this? Shouldn't we be more focused on getting to the car, grabbing that big hammer of Leon's, and then finding the demon creating this barrier and killing it?"

"He's right," Leon said. "We need to bring this barrier down before thinking of anything else."

"Very well," Samantha relented. Tristin's sigh of relieve was cut off, however, when she pinioned him with another glare. "But, you and I will be talking about this, and soon. Do you understand?"

"Y-yes ma'am!"

The group rushed down the hall, feet pounding along the carpet. They took a right at the T-junction, then found themselves in the lobby, or at least the front entrance. It couldn't really be considered a lobby. It looked more like a waiting room. A sofa and two chairs sat off to one side, surrounding a table. Near the "back" of the room was a desk, where a reception could be seen sitting down, his brown hair just barely peeking over the table. The entrance was a single push door made of glass. There was truly nothing about this place that most people would consider worth giving it the title of lobby.

It's not like I was expecting a 5-star hotel, though. Samantha sighed.

They ran outside. Their entire world became locked in a haze of red as they left the hotel. Everything about this world looked just as it would have if they were still in the human world. The buildings looked the same, cars still drove across the streets. There were even still people out and walking around. The difference lay not in the type of architecture, nor in the way the world moved, but rather, it lay in the haze of red, like the world had been engulfed in a layer of mist. Blood mist. All the buildings and objects, from the streets and sidewalks to the flora and fauna, was dyed crimson.

The parking lot did not have a lot of cars, about six all told; a red Ford, a green Torus, a Silverado truck, a dark blue minivan, a Ram with large tires, and a red Chevy pickup. That was it. Most of the people who were staying at Supercedes were truckers. Fitting one of those large, semi-trucks into a little lot like that was impossible, thus, most of the vehicles belonging to the people staying there were in parking garages located across the street.

Several demons were already there. Their bodies, moving with a sort of mechanical slowness, their joints cracking and snapping, swiveled about to face the group as they entered the parking lot.

"Ah, man! They're already here! And I don't even have my Sandalphon yet!"

"Oh, crap! This is really not good!"

"Sif!" Samantha shouted while Leon complained, and Tristin whined.

"I'm with you!"

Moving with a swift grace, Samantha and Sif rushed forward. Raven hair whipping out behind her, lashing with jerky movements, Samantha placed her right hand on the hilt of Zaphkiel.

The demons, a group of low-class entities called marionettes, began moving toward them on stiff joints. They were far too slow, however, and Samantha reached the first one, her blade flickering with a flash of red light as she smoothly pulled the weapon from its sheath at super-sonic speeds. It was re-sheathed a second later, as she was running past the first of her enemies, a resounding *click* echoing around them. Six slashes appeared on the marionette's body, which then fell apart and clattered to the ground.

Not one to be outdone, Sif leapt into the air, her body spinning around like an out of control dreidel. She fell upon her enemy, sinking her claws into the creature's face and tearing it apart. The demon landed on its back, and Sif used it as a springboard to launch herself into another flip. Her next target, a marionette that looked like a puppet with human flesh stretched over wooden body parts, was sliced apart when she cut into the thing with lightning quick slashes.

Her blue eyes narrowing, Samantha crouched down low as she found herself surrounded by six marionettes. They all clattered around her, their limbs moving with the kind of controlled, if spasmodic, movements of something being manipulated by someone else.

With her hand on the hilt of her blade, she took in a deep breath before, with speeds that made her blade appear to be nothing more than a long, graceful arc around her body, she unsheathed the sword and spun about in a full circle, and then re-sheathed it just as quickly. There was a moment pause. A gentle click echoed around her. Then all of the marionettes around her fell, their upper bodies soaring in one direction, while their lower halves clattered to the ground.

A quick glance around the lot showed that Sif was taking care of the last few. Her left arm swung up, slicing deep furrows into one marionette. The other arm came in, the gauntlet covered hand raised to block a dagger slash aimed at gouging her eye out. The tiny blade was caught between two of her claws, which she twisted, snapping the dagger in half. That same claw then penetrated the marionette's face when Sif thrust it forward. As she proceeded to yank the claws out of the head, she moved to the side, allowing the marionette she'd drawn deep lines into to shoot its fellow puppet. While bullet holes perforated the already defeated doll, Sif ran up, slicing her two claws in an X pattern across her body, destroying the marionette with the gun.

As the many ships and wooden party parts fell, Sif stood back up, her body relaxing.

"Looks like that's the last of them," Samantha commented. "Let's move."

With their enemies gone, Samantha, Sif, Tristin, and Leon ran over to the Ford F-150, a truck with a decent amount of power to it. It was an older model, a 2005, and looked a little used. Some of the paint was rusted and dull. There were scratches along the hood. The leather seats appeared worn, like they had been out in the sun for too long and the luster had begun to fade. Despite its beat-up appearance, it still ran just fine and didn't look like it would be giving out on them any time soon. That was the whole reason Samantha had bought it.

Leon was the first to reach the truck, his large, lumbering steps pounding the pavement as he raced to the back. Sandalphon was in the back of the truck, lying down where a large sheet of gray fabric was thrown over it. Upon grabbing the giant hammer, the big man began cuddling the weapon to him like it was a favorite pet instead of a 150-pound weapon capable of turning bodies into a fine paste.

"Oh, how I missed you, Sandalphon! You and I shall never be parted again!"

"Could you please stop that?" asked Sif, deadpanning. "Seriously, it's freaky."

"Say that after you've been parted with Daniel and Gladreel."

"Alright you three, listen up!" Samantha snapped, cutting off anymore extraneous conversations. "We're going to have to split up. Two of us need to go and find the demon upholding the barrier, while the other two stays here and guard our vehicle. Because Tristin is useless in a battle—"

"Don't say that about me in such a blasé manner!"

"—He's going to stay here."

"I mean, sure, it may be true, but it's still not nice."

"I'll stay here and keep Tristin from getting killed."

"Oh, my dear, sweet, beautiful boss lady! I knew you cared about me!"

"I don't care about you," Samantha scowled at the man. "I merely have need of your talents, and it would be a shame if you got yourself killed before I could use them."

"H-how cruel!" Tristin's hands grasped at his chest, clenching fistfuls of his shirt, pretending to suffer heartbreak.

Samantha ignored him.

"Sif and Leon, because you two have worked together on a number of missions and possess such superb teamwork, I want you to find this demon and destroy it. I'm not sure what kind of demon you'll be facing," she added. "All upper-class demons are capable of creating barriers like this that separate our world for limbo. Be careful."

"Hahahaha!" Leon laughed, a hearty, earth-shattering laugh. The lion of a man hefted Sandalphon over his shoulder, grinning like a loon. "Don't worry about us, Samantha! No demon is a match for me and Sif. We'll send that demon back to hell before you know it!"

"While my partner should temper his enthusiasm, I agree with him," Sif added in her own emotionless tone. "Upper-class demons are troublesome opponents, but any member of the XIII should be more than capable of vanquishing them. Just leave this to us."

"Right." Samantha nodded. "May God be with you both."

"And with you."

***

The silent streets were unsettling, more so because Leon could see the cars drive past but not hear them. Limbo was always a freaky place like that. You could be right next to a person, their wispy form just barely visible as they stood on the other side of the boundary, yet never hear them, never touch them. The cars ran on silent wheels, their engines inaudible. It was like watching those old black and white films before they got audio... except this was black and red.

Yes. Limbo was definitely disconcerting.

"It looks like the barrier is several kilometers across. How are we supposed to find this demon in such a big space?" asked Leon.

"I suspect when we run into the area with the highest concentration of demons, we will find the one controlling this barrier," Sif answered. She walked alongside Leon, her movements far more graceful than her companions. Likewise, unlike Leon, who appeared not be paying any attention to their surroundings, she was surveying everything with her hawk-like stare.

"Well, yeah, obviously," Leon said, rolling his eyes. "What I meant was, how are we going to find it? I don't know how far this barrier extends, but it looks like it goes out quite a way. We could be walking around for quite some time before we run into anything that will lead us to the demon who created it."

"Hmm... you make a good point." Sif frowned, her expressionless face seeming to gain some creases on her brow as she began to think. She looked down, then found herself staring at her chest. The frown grew before she shook her head and looked back up. "We should find a high vantage point with which to observe the city from, a tall building should suffice." She turned her head and looked around before finding what she was looking for and pointing at it. "I believe that building will work best."

Leon turned his head to look at the structure Sif had selected. A large, square-shaped building that was built upwards instead of outwards, not as big as a skyscraper, but taller than anything else in this area. There were seven windows, so it was seven stories high. They would get a clear view of the small city from up there.

"Yeah, I think that'll do," he admitted.

"Of course it will. Now come."

"Aye!"

Sif and Leon made their way up the building, taking the stairs and climbing to the top. There were several low-level demons that stood in their way, but all were easily dealt with.

"Man, more marionettes. These things aren't even a challenge."

"I would not worry about challenges. When we find the demon controlling the barrier, you will have the challenge you crave."

The roof of the building was a mass work of large metal boxes, cooling units and electric power boxes. Pipes ran along the structure, casting dark red shadows along the ground. The red-colored cement, shaped as large squares, was surrounded by a small wall that would not do a single thing to keep someone from falling off.

Their footsteps echoed loudly as they walked around. There was a strange quality to the echo. It was not a natural sound, but more like the kind you would hear when walking down a long tunnel. The reverberating of noise was a natural phenomenon in limbo. It probably had something to do with the dense atmosphere, which almost felt like they were wading through some kind of smoky substance that was thick enough to actually hinder them.

Gliding over to the ledge with swift, graceful steps, Sif looked out over the mass of buildings, her eyes narrowed, and her face set in a mien of single-minded focus. Leon lumbered after her, setting one foot up on the rise of the wall and placing his left hand over his head like a visor to block out the blood red sun.

"I'm not really the scouting type," Leon said, "What are we looking for?"

"We're looking for an anomaly," Sif answered. Leon glance out of the corner of his eye to see the woman glaring into the distance. Was she trying to burn a hole through the barrier or something? "You can usually see the energy being emitted by a demon when they are maintaining a barrier like this. It should be something like—found it! Over there!"

Leon followed Sif's finger until he, too, saw what she was talking about. Behind what looked like a shopping center was what almost looked like a large, red flame, a conflagration that rose into the sky, licking at the barrier, threatening to consume the world in its infinite inferno. Yet nothing burned. The "flames" did not move from their location, merely opting to stay in that one spot.

"I judge that to be about one... two miles out," Sif determined, nodding to herself. She then spun about and began moving back to the door that would lead them to the stairwell. "Come, Leon!"

"Right, right."

Leon turned around and made to follow Sif back down the stairs, but before either of them could even reach the door, the cement around them cracked right before several large, black *somethings* burst from the floor. When the creatures landed on the cement, standing crouched on all fours, Sif and Leon reacted by getting into their respective combats stances.

As Leon eyed the monsters surrounding him, he summed up his thoughts in two words.

"Ah, hell!"

***

Samantha barely found herself restraining a curse. It hadn't even been fifteen minutes, and already she and Tristin found themselves surrounded by several demons. While some might not be so hasty to jump to conclusions, it was clear to Samantha that whoever oversaw the demons in this sector of limbo had been waiting for their group to split up before sending anyone in to attack.

She eyed the creatures that had besieged them, trapping them in a small ring. They were quadrupedal beings. Large, sharp teeth revealed themselves behind the peeled back lips of an ugly muzzle. Greyish, decaying skin clung to the demon's thin body. Samantha could see their ribs. Each one had several patches of fur randomly populating their skin, but most of them looked like it had all been burnt off. Small, pointed ears sat atop their heads, swiveling each time they heard a new sound, and bloody, glowing orbs were situated in their eye sockets.

Hellhounds. An unoriginal name, but one that suit these creatures best. They were low-level dog demons. Individually weak, these beasts were often used to track enemies and wear them down with numbers. Many of the Casteless had lost their lives to hordes of hellhounds out on the field. They were the largest cause of death among rookies.

Crouching low, one hand on the hilt of her sword, the other on the sheath, Samantha shifted her feet across the ground. The hellhounds growled and barked, their snarling visage a mask of animalistic savagery. These creatures were nothing more than mindless beasts, relying on their instinct and lust for blood to get them through.

Samantha would have no trouble putting them down.

It happened in an instant. The crunch of gravel was what first alerted Samantha to the impending charge. With an out crying of howls, the hellhounds bound towards her and the car with long, loping strides.

"Oh, shit! Oh, shit! These things are coming!"

Samantha ignored Tristin as he cried out behind her, sitting within the trunk of the vehicle. She inhaled a calming breath, and then she released it all in one go, unleashing Zaphkiel at the same time. The blade sang as it was released from its sheath. The polished surface gleamed red in the light as it moved in an elegant arc that combined equal amounts of speed and power. It moved so fast that the blade appeared to be nothing more than a blur.

The first hellhound to taste the Orichalcum of her sword was the one on the far left. Zaphkiel sliced right through the creature's head, separated its entire muzzle from its body. The muzzle fell to the ground with a wet, meaty thud, crimson leaking from its severed end. The hellhound whimpered. It tripped over its own feet, causing to stumble and fall to the ground, where it began twitching in pain.

While the first hellhound survived, the second wasn't so lucky. Rather than slicing off the muzzle, Zaphkiel ended up cutting through its cranium. As the blade passed through its head like jello, the upper most part of its skull slid off along half of the pink, fleshy organ sitting inside. The hellhound didn't seem to realize it was dead for a second, but once that second had passed it, too, tumbled to the ground, where it twitched once before going still.

Both the third and fourth were taken out in a similar manner to each other. Zaphkiel, sharper than almost every sword in existence, cut through their torsos with ease, causing their hind ends to fly in one direction and their front end another. Blood sprayed from the wounds like broken fire hydrants, painting the parking lot in even more crimson colors.

The sixth hellhound managed to reach her, but Samantha was already prepared for it. Ducking under the monster as it pounced, she went down on her shins, her thighs pressed against her calves and her back against the ground. From her prone position, she plunged Zaphkiel into the demons stomach all the way out its back.

Rather than cause her to lose her sword, the blade slid right through flesh, bone, and muscle with simplistic ease. Like a fountain gone wrong, crimson mist shot from the nearly bifurcated body, coating Zaphkiel and Samantha in red. The hellhound barely made a whimper as it struck the ground, rolling along the pavement for several feet before coming to a rest.

Standing up, Samantha grimaced as she looked down at her clothes. They were soaking wet, covered in blood, and smelled awful. Blood always smelled horrible, but the blood of hellhounds had an acidic quality to it that reminded her of burning ozone.

"This is going to take forever to get out," she clicked her tongue in agitation. "If only I had just been a little faster."

"I think you look good in red," Tristin told her, only to be placed on the receiving end of her vitriolic glare. "Eek! I-I mean, if you want, I'll be sure to wash them for you! I'll scrub and scrub and scrub, until there isn't a single spot of blood left. Sound good?"

Samantha kept up her steely-eyed expression for a few more seconds, then sighed. "You're an idiot."

Tristin's shoulders slumped. "That's a pretty rude thing to say, you know."

Just then, a howl went up. The howl was followed by several more hellhound cries. And not long after that, the sound of padded feet thundering along pavement reached their ears.

"Oh crap! There's more coming!"

"Tch!"

Samantha disregarded Tristin's existence, pretending the idiot man wasn't even there. She flicked her blade clean, the blood dripping from her sword now joining the puddles forming on the ground, then resheathed it in a brisk, polished motion. She bent her legs. Lowered her center of gravity. With her right hand on Zaphkiel's hilt, left hand on the sheath, Samantha prepared for the coming storm.

It was going to be a long night.

***

With a shout of effort and power, Leon brought Sandalphon down on the charging hellhound, crushing its body and causing the pavement underneath it to dent. When he lifted his warhammer, it was to see that the demon was literally just a stain of blood and chunky looking pieces of oozing flesh.

Two more hellhounds bounded towards him with a loud yowl, as if angered by how callously he had killed their brethren.

Before they could reach him, Sif was there. The young woman rushed forward, her center of gravity low as she charged in. She wove her way in between the two hellhounds, her body twisting as she avoided their lunges. She then lashed out with her two claws, Daniel slicing through the torso of the left hellhound, spilling its blood and innards onto the street. Gadreel struck the hellhound on the left, tearing through its body with ease. Both creatures landed on the ground with wet, meaty thuds, tumbling along for several seconds before coming to an abrupt halt at Leon's feet.

"You're stealing away my kills, Sif," Leon said, complaining.

"I'm sure there will be plenty more demons to fight." Sif rolled her eyes. "Now, come on."

The two moved quickly. True to Sif's words, there were plenty more hellhounds coming their way. They poured in from side streets, the main roads, and other buildings. There was no telling how many of them there were.

The two of them made short work of the beasts, dispatching them with ease. They proceeded ever forward, heading toward the undying red flames of energy. The closer they got to the source of the barrier, the more hellhounds they found themselves battling. Swarms of the demonic dogs rushed them. It was like a never-ending stream.

Leon, his blood boiling for battle, rushed forward with a war cry. Following in his wake was Sif, the ever-calm expression on her face not giving away any of her emotions. The larger of the duo crashed into the demons with the fury of a storm. He swung his warhammer around his body at speeds that were barely perceivable by human eyes. Hellhounds were struck and sent flying through the air, their bodies broken beyond repair as they crashed into lampposts and walls.

As they drove forward, pushing through the horde of demonic hounds, Leon laughed. "Come on, you weaklings! Come and fight me! Just try and take me on! See where it gets you! Ah hahahaha!"

Sif would have rolled her eyes at the overly exuberant man, but she was a little busy killing. She dashed toward the nearest hellhound, leaning forward in order to increase her speed. The ugly creature didn't even notice her full-on sprint until it was too late.

When it did turn its head to look at her, Sif had already launched herself into an acrobatic flip that had her body twisting around. While at the apex of her jump, Sif's body was turned so that her head was pointed towards the ground and her feet the sky. She extended her left gauntlet, Daniel, during this time. The four sharp Orichalcum claws tore through the beast's head like a machete cutting through ice cream. No contest.

As blood from the four deep wounds arced out in an almost graceful manner, Sif continued her flip, twisting her body, and landed on the ground. She then threw herself into a forward shoulder roll, skipped up to her feet, and launched herself at the next hellhound in her path.

The bodies of hellhounds dropped like flies. Despite the number of beasts they killed, more kept coming. At some point, their forward progress was halted, as the number of enemies pouring into the street became too great. And some time after they were forced to stop moving, the two found themselves surrounded.

"Didn't think there would be this many of them," Leon grunted, his eyes taking in all the hellhounds that had surrounded them. He tightened his grip on his axe, his back pressing into Sif's. Hellhounds growled and barked and howled, their jaws snapping, drool escaping their mouths where it fell to the floor began burning a hole in that earth. "Got any ideas? Cuz I'm fresh out of those."

"There are too many here for us to take on by ourselves," Sif informed him. Her back muscles tightened as she lifted her gauntlet covered hands. "Perhaps one us should stay behind to keep these creatures off the others back as they continue toward the source of the barrier?"

"I'm not sure I like that idea," Leon admitted.

"Do you have a better one?"

"Not really."

The two got ready to open a path through the mob of monsters. While neither of them were too keen on being separated, especially since they had no clue what sort of monster was up ahead, they also realized there wasn't much of a choice.

However, just before the two could rush forward, the hellhounds quieted down. They stopped barking, the growls ceased, and the fierce expressions on their visages seemed almost calm. Leon would have wondered what happened, but he only had a moment to contemplate this new variable before something else happened, something that shocked the two former Executioners.

The hellhounds off to their left parted as a figure walked through them. This figure looked like man, almost human, with handsome features. His dark hair had a spiky fringe that rustled and swayed as he walked, hovering over two luminescent purple eyes. He was tall, and the clothing he wore emphasized his athletic physique. Boots clacked against pavement, the dull thud reverberating across the street. His pants, dark and slightly baggy, ruffled as he walked. He wore no shirt, allowing his defined chest and lean abs to be seen beneath a long black trench coat that flapped out behind him. On his back were two large black wings made up of thousands of feathers.

"Hmm..." The man hummed, his countenance amused. Bright eyes glinted beneath thick bangs, surveying to two former Executioners with a keen look. "I see now why the fifty-sixth purgatory penitentiary was so easily broken into. You two are Sif and Leon, if I am not mistaken. Two members of the XIII, the elite among Executioners."

"Who the hell are you?" asked Leon, readying his warhammer.

"Me?" The amused quirk to the man's lips grew larger. Placing his left hand at his waist, the man with black angel wings gave a very formal bow to the pair. "My name is Azazel." He straightened up, his smile growing. "It's a pleasure to meet you."

Sif and Leon stiffened as they heard the name. Azazel was the name of a fallen angel, one of the rebellious Grigori leaders in the time that proceeded the great flood. It was he who taught men the art of warfare, of making swords and knives and shields and coats of mail. He was also responsible for teaching the women how to deceive by ornamenting their body, dying their hair and painting their face. It was even said that he was the one who had introduced witchcraft to humanity and corrupted them. According to the bible, Azazel was defeated by Archangel Raphael and was chained to the jagged rocks of Duduael until the Day of Judgement. Azazel was considered to be a threat on par with Abaddon The Destroyer.

This was so not good.

"Sif," Leon leaned down to whisper in Sif's ear. Azazel quirked an eyebrow as he stopped several meters in front of them but did not use the distraction to attack. "Got any ideas?"

"Not really," Sif admitted.

"Damn."

"At least there's a silver lining to all this."

"And that is?"

"You get your challenge."

Leon stared at Sif for a moment before grinning like a loon. "Yeah. Yeah, I guess I am going to get my challenge, aren't I?"

They both turned to look at Azazel, who appeared calm and cool, imperturbable. "Are you two done strategizing or whatever? Cuz if so, I would like to get this battle started."

"Oh, you would, would you?" Leon readied his warhammer, hefting Sandalphon over his head before charging forward. "In that case, let's see you take this!"

"No, wait! Leon!"

Leon dashed forward with a loud battle cry. He swung the giant hammer down on Azazel's head, intent on crushing the fallen angel's skull.

That didn't happen.

Because Azazel stopped the warhammer with a single hand.

"What!?"

"Is this the strength of the much-vaunted Lionheart?" Azazel sounded most disappointed. "How pathetic." With an incredible burst of strength, the fallen angel shoved at the warhammer, causing Sandalphon and Leon to go flying backwards, skidding and stumbling along the ground, kicking up dust. "I had been told that you people were two of the strongest Warriors the Executioners had to offer, but if this is the strength of its top members, it's no wonder you people were destroyed so easily."

Leon growled. "You wanna see weak! I'll show you weak!"

He rushed in again, unleashing a furious yell that echoed across the vast cityscape. He brought his great warhammer, Sandalphon, down on Azazel again. And it was blocked, again. And again. And again. And again. Over and over Leon tried to smash the dark-haired fallen angel, and over and over the warhammer was stopped by nothing more than a hand.

The ground underneath Azazel's feet cracked as the incredible power behind each swing was unleashed. The air howled with the sounds of movement as the mighty warhammer was swung with impossible speed. Each attack sounded like thunder as it struck the hand, a booming earthquake, a natural disaster. Yet no matter how many times Sandalphon was smashed down onto Azazel's form, nothing changed. The man just stood there, taking each attack head on.

And then Azazel moved his right hand.

Sif did not know what happened. One minute Leon was getting ready to swing down on the man again, the next he was being sent flying backwards, a loud shout of pain escaping his mouth. The muscled human struck a wall on the opposite side of the street, causing it to cave in and crumble around him.

"Leon!" Sif shouted. She started to move toward him, worried that he might be dead. She was stopped, however, by Azazel appearing in front of her, his form flickering with the kind of speed no human could possibly hope to match.

The young woman jumped back, her claws coming up to defend herself. Azazel did not attack, though, and what happened next came as a surprise.

"Hello there, gorgeous," Azazel said, his voice modulated into a smooth overtone that actually had Sif's spine tingling. "My name is Azazel, leader of the Grigori, fallen angel, currently a self-employed agent trying make his way in the world." The fallen angel's body flickered again, and suddenly, the powerful entity was right in front of her, standing on bended knee. He grabbed one of Sif's clawed gauntlets and kissed it.

Sif's brain short circuited. "W-what?"

Azazel looked up at her, his eyes brimming with... something. Sif didn't know what that something was, but she was also positive that she didn't want to know.

"I enjoy going to the movies, traveling through parks, and taking long walks on the beach."

"Um..."

"I also like having sex. Lots and lots of sex."

"Eh?"

"Would you be interested in coupling with me sometime? I've been told that I'm a demon in the sack." The man's teeth sparkled as he flashed her a smile.

Sif stood there for several seconds, her mind in shambles. What was going on? Was he... was Azazel hitting on her? She stared at the man, still looking just as handsome and young as he had when he rebelled against God. His amethyst eyes sparkled with an unusual sheen, a burnished sort of luminosity that caused her loins to grow hot. There was a smile on his face, dazzling and radiant in a way she had only ever seen on Tristin when he was hitting on a girl. He wanted her, and, for that single moment, Sif wanted him, too.

"You... you..."

The smile widened. "Yes?"

"You damn pervert!"

Sif lashed out with Gadreel. The four-clawed gauntlet moved like greased lightning, her anger fueling the speed of her strike. It still didn't hit, as Azazel's body flickered again, and he appeared several yards back.

"I guess you're not interested," Azazel said. He looked almost sad. "Perhaps some other time." Sif just glared at him, causing the fallen angel to sigh. "Well, I guess I'm done here for now."

Azazel's wings gave a great flap, lifting him into the air. As he began to fly away, Sif snapped out of her stupor.

"Wai—hold on! Where do you think you're going!?"

"I've seen all I need to," Azazel answered. Sif was surprised he actually bothered to answer. "So I'm not interested in this battle anymore. Tell your friend that if he wants to have any hope of defeating the enemies that lie in your path, he is going to need to get much stronger. You are going want to start training again as well. You're fast, but you lack the kind of speed necessary to fight against opponents on the same level as I am."

Sif watched in silent shock as Azazel flew up towards the barrier's domed ceiling. There was a strange sound, like glass shattering, and then the barrier was gone, and Sif was no longer standing in limbo, but at the cross streets of West Center Street and North Main Street. She frowned as the people around her became distinct. Several people had noticed the hole that Leon had made when he was blown through the store. They pointed and whispered, but Sif couldn't hear what they were saying.

She was still confused.

What the heck had just happened?

***

Samantha's sword sung as she swung it through the air. She danced left and right, her body twirling as her sword flashed out. Every time it did, blood flew out of freshly made cuts, soaring through the air in almost graceful arcs before splattering on the ground.

She was no longer using Iaidō, the art of drawing and sheathing the blade to increase the speed of her attacks. Since the number of hellhounds attacking them had increased, she'd been unable to even conceive the notion of sheathing her blade. Instead she relied on a more basic sword-style, the first one she had learned. A common kendo stance used by Japanese practitioners of the sword.

Her sword flashed out, slower than before, but still too fast for any of the hellhounds to avoid. One of the beasts that had gotten a little too eager ended up getting its head sliced off. Another tried to pounce on her, but she twirled out of the way, to the left, her sword extending as she swung it at the demonic dog. When the blade passed through the beast like water, the hellhound fell to the ground, its two halves cut lengthwise.

"Heee!"

A strange squealing, sort of reminiscent of a dying pig, reminded Samantha to the fact that she was not alone. She turned to see Tristin, standing on the top of the truck, his leg clamped in the jaws of a hellhound, which he was trying to shove off with some vigorous shaking.

Were she not in the middle of combat, Samantha would have sighed. What a useless excuse for a person.

Sprinting forward, Samantha sank her blade into the hellhounds flesh, causing it to emit a yelp and let go of Tristin's leg. As the creature fell back to the pavement, she yanked her sword out of its hide, and then swung around in a full circle, decapitating the creature with ease.

"Th-thanks, boss lady," Tristin said in between his whimpers of pain. He was holding onto his calf, which now had several large puncture holes in it from where the hellhound had chomped down on him. Knowing the strength of a hellhound's jaws, Samantha also suspected his femur might be broken. "I-I owe you."

Samantha didn't respond, not because she didn't want to, but because several more hellhounds had leapt at them. The woman readied her blade, her hair framing her face as she dropped into her stance.

Just as she was about to unleash another series of lightning quick attacks, there was a strange, loud sound, like the shattering of glass. Samantha blinked. Then she blinked again when the barrier overhead broke into a thousand shards. The blue sky became visible again. The red haze that covered the city disappeared, as did the many hellhounds that had previously been surrounding them.

"W-what just happened?" asked Tristin, staring around in slight bewilderment.

Samantha merely smiled. "It would seem that Leon and Sif have accomplished their task."

"T-that's good, right?"

"Yes. Now all that's left to do is wait for them to return."

she brought up a hand and absently wiped at the blood on her forehead, some of it from her foes and some from her. When she pulled her hand away and brought it before her eyes, she looked at it in disgust. She then looked down at her clothes. There were a number of rips and tears on them from close calls. A few bloody scratches from where a hellhound had gotten a lucky hit. But other than those few wounds, she came out of the battle relatively unscathed.

Tristin... not so much.

"I'm going to have to ask that you stop bleeding on the truck, Tristin. Blood is acidic and will corrode the paint, and this is rental."

"Are you saying that you care more about the truck then your own beloved subordinate? How cruel!"

Samantha ignored the sight of Tristin crying. She knew he was exaggerating anyway. The man enjoyed hamming it up like nobody else. That said, she did help him stem the blood flow with a tourniquet. It would be enough to keep him from dying until they could give him proper first aid.

"Commander!"

Samantha looked up at the sound of her former title being called out by a feminine voice. Sif and Leon were entering the parking lot. Dark eyes narrowed when they saw that Leon was being supported by his smaller female compatriot, his body leaning over Sif's as she practically carried him on her back.

"Leon." Samantha looked at the bulky man in concern. "Are you alright?"

Leon grimaced. "I'm fine. I just got a little overconfident and paid for it."

"I see..." Not really seeing but understanding that Leon had lost and didn't really want to discuss it, Samantha turned to Sif for an explanation.

"We ran into Azazel," the other woman answered.

"Azazel!?" Samantha's eyes widened. "You're talking about the fallen angel? Leader of the Grigori?"

"Yes."

"What was he doing here? Azazel isn't a member of Satan's army!"

Azazel was one of the angels that hadn't been sent to Hell, but due to his earthly desires, he had not been allowed to return to heaven. He, along with Shamsiel, were the two leaders of the Grigori, a group of fallen angels that sided with neither demon nor human. That he had appeared before Sif and Leon was worrying.

"I don't know what he wanted," Sif said, grunting as she strained against Leon's weight. "But we may want to get going. When the barrier broke, Leon's state caused quite the commotion. I wouldn't be surprised if the police or the paramedics arrive soon."

Samantha wanted to ask more questions, but she realized that Sif had a point. Even if Leon had not caused whatever commotion he'd made, staying in this place any longer than necessary would not be a good idea. They had been found, so it would behoove them to keep moving.

"Very well. Get in the truck. We'll try and make it to our new headquarters in a single trip."

As Samantha hopped in, she started up the car. The engine rumbled to life as Tristin hobbled into the back seat. Sif helped Leon sit down in the front, before she, too, moved to the back. Glancing in the mirror to look at the two, Samantha was amused to note that despite not liking him at all, Sif was helping administer first aid.

"Ow! Ow! Ow! Couldn't you be gentler?"

"How is this for gentle?"

"OH GOD! MY LEG!!!"

"Stop crying, you big baby!"

Whether she was helping Tristin or hindering him was another matter entirely.

Without waiting to see if everyone had buckled in, Samantha tore out of the parking lot and made her way to the I-15. As they were driving, Tristin just had to ask, "Where are we going?"

"To our new headquarters."

"I knew that," Tristin said, pouting. When Samantha studiously ignored him, he frowned, and said, "What I mean was where is our new headquarters?"

"Nevada, just off the borders of Boulder City," Samantha said as sunlight reflected off the truck's paint.

Chapter 7

"We succubi have been around for many millenniums. Stories have been written about us since the dawn of time, legends of beautiful women who would seduce men and drain them of their essence. Even before the rise of Christianity, before Judaism became a religion, we succubi have existed, hidden among humans in order to survive."

It was early in the morning—not that either of them would know this since they were underground. In any event, that morning, Christian and Lilith found themselves sitting together on a small couch within a large library.

Because the couch was not actually made for two people, they had been forced to sit close together. Very close together. As in, Lilith was actually sitting on Christian's lap. That said, neither of them seemed to mind. The two love birds looked quite comfortable as they snuggled together.

If someone were to ask Lilith what she thought about her seating arrangements, she would gladly tell them it was the best seat in the house.

"Written history has us dated as far back as medieval times. Back then, they had ascribed to the belief that we were demons who appear in dreams and take the form of human women in order to seduce men through sexual activity. I do not know where people got the idea that we appeared in dreams, or where they came under the arrogant belief that our entire life goals were the seduction of men." An inelegant snort escaped her delicate lips. "The ego of men has never ceased to astound me."

As one of the many structures located within the succubus enclave, the library had been one of the very first buildings created. Like all structures of its kind, it was used to house, well, books. A lot of books. Lining every wall were shelves upon shelves of books. Running along the room parallel to the northern and southern cardinal points were more isles of more shelves filled with more books.

The only place of the library that did not have rows upon rows of bookshelves was the small sitting area located in the front left corner of the room. It consisted of only two small couches, a sofa, and a table for books to be placed on. The couch they were sitting on, made of a reddish-brown leather, creaked underneath them as Christian shifted at the insult. Lilith tried not to let out a giggle as she placed her hands over his more masculine ones as they rested against her stomach.

Standing in front of them, pacing back and forth across their field of vision, was none other than Clarissa. She had gotten the pair up bright and early that morning to begin their lessons, just like she had promised Lilith the night before.

Though it seemed to Lilith that she was getting a history lesson instead of instructions on how to use her powers. At least it was still interesting.

"Our earliest known history actually comes from the Jewish Bible. It was believed by many that it was Lilith, not Eve, who became Adam's first wife, and that she was created from the same earth as Adam, unlike Eve who was created with one of his ribs."

"B-but that's never been proven!" Christian suddenly shouted. Lilith winced. That had been loud. Didn't he know that her ear was right next to his mouth? "While that was written in the Alphabet of Ben Sira and onward, it was disproved fifty years ago by the Catholic Church!"

"And how was it disproved?" asked Clarissa, placing her hands upon her hips as she cocked them at an angle. "What sort of evidence did they have to disprove this theory?" When Christian remained silent, she shook her head in disgust. "That is the problem with you religious types. You always take the things that the Church says at face value. I bet if the Pope told you the sky was yellow, and rain was actually liquid shit, you would believe it."

Christian gritted his teeth, his body shaking a bit. Lilith recognized the signs of him trying to suppress his anger. He might not be loyal to the Church anymore, but he was still religious.

"I don't think that's a fair thing to say," Lilith said, rubbing her hands against his wrists, soothing his anger.

"What's not fair is how he interrupted me when I am trying to give you two a lesson," Clarissa said. "Now do not interrupt me anymore, or I shall take that as a sign that neither of you wish to learn the true history of the world."

Lilith watched Christian out of the corner of her eye. He took several shuddering breaths before slowly relaxing.

Clarissa nodded, as though acknowledging that he was willing to listen, and began pacing again.

"The Bible, like every other written form of human history that goes into detail about succubi, is incorrect. The truth of the matter is that no one knows where, why, when, or how we succubi came to exist. What we do know is this: many thousands of years ago, during the time of when the city of Babylon rose to prominence, there existed four beings, women, each one equally as beautiful as the others. These four went by the names Lilith, Mahalath, Agrat Bat Mahlat, and Naamah, and they had powers beyond compare. Men would bow before them, women worshiped them as goddesses, and it was said that they had abilities so far beyond modern day succubus that we might as well be a different species altogether. While the gifts they left us have become diluted and less powerful since their time, all succubus have been granted a number of abilities that can be used."

Lilith perked up at hearing about succubus having abilities. Clarissa stopped pacing, turned to face them, and held up a single finger.

"The first is our Aura of Allure. Most humans ascribe it to some kind of demonic magic, but the truth is it's a lot closer to science than any kind of magic. The Aura of Allure is nothing more than the releasing of pheromones, which are used to heighten the lust of men. This ability can vary in strength, depending upon the power of the succubus using them, but generally, pheromones only have a range of up to, maybe, five meters at most."

"U-um, excuse me." Lilith raised a timid hand into the air. It wasn't that she feared being yelled at or anything. No. Of course not. It was just that she didn't want to upset Clarissa by interrupting her.

"Yes, Lilith?"

"You say that the Aura of Allure only works for about five meters or so, but I've always seemed to attract people from much farther away. Sometimes there would even be occasions where someone from over a hundred yards away would come after me."

"She also has a tendency to make large crowds of men go crazy with lust," Christian added. "I remember when we spent our first day together, we ended up surrounded by a group of men who'd gone all post-apocalyptic zombie on us."

Lilith winced. She remembered that time. They had indeed been like zombies, only instead of wanting brains, they had wanted boobs, and maybe something else, too.

"I believe the reason you had such a far range and strong reaction is simply due to your own exceptional power," Clarissa said. She paused, then added. "While the powers of most succubus in this day and age pales in comparison to those of the original four, there have been rare occasions where a succubus will be born with great power. One such example is Meridiana, who helped Pope Sylvester II rise through the ranks of the Catholic Church. She was an exceptionally powerful succubus said to have inherited the original powers of Mahalath." Clarissa then looked at Christian. "Lilith's power is every bit as impressive as Meridiana's, which makes the fact that you were completely unaffected by her Aura of Allure very impressive."

Christian blinked. He then leaned down and whispered into Lilith's ear. "Did she just compliment me?"

Lilith tried not to, but she could not quite manage to stifle a giggle. "I believe she did."

"Stop talking out of turn!"

"Yes ma'am!" The two shouted in unison, almost snapping to attention like soldiers before a drill Sergeant.

Clarissa held up a second finger.

"Now then, the second power that all succubus have is the ability to transform into a sort of hybrid form. When in the hybrid form, a succubus's skin will generally change color—purple seems to be the most common, but there have also been those whose skin turns orange, red, and even green. There doesn't seem to be much of a reason for why certain succubus have certain skin color. At least, there is no reason that we can determine. When in this form, a succubus will also gain a pair of large, leathery wings that form out of her back, as well as a spaded tail, and the nails on their hands and feet can extend into sharp claws. This ability is generally useful when in combat, as it allows a succubus to utilize their full power, though they can only remain in that form for a limited amount of time."

Clarissa held up a third finger.

"The third power we possess is the ability to weave illusions. All succubus have the ability to cast illusions that affect one of the five senses. Some of the more talented among us even have the ability to affect more than one sense at a time. I myself can affect three senses at any given time. There have also been rumors of succubus who are so powerful they can actually turn illusions into reality, though I've not seen the evidence to lend this rumor any credence as of yet."

Putting her hand down, Clarissa looked at her two "students" with dark eyes.

"And these are the three basic succubus abilities that every succubus has. There are a few more, but they seemed to breed at random and are generally unique abilities that other succubus don't have.

She gave them a moment to absorb this information. Christian, in particular, seemed to be thinking especially hard. His brow was furrowed, red and green eyes narrowed, as he silently contemplated what they had been told. Lilith knew very little about her own race. However, Christian had knowledge about succubus that he'd acquired from the Catholic Church. That knowledge was probably being tested right now.

"Now, are there any questions so far?" asked Clarissa after a moment had passed.

Christian and Lilith looked at each other, stared into the other's eyes for several seconds, and then looked back at Clarissa.

They shook their heads.

"No? Good, then it's time we started training. Follow me, you two. Your training begins now."

***

Christian narrowed his eyes. There was a look of fierce concentration on his face. He could feel the sweat pouring down his skin in thick rivulets, trailing across his body like several small streams. Each time he swung his swords, droplets of liquid flew off his bare torso and hair, coruscating lightly in the lighting of the room. Swift feet shifted across the floor, never stopping for even a moment as he went through the motions.

The room Christian found himself in was the one of four training rooms located within the enclave. Because of the threat from monsters like those goblins, the succubus of this enclave had comprehended the need for such training grounds. It was impossible to protect one's home unless they had strength, after all.

Carved into the rock wall of the cavern, the training room was an expansive chamber. It was longer than it was wide. Much of the floor was covered in blue mats, soft yet unyielding. Sparring mats. The walls were mostly bare, with only a few racks containing wooden training weapons resting against them.

This room, Christian had been told, was the training room the succubi use to practice and study close-range combat. Hand-to-hand, sword-styles, nagitana jutsu, combat using a pole-axe, knives, staffs, and any other type of melee weapon a person could think of. It was in this room that the eternally beautiful women of this enclave were trained in their use.

Christian had decided to do some shadow sparring while Clarissa helped Lilith. It was not the best way to train, especially with his style. Presenting false openings and then pretending someone was attacking them was a half-assed way to train at best. This forced him to train in a more standard fighting style, which in his mind was just as bad. His body wasn't as used to moving in the basic dual wielding styles used by most people. It didn't help that his blades were both the same length and weight.

When dual sword wielding, it was a common practice for the blade in the offhand to be smaller and lighter than the one in the primary hand. The reason practitioners of the dual wielding styles used a smaller blade in the offhand was because their primary arm was stronger than their second arm. Thus, when someone used two swords of the same length and weight their arms became imbalanced. This not only creates unintentional openings that could easily be exploited but would cause the secondary arm to tire more quickly, eventually making them useless in combat.

A dual-wielder cannot fight with only one arm.

Christian had trained his body extensively to be equally strong on both sides. Years upon years of intense training had ensured that his right and left arms were equally powerful, equally capable. He was also naturally ambidextrous, so that helped. Even so, it had taken a lot of time, effort, blood, sweat, and broken bones to reach this point, but

Christian was proud to say that he had no weak sides, neither the left nor the right.

This was just another reason why training in the standard fighting style was more difficult for him than others.

It was as much of a weakness as it was a strength, Christian had to admit.

Still, he trained as best he could. Now, more than ever, it was important to keep himself in top form. No. Simply maintaining his strength wasn't enough. If he wanted to protect Lilith, then he needed to be stronger, far stronger than he was now. Asmodeus had shown him that he did not have the strength to protect her. And so, he had decided to train.

Besides, it wasn't like he had anything better to do.

While his body moved of its own accord, muscles straining and stretching, pushing and pulling, he took glance at the other two people in the room.

Lilith was standing several feet away, Clarissa in front of her. The young woman had a look of intense concentration on her face.

Well, Christian called it a look of intense concentration, but the truth of the matter was that Lilith actually looked kind of constipated. Her cheeks were puffed up like a chipmunk. Her eyes were narrowed. She wore a large frown. Her face was a deep red. Her body was shaking. She looked like she wasn't even breathing.

"Don't stop breathing, foolish girl!" Clarissa scolded the young woman. "You need to relax. In order to change into your hybrid form, you need to reach a balance within yourself. You can't do that if you are not totally relaxed."

"This... is a lot... hard... er... than it looks..." Lilith puffed and panted, huffing from a lack of oxygen.

"Breathe, Lilith!"

Lilith sucked in a deep breath, her shoulders heaving.

"Honestly," Clarissa shook her head. "You've been standing there for fifteen minutes, holding your breath. Do you truly believe you're going to be able to transform when you're like this? All high strung and tense? To transform, you must balance both aspects that come from being a succubus. Love and lust. These two aspects of succubus are both equally important. Without one, the other is useless. If your love is stronger than your lust, then your powers grow weak. If your lust is too great, then you become nothing more than a monster. And when that happens, your physical body will reflect your inner lusts and you'll no longer be able to go back to your regular form."

"So... so what you're telling me is that if my lust gets the better of me, I'll become a monster?"

"That is exactly what I'm telling you. Succubus who go out into the human world without taking the necessary precautions almost always find themselves turning into monsters. They live amongst men, their minds and hearts full of hopes, and their auras uncontrollable. Men lust for them, incapable of controlling their urges as their senses are overwhelmed by pheromones. When the evil nature in the hearts of men overcome a succubus, they become consumed by those natures. The lust inundates them in a deluge, changing them, transforming them into mere shells of who they should be. They become monsters who consume the souls of men through acts of lust. In other words, sex."

"Are you saying its men who cause succubus to become monsters?" asked Christian, having finally stopped his training in order to listen in on what was being said.

"But of course," Clarissa said with a devious smile. "Did you think succubus were simply born evil? That the moment they are brought into this world, they have a desire to drain men of their essence, leaving them nothing but empty shells devoid of life?"

Christian's tongue was halted before it could even begin speaking. "Uh, well..."

"Do not be foolish, Christian Crux. No succubus has ever been born evil. We are beings of nature, born of Gaia and nurtured in the earth's embrace. Good. Evil. Nature does not recognize these concepts. Evil is born unto the hearts of men, and it is men who give birth to true evils."

Narrowing his eyes, Christian glared at the woman. "So, what? You're telling me that all men are evil?"

"Were you even listening to what I said? Evil is a concept created by man, but man is not evil itself. Just as the concept of evil was created by man, so too, was the concept of good. While there are no such thing as good men, that does not mean all men are evil. Most straddle the line between these two concepts, shades of gray that are neither one nor the other. These humans make up most of your world. Some border the dark more than the light but most walk along the middle ground. Even then, when introduced to outside stimuli, it is very easy for these men to give into their desire: wrath, avarice, sloth, pride, lust, envy, gluttony."

"The seven deadly sins." Christian placed a hand on his shoulder, stretching it out. "Yes. I suppose I could see how that would work."

"Oh? Giving in so easily?" Clarissa raised a dainty hand and smiled behind it, her eyes crinkling. "I'm surprised. I expected you to argue more in favor of humanity."

Christian closed his eyes. "It's kind of hard to argue with you when I've seen the proof of your claims."

Even now, he could still remember how all those men in Seal Beach, even supernatural beings such as werewolves, had acted around Lilith. He could not believe that all those men had been evil. However, her out of control Aura of Allure had overwhelmed them, causing their darkness to get pulled to the fore.

"I see." Clarissa waited, as if expecting him to say something, but Christian remained silent.

"Clarissa?" Lilith started, causing both Christian and Clarissa to look at her. "What would have happened if those men, I mean, if they had actually managed to..."

"If they had actually managed to rape you?" finished Clarissa when Lilith trailed off.

The blond shuddered but nodded. Christian, seeing the way the young woman was shaking, moved over and wrapped an arm around her shoulder. Lilith sighed, content, leaning into him.

Clarissa smiled. An actual smile, which Christian was surprised to note he had never seen on her before.

A small frown had appeared a second later.

"If any one of those men had managed to rape you, their darkness would have consumed you. You would have turned into a monster whose sole purpose was to consume the essence of men. You would have drained men over and over and over again, until the Executioners discovered and killed you." Clarissa tilted her head, then shrugged. "To be honest, I am kind of surprised you managed to last long enough to find a mate."

"You've called me that before," Christian said, then blinked when he felt something small and wet run up his neck. After a short pause, he looked down and found Lilith licking his neck. "What are you doing?"

"Um..." Lilith looked at him, blinking. Then she blushed and buried her face into the crook of his neck. "N-nothing... sorry..."

"It looks like she's horny," Clarissa stated.

"Don't say that in such a scientific tone of voice! In fact, don't say that at all!" Lilith shouted.

"It's been a while since she had sex with you, hasn't it? She's probably hungry."

Despite himself, Christian blushed at the implications. "I thought you said she didn't feel the need to consume men of their essence."

"And she doesn't," Clarissa admitted, and then added, "but you are special. You are her mate. That makes you very different from some random male. Succubus need sex to survive. Having sex with her mate is necessary."

Lilith took in a deep breath. Christian shuddered when her released breathing hit the back of his neck. Was she... was she smelling him?

"I'm not sure I understand what being a mate is," he said, trying to ignore Lilith.

Clarissa nodded and hurried to explain. "Succubus have always looked for men who are not affected by their Aura of Allure. It is these men, those precious few who can remain themselves, who do not give into their lusts when we're around, that make the only males that we can safely mate with without being tainted by the darkness of humanity."

Christian's spine tingled as Lilith pressed herself against him. He wondered if her heaving bosom had always been so... squishy. It felt like two marshmallows were pushing into his torso.

"Back in ancient times, Succubi would call these men their Destined Ones, believing that it was their destiny to meet and fall in love with them." Clarissa snorted. "Destiny has nothing to do with it. We've learned that now. Those who we call Destined Ones are, in actuality, just humans who are genetically predisposed toward not being affected by that specific succubus's Aura of Allure. It's science."

Lilith shook her head as if trying to dispel her lust. She looked at Clarissa with half-lidded eyes.

"Science?" she asked.

Clarissa nodded, her eyes twinkling. "Yes, science. A person's genes are a lot like a person's fingerprint. Each one is unique. Oh, there may be some similarities between relatives certainly, but even then, no two person's genes are completely the same."

"So what do a person's genes have to do with succubus and being one's mate?" asked Christian.

"Compatibility."

Christian and Lilith shared a look. They frowned. Then they looked back at Clarissa.

"Compatibility?" they asked at the same time, though Lilith's voice sounded more like a sigh. Christian grimaced. She was sniffing him.

Smiling, Clarissa said, "Yes. Certain men are compatible with certain succubus based upon the genetic coding in their DNA. Basically, when these men meet a succubus who shares a genetic makeup that is compatible with their own, they find themselves unaffected by that succubus's Aura of Allure."

Christian slowly nodded as he began to understand what she meant. "I see. Then if that man were to meet a succubus who they are not compatible with..."

"Yes, they would be affected," Clarissa wore a devious smile. She then tossed him a wink. "Good thing the succubus you ran into was Lilith and not someone else, isn't it?"

"Yeah."

Christian and Lilith shared a smile. However, a curious look overcame Lilith's features. She turned her head to look back at Clarissa, a question on her lips.

"If the only reason Christian wasn't affected by my Aura of Allure is because he's genetically compatible with me, why is he not affected by you and the other succubus here?"

"Two reasons," Clarissa said, holding up a hand with two fingers. "The first is because you've already mated with him." Christian and Lilith blushed at her insinuation, causing her to giggle. "This grants him a form of immunity against the Aura of Allure of other succubi, sort of like you marking your territory to let others know that he's yours."

"You make it sound like I'm some kind of possession," Christian complained.

"The second reason is because all of the succubus living in this enclave, minus a few of the young ones who have yet to undergo training, have control over their Aura of Allure," Clarissa turned away from them to look at the training hall. "This enclave was built in secret to be a place where succubus can train their powers, until they are ready to head into the human world and find their mate."

"What's so important of finding a mate?" asked Christian.

"Have you not figured it out yet?" Clarissa raised an eyebrow. "Succubus need love to survive. While most humans believe succubus only live to seduce and sleep with men, the truth is that sex is only half of what we succubus require to sustain ourselves. Sex gives us succubus the energy we need to use our powers, but it's love that allows us to live. Succubus who do not find a mate by the time of their twenty-first birthday will wither away."

Clarissa paused to let that hard truth sink in. Then she sighed.

"Of course, most succubus end up getting raped and turn into monsters before they turn twenty-one. Very few succubi live long enough for it to matter."

Christian and Lilith didn't say anything at the sobering thought. It was not pleasant, and they had no desire to continue discussing such a depressing conversation.

Clarissa must have sensed this and changed the subject. "Now then, I believe it's time you two went back to your quarters. Lilith looks like she's going to jump you."

It was only after Clarissa said this that Christian realized what she was talking about. During their conversation, Lilith's breathing had gotten heavy, her eyes were half-lidded with lust, and her cheeks had become a warm shade of pink.

She was also licking his neck again.

"Oh, boy."

"Oh, boy indeed," Clarissa paraphrased him, a small grin on her face.

***

Christian's back slammed hard against the door to his and Lilith's bedroom, causing a slight jolt to travel up his spine. He ignored the brief moment of pain, or rather, it was simply impossible to focus on the pain when there was a very soft, luscious pair of lips attacking his mouth. He could feel Lilith's tongue pushing against his teeth.

It had been difficult getting back to their room. Lilith had become rather fervent in her desire to copulate after they left the training hall, and he'd been forced to keep himself in check and move them along as the young woman began biting his ear and licking his neck. It had been difficult, almost impossible, to even focus, but somehow, he'd made it to their bedroom.

Or at least the doorway that led into the bedroom.

Even though he had been prepared for it, Christian was still surprised by the intensity of Lilith's assault. There were times when she would get like this, usually if they had gone a day or two without having sex. Even so, the vigor of her kiss was rather astonishing. Her lips, softer than velvet, were like fire, and he was getting seriously burned.

He tried to fight back as much as he could. He tried to match her passion with his own. He really should have known better. Perhaps it was a succubus thing, but when Lilith got like this, there was no keeping up. All he could do was ride out her ardor until the end and hope he had enough stamina to last.

As Lilith's tongue traveled down the furthest recesses of his mouth, their saliva mixing as her tongue fought with his and rubbed against him in all kinds of delicious ways, Christian tried to find the doorknob with his left hand. It took a while, far longer than it should have, especially when Lilith's hands cupped his crotch over his jeans. Then it became practically impossible. Her actions were too distracting. He still managed it, eventually, after nearly a full minute of searching, and was able to turn the doorknob.

It was too bad he hadn't accounted for the fact that Lilith was shoving him against the door. As the hinges moved, the door swiftly opened, and Christian and Lilith spilled into the room. Christian landed hard on his back, Lilith on top of him. She hadn't stopped kissing him. Even now her tongue was exploring his mouth, ravishing it in ways he'd not seen from her before.

At least he knew why. The young woman was hungry.

Trying to focus on both Lilith and the door, Christian looked over at his feet and kicked them at the door to close it. He would have liked to lock it, too, but that really didn't appear to be in the cards at that moment. So he decided to forget about that and gave into his instincts. That was the only way he would be have any hope of keeping up with Lilith.

His hands went to the small of her back, moving into the gentle dip along her lower spine, where he began to message it with two fingers. Lilith practically purred, her back arcing, her jean covered crotch grinding against his left thigh. He could feel his pants growing wet. The heady scent of something sweet was beginning to permeate the room. It made him light headed.

Christian slid one of his hands down the smooth surface of her back to grasp her firm derriere in his. Lilith's rear end was magnificent. Even though he was touching it over her clothes, his fingers sank into the plentiful flesh of her round yet pert ass. He groped and squeezed her butt cheeks, admiring the way it felt underneath his palm and calloused fingers, firm yet soft. Lilith moaned into his mouth. It was a lovely sound that traveled through his ears like the sweetest of symphonies, increasing in volume as he began helping her body move across his thigh.

A pair of hands, warm, soft, and oh so delicate, plunged underneath his shirt. Nails scraped against his pectorals and abs, leaving shivers in their wake and forcing a low, guttural groan to leave his mouth. He thought he could feel Lilith smile against his lips, but he couldn't be sure as her tongue was still plunging itself into the depths of his mouth.

It was while he was lying there, letting Lilith pretty much do what she wanted with him, that he decided he didn't really feel like being on the bottom today. She was on top far too often for his tastes, and a change of pace would be nice. So, using his superior strength, he flipped the two of them over so that she was lying on her back and he was on top. Lilith made a pleased sound, halfway between a mewl and moan, the hands that were on his chest and stomach moving to his back.

The kiss soon broke and the two gasped for air. Christian pulled away, a small string of saliva connecting them. The connection only broke when Christian sat up. It was only long enough so that he could remove his shirt and toss it away, but Lilith still gave a whining complaint. He almost didn't have enough time to throw it somewhere when she grabbed the back of his head and pulled him back down.

The battle of tongues began anew, and while this was happening, Christian grabbed at Lilith's shirt, pulling at it. Despite her mind being in an obvious haze of lust, Lilith understood his desire and arced her back until it was off the ground, allowing him to pull her shirt over her breasts. They were clad in a pink bra with a front clasp keeping them closed. Christian ignored the clasp for now, instead setting a firm hand on one of the two proud mountains on her chest and giving it a firm squeeze. Lilith's approval was muffled by his mouth and the sounds of saliva being exchanged in a wet, sloppy kiss. But soon even that wasn't enough. Christian wanted to feel more of her, and he didn't want a piece of annoying fabric in the way.

He went to the clasp. By now experienced fingers undid the catch quickly, allowing her incredible, shapely breasts to spill free. The two large mountains shifted to either side of her chest. He was vaguely reminded of water balloons. Never in his life had he ever seen a more magnificent pair of breasts.

Christian reached for Lilith's left breast. He cupped her breast, hefting it up, his thumb running over her nipple until it hardened into a stiff point. The music that absconded from Lilith's mouth increased in volume and frequency, to the point where he could actually feel the vibrations in his mouth.

While some part of him wanted to continue kissing Lilith until they passed out from lack of oxygen, another, much larger part, really wanted her breasts in his mouth. He pulled his lips off hers, ignoring the petulant whine she released. He licked the saliva that had begun to drip down her cheek, almost grinning when she shivered.

Lilith might have wined out loud, but he could still hear the voice in his head, the one that sounded like Lilith, telling him what to do. This, he realized, must have been part of what it meant to become a succubus's mate.

He made his way toward his prize with his mouth, his tongue trailing a wet, glistening path down her neck, stopping only to lightly nip at her pulse points. He moved along her collarbone, his lips and tongue paying particular attention to the curvature of her elegant clavicle. Lilith squirmed beneath him as he kept moving. Blazing a path down the center of her chest, Christian soon swerved to the right. There, he found her breast, capped with a light pink nipple. It was beautiful. Perfect. Just like her.

And he really, *really* wanted his mouth on it right that instant.

He leaned down. Rather than simply placing his lips over her nipple and suckling on it, he swirled his tongue around it, licking around her areola. The gasp that swept out of Lilith's throat was followed by a low, throaty moan. The hands that had been scratching his back went to the back of his head and pulled him down, practically shoving his face into her. He could taste her skin, salty but sweet. Perspiration had broken out on her skin. He lapped at it. Lilith shivered. Once her nipple was covered in saliva, Christian took it into his mouth and gently scraped it against his teeth, eliciting a loud cry from Lilith.

With his mouth occupied, his hands were free to explore, which he took to doing with great relish. His palms and fingers flowed across smooth skin, sweeping down her flat belly. Goosebumps broke out underneath his touch.

He soon reached the hem of Lilith's jeans. He worked his hands underneath them, slipping inside both her jeans and panties, roving down before he finally found what he was looking for, a soft pair of lips that were already puffy and wet with arousal. He cupped her sex in the same way she had been cupping his crotch just a little while ago. He rubbed his hand along the entire length of her mound, feeling it come away with a slick coating of her juices. He then let two fingers pressed up against her lips, stroking her, causing her hips to buck against his hand. More juices flowed out from inside of her, trailing into her butt crack, and the jerking of her hips grew wilder. When he felt she was sufficiently wet, he slipped a finger inside.

Lilith unleashed a loud, keening wail as he curved his finger against the walls of her passage, finding her sweat spot and giving it a firm caress. Her hips jerked. She lifted her thighs into the air, spine arcing, as if humping his hand and released another loud cry. He was sure their neighbors could hear them. Christian knew he should feel embarrassed or something, but for some reason, he really couldn't find it in himself to care today.

A second finger was inserted inside of her, which he began to pump in and out. A wet sucking sound issued from her sodden entrance. It was barely audible above Lilith's panting moans and his groans.

He moved his thumb, pushing it against her hood and working out her clitoris, which he started stroking. Lilith's body began shaking, her hips bucking and jerking as she humped his hand. The area between her legs was hot, and his hand and fingers became coated in more than just her juices. Sweat began breaking out on her body, a shimmering coat that looked exceedingly fetching on her.

The shaking increased, as did the humping and the bucking and the wailing. He felt her passage clamp around his fingers, a vice that made working them inside of her hard. Thankfully, the deluge of liquid that rushed out allowed him to slip his fingers out of her as well.

Christian leaned up, his mouth leaving her breast, so that he could watch Lilith as her body was wracked with small twitches and spasms. It was always a stunning sight to see her come down from an orgasm. He loved watching the way her chest heaved and shuddered, loved seeing the glimmering coat of sweat that broke out on her skin, and the way her eyes glazed over slightly. Because she was normally the one in charge during sex, he only got to see this after everything was said and done, and he was often too tired to care when that happened.

He needed to take this opportunity while he could.

"Christian... I need you... in me... right now..."

Lilith's voice, a panting whisper filled with love and desire, an enchanting promise of unfathomable pleasure, caused him to shiver. He was also surprised that she could talk at all. He'd been sure her lust had consumed her before they even entered the hallway.

Maybe the orgasm had brought her mind back from the brink? It was food for thought.

"Actually, would you mind if I tried something first?" he asked.

Lilith whined and shook her head. "N-no. I need you now."

"And you'll get me, but I want to do something else for you first. Please?"

"F-fine but make it quick."

Lilith didn't take long to think about it. She probably didn't have the brain capacity to think about much at that moment. He supposed that was what happened when a succubus was overtaken by their need to feed?

Moving down her body, Christian first took off her shoes. He slipped one shoe off her left foot, then other, and set them aside. Then reached her hips, where he unzipped her jeans and hooked his fingers underneath both pants and panties. Lilith raised her hips into the air, allowing him to pull both articles of clothing off in one go, exposing her lower body to the elements.

Lilith shivered just a bit, but that stopped when Christian put his mouth over her wet pussy lips and began to kiss her like he would her other mouth. Her thighs clamped around his head, and her beautiful singing voice bounced off the walls as Christian's tongue penetrated her folds, pushing its way inside of her.

This was his first time doing this, so he wasn't exactly sure what he was supposed to do. The voice inside of his head had also gone silent. He strained his ear to listen for any verbal cues that would let him know what Lilith liked. It was difficult to figure out if there was anything she didn't like. Maybe it had something to do with the whole "mate genetic compatibility" thing Clarissa was talking about, but Lilith seemed to like everything he did.

Deciding to just do what came naturally, he allowed himself to enjoy the act. He inhaled her scent through his nose, savoring the unusual smell that was like a combination of vanilla and strawberries. He didn't think women were supposed to smell like this (not like he had experience with anyone else), but he figured it was also due to her being a succubus and them being compatible. His nose soon grazed against the cluster of nerves that were sticking out of her hood. Lilith's cries were magnified as he rubbed his nose against her clit.

Another flood rushed out of her. The intense tremors that afflicted her body spiraled as she climaxed, and then she came down, her entire body slumping. Her legs relaxed, allowing him to remove his head from between them. As he sat up, absently wiping at the fluids soaking the lower half of his face with his fingers, which he then stuck in his mouth to suck clean, he looked at Lilith's face and had to smile.

Glazed over eyes and a mouth opened in a little "o" made up her face. There was a healthy glow on her cheeks, and her body was flushed a slight pink. She shone with a light, glistening coat of sweat, her body sparkling in the lighting of the room, and her body was heaving, sucking in deep, lungsful of air, as if she had just run a marathon without training. She looked both exhausted and pleased.

Christian wondered if it would be vain of him to feel proud.

He looked around, noticing that they were still on the floor. Not wanting to have sex on the floor when there was a perfectly soft bed next to them, he scooped the young woman into a princess carry, letting her head rest against his shoulder, and walked over to the bed. He set her down and climbed on as well, lifting her legs before letting them rest over his thighs, then positioning himself at her entrance. He didn't enter her. Not yet. Instead, Christian chose to lean over her, his left forearm holding him up, while he caressed Lilith's face with his right hand.

"Christian..." she mumbled, closing her eyes and leaning into his hand at the same time.

"Yes?"

"If you do not stick that thing in me right now, I am going to hurt you."

Christian blinked. "You're acting awfully violent today."

"Christian..."

"Got it, got it."

Not wanting to upset Lilith, who was, quite clearly, still hungry, Christian pushed himself against her, entering her and allowing for the consummation of their minds, bodies, and souls. Lilith practically melted. She sighed as her body relaxed. Her lips stretched to accommodate his girth, while her insides conformed around his thick shaft.

No matter how many times they had sex, she was just as tight, just as amazing, as the first time they had done it. Her wet, well-lubricated walls clamped around him, but it didn't hurt. Christian could feel her, all of her, surrounding and all-consuming and absolutely perfect.

They lay like that, connected and content, before, on an unspoken signal they began to move.

Two minds soon became one. Two hearts connected. Bodies melded together, slick, wet, and wonderful. Reality blurred as lines were crossed. Christian moved inside Lilith and Lilith became a part of Christian. Worlds were born, and stars went nova behind heavy lidded eyes. Every moan, gasp, groan, and grunt that accompanied the sounds of two people locked in a passionate dance where time, space, and the universe came together in an explosion of energy and passion.

All good things come eventually come to an end, and theirs came quickly. Lilith tightened around Christian as he unleashed himself inside of her, making motion almost impossible, until her orgasm ended, and her walls loosened around his cock.

His body spent, Christian rolled over, pulling himself out of her with a wet pop. He lay on his back, staring up at the ceiling, his breathing heavy, with several droplets of sweat coalescing and trailing down his skin.

After several seconds of resting, he regained his ability to speak, and said, "Lilith... I know you might still be hungry, but do you think you can wait a bit for me to recover before we go at it again?"

... No answer.

"Lilith?"

Christian turned his head to look at Lilith. He blinked, then frowned when he saw that her eyes were closed, and her breathing was deep and even. She was asleep.

"So much for being hungry."

He sighed. At least he didn't have to go another round. He loved making love to Lilith, but there were times when she was just too much for him to handle, especially when she wanted to go at it several times in a single night.

Damn succubus stamina, he grumbled internally before rolling over onto his side. Lilith, as if feeling his movement, rolled over until she was facing him and snuggled close. He wrapped his arms around her and slowly drifted to sleep.

***

Tristin stared out of the backseat window of the Ford F-150 as Samantha drove it down an innocuous looking street. There wasn't much to see outside. Just dirt, dirt, and more dirt. And some buildings off in the distance—Boulder City, Tristin presumed, though he didn't know for sure. He didn't really care to know either, so it was all good.

"We there yet?" he asked, more to amuse himself than because he thought they were getting closer. Well, they had to be getting closer, right? That was the whole point of driving. To eventually reach their destination.

"No," Samantha answered. She sounded a little exasperated. Tristin couldn't figure out why. Surely, it wasn't because he'd already asked this question fifty times in the last hour. No. Of course not.

"...How about now?"

"Tristin!"

"Sorry, sorry. I'm just so bored."

Hm. Maybe he should be a little more cautious when trying to annoy Samantha. She took most of his ribbing well for such a serious woman—about as well as Christian, which was probably why he teased her. Then again, if there wasn't the possibility of potentially lethal actions taken, wouldn't that make messing with her less fun?

"You should learn to loosen up, boss lady."

"Hahahaha! Tiny has got a point!"

"Who the hell are you calling tiny?!"

"Lighten up a little, Samantha! You keep frowning like that and you'll get wrinkles."

"I don't want to hear that from someone who's always laughing like a loon." Samantha scowled. Both Leon and Tristin just laughed.

"Ugh, men," Sif muttered in disgust.

Tristin found himself looking at the lady. Well, he found himself staring at her breasts at least. He didn't think anyone would blame him. They were big, and he was really horny. How long had it been since the last time he had sex anyway? At least a month. He was beginning to run low on energy.

"There's nothing wrong with having a dick, Sif," Tristin said, grinning. Sif just looked at him like she wanted to stab him in the face, which honestly wasn't all that different from how she normally looked at him, except maybe with a bit more vitriol.

He got the distinct feeling that she didn't like him.

Hm.

The expansive desert landscape soon revealed something in the distance, which Tristin noticed almost as soon as it came into view. At first, it just looked like a blurry, indistinct, and shapeless mass that wavered in the heat. It wasn't until they got closer that he realized what it was: a very small, abandoned warehouse.

The place was surrounded by a fence with barbed wire prickling the top. Several blue dumpsters lay scattered about, grimy, covered in rust, and suffering some serious wear and tear from having been out in the sun too long. Large stacks of something, Tristin didn't know what, also lay half-haphazardly sprawled around the exterior of the warehouse.

The warehouse itself consisted of three buildings. The largest of them, the one in the center, looked like a stereotypical warehouse, large and square and without a hint of elegance to it. The walls were made of metal, which had rusted over from not receiving a proper cleaning in what had to be decades. Likewise, the slanted roof was made of metal that had been oxidized from the sun beating down on it. The other two buildings were smaller. One just looked like a gray square with a door and two windows, while the other appeared to be a smaller warehouse painted white, with chips of paint peeling off and only a single entrance.

So this was the Executioners new secret hide out, huh? The whole thing looked like a giant cliché, but Tristin supposed beggars couldn't be choosers.

They pulled up past the fence, which had not been locked, and then parked the truck.

"Alright, everyone. Get out," Samantha commanded, putting her own words into action.

Tristin followed her with the other two as they were led into the large warehouse building. The space inside was pretty empty. There really wasn't a whole lot to the place. Cement floors, metal walls and ceiling, a couple dozen boxes that ranged in size from as tall as Tristin's calf to nearly two times larger than he was.

Samantha led them to a spot in the center, surrounded by four of the large boxes. She knelt upon reaching an area that really didn't look any different from any other spot in the warehouse. It wasn't until she pushed a depression on one of the large metal boxes, which slid open to reveal a handprint scanner, that Tristin really began paying attention.

After Samantha placed her hand on the scanner, there was a moment of silence, then a slow, grinding noise echoed around them. Tristin peered down at the floor as it began to shift. A section of it moved inwards before the rectangular section shifted to the side at a sluggish pace to reveal a set of stairs.

"A secret staircase hidden in a warehouse, huh? Very secret agent of you," Tristin complimented as Samantha, followed by Leon and Sif, walked down the stairs. The stairwell was well-lit, which was nice. Tristin didn't want to trip down the stairs. He might be a big-time player who could convince any women (or almost any women) that he was the smoothest operator in the history of ever, but he was about as graceful as a ponderous panda trying to play on a swing set.

At the end of the stairs was a hallway with a sliding door at the end. Samantha, Leon, Sif, and then Tristin all passed through to the other side.

Tristin looked around, eyes wandering. Low ceiling. Cement walls and floor. It looked like they were in some kind of office space. There were a number of cubicles with people Tristin recognized as fellow intelligence agents sitting in them, typing away at what appeared to be very standard PCs. This place was a far cry from their old

Headquarters, and not just in aesthetics. He sighed. At least the room was well lit.

"Not much to look at, is it?" Tristin couldn't help but comment, much to Samantha's consternation.

"Don't complain," Samantha said, a small vein pulsing on her forehead. "This place was never meant to be a true base of operations. It's a fallback center in case of emergencies. Taking that into consideration, this place is better than what most organizations like our own would get."

"Well, I guess that's true," Tristin admitted. He then gave the raven-haired woman a cheerful grin. "That's my boss lady! Always prepared for every occasion."

Samantha just rolled her eyes at him before turning her attention to Leon and Sif. "Why don't you two head back to the barracks? Tristin and I have something we need to discuss."

Tristin felt a chill run down his spine as Samantha looked at him. There was something highly disconcerting in her gaze, those fierce blue eyes that held within them all the warmth of a glacier. Oh yeah, he was in big trouble.

"Sure thing," Leon said, turning toward a corridor on the far side of the office. "Come on, Sif."

"Commander," Sif gave Samantha a respectful nod before she followed after her partner.

"They make such a cute couple," Tristin said with false cheer.

"Don't let them hear you say that," Samantha said. "Now come on. Follow me." The young woman turned down one of several corridors, her black hair swaying behind her. Tristin sighed. Gathering his courage, he prepared to play the piper, as it were, and followed her.

She led him into a small office, one that looked a lot like her old office, except the walls, floor, and ceiling were made of gray cement instead of marble and plaster. The only thing he didn't see hanging on her wall was her sword, Zaphkiel, which Samantha set against her desk, ready to be drawn at a moment's notice.

Samantha sat down at the small desk, her hands clasped in front of her. She looked calm, too calm for Tristin, who felt something like a thrill of fear run down his spine. He wondered if this was going to be the last sunrise he ever saw.

"Now then, Tristin," Samantha began, "you are going to tell me how it is that you did not become incorporeal when that barrier was put up. I'm very interested in knowing the truth."

At those words, Tristin gulped.

Yeah, he was so screwed.

Chapter 8

My body was burning. Fresh blood poured down sharp cuts, deep and painful, like the sting of a thousand bees, or the bite of a cobra. The ichor flowing down my body made my clothes cling to my skin. A wound on my scalp caused more to trail down my face, forcing me to close my right eye, lest I get some in it.

All around me lay dozens of corpses. Most of them had been burnt beyond recognition, charred bodies that didn't even look human. They were scattered across the sight of what could only be a war zone. Buildings lay in ruins. Cars were crushed beyond recognition. The large bridge that had once stood over the Colorado river had been destroyed, the pieces scattered in large chunks, with some sticking out of the river like stakes impaling a snake.

I was not one to swear; swearing was a sin, but I really felt like doing so right now. The battle had been going well enough at the beginning, or so I thought. The team of Executioners that I was with had managed to trap our quarry in a net, closing in on them. Just as planned, we had attacked simultaneously. He fired a long-range barraged designed to disorient and confuse our enemy. Everything from rockets and missiles to grenades and machine gun fire had assaulted the demon all sides, creating a series of explosions so powerful that our enemy had been engulfed in a blaze large enough completely engulfed the monster.

Unfortunately, we had underestimated our enemy. Before even a second had passed, the fire was dispersed by a burst of incredible power. The air had whipped about us fiercely, a hot gust that caused our skin to sear and small cuts to tear apart our clothes.

It was only after the gust passed by that we were able to see our enemy, unharmed, floating in the air, their arms crossed with arrogant nonchalance.

Abaddon The Destroyer, one of the Knights of Hell, was a being whose power far surpassed those of most supernatural monsters. This was why our plan had been to destroy him with a barrage of firepower so great it simply overwhelmed him before he could mount a proper defense. The idea had seemed sound, at least until now.

After withstanding our barrage, allowing us to use up all of their ammo in a futile attempt at destroying him, Abaddon laughed at us, and then proceeded to decimate our forces. I had been able to survive thanks to my unique fighting style, even though it was still in development. The others had not been so lucky.

Gasping for breath, one hand holding my side, pressing against the growing stain of dark red from where a fragment of burning hot metal had pierced through my skin, I stared up at the floating figure with horror.

Powerful black wings flapped behind them, each flap caused the air to burst, sending more searing heat in my direction and making my skin blister. Dark red skin gleamed brightly, not possessing a single scratch. His hair, thick locks of darkness that lay clumped on his head, swayed in the breeze created by his own powers. Bright, glowing red eyes seeped with amusement as he stared down at me.

I tried not to let on how frightened I was, but I'm not sure I was successful. I could feel my legs shaking and my body shutting down from shock. I couldn't believe how easily we had been beaten. We never stood a chance, from the very beginning. Abaddon had taken everything we could throw at him and dished it back one-hundred-fold. He had torn through our ranks like we were a bunch of stuffed teddy bears. My comrades broken bodies lay around me, twisted and charred lumps of flesh, a testament to this monster's power.

There was no one else around besides me.

I was the only one left.

*"**Poor, misguided humans.**" Abaddon's voice was deep, cracking like distant thunder. It reverberated inside of me, shaking me to my core. "**Did you really think you could defeat me?**"*

His words struck a chord with me. We never should have fought this battle. It had been a hopeless crusade from the very beginning. Now everyone besides me was dead, and I would be joining them soon enough.

'Giving up already?' a voice called from inside of me. 'How pathetic.'

"W-what?" I looked around as the voice resonated around me, but I could find no one there. No one except for myself and Abaddon. "Who is there?"

'Do you want power, boy? The power to defeat the one who frightens you? The power to avenge your fallen comrades? I can help, you know? I can give you that power.'

"Y-you can?" I didn't know who this voice was, but at that moment, I wasn't really sure I cared. This voice was offering me power. But could it really grant me the power to defeat Abaddon? How could a voice give me anything? It was just a voice.

'Of course,' the voice assured me. 'I can give you more power than you ever dreamed of. So how about it? Would you like me to give you the power to avenge your comrades?'

I thought about his question, and my situation. My comrades were dead, and I would be, too, unless I did something. I couldn't afford to die here. Not yet. Not now. Not when I had so much that I needed to live for.

And so, I made a choice.

"Ye-yes. Give me power."

'Good. Then take my power and make Abaddon pay for what he's done to your comrades. But, before you receive it, know this: All power comes with a price.'

I didn't have time to question the voice's words. From that moment on, the world around me changed, and the battle between Abaddon and myself commenced. My body overflowed with power. All the wounds on my body healed, sealing up with a loud hiss. My limbs strengthened. It felt like they were made of orichalcum.

With this power, I was able to match Abaddon blow for blow, and then, slowly, I began to push him back. Abaddon howled at me in rage, but I gritted my teeth and continued to fight using every ounce of strength in my body. I would not let this monster win!

While I fought against Abaddon, dark, braying laughter that sent chills down my spine echoed inside of me, reveling in the carnage and death around me.

***

The next morning, after he and Lilith took a shower together, the pair made their way to the cafeteria/restaurant for breakfast.

Almost as soon as they arrived, Lilith found herself surrounding by several dozen blushing and curious succubus. Christian was pushed away from Lilith by the overly rambunctious women. He tried to keep with her, but it proved impossible to wade through the massive gathering of bodies. They couldn't even get a word in edgewise, as the group of succubi had not only crowded around Lilith, but they were asking her questions he didn't think they had any right to ask.

"Hey, hey, did you know how loud you and your mate were last night?"

"You guys were really loud."

"Did you two have sex? You did, right? Right?!"

"What was it like?"

"Did you enjoy it?"

"What kind of question is that, Catie? Of course, she liked it. Did you not hear her screaming?"

"I wonder, is sex always that loud?"

It seemed that all women, even Succubus women, shared a need to gossip and ask invasive questions. Christian remembered reading something about this once. That said, he'd chalked it up to fantasy. He'd never assumed something that happened in his light novels could happen in real life.

Ch-Christian!" Lilith cried out, her face flushed bright red as she waved her arms in the air. "H-help me!"

"Uh... Sorry, but I think you're going to have to deal with this one on your own." Christian felt bad for Lilith. He really did. But this was beyond his ability to deal with.

Ask him to slay a monster? Sure, he'd do that any day, and he'd do it with style.

Ask him to deal with a horde of women who also happened to be succubus as they gossiped about his sex life? Yeah. Not happening.

"Wh-what!? You can't leave me here! Christian? Christian!"

"I'll grab you some breakfast and save you a seat." Christian waved at Lilith as she was engulfed by "The Horde" and began making his way over to the buffet table. He grabbed a tray and two plates, then began loading up their food. For Lilith, he chose light foods, a small scoop of scrambled eggs, a slice of toast, some fruit, and some orange juice. His own meal was decidedly larger, a heaping helping of eggs, three pancakes, and several sausage links, along with a large glass of milk.

Christian's stomach gurgled, alerting him to how hungry he was. Having sex with a ravenous succubus really did a number on one's appetite.

He made his way over to one of the tables, the one occupied by Andrew, who was already scarfing down the mountain on his plate with the voracious appetite of a wolf. Or a werewolf.

"Andrew," Christian greeted as he sat down, placing his tray on the table and setting both his and Lilith's plates out.

The man paused mid-scarf. He looked at the younger man, then swallowed his food.

"Christian," he grunted, sounding displeased. "Do you know how loud you and Lilith were last night?"

"Uh... is that a trick question? Because I'm pretty sure I realize that Lilith and I were a little, erm, ah, noisy, last night."

"A little?" Andrew rolled his eyes. "Kid, someone playing their music loud enough that I can hear it through the walls when my room is right next to theirs is a little. You and Lilith were so loud that I could hear you six rooms down."

Christian's face became hot with embarrassment. Had they really been that loud? Truly? He wasn't sure whether to feel humiliated that people now knew more about his and Lilith's sex life than he ever wanted them to, or proud because he'd made Lilith scream loud enough to be heard six rooms down. Maybe a little both, though he did his best not to let Andrew know what he was feeling. He tried to at least maintain a composed expression.

"Alright, fine. So, Lilith and I got overexcited. You can't blame me."

Andrew took one look at him, then one at Lilith, before going back to him.

"No," he admitted, shaking his head, his shaggy hair swaying with the motion. "No, I can't. And I don't care what you and she get up to in private, but you should at least be a little more considerate of the people sleeping in the rooms around you."

"Right. I'll remember that."

And he would. Christian had no intention of letting anyone else know any more about his private life with Lilith. He didn't know if he would be able to live it down if other people knew about the sort of things they got up to, last night's sexcapades aside.

Christian waited for Lilith to eventually free herself from the horde of women, who were broken up by Clarissa when she stepped into the cafeteria by telling the girls they only had a few minutes before going to their assigned stations, and that they should use the time wisely by eating instead of pestering a girl about her sex life. She also told Lilith that she should be more mindful of where she was in the future when deciding to copulate with her mate, leaving a blushing blonde succubus to sit down at Christian's and Andrew's table.

"Here," Christian said, sliding the plate with the smaller food portions over to her. Lilith just huffed, grabbed her fork, and began eating in silence. Christian sighed. "You're mad at me."

"What gave you that idea?" Lilith asked.

"Maybe the fact that you're stabbing the scrambled eggs like you're trying to kill them."

"Hmph! If I'm mad at you, then you only have yourself to blame."

"Look, I'm sorry about leaving you with those women, but there really wasn't much I could do."

"You could have pulled me out of there. You could have told them to back off and give me some space." Lilith looked at him from the corner of her eye, then back at her plate. "But you didn't do either of those. No, instead you left me there. Do you know how embarrassing it was to be asked all those personal questions?"

"Pretty embarrassing, I'd imagine."

"Beyond embarrassing," Lilith countered, "And the next time you leave me high and dry like that, you're sleeping on the couch."

"But we don't have a couch."

"Then you're sleeping on the floor."

Andrew watched the two banter back and forth before letting loose with a hearty laugh. Christian and Lilith stopped arguing to look at the big man, who calmed down a second later to say, "Did you know that you two act like an old married couple?"

Christian and Lilith shared a look.

"Do we really?" asked Christian, embarrassed and pleased at the same time. Lilith appeared much the same. She was blushing, but there was a beaming smile on her face.

"Yes. You do."

"Good to know... I guess."

Breakfast continued, and Clarissa soon joined the trio at their table. She sat down next to Andrew, putting a bowl of fruit in front of her. With her back straight and her bearing proper, the olive-skinned female looked like a reigning monarch. If her chair wasn't small and made of plastic, he might have mistaken her for one. She really did have a regal bearing.

As she began to eat, taking single slices of fruit and sliding them into her mouth, Clarissa started to make light conversation. "Christian, I have already spoken to Lilith about this, but I felt I should also speak to you as well."

Christian looked up from his food. "What is it?"

"While I am pleased to know that you are taking your duties as Lilith's mate seriously, I really don't want to hear you two when you're copulating. So, from now on, please try to keep your volume down when you are having sex."

Christian wondered how many times his face could get red in a day, because he was pretty sure he'd just broken a record of some kind.

"Maybe you should just think about sound proofing your rooms or something," Christian said, mainly because he had nothing else with which he could defend himself.

"They are sound proofed," was Clarissa's dry response.

Christian needed a moment to register those words.

"O-oh..."

"Yes, 'oh,'" Clarissa's tone took on the same quality as a desert. She smiled when both Christian and Lilith had the decency to look embarrassed and ashamed. "Still," she added, "I believe we can take this as a good sign. You are clearly an extraordinary lover."

"I-I wouldn't know about that," Christian mumbled. Would it be unmanly of him if he admitted that he wanted to sink into the floor? "I mean, I haven't, ah, been with anyone other than Lilith, so..."

"Yes, well, that matters little when dealing with a succubus," Clarissa informed the young man. "You are her mate, which means that each time you two have sex, you get better simply by virtue of the connection you share. I'm sure you've felt it by now," she added upon seeing Christian and Lilith staring at her. "That connection is a side effect that happens during the energy transfer. When you two are connected, you, Christian, are not just giving Lilith energy to help sustain her life, but also bonding with her on a level that is far deeper than anything anyone who is not mated to a succubus will ever experience. It almost feels like you're sharing the same soul, right? Like your minds, hearts, and bodies are connected as one?"

"Yes," Lilith said, leaning toward Clarissa, her eyes sparkling with fascination. "Have you experienced the connection before, Clarissa?"

"Of course. You don't get to be my age by not having several mates in your lifetime."

"And just how old are you?" asked Andrew, only to yelp as Clarissa's heeled foot dug into his toe.

"That is not something you should be asking a lady, Andrew. I expected you to know better."

"Sorry, I was just curious. You made it sound like you were, well, a lot older than you look."

"And it is still not something to ask a woman."

"Alright, alright. I'm sorry. I won't ask again."

"Good."

Christian leaned over, his lips caressing Lilith's ear as he whispered, "Now who's acting like an old married couple?"

Lilith giggled.

"Did you say something, Christian?" asked Clarissa.

"No, ma'am."

"Hmm..." Christian squirmed under the woman's scrutinizing gaze. It was difficult to maintain eye contact with her. She thankfully decided not to pursue the issue any further and instead looked at Lilith. "Lilith, today we will not be studying your succubus powers."

"What?" Lilith stared at the woman with slightly wide eyes. "Why not?"

"Because you are not the only succubus who is in need of my teachings, and due to the nature of the training, I can only instruct you one-on-one. I must divide my time between yourself and a few of the young girls who were brought here recently."

"Oh... I see..."

"Do not get too down, though," Clarissa, upon seeing Lilith's slumped shoulders and despondent visage, added. "I have tasked someone else to give you lessons on something aside from your succubus powers after breakfast." She smiled. "I'm sure you'll find it beneficial."

As Lilith shivered a little under the disconcerting smile of Clarissa, Christian found himself glad that he was not on the receiving end of that smile. He also made a mental note to make sure he never found himself under it either.

***

After breakfast Lilith found herself in a long, rectangular room that had been lovingly dubbed "The Shooting Range." It wasn't a very original name but considering every wall within the room was loaded up the wazoo with what looked like every gun imaginable, Lilith could see why it would be called that. It was quite apparent that this was the place where long-range fighters learned how to use various types of guns. And bows. And throwing knives. Lilith even saw some kunai hanging on the wall.

There was only one section that was not covered in long-range weaponry. The entire left side, where a wall would have normally been, was instead a space with several segmented zones separated by cement walls. They were kind of like stalls. Each little cube had a small, two-foot wall rising from the ground, keeping people from going further. Beyond that was the rest of the room, which extended at least a hundred more yards. Lilith could make out what looked like several people shaped dummies near the back of the expanded space.

She was learning how to use a gun today, which was too bad, because she would have really liked to learn how to throw a kunai.

"I'm sure you know what a gun is, so I'm not gonna be going into some big lecture about them," her instructor for the day began. "There are many different types of guns; rifles, shotguns, handguns, machine guns, and many different sub-types of each gun such as 9mm pistols, magnums, revolvers, and the AK-47."

Heather Locklear was a woman with a very no-nonsense aura to her. Despite the "you'd better run if you don't want to die" vibe that Lilith was getting from her, she had to admit that the woman was every bit as gorgeous as she was, maybe even more so. Long, straight, silvery blond hair hung from her light in a messy tangle that somehow looked natural and sensual, like she'd just finished having a night of hot, passionate sex.

"Today, all we're going to be doing is having you try out different guns to see which one works best for you. Now come over here."

Lilith followed Heather over to a table, which already had several guns sitting on it. Some were small, some were large, some had long barrels, and others didn't. A few looked like they were supposed to be held with two hands. Most of them were black and gray. Lilith didn't recognize any of them.

"Since you're a beginner, we're going to start off with something easy," Heather told her, picking up one of the smaller guns. Shaped like an L, with a handle, a trigger, and a barrel, it really didn't look all that different from any other gun to Lilith. "This is the Beretta M9, a 9mm semi-automatic pistol. It has an effective firing range of fifty yards, a fifteen round detachable box magazine, iron sightings, and short recoil. This gun was adopted by the United States Armed Forces in 1985."

"Uh..."

All of that flew right over Lilith's head. 9mm? Fifteen round detachable boxes? Short recoil? This woman might as well have been talking rocket science.

Heather seemed to realize this. The woman sighed, placed one hand on her forehead, and then gestured for Lilith to follow.

"Why don't I just show you the basic functions of the gun and we'll go from there?"

Lilith nodded and followed Heather, who soon tried to explain the functions of this particular gun to her.

***

That day was the first day Christian found himself separated from Lilith for more than a few hours. It was an unusual experience, and kind of unpleasant, if he were honest. He'd gotten used to having the young woman by his side, a constant presence that let him know he was not alone. Now that she was gone—off with some woman who had a severe look on her face—he found the lack of her companionship disconcerting.

Despite this, Christian knew it would be good for them. He didn't think it was good for Lilith to have just him as a companion. Making friends among her fellow succubus would be beneficial. It was the whole reason—or at least part of the reason—that he'd not run interference that morning when all those succubi had surrounded her. Lilith needed to step out of her comfort zone in order to grow.

Besides, he had something that he needed to do, and he wanted to deal with it alone.

"Clarissa," he greeted after having finally found the woman. She was in the same training room that they had been using yesterday. He should have checked there first. It would have made everything so much easier. Instead, he had gone to just about every other building he could think of before deciding to come to this one.

Just as she had told them that morning, Clarissa was working with one of the younger succubi. It was the redhead; the one Christian had saved during the battle against those goblins.

Now that he was no longer in a dark, dank cavern or lost in thought, he could see that the female was one of extraordinary beauty; she possessed pale skin with a smattering of freckles on her nose surrounded by dark red hair, and her eyes were a vibrant green. Her face was somewhat rounded, youthful. Now that he was getting a good look, Christian quickly determined the girl to be even younger than he had estimated. Maybe sixteen at the most. Her body was not as curvy as the other succubus he'd seen so far, which also clued him in on her age. Though, perhaps unsurprisingly, she still a more generous figure than most girls her age did.

"Christian," Clarissa greeted, turning to face him. The redhead also looked at him, but only for a second. After that, her face turned a shade of red that nearly matched her hair and she looked away. Christian would have wondered what was wrong with her, but he honestly didn't care enough to ask. "Can I help you?"

"Yes, actually. I wanted to talk to you about something you said when we first met."

"You are referring to when I referred to your inhuman origins?"

"Yes. You mentioned that my right eye is not human, and you said something about above normal healing."

"Indeed, I did," Clarissa said, nodding. "Are you telling me that you're beginning to believe me when I say you are not fully human?"

"I never said that." Christian scowled. "I just want to know how you came to the conclusion that I'm not human."

While Christian would never admit this to Clarissa, the truth of the matter was that he was beginning to wonder about his own origins.

It wasn't something that he'd ever thought about, so it never occurred to him, but his father had numerous inhuman features. He had looked human enough, but there had always been some discrepancies between him and normal humans. His eyes, for one. Clarissa was correct in that humans did not have red eyes, unless they had pigment problems, such as albinos. There had also been his father's teeth, razor sharp incisors that looked more like those found on a shark than a person. His father's skin had also been a rusty red. Christian used to think of it as a weird tan, but maybe that wasn't the case.

Aside from his father's appearance, there was also...

"Then you know what you have to do, right? You have to kill him. End his life. Then he won't be able to take Lilith away from you."

Christian shuddered as he remembered the voice that had whispered in his ear during his battle with Asmodeus. It had commanded him to kill, to destroy the demon who stood before him, to murder the creature that dared to hurt Lilith. His eye had stung, and his blood had boiled. His vision had changed, too, showing him Asmodeus's weakness, the one spot on his body that could defeat him.

He also remembered the feeling it gave him. Just before Asmodeus had exploded, Christian had felt a sense of elation, of joy, the kind that came from death, from killing. He had enjoyed killing Asmodeus, loved it even. The feel of his blade sinking into the demon's flesh, the screams of outrage and pain that emitted from the demon's mouth, all of it had felt incredible, wonderful. It had been euphoric.

That frightened him. It scared him to think that he could take such joy in the killing of others, even if the person he killed was a demon.

This wasn't even the first time that had happened either. It had occurred before, a similar instance happened when he'd been fighting Asmodeus in his human form on the train, and another time during his battle with Abaddon. He'd heard the voice after everyone else that had been involved in that battle was killed. The Destroyer had been about to kill him, and the voice had come, asking him if he wanted the power to survive, the power to avenge his comrades, the power to defeat the Knight of Hell. It was thanks to that voice that Christian had been able to kill Abaddon and Asmodeus.

Yes, that was not natural. Not human. Humans did not hear voices in their head. They did not gain powers like that.

"I said not fully human," Clarissa told Christian, her tone chiding. "I suspect you carry some demonic blood in your veins. Tell me, does your eye have any special properties other than its unique color?"

"Well, yes, it does." Christian reached out a hand on and placed it underneath his eye. "When I focus on it, I can see perfectly even when there's very little light. Depending on how hard I focus, I can even see a three-hundred and sixty-degree view of my surroundings, though I can't use it for long because my head starts to hurt."

"Information overload is like that," Clarissa informed him. "There is a reason humans can only see in a one-hundred and twenty-degree arc. The human mind is not made to comprehend more than that. Your headache is likely being caused by your mind trying to grasp more information than it can handle."

"But wouldn't that mean I'm human?"

"Yes and no. Like I said, you are part human. It is the human part of you that has trouble comprehending that power. Tell me, how long have you had that power?"

"Ever since my battle with Abaddon," Christian admitted with a shrug, causing Clarissa to nod.

"I see, and are there any other abilities that you possess?"

"I don't think so."

"What about your healing?"

"My healing?" Christian looked puzzled for a moment, then shook his head. "I don't have any healing powers."

"Then how is it that you healed from your injuries so quickly?" asked Clarissa. "You healed from grievous wounds that most people would not have walked away from at all, and you did so in under a week. That is not natural."

"It's because of the nanomachines inside of me," Christian defended, "My physician—former physician—Doctor Anastasia Pierce, used some kind of cream filled with nanomachines that worked their way into my skin and bloodstream. They heal injuries by manipulating skin and muscle cells to regenerate damaged tissue and increase the production of red blood cells." Christian then paused, frowning. He looked down at his hands, clenching and unclenching them. "Though it is strange. The nanotech should have been used up weeks ago. I am surprised they're still inside of me."

"Are you so sure it's the nanotech at work now?" asked Clarissa.

"Of course, I am." Christian frowned. "What else would it be?"

"I have a book in the library that I believe you should read," Clarissa said with an expression that made a chill run down Christian's spine. "It may help you understand just what you are. Maybe then you'll begin to accept that you're not one-hundred percent human."

Chapter 9

*B*efore the New Testament firmly established Satan as the ruler of Hell, it was often said that Belial was the one in charge. In the Old Testament, the word "Belial" held the meaning of worthlessness or wickedness, but later came to be used as a proper noun for the Devil or Satan.

According to the Dead Sea Scrolls, The War of the Sons of Light and the Sons of Darkness, he was the uncontested ruler of the dark side: "But for corruption thou hast made Belial, an angel of hostility. All his dominion is in darkness, and his purpose is to bring about wickedness and guilt."

The demon of lies, he was acknowledged as a source of great evil, and even as the lord of all demons. Some apocrypha declare that Belial was created next to Lucifer and that he was the King of Hell governing eighty Infernal Legions. Others credit Belial as being the father of Lucifer and the angel that convinced him to wage a rebellion in Heaven against God, and that as such, he was the first of the fallen angels to be expelled.

Deceitful and evil-hearted, Belial was once considered Beelzebub's equal, but by medieval times he had been relegated to one of the lesser demons of Hell. In the apocryphal the Martyrdom of Isiah and in the Gospel of Bartholomew, he is labeled as the demon of lawlessness: "And Manasseh turned aside his heart to serve Belial; for the angel of lawlessness, who is the ruler of this world, is Belial, whose name is Mantanbuchus."

While there are many different opinions and beliefs about Belial's origins and ranking among the demon hierarchy, what we do know is that he is a powerful demon who is said to be on par with the Seven Demon Kings. It has been theorized by demonologists that he might actually have been one of the Seven Demon Kings at one point in his life but was demoted or killed during one of the many conflicts that happens between demons.

Belial is said to often appear as a man in his middle years, with graying sideburns and a sharp goatee. His eyes are purportedly white, all white, with no pupil or iris, and his skin is the color of darkness, so black that all light that touches him is consumed. Like all demons, there are two wings on his back, remnants from the time when he was supposedly an angel under God's rule.

Belial is known to possess a trident of incredible power, one capable of piercing anything by distorting reality. Some believe this trident to be Gae Bolg, a spear wielded by Cu Chulainn, the famed Hound of Ireland. Others think Gae Bolg is merely a part of the trident wielded by Belial. Regardless of what mythos are to be believed, it is well-known that the trident wielded by Belial is one of incredible power.

Like many demons of his class, Belial is known for possessing incredible amounts of raw power. It is said that with nothing but a wave of his hand, he can create hellfire powerful enough to wipe out several dozen acres of land.

He is also known for his ability to steal the powers of others. It is said that drinking even a single drop of blood is enough for him to gain all the powers someone else has, be they demon or something else. This, above all else, is what makes him such a terrifying enemy.

Christian closed the book in his hands with a loud snap. He flipped the book over and brushed his fingers against the cover. Dull and worn, its cover the color of rust, the book *A Study in Demonology* was one that Clarissa had suggested he read. She told him it might contain the information he was looking for, the knowledge that would help him determine his possible origins.

He had no clue why she would have bothered suggesting such a book. There was no way he could have demon blood in him. There just wasn't. He was willing to accept that, maybe, possibly, his father wasn't quite human, a vampire or a werewolf perhaps, but a demon? He just couldn't see it.

Demons were said to be the one true evil. Angels that had fallen from grace and decided that, if they were going to be cast out of Heaven, they would have their revenge on God by going after the humans that God had created. They were wholly different from the fallen angels, those that had been cast out of heaven but instead of using their powers to harm humans, they merely used them to indulge in their own human desires.

Of course, the fallen angels who became demons were just the higher-ranking demons. They had been born with their power and attained their ranks by stint of their God given abilities. The other type of demon were the ones who formed the middle and lower ranks. They were humans who had lost their humanity, either sometime after death or, in rare circumstance, before it. Those were the demons who no longer looked even remotely human, their desire and powers having transformed them into something grotesque.

Either way you looked at it, demons were evil. There was just no two ways around it. Christian was willing to accept that he was wrong about succubus, and he was even willing to accept that there were probably werewolves, mermaids, vampires, and other entities of the supernatural world who were not evil. But demons? No. He was not willing to accept that any of them were good.

My father, a demon? Yeah, right. If the idea wasn't so insulting, it would actually be funny.

His father had been a good man, willing to protect his family with all his might. He had also been an oaf, a klutz, and an idiot, according to Christian's mother. There was no way his father had been a demon. He refused to believe it.

That was not to say that all the information within the book had been useless. While he didn't think he was related to any demon, the part about Belial's ability to steal powers struck a chord with him. Christian recalled his battle with Abaddon, how after the battle his red eye had gained the ability to see in the dark and, after practice, he was able to see a full 360 degrees. There was also those nanomachines. They were long gone from his body, or they should have been gone, yet he still healed abnormally fast, especially during the times he heard that voice asking if he wanted power.

He also had that strange energy to consider. Whenever the voice gave him power, he felt a strange kind of energy rushing through his body. It had empowered him for a time, allowing him to perform feats that were beyond him, sort of like how those Executioners who used enhancement drugs were strengthened, he imagined.

But what sort of energy was that? It felt familiar to him, but at the same time different than anything else he'd ever felt before. It was contradictory, a paradox that he couldn't make heads or tails out of.

Christian leaned his head back against the headboard of the couch and sighed. Even if this book had given him a few ideas about what kind of powers he might have, it left him no closer to finding what sort of supernatural creature's blood was running through his veins.

What supernatural entities did he know of that had the power to copy other supernatural powers?

Christian knew about plenty of creature's, from vampires to werewolves, trolls, goblins and more. He must have fought and slain over five dozen different types of supernatural being during his time as a Warrior for the Executioners, but he couldn't for the life of him think of one that had the ability to copy or steal powers. Vampires had supernatural strength, werewolves speed, goblins were a race of bloodthirsty and greedy creatures, trolls were large and physically imposing, and ogres were able to spit out terrible globs of highly acidic saliva that could melt through concrete in seconds.

Yes, Christian had a well-spring of knowledge about the supernatural world, or at least knowledge about the various powers and abilities of specific supernatural creatures. Yet, even with all the information he had acquired in his life, he couldn't recall a single entity that had the power to copy or steal powers and abilities.

He raised his left hand and touched underneath his red eye, and suddenly, his lips quirked up as an amusing thought occurred to him. "Maybe my father was an Uchiha," he muttered, then snorted a second later and shook his head. Jokes wouldn't help him here.

He frowned, and he pondered. Maybe he should speak to Clarissa again. She at least seemed to have an idea on what kind of blood might be running through his veins.

Then again, she was also the one who directed him to the book on demonology, so maybe not.

"There you are."

A voice came to him, familiar and enchanting. It brought a smile to his face and pushed his current quandary to the back of his mind. Even the tension in his shoulders began bleeding out of his posture.

He moved his head off the headboard of the couch, no longer looking at the ceiling, but instead at the vision of loveliness, of a halo framing unblemished porcelain skin, of a pert nose, of sparkling emerald eyes, and a dazzling smile. Actually, she was kind of pouting at the moment, but that hardly bothered him beyond wondering what was getting her down. Such was the power of love, he supposed.

"I've been looking everywhere for you. I thought you would be in that training room again, but no one was there when I arrived."

"Sorry. I would have told you that I'd be in the library, but it was sort of a spur of the moment thing."

Which he guessed was true, in a roundabout sort of way. It was his spur of the moment decision to speak with Clarissa about her words on how he wasn't fully human that led to her taking him to this library and giving him the book on demonology.

"It's fine," she said, smiling as she walked up to him, a very slight sway to her hips. When she reached the steps, she lifted her left leg and set her knee on the couch. Then she lifted her right leg and that knee was also set on the couch, but on the opposite side of Christian. The young woman slowly crawled up until she was straddling his hips, and then she leaned forward and placed a kiss on his lips.

Christian took the time to enjoy the kiss. Chaste as it was, it still lingered on his lips for several long seconds. When they broke again, Lilith's arms slowly went to his neck and her forehead pressed against his.

"How was your lesson this morning?"

"It wasn't something I can say I enjoyed," she mumbled, the pout returning. "I had this really strict woman, Heather Locklear. She was teaching me how to use a gun."

Christian felt his mind stop for a second, then restart with a sudden blink. "She taught you how to use a gun?"

"Well, not really taught. She showed me some stuff, like the different parts of a gun, how to load and unload a clip of ammo. Where the safety switch is. Oh, and she taught me how to hold a gun. That part was interesting at least." Lilith smiled for a moment, then shifted, her face going somewhat neutral, her eyes revealing that she was thinking. "Guns are heavier than I expected them to be. Even the small handguns."

"That's because guns are made of metal," Christian pointed out. "Metal tends to be heavy. You also have to take the bullets into account. A single cartridge of ammo adds a couple dozen grams to it, give or take. That might not seem like much, but because of the material, well, they feel heavier than if you were to get the same weight from a bag of flower or sugar. It has to do with gravity's effect on metal because it's such a dense material, or so I was taught."

"I hadn't realized you knew so much about guns," Lilith said after a moment.

Christian raised an eyebrow. "I do have two guns, you know? And I use them pretty often."

Lilith's cheeks turned red. It was just on two spots, giving her a kind of rosy appearance. Christian thought it made her look adorable.

"I know. I just meant, well, I know you have those handguns of yours, and I know you're a really good shot. I've seen you shoot. What I meant was that I didn't know you were knowledgeable about guns in general."

"It's foolish to give someone a gun, teach them how to properly shoot and not blow their own foot off, and not teach them the basics about guns in general. Every Executioner must undergo gun safety classes, where we study the different types of guns, how they work, the mechanics behind them, and why one is more preferable in one situation as opposed to another. That sort of thing. Even if, like me, an Executioner only ends up using one type of fire arm, by learning about all the other ones, we have working knowledge that could help us in the field. Some of the creatures that I've fought against have wielded firearms, hoping it would give them an advantage."

"Did it?" asked a curious Lilith.

Christian shook his head. "No. At least, not when I was dealing with them. Anyway, why are they teaching you how to use a gun?"

"So that I can protect myself, I guess. You know, in case you get incapacitated or something."

Christian frowned. That line of reasoning was sound—and very possible—but somehow, he felt Lilith was hiding something from him.

"Lilith? Is there something you're not telling me?"

"Of course not," Lilith was quick to say, maybe even a little too quick. "Why would you think that I'm hiding something?" Christian continued to frown at her, causing Lilith to bring out her secret weapon.

Her eyes grew large and... teary. He would have said that her large eyes reminded him of a kicked puppy, but there was no way someone as drop dead gorgeous as Lilith could look anything like a dog, or any other kind of animal. Regardless, this fact did not stop the expression from being any less powerful.

As the old saying went, it worked like a charm.

"Don't you trust me?"

Christian grimaced and tried looking away. It was difficult to concentrate on anything when she was looking at him like that, and it made his heart clench, which was just an unpleasant experience all around.

"I do trust you," he relented. "I guess I was just expecting something more profound."

"More profound?" Lilith seemed to find his words amusing, if the quirk to her lips was any indication. He didn't see what was so amusing, but he didn't have any intentions of inquiring about it either. "Like what?"

"I don't know," Christian shrugged his shoulders. "I wasn't really sure what to expect. I guess I just thought there would be a deeper reason. I'm not saying self-defense isn't a good reason," he added. He didn't want her to think that he found her reasons flimsy. It was a good one. "Self-defense is really one of the only justifiable excuses someone can have for wielding a gun, but I had assumed your reason for wanting to learn how to use guns might have been symbolic or something. To be honest, I'm kind of surprised that I never taught you to use a gun myself."

Lilith looked started. Her eyes went somewhat wide, and her lips parted in surprise. "You would do that?" she breathed, sounding shocked for some reason. Though just why she would be surprised by this, Christian didn't know. "Teach me how to use a gun, I mean? You would teach me?"

"Yeah, sure." Christian wondered why she looked so happy to hear him say that. It wasn't that big of a deal, was it? Well, so long as she was happy he supposed it didn't matter. "Though I can only really teach you how to use handguns. I know the basics about every type of gun, but I only really know how to use handguns."

"That's fine." Lilith beamed at him. "I don't mind. Handguns are just fine. Heather said I wouldn't be good at shooting any of the other guns." She pouted again, her cheeks puffing up like a squirrel with an acorn in its mouth. "Something about the recoil or whatever she called it being too much for me."

"That makes sense." Christian nodded to himself, until he saw Lilith frowning at him. Then he endeavored to explain himself. "Handguns are generally the easiest to use because they don't have much recoil, meaning they don't kick as hard. Did your instructor have you fire a gun?"

"No." Lilith shook her head. "She just showed me what kinds of guns there were, and the had me hold them and stuff."

"I see. In that case, I'll show you what she meant by recoil tomorrow when I start teaching you."

"Tomorrow?"

"Would you like to start later than that?"

"Ah! No, no." Lilith raised her hands and waved them in front of her face. "I didn't mean to make it sound like I wanted to start later or anything. I just thought we'd be starting sometime today."

"We could," Christian acknowledged before the hands lightly resting on her hips tightened their hold on her, digging lightly into her lovely porcelain skin, eliciting a soft gasp. Christian smiled. "But I had been hoping we could spend some time together doing something other than learning how to shoot guns."

Lilith, upon hearing his words and the invitation in them, gave him a smile of her own.

"I would like that," she said.

***

"Are you sure this is a good idea?" Tristin asked, for the one hundredth time—or at least, it seemed that way to Samantha. "I mean, I'm as up for an on-sight investigation as much as the next guy, but that's only when I'm not the one going."

"Do you ever stop complaining?"

Samantha scowled. She was beginning to regret having him tag along with her. She would have been better off asking Sif and Leon come with. Yeah, that would have been a great idea, except neither of them had Tristin's intelligence and deductive abilities.

Most people thought that the pretty boy's only talents were hacking and sexing up women—which Samantha had discovered when she walked in on him seducing one of the few female Assassins that she managed to escape Los Angeles with (She had wanted to strangle him when she saw him and that girl mid-coitus) —but Tristin had more talents than just those two. The man was an analyst genius. He was a modern-day Sherlock Holmes with an IQ and the eccentricities to match.

She needed those abilities. She needed that talent.

It was really the only she hadn't killed him already.

Though she could do without the eccentricities.

"I don't like this anymore than you do," she continued. "But this might be the break we're looking for."

They were walking down the streets of Las Vegas, a place Samantha never thought she would have been caught dead in. It was too bad circumstances had forced her to the place people called Sin City.

Evening had come and gone some time ago. The sky, no longer painted in color, was a dark blue nearing black. Much like Los Angeles, it was nearly impossible to see the stars that had come out. All of the lights from the city were nearly overpowering, perhaps even more so than what could be found in Los Angeles. Neon lights cast a brilliant luminescence of obnoxious colors that offended Samantha's senses and forced her eyes to squint. She never did like the bright lights of the big city, especially when they were this glaring and made it feel like her retina were being burned.

Despite how late it was, the city was still alive with lights and people and all kinds of ruckus. The neon signs pointing to one thing or another, shops or casinos or what have you, radiated down on them with the incandescence of a flash bang. People walked out of large buildings, most looking depressed, but a rare few holding a wad full of cash as they skipped along, a brilliant smile lighting their faces. Some of those lucky gamblers had a woman on their arm, and some even had two. Cars drove down the streets, moving lights that flickered across the roadways like fireflies.

Because of how conspicuous they both were—they were rather well-known in certain circles—she and Tristin were in disguise. She was wearing clothes that, had someone suggested she wear them months ago, she would have seriously considered shooting them in the face, sin be damned. Wrapped around her thighs were a pair of really short jeans. Really, *really* short jeans. They rode all the way up her hips, settling just a few centimeters short of her butt. If she were to bend over, Samantha was sure her glutes would be hanging out of them.

How she let Tristin talk her into these jeans was beyond her.

She also had a sleeveless white shirt on. It, too, wrapped around her body, much like the shorts. Samantha was only glad that she did not have breasts as large as Sif's, or she would have been unthinkably uncomfortable. Her raven hair was also done up in twin pig-tails, which made her look like some kind of California valley girl.

Samantha had never been more embarrassed in her life.

And she was going to kill Tristin for convincing her to humiliate herself like this.

She looked over at Tristin and scowled. Unlike her, he was dressed stylishly. Dark blue jeans with a number of strategically placed rips. A black button up shirt with the sleeves rolled halfway up and the first three buttons undone to show off his chest. A pair of slick black shoes clicked against the ground, and expensive looking sunglasses settled neatly on his face.

Samantha had no clue where he had gotten those sunglasses. She certainly hadn't given them to him.

"Well, yeah, that's why I said I have no problem with us going out to do some scouting," Tristin said. "I just don't see why I have to be the one to do it."

"Because you're the best intelligence analyst we have," Samantha said. "And there was absolutely no way I was going to leave you unsupervised at the base. The last thing I need is for you draining all of my Warriors and Assassins of their stamina." Sif and Leon were the only ones who could keep Tristin in line aside from her, and both of them were already out following another lead they had gained.

"I would have only drained the women." Tristin pouted at her, causing Samantha to glare harder. Times like these made her wish she had the ability to shoot laser beams from her eyes. "Whoa, now. Ease up on the death glare, boss lady. I'm only kidding. I don't know if you know this, but I'm very selective with the partners I sleep with. I won't screw just anybody."

"You are so lucky that I can't afford to kill you," she said, gripping the case that contained Zaphkiel tightly enough that the handle began to creak.

"Because you need me, right?" Tristin grinned.

Samantha clenched her teeth. If she didn't have need of his talents, she would've ripped that cocky, arrogant smirk right off his face.

"That's right. I'm going to need you, not just for your hacking skills, but for your analytical abilities and deductive reasoning as well."

"Right! So, what am I doing again?"

"Weren't you listening to me the first time I explained this?"

"Mmm..." Tristin looked up at the sky, thoughtful, then glanced back down. He winked at a pair of women as they passed, causing them to break out into feminine giggles. Samantha scowled, then pinched his arm, hard. "Yeowch!" He rubbed the large red welt she had given him, pouting. "What was that for?"

"For being a pig."

"Are you just jealous." Samantha's glare turned murderous, causing Tristin to shriek like a little girl. "Eek! I mean, ah, ahaha! Of course, you're not jealous! Why would I think something like that? Hahahaha!"

Samantha sighed and rubbed at her forehead. She was beginning to understand why this man pissed Christian off so much. She could practically feel herself aging just walking next to him.

"Pay attention, because I'm only going to say this once more. We're going to be infiltrating the Las Vegas News station. There were rumors a while ago—rumors that you found out about, I might add—that something happened here about a few weeks ago. The news station said that an oil truck crashed into a building and caused a massive explosion, but there was a discrepancy with the damage reports. We're going to find out the truth."

"Which is why you need me, right?" asked Tristin.

"Yes, with your abilities to hack into any network, it should be a cakewalk for you to work your way inside this one. Unfortunately, because we no longer have the technology that we did under the Catholic Church's backing, we don't have the ability to hack a system remotely anymore. At least, not with the guarantee of our own network remaining undetected."

The hidden base in Boulder City was the only one they had left. If that fell, then the Executioners would be taken out. It was better to remain safe and hack into a network, even an unsecured one like this, on sight instead of trying to do so remotely.

"After that, I'm going to need you to analyze all the information you gathered to find out everything you can about that incident, and whether or not one of the Executioners who survived might have been involved."

"Yeah. Okay. I see why you would need me here. Alright!" Tristin pounded the fist of his left hand into the palm of his right. "Let's do this!"

"Don't get too excited now," Samantha muttered, rolling her eyes.

The Las Vegas News Station was a large building, one of the few non-hotel buildings that stood over thirteen stories in height. Made of brick, steel, and large, gleaming windows, there was nothing overtly unique about the structure, other than it being larger than a clear majority of the architecture around it. Samantha and Tristin slowed their walk as they came up to the front. It wasn't guarded, but they didn't enter right away either.

"Do you have a plan to get me into the system?" asked Tristin.

"I'm working on it."

"You mean you don't have one?"

"I said I'm working on it." Samantha scowled. "Just stop complaining and follow me."

The doors slid open and Samantha walked inside, Tristin trailing in behind her. The first floor looked like some kind of reception room. It was pretty empty, which was why she had decided to infiltrate it at night. Only people who worked the nightly news would be working.

Her black boots tapping against the white tiles of the floor, Samantha made her way to the other end of the room, where a set of elevators were stationed. She hadn't studied the layout of the building beforehand because they had been unable to get a map, but she imagined all the work stations that were connected to the network were up there. It would also be more secure than using the one behind the receptionist desk, which anyone would be able to see them use.

Unfortunately, before she and Tristin could get too far, the receptionist sitting behind the desk called out to them. "Excuse me! Office hours are closed. If you wish to make an appointment or something, I suggest calling in next time. Or, if you have some news you think we'd be interested in reporting, just send us an email at myvegasnews@news.com and if we're interested, we'll contact you."

Samantha swore. She had hoped the woman would have been distracted, as she had been looking at her computer when they walked in. She should have expected this, though, and it would be just their luck to get caught before they could go too far. It had been too much to hope that no one would notice them trying to make their way to a higher floor. Neither of them were particularly stealthy.

Well, there was nothing she could do about that now. They had been spotted. All that was left to do was change their plans accordingly and hope for the best.

She walked up to the receptionist, a middle-aged woman who wore far too much make up. Samantha assumed she was one of those women who tried to make themselves look prettier than they really were. Perhaps she thought that by covering her face in so much powder that it was impossible to see her skin, some man would take notice of her.

Or maybe she just liked wearing a lot of makeup.

"I'm sorry," Samantha's tone was apologetic as she bowed to the woman. Too much makeup or not, there was no need to be rude. "But I'm going to need you to go to sleep now."

"Wha—"

The woman barely had the chance to open her mouth and utter a slight squeak before Samantha rushed behind the counter and bashed her across the forehead with her sword case. The resounding "crack!" that resonated around the room as a result was far too noisy, a deafening roar as opposed to a muted smack. Samantha was only thankful that no one was in the room with them.

The woman's head snapped backwards, lolled around for bit, then came down as she slumped forward. Samantha caught her before she could face plant against the computer. She then slid the woman off the chair and leaned her against the wall, out of sight from anyone who might walk in.

"That was pretty inelegant of you, boss lady."

"Shut up. Can you hack into the network from here?"

The man brushed back his blond hair, thinking. "I can, but are you sure you don't want me to do this in a more secure location?"

"I'm not sure we have the time anymore. Someone was bound to see what just happened." Samantha then pointed out three different security cameras located in the room; one was in the left corner near the entrance, another was hidden behind a potted plant, and the last was directly above their heads. "Just make it fast."

"Alright then." Sitting down, Tristin cracked his knuckles before placing his hands against the keypad and beginning to type. "Let me work my magic and see what I can find."

Samantha watched as Tristin's hands flew across the keyboard. His fingers seemed to blur together as he began pulling up dozens of screens, folders, files, and all kinds of things. Samantha was not unknowledgeable about computers, but she couldn't for the life of her figure out what half the stuff he was pulling onto the monitor was.

"How long is this going to take?"

"Patience, boss lady. I've already hacked into the system, though I wouldn't call it hacking since it's only a standard password-based security system." He frowned. "I guess that isn't very surprising. This isn't a military network or something. Anyway, just because I'm in the system doesn't mean pulling up all the relevant information you want is easy. It takes time to do this."

"Couldn't you just download all the information in their database and sort through it later?"

"Do you know how much information is in a news station's database?" asked Tristin, the sarcasm in his voice so thick it couldn't really be called sarcasm. "News stations like this have millions of gigabytes of data. Every single scrap of news they've ever told is stored in their network, and Las Vegas News was founded over thirty-five years ago. That's over thirty-five years' worth of news to store. Do you really want me to download all of that and sort through it later?"

"I see." Samantha coughed into her hand, partly to hide her embarrassed. "In that case, keep doing what you're doing."

"Don't worry. I plan to."

"Also, your sarcasm wasn't needed."

Five minutes later, which was five minutes too long in Samantha's opinion, Tristin leaned back in the chair and sighed.

"Did you find something?"

"No. It looks like whatever files they might have had on the incident were deleted. That, or they never existed in the first place. It's quite possible that the Las Vegas News really did believe the incident was nothing more than a fuel truck crashing into a building."

"Do you really think that's the case?"

Tristin hesitated for a moment, then pressed on, his manner surprisingly serious. "No. The rumors Leon picked up at that bar the other day about a demon wrecking the city may have been the ramblings of a drunken fool, but there had been several dozen unrelated deaths the week before the explosion. The deaths weren't accidents either. They were murders. Coincidence? Hell no." Tristin ignored the scolding expression on Samantha's face. "There is also a small note stating the police department was attacked. The building itself was damaged and several officers died, including a number of officers from the Los Angeles Supernatural Investigations Unit."

"That's nice and all, but it still leaves us with a problem. We don't have any information regarding the incident that left an entire block of the city in ruins."

"Oh? Is that what you two are looking for?"

Samantha and Tristin stiffened. They both looked up to find themselves staring at a man adorned in expensive clothing. A white top hat with dark velvet around the base covered his messy black hair. He wore an elegant white suit with a white undershirt beneath it, and a dark purple tie. Wrapped around his shoulders was a long cape that went down to his calves, the dark purple inner lining giving it a velvety appearance as it fluttered in a breeze. One purple gloved hand was tapping a cane against the ground, while the other was absently stroking his goatee. Bright, inhuman yellow eyes stared at them from beneath a fringe of bangs.

He stood in front of the receptionist's desk, surrounded by several marionettes, all of which were dressed to look like security guards.

They were also all carrying guns.

"If you had wanted that kind of information, you should have just asked," the man continued, lips peeling back in a dangerous smile that revealed sharp canines. "I wouldn't have given it to you, of course, but asking never hurt anyone."

"Samantha?" Tristin's whisper sounded far louder than it should have. "I think we've been caught."

"Really? Thanks for telling me. I hadn't noticed."

"Do you know who this guy is?"

"Not a clue."

"This guy" smiled at them, showing off his sharp teeth. "I suppose introductions are in order. It would be rude of me not to let you know the name of the man whose about to kill you." While Tristin let out a mouse-like squeak, Samantha narrowed her eyes, her fingers tightening around the handle of her case. "My name is Mephistopheles, but you may just call me Mephisto, if you'd like."

Samantha sucked in a breath. Mephisto was a high-class demon, much like Abaddon had been. Unlike the demon that Christian had killed, very little was known about this one, except that he served Satan as a sort of information broker, or something like that. The fact that he was there, standing in the Las Vegas News Station, lent weight to Tristin's deduction about what happened several weeks ago.

That fact didn't make Samantha happy at all. Not anymore.

"What is Satan's information broker doing here in Las Vegas?" asked Samantha.

"Information broker?" Mephisto laughed. "My dear woman, I am more than just a simple information broker. I won't be letting you know what I do, that would be telling. Suffice it to say that I am integral to Lord Satan's many projects. As for what I am doing here, well..." he smiled. It wasn't a pleasant smile either. Must have been the teeth. "I heard from a reliable source that a couple rats were scurrying around Las Vegas. Being the man that I am, I thought I'd do Lord Satan a favor and get rid of them."

Samantha felt like swearing—she didn't even care that it was a sin. Nothing had been going her way ever since she arrived in Las Vegas. Tristin annoyed her to no end. The sight where the "oil truck explosion" had taken place revealed nothing but giant crater and ruined buildings that were in the middle of reconstruction. And now she was here, standing before a demon of incredible power, with a scared intelligence agent quivering behind her, and half a dozen marionettes pointing shining, black barrels her way.

"We're so screwed!"

She didn't want to admit it, but Tristin might very well be right.

What a predicament.

Chapter 10

"Boss lady, I really, *really* hope you have a plan to get us out of this."

"Maybe if you'd shut up, I would be able to think of something."

If the situation weren't so serious—not to mention potentially deadly—Samantha would have rolled her eyes. Here they were, caught between a rock and a hard place, or a desk and several dozen demons pointing guns at them, and Tristin still found it within himself to complain. There was just no pleasing the man.

She eyed Mephisto, noting the smooth lines of his face, all hard planes and sharp angles. He would probably be pretty handsome if it weren't for his pasty white skin and yellow demon eyes. She wasn't necessarily observing him for his looks, however, but rather, she was looking for something that might help her find a way out of this mess in a way that would leave her and Tristin with their lives intact.

Unfortunately, she couldn't find one. She didn't know what his powers were. She didn't know what his weaknesses were. She didn't even know what he did for Satan—because apparently their information was wrong. In short, she knew absolutely nothing that would help them.

What would Christian do in this situation?

"It's such a shame to be killing off one as beautiful as you," Mephisto harped to her. At least, she hoped he was talking to her. Samantha really didn't want to think about a demon who batted for the other team. That would just be weird.

"You flatter me," Samantha said, stalling for time. She needed to keep him talking. The longer he conversed with her, the more time she had to think. "Are you sure you can't tell me what I want to know? My partner and I are going to die anyway—"

"Oh, so now I'm your partner. I see how this is. We're only in this together when the pooch has been screwed up the ass with a crow bar."

"—Couldn't you at least give me some closure by telling me what I want to know?" Samantha finished, her right eye twitching violently. Did Tristin really have to be so crass? And hadn't she told him to watch his language around her? Honestly. If they got out of this alive, she was going to smack his head so hard that all those people who became possessed in horror movies would be green with envy when his head spun around like a top.

"Hmhmhm." Mephisto had an unusual chuckle, close mouthed and rumbling from deep within his stomach more than his throat. "That kind of word play might work on other demons, my dear, but not on me. I know that you're only asking me because you think you can escape from this hopeless situation. But I do give you points for trying. Were I a teacher, I would have presented you with an A for effort, if nothing else."

"You can't blame a woman for trying." She continued to stall. He might not be willing to give her the information she was looking for, but if she stalled him, they could still make it out of this without losing any limbs.

"No, I suppose I can't," he said. While he talked, Samantha ran through a mental checklist of all the items she had on hand. There was Zaphkiel, her trusty sword. There was Araton, her revolver, hidden within her left boot. It was only good for one shot, so that was a no go. What else did she have? Not much. Some lint. A few pennies and... oh! Didn't she give Tristin a flash bang just in case they ran into trouble? "Still, you can't honestly expect me to just hand over that kind of information, do you? Why, the trouble I would be in if I told anyone would be astronomical!"

Wanting that flash bang, but not wanting to give her intentions away to Mephisto, she tapped Tristin's foot with her own. The man blinked, a sign that he knew she wanted something from him, which she saw out of the corner of her eye. She then gestured toward his pocket, keeping her hand below the desk.

Tristin seemed to get it—at least, she hoped he was getting it. He reached into his pocket, careful not to make any sudden or jerky movements that would let the demon in front of them know something was up.

And while the blond pretty boy was trying to find the flash bang she had given him, Mephisto was still talking. "He would probably kill me! And, no offense, but my life is way more important than your own."

Like all demons, it seemed this one also had a love for listening to his own voice.

Pretty soon, Samantha had the flash bang in her hand. She continued listening as Mephisto prattled on—and boy could he prattle. She primed the charge, not bothering to set a timer.

And then she threw it. Without warning. Without even a hint of thought, she fast-balled the tiny sphere right into Mephisto's face.

Despite his surprise, evident by the widening of his sickly yellow eyes, he still managed to catch the thing in his hand. Too bad for him that did nothing. Just as he was about to open his mouth, the entire interior of the reception room exploded in a shower of light.

There was a loud scream. Several actually. Or maybe that was just her imagination. Samantha, her eyes already closed, reached out to the last spot she had seen Tristin. She grabbed something soft, with a fabricy feel—his shirt, then—and yanked him behind her. There was a yelp, followed by the thudding of stumbling feet. She could feel Tristin almost fall over. She yanked him again, harder this time, forcing him to move along with her as she sped out from behind the desk.

Using the mental map she had created during Mephisto's rambling, Samantha did her best to avoid the areas that she knew had previously contained marionettes and Mephisto. Ears straining to hear any shifts in her opponents' positions, all she could hear was the dull pounding of hers and Tristin's feet and the hammering of her own heart.

"Damn Executioners! Kill them! Shoot! Shoot!"

Samantha, running for her life, tugging along a terrified intelligence agent, almost snorted when Mephisto ordered his puppet demons to shoot them. Demons using guns? What an absurd notion. Not that she couldn't see why. Marionettes were just that: puppets. They were low-class demons with no powers of their own. They were only good for cannon fodder and swarming enemies. If you wanted them to do some damage, you had to give them weapons.

Most gave the Marionettes swords, but it seemed at least one demon had wizened up and decided to up the ante by giving his puppets a couple of AK-47s.

Samantha hissed as the sting of a bullet grazing her arm ran through her. A yelp behind her informed her that Tristin had also been shot.

"Dammit! My ass! They shot me in the ass!"

And he had apparently been shot in a very unpleasant area.

She was still going to scold him for language.

Changing from a straight forward run to a swerve, Samantha grit her teeth. Bullets blazed all around them. She could hear them as they struck the floor, shattered glass, and pinged off the walls. She could practically feel the air currents as near misses ruffled her clothes. Yet she kept on her course, her mental map telling her she was only a few feet from the exit.

Then they were out. Samantha's eyes opened to be greeted by the perpetual lights of the city. She didn't stop to admire the sight—not that she would have even if she *wasn't* on the run from a high-class demon —and instead bolted to the left, running past the building and around the corner. She kept running. Running and running and running. She had no clue how far. The length didn't matter. She just had to run far enough to make certain they had escaped.

Just as Samantha was beginning to feel safe, a dreadful feeling overtook her. Abhorrent and terrifying, it washed over her like a rip tide threatening to pull her under. Her mind, her body, and even her soul shook as the power, arcane and mighty and unbelievably overwhelming, rushed across the cityscape.

Sin City was engulfed in red. The buildings, the cars, the streets, the sidewalks, everything blurred together in a crimson haze. The people walking down the streets, denizens of the city, dispersed into particles of red light, becoming ghostly images, a spirit form that reflected their inner selves. The dark sky, once a midnight velvet, became stained with blood.

A barrier. Mephisto had set up a barrier. Damn him.

"Come on."

Samantha continued dragging Tristin behind her. She could hear the blond man panting and whimpering. A pang of sympathy raced through her, but she quickly squashed it, remembering that this man was annoying and deserved getting shot in the backside. She should be thanking the marionette that had done it.

"S-Samantha," Tristin gasped, his feet scraping against concrete, stumbling, tripping, and forcing her to make up the difference by increasing the strength in her stride. "I don't think... I can't go on much farther."

"Just a little farther, Tristin. Then we'll rest."

Times like these made her really hate her job, but Samantha tried to look at their predicament in a positive light. Every bad situation had a silver lining. Their situation was bad, yes, but it could be worse. Demons couldn't sense them when they were inside of the barrier, which meant that if they could find a place to hide, they could rest and come up with a plan to escape.

Even better, Mephisto was probably the one who cast the barrier. Demons couldn't move once they had set up the barrier or they ran the risk of disrupting it. Creating a barrier like this required a constant stream of energy to be emitted from the demon who did the casting. It had to be strong and steady. It couldn't fluctuate, which would happen if Mephisto moved from his spot. That meant the only thing they had to worry about were those marionettes and whatever other horrors the demon had in his legion.

Shelter was found in an alley behind a church. It wasn't a real church, but one of those Las Vegas churches that people eloped in. That was too bad, as Samantha would have liked to pray, even if her faith had been shaken by recent, ground breaking events.

At least the place was decently clean. The ground was a little dusty, sure, and there was an odd smell coming from a sewer vent several meters away, but that seemed to be the worst of it. A door leading into the church stood a few feet from them. Perhaps they could slip inside. She didn't want to remain outdoors. The red sky that formed from demonic barriers always gave her the creeps.

"Here." Samantha directed Tristin over to the wall. "Lay down on your stomach. I need to see the bullet wound."

Tristin, for once, did not respond with something marred by cheerful sarcasm, or just sarcasm in general. He merely whimpered and did as he was told.

Not for the first time, Samantha compared Christian to Tristin. The two had arrived in her care only days apart, joining her Executioners in two different branches, and they couldn't have been more different.

Tristin was cheerful to the point of obnoxiousness. Right from the very beginning, he had been a problem child. He didn't care for the Catholic Church. He didn't believe in God or that Christ was the savor.

He had no trouble going out, flirting with, and sexing up women for his own pleasure. She was even sure that he flaunted this fact because he knew they couldn't do anything. They needed him. They needed all the help they could get. Every week he found a different batch of women to sleep with. Where he met them she didn't know, nor did she care to, but it had been infuriating to call for him, only to find out that he'd gone out that night to get himself laid.

Presenting a stark contrast to the cheerful sexual deviant was Christian. He was serious to the point where he seemed moody most of the time. Straight-laced and a strong believer in following the rules, Christian had thrown himself into his training, his tasks, and the Catholic Religion. He became everything a Warrior should be. He was not just a strong fighter but also a scholar and a man of God. The only thing that had bothered her about him was his unhealthy obsession for light novels and Japanese pop culture, but she could overlook that in light of his accomplishments and piousness.

And yet it was Christian who ended up running away with a succubus, forsaking his duty for a monster. It was Christian who abandoned her when she needed him most. Furthermore, it was Tristin who was here, right now, having taken a bullet to the butt, whimpering in pain, who had helped her the most.

How was that for ironic?

"S-Samantha..."

Samantha snapped out of her reverie and focused on the task at hand.

"I'm here. Let me see your injury."

With Tristin's help, Samantha managed to work the man out of his pants. If it weren't for the small issue of them being trapped in a barrier with a high-class demon, Samantha was sure she'd have been blushing, or raging. Definitely raging. This was the first time in her entire life that she had ever seen a male's lower half. Unlike a good deal of Executioners who'd lost their virginity, she had never bedded anyone.

Samantha tried to ignore the fact that Tristin's rear end was being practically shoved in her face. His skin was a lot paler down there than it was anywhere else. Probably because he never got any sun there. Leaking from a small wound in his left glute was blood. It trailed down the pale flesh, a tiny trickle.

"This is the injury you've been whimpering and moaning about?" A large vein pulsed on her forehead. She could feel her right eye twitching with violent intentions. "This tiny, little, measly wound is what you've been crying over?"

"Uh..." Tristin appeared to be at a loss for words. He also wasn't whimpering anymore. "It, um, really hurt? Hehehe..."

"Tristin," Samantha said, her voice a terror inducing, sibilant hiss.

"Um, yes?" Tristin's reply was meek, afraid, perhaps even petrified. His body began to quiver, which was easily visible since his pants were hanging around his ankles, along with his boxers. Yeah, he knew he was screwed. And he knew that she knew that he knew he was screwed.

"You and I are going to have a very long talk when we get back to base."

Tristin just gulped.

***

The next morning brought with it a bright new day. At least, Lilith thought so. Sure, she couldn't actually "see" the bright new day because, well, she was living in the middle of an enclave built underneath a park. It was hard to see true daylight when you were surrounded by rock, but that was a form of semantics she didn't care to get into that morning.

Sitting up in the king-sized bed that she and Christian had been given for the duration of their stay—they had no clue how long it would be—she and Christian shared breakfast in bed.

"Here, Christian. Try this," Lilith said, turning to face him as she tilted her head slightly. That was what she was supposed to have said, were her mouth not currently full of a French toast stick, or at least half of one. The other half was sticking out of her mouth, wiggling about as she moved her lips in what she hoped was an enticing manner. What her words actually came out sounding like was, "mer mimim. my miff," or something close to that.

Christian shook his head. "You know, the more time you spend here at the enclave, the crazier your ideas get."

At least he seemed to understand what she wanted, if his words were any indication. They still made her pout—or would have if her mouth wasn't full of food. Surely he had to know why she was doing this. While not exactly a standard, this sort of thing happened in light novels all the time, though it was normally with pocky and not French toast.

"Muu." Lilith tried to put on a sulky look, but she was pretty sure she had failed because she *still* had a piece of French toast wriggling around in her mouth. "Mom om, mimim. Murry mup mam meaff."

"Alright, alright."

Christian had the audacity to laugh at her. The smile he gave her offset what could only be him mocking her, but only a little. She was so getting him back for laughing at her idea.

Those were her thoughts, until he leaned over and placed the other end of the French toast in his mouth. He then began to nibbling on the food at a maddeningly slow pace. Each second that passed caused his face to move closer by an inch. An inch! Couldn't he hurry this up? Was he that dead set on making her suffer?

Torture her like this, would he? She was definitely going to get him. Christian wouldn't know what hit him by the time she was done.

Eventually, after an excruciating amount of time had passed, Christian made it all the way over to her. Joy overflowed, singing within her like a quire of angels. She was so happy that she closed her eyes. She would have puckered her lips, too, but with the French toast in her mouth, that was kind of impossible.

So she sat there and waited.

And waited.

And waited.

And then she waited some more. When there were no lips pressing against her, she opened her eyes and saw Christian, sitting on the bed, his face no longer inches from her own, swallowing the last bite of French toast.

"That was good," he said, smiling at her, his eyes alight in a way that would have sent his former commander, some lady named Samantha, into epidemic seizures. "Thanks for sharing your breakfast with me."

Lilith swallowed the food in her mouth and narrowed her eyes. "You were supposed to kiss me."

"Was I? Oops. My bad."

Christian's innocent mien didn't fool her one bit. She knew that he knew what she wanted, what her goal had been. Her mate was teasing her. He was actually messing with her. When did this happen? How did this happen? Had Christian become a flirt when she wasn't looking? And did he know that she secretly enjoyed it?

Maybe this was part of the bond. She knew that by connecting with Christian, she was given energy and a little of Christian's strength and confidence flowed into her through it. Did that connection work both ways? Well, it had to, of course. When they were connected, she could sense the flow of thoughts between them, the link that was conceived when they were one. She felt what he felt and vice versa. That was what made it so powerful. It wouldn't be a stretch to assume that Christian saw into her thoughts as well, that he knew of her desires. He might have even seen her mental checklist, which she had dubbed "Things I Want to do With a Man if I Ever Get the Chance."

This entire scenario was one of them.

"I hope you don't think I'm going to let you off just like that," Lilith said, her tone going slightly dark. Christian didn't get scared. Lilith knew she wasn't that scary. And the purpose wasn't to scare him anyway.

"Oh? And what are you going to do about it?"

"This!"

With nary a thought, Lilith hurtled herself at Christian, crashing into him and knocking them both off the bed. Christian hit the ground, emitting a loud "oof!" as all the air was driven from his lungs. Lilith landed on top of him. She barely gave the young man enough time to suck in a breath of oxygen before she was on him, smashing her lips, her tongue shoving its way past his teeth to get to the warm cavern behind them.

Rather than put up a struggle, Christian simply breathed through his nose. His arms tightened around her waist, pulling her to him. Lilith had to shift her legs, as they were still partly on the bed, but she was soon straddling his waist. She let her hands roam over his shirt, shamelessly feeling him up. She loved her mate's body. It was hard as granite, firm and unyielding and muscular. Not to mention those abs...

She would have loved him even if he had was ugly as sin, but she was truly glad that he wasn't.

In most normal circumstances, this would have been the point where their kiss heated up and they began ripping each other's clothes off. Christian had to put an unfortunate stop to that before things got too far.

"Sorry." He at least had the decency to apologize, no doubt seeing the look on her face. "But I don't think I can go a round with you this morning."

"Why?" Lilith asked, tilting her head, worried. "You're not tired, are you? Am I draining you?"

She had learned that one part of what made a succubus's mate special was that the succubus they were compatible with did not drain them of their essence. They merely took the excess energy that all human beings produced naturally. But what if that wasn't the case? Had she been lied to? But why would they lie about this?

"No, no. Nothing like that," Christian assured her, making her sigh in relieve. It was shorted-lived relief. She still didn't know why he was refusing her.

"Then why?"

"Because I'm feeling a little..." Christian paused, his face scrunching up. He was probably searching for the most diplomatic response possible. "...raw," he decided on, "down there."

"Raw?" Lilith felt lost. What did he mean by "feeling raw?" Raw normally meant something along the lines of uncooked or unprocessed meat, didn't it? No, wait. It could also mean tender and painful. So, did that mean... "Oh," she said, finally getting it. Her eyes widened. "Oh!"

"Yeah..." Christian looked just a little embarrassed. Lilith felt much the same. "I... think we might have been going for a little too long last night."

Lilith understood what he was talking about. Last night they'd made love. Not all that unusual, all things considered, but last night they had made a lot of love. Four hours' worth of it, in fact. That had to be a new world record. She didn't know of any couple who'd lasted that long. Granted, she didn't know any couple other than them, but her point still stood. Weren't most women complaining about their man's lack of stamina? Stacy always complained about "minute men."

Her Christian was no "minute man," that was for sure. She didn't know if his stamina on the battlefield helped increase his stamina in the bedroom, but he was always an energetic lover. That said, it seemed like they had made love so much that his crotch was actually hurting.

"Then I guess we should get up," Lilith said, a tad reluctant. She still wanted more, but she also knew that if they stayed that way, things would get out of control very quickly.

"That's probably for the best," Christian agreed. So, with a sigh, Lilith stood up, then helped Christian to his feet.

They took a shower, helping each other wash those hard to reach areas. It almost ended up becoming something more, but their willpower held—even if a few cracks formed, and they soon made their way into the shooting range.

This was the first time Christian had been in the shooting range. When he saw all the weapons that lined the walls, a whistle escaped his lips.

"Wow. This is really impressive. You don't see many places that have such a variety of firearms."

"Was it not like this with the Executioners?"

"Not really." Christian shook his head. "The Executioners were never in the business of hording weapons. Ammo maybe, but not weapons. We had a weapons supplier who would send us standard equipment whenever we needed it. When an Executioner was worthy of it, the Science Division would make them custom weapons like my guns and swords."

"I see." Lilith hummed. "So it's not like here, where you have a bunch of weapons and choose the one for you. They fit you with a weapon they feel works best and will customize your weapons if you become good enough."

"More or less. Anyway, why don't you show me the guns Heather explained to you and which one you two felt worked best."

"Okay."

Lilith led Christian over to the wall that had only handguns attached to it. She searched for a moment, her nose wrinkling and her eyes squinting as she tried to remember which gun they had decided she should learn to use. Most guns looked the same to her. They were just a bunch of L-shaped objects with a trigger. It was only after remembering the discussion she and Heather had shared about how to determine which type of gun was the best fit for her that she found the gun she was looking for.

"That's a Glock 19," Christian determined after taking a moment to look at it. Lilith handed him the compact weapon. He turned it over in his hands. "This weapon is actually used by many of the female Assassins due to its reduced dimensions and versatility. I myself have never used one, but they're supposed to have very little recoil. I know that the LAPD uses this gun as a backup weapon when on the field because of how easy it is to conceal."

"So it's a good gun?" asked Lilith. She had actually heard all of this from Heather, but it was nice to hear Christian confirm the other woman's words. She trusted him more than she did some woman she had only met once.

"Yes. It's a good gun. Great for people who've never fired a gun before and specifically designed with women in mind. You could easily conceal this in your purse or something of that nature." He stopped talking and looked up at her. "You said she hasn't shown you how to use it yet?"

"That's right." Lilith nodded in affirmation. "All she did was show me the guns on hand and help me find the one best suited for me."

"Right. In that case, why don't we get started? Did she show you where they keep the ammunition?"

"Um..." Lilith reflected on yesterday for a moment before the light bulb went off in her head. "She did! The ammo is over here!" She led him to a series of drawers embedded in the wall. After running her index finger up and down, humming and trying to remember which drawer had the ammo for the handguns, she eventually grabbed the second to last drawer and pulled it open. "Here they are."

All the ammo was neatly stored inside a set of boxes, organized by type. Lilith watched as Christian grabbed several clips of ammo, four in total, and then closed the drawer.

"Come on," he said, taking her hand with his free hand, the one not carrying the ammo, and leading over to the nearest shooting station.

The stations were rather plane. Just a tiny cubicle large enough for maybe two people to stand in side by side. In front of the station was a square of cement rising out of the ground, acting like a table. It was the table that Christian set the guns and ammo on. He then turned to her and tried to adopt a pose like what people might expect to see on a teacher.

"Okay, the first thing I'm going to show you is how to load and unload the ammo clips from your gun..."

Thus began Christian's instruction on how to properly use a gun. It was kind of boring, if Lilith were honest with herself. She just wasn't interested in guns. They held no appeal for her. She still paid attention to everything he said, though, and not only because it was Christian speaking, but also because she knew it was important. If she planned on being useful and helping Christian, then she needed to know how to use a gun.

It was just logical.

The first thing Christian showed her was how to load and unload ammo from the gun. It was a straightforward process. Use your palm to push the clip of ammo into the butt of the gun. Grab the slide. Pull it, and let it shift into place. To unload, just push the magazine release. Easy. It was after he taught her how to load and unload magazine clips that the lessons became interesting.

"Now that you know at least the basics, let's actually get to shooting it. Here." He moved behind her and placed his hands on her shoulders. "The first part about shooting is that you need to get into the proper stance. Put your dominate leg to the rear. This way you have it acting as a support. That's it. Now shift your torso, not fully facing forward, but at a sort of candid angle. There. Just like that. Now, hold the gun and extend your dominant hand and then put your non-dominant hand over your dominant hand. Excellent. Remember to keep your non-dominant arm bent. There you go. Good."

While he spoke to her, Christian pressed his chest against her back. The hard muscles of his pectorals and abs as they pressed into her were impossible to ignore. His arms and even his legs were taking her limbs and directing them as he talked her through the process. Lilith could feel his hot breath hitting her ear. His voice was a sweat whisper filled with promises, or so it seemed to her, and it was driving her crazy.

If he didn't let up soon, she was going to jump him right there in the shooting range.

"Think you've got the hang of it?"

Christian's question snapped Lilith out of her thoughts on how she wished they were back in their bedroom, where she could tear off his clothes and...

"Lilith?"

"Y-yes?"

Christian looked at her with an odd inflection on his face. Could he see how hot and bothered she was? Probably. Lilith wondered if he knew that the reason for it was him. Most likely. There wasn't anything aside from Christian that made her so hot under the collar.

"Try not to get too distracted now," he teased. Lilith would have pouted at him, but she couldn't really find the necessary strength. Just thinking about something other than how nice his arms felt around her, or his chest pressing into her, was taking up more brain capacity than she thought possible. He must have seen this too because he stepped away, just a little, much to her disappointment. "Why don't we try having you fire the gun? I'll watch and correct you whenever you make a mistake. Sound good?"

"I guess."

Was it wrong that she was beginning to regret asking Christian for lessons? She loved spending time with him, but dammit, she wanted to spend time with him, not spent time learning how to shoot guns.

Just then, as Lilith was about to try and remember everything Christian had told her, the alarms suddenly began blaring.

"W-what is...?"

"It looks like something has breached the perimeter of the enclave," Christian said to Lilith's unfinished question. He looked over at her, then at the gun in her hand. "It looks like we'll have to continue this some other time."

The two of them left the shooting range to search for Clarissa, or someone who could tell them what was going on. Lilith, on impulse, stashed the still loaded gun into the back pocket of her jeans. It would have still been noticeable because her jeans fit her so well, but she managed to hide the bulge in her back pocket by covering it with the hem of her white shirt.

It took some doing, and Christian had to ask more than one person, but they eventually found Clarissa. She was in the command room, a centralized hub that controlled all the security measures they had put in place to protect the enclave. Built almost like a war room, it had a large table in the middle with a built-in map of the entire underground, including all the tunnels they had discovered. Along the walls were monitors and screens flashing with information and video feeds from cameras installed inside of the cavern tunnels. Most of the monitors were in shades of green, night vision, because the caves interior was so dark that it was impossible to see with normal cameras.

Clarissa was standing behind a young woman working at a monitor. She looked worried. Anxious even. Lilith could see how tense her shoulders were. Something was definitely unsettling her.

"Christian, Lilith," Clarissa noticed their presence and greeted them. Her eyes flickered to Lilith for a second, making the young woman remember that she was supposed to have met with Clarissa to practice her transformations that morning. Oops. "It's good that you are here," she said to Christian. "I was just about to send someone to get you. I've already sent someone to fetch Andrew."

"I'm guessing from the alarms that we have some kind of problem?" Christian asked.

"It's more than just 'some kind of problem.'" Clarissa looked grave, graver even than the last time they had been attacked. "The goblins have gathered in mass and are launching a two-point assault. One in the northern quadrant of the tunnels. The other in the southern quadrant. We have been unable to determine their full numbers, but so far we count at least five hundred in each group."

Lilith balked at the size of the attack groups. The enclave consisted of exactly 215 succubi. That meant the force coming to attack them was five times larger than their own forces.

"A pincer attack with one thousand strong?" Christian asked, frowning. "I didn't know they had those kinds of numbers."

"They shouldn't, and that's what's worrying." Clarissa worried her lower lip, drawing just a little bit of blood. "The goblins have not been here as long as we have. While we have been living in this enclave for nearly thirty years, they arrived roughly eight months ago, burrowing their way in on the opposite side of the lake and going deeper than even we dared to do when we built this enclave. Our rough estimate of their numbers put them at a couple hundred, maybe five hundred at most. Not enough to launch a full-scale assault, especially as their numbers have dwindled since we began fighting them. This sudden rise in numbers is troubling."

"Then something has changed," Christian determined.

Clarissa gave him a grim nod. "Either they were concealing the numbers they had, or the number of goblins has expanded since then." She paused. "That said, even if they had this many goblins, it doesn't make sense for them to launch a full-scale assault now. Something else must have changed. Perhaps they have a secret weapon they plan on bringing out."

"But what about that attack the other day?" asked Christian after Clarissa finished listing off possible reasons for this new, two-pronged attack. "If they had a weapon, why use it now and not two days ago? If they had manpower, why send a force of what was probably two-hundred strong and not do this the day before? They would have had a larger advantage."

"I don't know." Clarissa's expression, already quite pensive, grew steadily more concerned. "It could be this is a weapon they only discovered last night, or maybe some reinforcement arrived after the battle, or perhaps they are just growing impatient and have decided to go for an all-out push. We have been fighting against the goblins for nearly six months now, ever since our first contact with them ended in bloodshed."

Lilith stood there, listening as Clarissa and Christian conversed, not even paying attention to her. It was like they had completely forgotten she was even there.

Anger welled up inside of her. And jealousy. This wasn't the first time such a thing had happened. Every time they were confronted with a serious problem, Christian would go into this strange battle mode of his and start talking to the other people involved, ignoring her. She didn't like it. Not one bit. She especially didn't like it because almost every single person in charge when their life hung in the balance seemed to be a woman.

"What if that last attack was just a probe?" asked Lilith. She needed to speak up so they would stop ignoring her.

Her words caused both Christian and Clarissa to freeze. Their heads swiveled to look at her, and Lilith suddenly began to think that maybe speaking out as she just did was not one of her best ideas. The look in their eyes was so intense that she actually thought she could feel heat radiating from them.

"A probe, you say?" Clarissa inquired, her dark eyes boring into Lilith. The potency of the older woman's gaze had her nearly freezing in place.

Swallowing the sudden lump that welled up in her throat, Lilith nodded. "Yes, a probe. This last attack could have simply been designed to see how strong you were, how quick your response time was, how well you responded to their attack, things like that. They could have been testing you in order to plan for their real attack."

"A feint designed to analyze our fighters' prowess and plan accordingly," Clarissa murmured, a hand reaching up to cup her chin. "Yes, that is certainly a possibility. One that I had not thought of." She brought herself out of her reverie, and then smiled at Lilith. "You have a very analytical mind, to be capable of developing a theory like that on the spot so quickly."

Lilith felt heat rising to her cheeks. "Thank you," she mumbled before noticing something out of place. Christian. He was staring at her with an odd look, one that she couldn't quite place. It felt almost like he was looking at her as if she was some kind of foreign entity that he had never seen before. "Christian? Is something wrong?"

Christian's eyes blinked rapidly. He shook his head.

"No, nothing's wrong. I was just thinking about something."

Lilith frowned, but she didn't have time to question Christian as he turned to back to Clarissa.

"If the attack two days ago was indeed merely some kind of test to see how our defenses hold up, then that means this next attack is going to be with the purpose of wiping the enclave out."

"Yes. Those are my thoughts exactly," Clarissa said. "That is why I want you to lead one of the two groups we will be sending out."

Both Christian and Lilith stared at the woman in shock.

"Me?" asked Christian.

"Yes. You will be heading the group with Heather Locklear. Your task will be to defend the southern quadrant. The south is one of our most important locations. It is where the exit to our enclave is, as well as the location where we have stored all of our larger equipment, such as vehicles and spare parts." Clarissa frowned. "I do not know how they managed to get all the way over there without tripping one of our detectors, but it matters not. That location must be defended at all costs."

"I understand." Christian nodded toward the woman, his expression solemn and determined. Lilith could see the way he set his jaw, the narrowed angle of his lips. He only got that look a few times since they had met. It had been most prevalent during the disaster with the No Life King, Damien, right before the battle that had nearly ended in his death.

Lilith felt something unpleasant settling in her stomach.

"Good," Clarissa said. "In that case, go meet up with Heather. She will likely be in the weapons room in the southern quadrant. Chances are good she is already rounding up the rest of our forces. Just relay the orders I have given you. Unlike some of the other succubus here, she will follow your lead."

"Right."

Christian nodded, then turned to her. Lilith looked up at him, her mind struggling. She wanted to tell him not to go. She wanted to say he didn't have to do this, that he should just stay with her, where she could keep an eye on him and make sure he didn't do something reckless. She wanted to say that, but she couldn't, because Christian didn't give her the chance.

Leaning in, he pushed his mouth against hers in a brief but fiery kiss. It caused her lips to tingle pleasantly. When he pulled back, he gave her a smile, and said, "I'll show you how to use that gun later, okay?"

Lilith didn't get the chance to respond before he was running out of the door and down the hall. She stared at the slowly closing door, her eyes wide as she tried to determine what she should do. Did she go after him? Did she stay there and wait?

She really had no desire to stand there, waiting around for him to return. Lilith had been forced to wait for him the last time he'd gone off to fight the goblins and had detested it. She disliked the feeling of helplessness that had come to her while she sat around with nothing to do but twiddle her thumbs. She despised how her mind had been kept in a constant state of distress, as apprehension clawed at her nerves, mangling her senses and making it impossible to think positively as dread welled up in her chest. She did not want to feel like that again. Not now. Not ever.

"Excuse me, but I have something I need to do," Lilith said, nodding to the leader of the enclave before spinning on her heels and making for the door.

"You are going after Christian, aren't you?"

Lilith stopped but did not turn around.

"If you wish to go with him, I will not stop you," Clarissa continued. "But if it is truly you're desire to follow him, then know this: as of right now, you have neither the skills necessary to defend yourself nor the will that is required to take the life of another. You will be, for all intents and purposes, a sitting duck. Following Christian right now could very well end in your death, or Christian's death because of the distraction your presence will bring him. If you are willing to risk both your life and his, then you may follow him."

Lilith stared at the door, incertitude filling her, making her hesitant as she became unsure of her course. Was what Clarissa said true? Would she really be putting Christian in danger by going after him?

She didn't want that. She didn't want him to get injured or die because of her, but she couldn't just stand there, waiting for him in silent worry, hoping that he would return to her. She couldn't bear the thought of him going out there and possibly dying, while she sat safe and sound inside the enclave.

In the end, it all came down to a choice. What did she want to do? Did she want to go after him, regardless of the consequences, simply to satisfy her need to be by his side, regardless of how powerless she was? Or did she stay there, anxious and worried and powerless?

Lilith hesitated for a second longer, and then she rushed out of the door, following Christian.

Chapter 11

Tristin woke up to the feeling of someone lightly kicking his side. It didn't hurt, not really, but it did cause his body to jerk. Whoever was doing the kicking knew where to kick. They managed to hit a cluster of nerves, the ones just below his ribs, and the jolt to his body's nervous system had him awake before he could even make the typical "just five more minutes" response that most teenagers gave their parents.

That was probably a good thing. He wasn't a teenager. Not to mention the person who did the kicking had violent tendencies when she was ignored, at least regarding him.

He wondered why that was, but then he pushed the thought aside as he sat up, blinking and groaning. Last night had not been the most pleasant of nights. There were cramps in his back from the hard wood floor. He had a creak in his neck from where he slept wrong. And that wasn't even mention how sore his ass cheek was. It felt like someone had shot him in the butt, and then someone else had taken a pair of pliers and pulled the bullet out of his aforementioned glutei.

Which was closer to the truth than he would have liked.

"Stop sitting there like some kind of idiot, Tristin," Samantha scolded him. He looked up to see the woman looming over him, her eyes penetrating deeper his than any steel blade could ever hope to do. "I need you to get up."

"Ugh," Tristin groaned but nonetheless stood as commanded. Samantha had been getting more violent as time passed. He supposed a part of that was his fault, what with the teasing and the complaining and the whole keeping a dark secret from her for several long years bit. That sort of thing didn't endear him to people.

In his defense, teasing was a part of his nature, he really wasn't suited to this kind of work, so it was his right to complain when tasked with doing it, and that secret would have gotten him killed if she'd discovered it before the Executioners had been betrayed by the Catholic Church. She could stand to be a little more understanding.

"Come on," Samantha commanded as they walked out of the small closet space they had taken up residence for the night. Raven hair swishing about, she peeked around the corner of the church to see if there were any enemies. Tristin stood behind her, blinking, too tired to even stare at her ass, which was an admittedly appealing prospect.

Samantha might be an uptight bitch—at least to him—but she was one of the hottest women he had ever met.

And he had met a lot of women.

"Wh-what time is it?" he asked, yawning as he followed Samantha into the church proper. Despite the place being a church in appearance only, it did look sort of like a place where people might come to worship God. There was an isle between two rows of long, wooden benches, the thick red carpet giving away its purpose. A statue of Jesus Christ nailed to the cross was situated in the back of the church, pressed up against the wall. The room also had a podium, just like a regular church would have. If it weren't one of nearly six dozen located on this city block alone, Tristin would have almost believed it was a normal church.

"It's a little past five," Samantha answered, her dispassionate voice echoing a little due to the room's acoustics.

"Just a little past five." Tristin balked. "You mean to tell me that we grabbed less than four hours of sleep?"

"Yes."

Who the hell runs on four hours of sleep? Tristin could hardly function without a full eight hours. Didn't Samantha know that? How did she expect him to keep up with her when he'd gotten so little rest?

"Couldn't we have slept for at least a few more hours? You know, like at least four?"

Standing by the back door, Samantha turned around to glower at him. "You obviously do not understand the situation we are in right now, Tristin, so allow me to spell it out for you. We are trapped inside a barrier, the enemy is searching for us, and if we do not leave this place soon, they will find us and then it will be all over. You'll get your rest, but it'll be an eternal rest."

"Eternal rest sound pretty damn good right about now," he shot back, only to receive a smack on the head. "Owch!"

"Mind your language, especially when you're in a church."

"It's not like this place is a real church."

"That doesn't matter. Real or not, it is still a church, and I won't have you disrespecting God by swearing in a place meant to bind two people in holy matrimony."

"Whatever," Tristin grumbled. Cripes this woman was a fanatic. Even Christian wasn't this bad. He believed in God, sure, but he didn't blow his top and get violent when Tristin said something insulting.

Then again, he and Christian had known each other for years before they joined the Executioners. Samantha hadn't.

He missed his best friend.

With a disheartened sigh, he followed Samantha as she led him out the back of the church. His butt was still sore—just walking hurt. Samantha had not been gentle when she used a pair of pliers she'd found inside of the church to pull the bullet from his bum, nor had she been tender when she cleaned it.

At least his butt wouldn't be getting infected any time soon.

He still wasn't sure if that was a good thing.

"Follow me and be sure to stay as silent as possible," Samantha said.

Tristin nodded, even though the woman couldn't see it. "Right."

They crept along the alley, moving as cautiously as possible. There was a pile of trashcans near the entrance, which they hid behind. While Tristin huddled down, knees pressed against his chest and arms around his knees, Samantha peeked out into the street beyond the alley.

"I can't see anything from here," she determined after a few more seconds of staring. She crouched back down and began moving further into the alley again. "Come on. We need to find a higher vantage point."

Tristin sighed, but he didn't put up a fight and followed the woman as she moved. What else could he do? Go out on his own? Not unless he wanted to get ripped apart by demons.

They passed the church, climbed over a small wooden fence, and made it to another alley. Grayish walls with stains and cracks closed in around them. The buildings were tall enough to keep much of the red barrier concealed from their view, unless one were to look directly up. Pipes, shoots, and tiny metal boxes covered some of the walls on either side, casting strange shadows that morphed and shifted to create inorganic patterns that defied all sense of reason, or maybe it was just Tristin's mind playing tricks on him. Demonic barriers had a way of messing with a person's head if they weren't careful.

Samantha led him to a ladder attached to the building on their left. She then turned to him and gestured to it. "You go up first."

"What?" Tristin blinked. "Why?"

"Because you're a lecher, and I don't want you staring at my backside while I'm climbing up."

Tristin felt like pouting, but he couldn't deny that the woman had a point. That did sound like something he would do.

"Alright, fine. I'll go first."

Tristin grabbed the rungs, grimacing. The bars were cold and covered in rust. He could feel his hands getting grimy and disgusting just from touching them. Repulsed, he was almost tempted to let go.

"Hurry up, Tristin."

Almost because Samantha was standing there, and he knew she would not let him get out of this. So he climbed up, putting one hand above the other, planting his feet on each rung as he climbed up, reminding himself that no matter how unpleasant it felt, the consequences of not climbing would be much worse.

When he arrived at the top, he scrambled onto the building, tempted to kiss the pavement. Samantha appeared on the roof several seconds later, having been following close behind. While Tristin was content to simply sit there on the roof, Samantha was not, and she walked over to the edge of the building, crouching down and peering over it to see if she could spot something that might be useful.

Tristin watched Samantha for a few seconds more, then turned his attention towards the sky. Red. He was really beginning to hate that color. It represented just about everything he didn't like. It was the color of the first thing he could remember of his past, of waking up with no recollection of who he was or where he was or how he even got there, of blood splattered against the floors, walls, ceiling, and himself, of two corpses that he did not recognize, lying on the ground, ichor pooling around them to form thick, sticky puddles.

Unlike most members of the Executioners, Tristin had not joined because he enjoyed battle and bloodshed. Much like how Christian had joined because he felt he could help humanity, Tristin had joined because he felt he could help Christian.

Ever since the time when they were young, and Christian had stood up to several bullies who were picking on him because his genetics made most men hate him, he'd felt a sense of kinship with the young man. It was amusing. Christian was the only male he could really put up with. Even Leon grated on his nerves.

Unlike most men who often felt like he was encroaching on their territory, Christian didn't even seem to realize he had a territory for Tristin to encroach on. He suspected that the reason for this lay in Christian's genes. It was the very same genetic code that made him immune to Lilith's allure.

Or maybe Tristin was just over thinking things. That was always a possibility.

Movement alerted him to Samantha crouching down next to him. The woman had her game face on as she unlatched the lock on her case and pulled out all the items therein.

"Alright." She set her sword down and grabbed a folded-up sheet of paper. It was a map, Tristin soon realized as she unraveled the item and spread it across the rooftop between them. "This is where we are." Samantha pointed to a building on the map. "Currently, there are sixteen marionettes patrolling the street in our general location here, here, here, and here. They seem to be moving in groups of four. I suspect each group farther out are also grouped in groups of four, though I can't be certain."

"It looks like they have us mostly surrounded," Tristin said, his manner neither joking nor complaining anymore. Now just wasn't the time for that. "They've blocked off the four crossroads for this block. If we're to base the movement of these four groups with what the others have done, then they are likely doing the same with every city block."

"Those were my thoughts as well," Samantha said. She seemed pleased for some reason, or at least satisfied. Tristin wondered why. "We won't be able to get out of this without fighting, and I suspect that they have four to each group for a reason."

"Three to send after us as a distraction. One to alert the others to our location."

Samantha nodded.

"Right."

"So then, what should we do?" Tristin scratched the back of his neck. "I don't think I need to tell you this, but I suck at fighting. And while I'm awesome at gathering intelligence and analyzing it, I suck at formulating plans."

"Do not worry about that." Samantha waved off his concerns. "I've taken your lack of fighting prowess into account. The key to getting out of this will be in my ability to kill all four marionettes in each group before they can get off a warning. Surprise will be our best ally here."

"And what comes next?"

"We'll make our way back to the News Station. That's likely where Mephisto is. He'll be immobile as long as he's maintaining the barrier. Dealing with him will be easy, provided he doesn't have any nasty surprises waiting for us."

"Gotcha. Guess this means my job is to simply stay out of your way while you do your stuff."

"Glad to see you understand." Samantha grabbed Zaphkiel as she stood to her feet. She left the case on the ground. "Let's go. I would like to escape this barrier before the hour is up."

Their plan in place and a destination set, the two ran over to the roof of the building. There, Samantha leapt onto the next building several feet over. She landed, her knees bending, and then turned around and gestured for Tristin to follow her. He did so, grimacing as he leapt across the small chasm. When he landed on the roof of the other building, he winced, feeling a jolt of pain travel up his legs and into his brain.

How Samantha and Christian could do this so easily was beyond him.

Continuing to travel along the roofs, the pair eventually reached the end of the city block. They crouched down behind a small cement wall that hid them from the view of anyone who looked up. Samantha was peering over the edge, carefully looking down.

"Four marionettes," she murmured to herself, eyes narrowed. "This is going to be more difficult than I thought."

Wanting to know what she meant, Tristin also peeked onto the street below. All four marionettes were spread out several yards apart. That was too far for someone to take them out in a single blow. If Samantha wanted to kill them, it would have to be one on one, and that would give one if not all three of the others time to escape. If Samantha wanted to have any hope of killing them, then they would need to find some way to make them all clump together.

His mind turned the problem over, but he couldn't see a solution. Fortunately for him, Samantha did.

Putting her fingers to her lips, her cheeks puffed up and a shrill whistle was released. Oddly enough, the whistle did not sound like it came from her lips, but somewhere down below. Ventriloquism. She was throwing her voice.

"I didn't know you knew how to do that," Tristin said.

"There are probably a lot of things I can do that you don't know about."

"Touché."

The four marionettes swiveled about and moved toward where the whistle appeared to have come from, directly beneath the building they were on. Tristin almost shook his head. Marionettes might make great cannon fodder, but they were pretty stupid.

From the corner of his eye, Tristin saw Samantha ready herself. Her left hand had a tight grip of Zaphkiel's sheath, while her right rested against the lip of the rising wall. She released steady, even breaths, causing her shoulder to move up, hold, then go down as she exhaled. She did this exactly three times, and then jumped, throwing herself over the side of the building.

Tristin leapt up as well, but not to jump off the building. He leaned over and looked down, watching Samantha. The woman descended quickly. Her midnight hair whipped around behind her, right hand moving to rest on Zaphkiel's hilt. He imagined she must have looked like some kind of avenging angel from the marionettes' position.

She removed her sword from its sheath. Tristin could barely see it. To him, it looked like a mere flash of light.

She landed on the ground and threw herself into a forward roll. As she came to her feet, Tristin noticed that she was already sheathing her blade. There was a click, soft, like whispering wind, and it yet somehow resonated throughout the street. A second later, all four marionettes fell apart, their bodies sliced into exactly four segments.

Tristin whistled.

"Tristin," Samantha called up to him. "Hurry up and find a way down here. We need to move before we're spotted."

"Right."

Tristin searched for a ladder or something he could use to climb down. When he realized there were no ladders he swore, and then began to search for something else that could help him down.

He eventually found that something in a metal pipe that connected the roof to the ground. It was hardly the ideal way of descending from his position, but he had little choice in the matter. He swallowed his fear, ignored the queasiness inside of his stomach, and began climbing down via the pipe. At least, that was his plan. Sadly, bad plans had a way of going awry when you least expected them to.

In the red light of the barrier, it was hard to notice that the pipe was covered in grime and thus slippery. Rather than climbing down, Tristin ended up sliding down. Without being able to stop himself, he moved quickly to the bottom, a shriek of fear proceeding his descent. He then crashed into the ground. His legs and knees gave out quickly as he fell to the floor in a heap of twitching limbs.

Dizzy, hurt, and trying to figure out why everything looked so blurry, Tristin didn't see Samantha come up to him until she was grabbing his arm, dragging him to his feet.

"Hurry up, Tristin!" She snapped, angry for some reason. "Thanks to that racket you made, I'm sure that every marionette within ten miles of us now knows where we are."

Tristin would have retorted, regardless of how true her statement was, but he was still dizzy. Of course, Samantha wouldn't have given a chance to dispute her claim anyway. She was already dragging him out of the alley he landed in, her feet pounding against pavement and forcing him to run along behind her with a stumbling gate as he nearly tripped over his own two feet.

True to Samantha's prediction, it seemed his horrified yell had indeed caused a good portion of the marionettes scouring the barrier covered city to home in on their location. They were forced to fight a running battle, or rather, Samantha was forced to fight a running battle and protect him while they tried to make it out alive.

The woman was like a swift and powerful wind blowing through the trees. Her black hair flowed behind her as she wove across the streets. Her blade flashed out of its sheath, slicing apart marionettes like they weren't even there, like they were made of paper. It would then move back into its sheath seconds later, only to flash out again when she reached her next target.

Yet even with Samantha doing everything in her power to kill off their pursuers, it was not long before they found themselves overwhelmed. Left with no other options, the two of them were forced into another alley. This one, situated between several towering buildings, was cleaner than most, with only a small series of trash cans set against their left. It also had a locked gate that lead to some kind of courtyard connected to what appeared to be a casino.

Samantha sliced apart the chains that locked the gate, kicked it open, and ran inside.

"Come on!"

Tristin followed her advice. He ran in swiftly, leaving the gates wide open. It wouldn't do any good to close it now that the chains locking it were in pieces.

They ran over to the nearest door, Samantha kicking it open and hurrying inside. Tristin proceeded in after her, his heart hammering in his chest, fear and adrenaline mixing together in his veins.

The room they entered was a casino. Slot machines were lined up in neat little rows. Tables where people played poker, roulette, and many other games of chance dotted the areas that were clear of machines. There was also a bar near the center, large and made of wood, with around three dozen cushioned stools arrayed around it. Near the father corner to their left sat a small stage with several instruments set out around it.

Wisps of red energy wafted around the room. Their forms shifting in and out of focus. Humans. This place was inhabited by many humans, their physical bodies incapable of reaching the separate world he and Samantha found themselves in, but still existing alongside of them like two sides of the same coin.

As Tristin continued running, the first few marionettes burst into the room. Samantha spun, Zaphkiel hissing out of its sheath. Light flashed, a bright red that blinded the eyes. Then it faded with the sibilant sound of it being resheathed.

The marionettes fell apart. Samantha ran to catch up to Tristin, and together, the two rushed out of the main casino and into the main lobby.

Looking more like the entrance hall to a grand mansion of the sixteenth century, the lobby was open and spacious. Gleaming marble tiles created intricate designs along the floor, patterns made to appear organic and cost a fortunate to have made. Large columns made of granite climbed up to the roof. Their intricately carved designs crafted at the top let everyone know they were there for decoration and not actual support. A sweeping staircase led to the second floor, with enough red carpet to make anyone walking on it feel like a star. A counter lay on the opposite side, built into the wall, where people could get their card keys to access their rooms. The room was very beautiful and extravagant.

It was also filled with several dozen marionettes.

Samantha and Tristin were forced into an abrupt halt. The path they had used to enter became blocked off as more marionettes streamed in. They were surrounded by a dozen puppets, their almost human looking faces staring down at them with emotionless glass eyes, wooden joints clacking and snapping with each movement.

As Tristin found himself staring down the barrel of several dozen guns, he gulped, and found himself leaning into Samantha so he could whisper, "I really, really, *really* hope you have some kind of plan for getting us out of this."

The look of defeat on Samantha's face did not bode well for him.

"I wish I did, but against this many marionettes..." She trailed off and shook her head. "I can't protect you and escape at the same time."

Well that just sucked.

"So you're going to leave me here." Tristin felt strange. The fear left him. In fact, everything left him. An unusual emotional numbness spread from the center of his chest, engulfing him. He wondered if this was his way of accepting his death. A smirk appeared on his face. "Heh. Hehehehe. I guess I should have expected this to happen. It makes sense. I would only slow you down."

"Tristin, do me a favor and shut up." Tristin blinked. His mind came to and his heart jumped. Samantha was scowling at him. "I have no intention of leaving you. You may be a jerk, a lecherous, filthy, disgusting little—"

"You are so nice, you know that?"

"—monster, but you are still my subordinate. And in case you have forgotten, I never leave those under me to fend for themselves, especially when they aren't capable of it."

"You really know how to make a guy feel special," he said, his voice dripping with cynicism. "Truly. I practically feel my heart bursting with all of the lovely things you have to say about me." A small, soft smile, so unlike Tristin that he actually scared himself when he felt it appear, crossed his face. "Samantha, thank you."

Samantha blinked. "Did you just call me by my name?"

"...No."

"Yes, you did. I just heard you call me Samantha."

"You must be hearing things."

"Look at how touching this is," Mephisto said, the marionettes by the door parting to allow him admission. He walked over to them, his footsteps calm, composed, and deadly. "You two seem to be having such a nice, precious bonding moment that I almost hate having to break it up."

"How are you moving?" asked Samantha, her eyes wide. Tristin understood her shock. Mephisto shouldn't have been able to walk and maintain a barrier at the same time. It went against everything they knew about that particular ability.

"My dear. You should know that not everything you know about us demons is accurate." Mephisto's tone was patronizing. "The fact that I am standing here before you now is proof of this." He spread his arms wide, as if to emphasize this fact.

Chills traveled up Tristin's spine. Fear. Primal and all-encompassing. It consumed him. He wanted to run, but his legs had turned into led. He wanted to scream, but his throat was constricted, his air passage blocked. He wanted to cry, but the tears wouldn't come. He wanted to do so many things, but the fear, the terror, the overwhelming and insurmountable self-assured knowledge that he was going to die held him in place.

Was this what Christian had felt the first time he'd gone out into the field? Had this terror overwhelmed his friend when he found himself alone, fighting against a demon that could destroy cities with ease?

Probably not. His friend had never feared death. Sometimes, he almost thought Christian was walking toward it, seeking his end in order to atone for sins he had not committed.

"Now then." Mephisto's smile revealed his sharp fangs. On his pale face, and combined with those sickly yellow Sith eyes, he almost looked like a vampire instead of a demon. "I do believe it is time we put this little chase to an end. I'll admit, it has been fun. You gave me the turnaround and evaded my grasp longer than I care to admit, but the fun, I'm afraid, has officially come to an end."

There was a soft creaking, the leather that wrapped around Zaphkial's handle straining in Samantha's grip. The soles of her boots slid across the floor, squeaking as she lowered her stance. Right hand on the hilt of her sword, left hand holding the sheath, it was clear that the woman was not going down without a fight.

Tristin, despite his own terror reducing him to silent quaking, felt admiration for this woman. That she could stand in the face of her demise, look death in the eye without a hint of fear, was impressive.

He wished he could be like that, even if it was the pipe dream of an idiot. Unlike Christian, who seemed to rush toward death with near suicidal tendencies and had actually created a style based around that concept, and Samantha, who accepted her death but was determined to make her enemies work for it, Tristin was a coward. He didn't want to die.

"Kill them."

Time seemed to slow. Tristin could actually see the marionettes' fingers as they started to squeeze the triggers. For some reason, his life did not flash before his eyes, making him suspect that sort of thing only happened in movies and books. What did happen, however, was that he finally resigned himself to his fate. There was no escaping this end.

And then a miracle happened.

The sound of shattering glass rang loudly in everyone's ears. He, Samantha, and even Mephisto looked up in shock to see the large glass roof, with its beautiful tinted windows, shatter as a pair of black boots crashed through it.

A figure attached to those boots descended to the ground, a black coat whirling around their body. As glass rained down all around them, causing both Samantha and Tristin to raise their arms over their head, the figure hit the ground boots first. The marble cracked, the noise echoing along the chamber, accompanied by the sounds of a thousand glass shards hitting the ground.

Black coat ruffling, the figure stood up, revealing it to be a man, his face youthful and pale. His chin was sharp and pointed. Icy blue eyes stared out from underneath finely combed bangs. His hair, long and dark, the color of midnight, created a startling contrast to his pale face.

His clothing matched his features perfectly. His black coat, long and flowing down to his knees, looked like the suede jacket of a nobleman from the renaissance era. Black boots ran halfway up his calves. Branded and buckled, they shone as if just polished.

Most girls would probably consider him handsome, Tristin thought with a pang of jealousy, but there were three aspects about him that stood out the most.

His ears. They were pointed and elven. A most unusual feature on anyone, regardless of species.

And his eyes. Bright yellow irises shone with a brilliant luminescence. They radiated power. Dark power, which was emphasized by the lack of white in his eyes. The entire sclera was black.

The third aspect, and probably the most important, were the black angel wings that stretched out behind his back. Four sets of two black angel wings. They flapped and extended to at least three feet in length before retracting.

"A fallen angel," Samantha practically hissed.

Tristin shared her trepidation. Things were already bad enough with just Mephisto and his puppets. Adding a fallen angel to the equation, and one that was a leader of the Grigori, if the eight black wings were any indication, was just asking for shit to hit the fan.

"Kokabiel!" Mephisto snarled at the fallen angel before them.

Tristin felt like a bolt of lightning had struck him. This was Kokabiel? The Kokabiel? The strongest warrior to have graced the fallen angels? A being that was said to have been birthed by God for the sole purpose of slaying demons? That Kokabiel?

"We are so screwed," Tristin muttered. Samantha did not argue with him.

"Good evening, Mephisto." Kokabiel's smile was that of a predator about to pounce on his prey. "I hope you are up for another battle. I am rather interested in paying you back for that scar you gave me two hundred years ago." The fallen angel pressed a hand against his chest, perhaps where the aforementioned scar was.

Mephisto looked nervous. A trickle of sweat, shining in red in the light, ran down his face. "How did you get here? I would have felt it if you broke through my barrier."

"You are assuming that I broke through your barrier at all," Kokabiel said, still smiling. "I have been in Las Vegas for a while now. When your barrier went up, I was already inside of it."

A grimace crossed Mephisto's face. "I am only here for the humans."

"And I am here to stand in your path." A brilliant light flared in the palm of Kokabiel's hands. The light, which took the form of two spheres, elongated and sharpened into a pair of wicked-looking spears, which the fallen angel clasped in his hands. The smile grew wider. "Now dance with me."

Kokabiel was swift to move on the offensive. He rushed forward, his feet seemingly gliding over the ground. He thrust out his left hand, stabbing a marionette through the chest and causing it to burst into ashes less than an instant later. He then spun around, the spear in his right hand slashing the head off another puppet, which also became naught but ashes.

So, that was the fabled spear of light, a gift only the angels and fallen angels possessed. It was supposedly the last remnants of their God-given powers. What a terrifying ability.

As Kokabiel took the fight to Mephisto, who was forced to block the attack with his cane, Samantha darted forward. Keeping her body low to the ground as she ran about in a zigzag pattern, the woman reached the first group of marionettes in her path.

She released her blade from its sheath. As she thrust Zaphkiel forward, penetrating the face of a marionette, she brought the sheath down on the head of another. One demon went down like a puppet with its strings cut. The other was sent stumbling backwards. It righted itself, but soon found its head removed as Samantha's sword sang out with a horizontal slash that went straight through its neck.

She spun around, then, ignoring the marionette as it clattered to the floor. Her next target, a puppet to her immediate left, tried to raise its gun and shoot her, but she divested it of its hand and then bisected it from the left hip to the right shoulder. In that same exact instant, she was already thrusting her sheath into the eye of another, shattering the glass ball with ease and making it tumbled backwards into a heap. Samantha then rotated a full 360 degrees and bent low, Zaphkiel extending out, cutting off the legs of six marionettes that were about to shoot her.

Moving to her feet, the woman was quick to reach a new target, her body spinning and twirling like a ballerina dancing in a ballet. Her dance was much deadlier than a ballerina's, as the demons in her path soon found out. With grace, power, and speed, Samantha Gale carved a path through the marionettes that were still trying to bring their guns to bare, the woman never giving them a chance as she moved constantly, making getting a bead on her impossible.

Yet even the most powerful warriors eventually slow down, and Samantha was no different. The sound of a gunshot going off echoed like a thunderclap. Samantha yelped, then stumbled, the grip on her sheath slackening. As it fell to the floor, the woman grimaced, ignoring it and dashed to her next target.

Tristin found himself ducking down on all fours after the first gunshot went off. Unlike Samantha who began fighting with twice her usual viciousness, he began trying to crawl away from the battle. He moved on hands and knees, doing everything humanly possible not to shriek like a little girl as the sounds of battle and Kokabiel's insane laughter reverberated all around him. He didn't want to be caught and killed because he couldn't keep his mouth shut.

Sanctuary was found in the form of the courtesy counter. He quickly hid behind it, ducking down, his hands over his head and his eyes clenched shut. Blood was pounding in his ears, rushing to his head. Dizziness warred with terror that only increased as the sounds of battle continued.

He had no clue how long the battle lasted, how long the explosions thundered around him, or the length of time Kokabiel's laughter continued. He didn't know. Time was indeterminable to him. Yet the battle did cease. At some point, the sounds of fighting stopped, the gunshots disappeared, and even the laughter was no more, almost like it had never happened.

Tristin peeked out from above the table. The marionettes were gone, either lying broken on the ground or turned to ash by the power of Kokabiel's light spears. Mephisto was nowhere to be found. The barrier was still up, surprisingly, or maybe the fallen angel had put his own barrier in place. That, too, was a possibility.

Samantha was standing there, in the center of broken puppet bodies, blood dripping from a wound on her forehead, her left arm hanging uselessly by her side. The clothing she wore had several rips on them, the left strap was torn, the lower half below her breasts had been ripped off to reveal her toned stomach. Several nicks and cuts ran along both her arms and torso, the wounds leaving small trails of blood that roved across her porcelain skin.

Despite this, she stood tall, facing down Kokabiel, who stood in front of her, prepared to fight.

"Be at peace, Executioner," Kokabiel said, raising a single hand. "I am not here to fight."

Samantha did not look convinced. "Then just what are you here for?"

"You are asking the wrong person." Kokabiel's smile was somewhat self-depreciating. "I know not why I am here. It was merely on Azazel's orders. 'Go to Las Vegas. There, you will eventually run into two humans, members of the now defunct Executioners of the Catholic Church. You are to aid them in any way you can.' was what he asked of me."

"Azazel asked you to protect us?" Samantha appeared shocked. Truly shocked. Tristin didn't blame her.

"Indeed." Kokabiel nodded. "Though why he asked me to do such a thing, I've not a clue." He shrugged. "I never know what goes through that man's mind anymore. And it's not like I truly care. My only desire is to find and fight powerful opponents. So long as I can do that, nothing else matters."

Huh. So Kokabiel was a battle maniac? Somehow, Tristin should have figured that. Wasn't he an angel originally bred for warfare and strife? That was probably why he had fallen in the first place.

"Azazel did want me to pass along a message for you," Kokabiel added, causing Samantha, along with Tristin, to perk up. "He wanted me to tell you that the person you seek is located underneath Yellowstone Lake."

"Christian," Samantha muttered, her voice soft but still loud enough for Tristin to hear. What the hell was his friend doing all the way over in Yellowstone National Park? And why exactly was he under a lake?

"He also mentioned that after you find the person you seek, he wishes to meet with you two in order to discuss your coming war against the Catholic Church."

"We're not waging war against the Catholic Church." Samantha scowled.

"Then you intend to let them destroy you?" asked Kokabiel, his voice placid, as if discussing the weather.

"Of course not," Samantha practically spat. "But our enemy is not the Catholic Church. It's—"

"I am not here to argue semantics with you, Executioner." Kokabiel appeared the bastion of calm to Samantha's stormy rage. Not a single feather on his wings were ruffled. "I am merely here to aid you in your time of need, and to pass along the message that my leader has requested of me."

"Fine then," Samantha spat. Her entire body shivered from head to toe. Tristin suspected that the only reason she had not launched herself at the fallen angel was because she knew her death would be a foregone conclusion if she did. "You can tell your leader that I have no intention of ever meeting with him."

"I will be sure to tell him that, then." Kokabiel shrugged, looking like he couldn't care less. He probably didn't. The fallen angel appeared to care for nothing other than the chance to fight strong opponents. "Though you would be wise to heed his request, and you would be unwise not to meet with him. Azazel is many things, eccentric and atypical being but a few aspects to him. Above all else, he is knowledgeable about the world and the new situation we find ourselves in. It would be remiss of you not to at least hear what he has to say."

Samantha said nothing, but the way she clenched her hands into fists, which were shaking, told Tristin all he needed to know about her emotional state.

"Regardless, I have now finished my task, so I shall take my leave." With a powerful flap of all eight wings, Kokabiel took to the sky. As he reached the shattered glass roof, he paused, then looked down at Samantha while Tristin walked over to her. "Should you choose to meet with Azazel, you will find him at the Old Faithful Snow Lodge and Cabins in Wyoming two weeks from now. He will remain there for a month. I recommend you go meet with him. You will be sure to find it... enlightening."

Kokabiel put on a sudden burst of speed. There was the sound of shattering glass. The red haze that had been hovering over the world was lifted. The bodies and pile of ashes disappeared, but the damage remained as the barrier that separated Tristin and Samantha from the real world was released.

And that's when Tristin realized just what kind of chaos their battle had unleashed. Even if people couldn't see the battle that had taken place, the damage done to the walls, floor, ceiling, and columns had caused everyone to panic. People were running every which way. They shouted and cried, panicking. It was a threnody of voices striving to be heard over the cacophony of pandemonium.

"I think it would be best if we get out of here before anyone notices us," Tristin whispered.

Samantha couldn't help but agree. "That is the first good idea I've heard from you in a long time."

The two made their way out of the casino filled with overwrought, panicking patrons. They stepped onto the street, doing their best to remain nonchalant, which was much harder than it looked because there were a lot of people doing exactly what they were doing: getting the hell out of dodge. At least the massive amount of people helped conceal their presence.

A thirty-minute walk in silence brought them to the car they had used to get to Las Vegas, the F-150. Both entered. Samantha sat in the driver's seat, started the engines, and took off, peeling out of the parking garage and onto the street.

In the silence, with only the sounds of the engine thrumming beneath them, Tristin asked a question. "Do you think we should meet with Azazel?"

"Of course not." Samantha's scowl came back with a vengeance. "There's no way we're ever going to meet up with a fallen angel. They can't be trusted."

Tristin wanted to point out that it would be foolish not to go, and that Kokabiel could have killed them if he wanted to but hadn't, proving that there may be some benefit to meeting with the Grigori leader. He didn't because he had no desire to get hit on the head.

"Are we at least going after Christian?"

Samantha hesitated, then said, "we'll see."

Despite her answer, Tristin found himself feeling hopeful. It might not have been a yes, but it certainly wasn't a no. He really did want to see his friend again.

What a reunion that would be.

Chapter 12

Christian passed through a doorway. The room he found himself in was fairly large, not quite as big as the training hall where he had taken to practicing with his swords, but still a decently spacious area. Much of the room looked the same as all the others. The floor, walls, and ceiling were all made of stone, having been literally carved into the rock of the cavern. Several lockers were situated to his immediate left, and several drawers built underneath a couple dozen racks containing guns of just about every shape and size were on his right. The drawers most likely held ammunition.

There were many women already inside; all of them were adorned in skin tight black clothing that conformed to their figures, leaving little to the imagination. It looked almost like they were wearing a pair of black spandex shorts, or maybe some kind of leather since it looked awfully shiny and creaked as they moved. Their shorts didn't go very low, stopping several inches below their butts. They were so short they looked almost like bloomers. Much like their shorts, their shirts were also made of black leather. They were sleeveless but connected to a pair of black gloves that went all the way up to their forearms. The outfits were finished off with a pair of black boots that extended well past their thighs.

Each outfit also had a pair of holsters strapped to their thighs, two handguns nestled snuggly inside. Some of the women were also carrying other weapons: submachine guns, AK-47s, one of them even had a SPAS-12 combat shotgun strapped to her back. While everyone had a long-range weapon, several also possessed close-range weapons such as swords, knives, daggers, and all manner of bladed paraphernalia.

One thing Christian noticed about these women was that he did not recognize any of them from the battle against the goblins. The difference in dress code may have had something to do with it. Did that mean these females formed a different squad? Perhaps a special forces unit of some kind? They looked older, or at least more experienced, than the ones that had been led by Clarissa.

As Christian entered the room, every single female turned to look at him. While he would never admit to being afraid when under the gaze of what appeared to be two dozen females, he would at least confess to feeling unnerved by their unblinking gaze. Unlike the other women he'd run into during his stay in this enclave, who looked at him with animosity, curiosity, or a combination of both, these ones seemed almost emotionless. Yes. It was definitely disturbing.

"You must be Christian."

One of the women walked up to him. She was taller than most, and her long, silvery blond hair flowed behind her back, soft and shimmering, like a curtain of satin. That same hair framed a face that was lovingly carved out of alabaster, with high cheek bones and a long, straight nose. There was a scar going across her right eye, but it didn't detract from her appearance in the least. It may have had something to do with her figure. The woman was all sensual curves and extraordinary elegance combined with incredible muscle tone and a lean, flat stomach. She reminded Christian of those Amazonian women he'd read about in stories.

She was packing heat like an amazon warrior princess, too. Strapped to her thighs were two automatic pistols. Lying horizontally across her back was an M4 machine gun. She also had a pair of long daggers with curved blades strapped across her upper back in a cross formation to form an "x" similar to how Christian wore Rafael and Michael.

Like the others, she was wearing the leather shorts, a sleeveless shirt, gloves, and boots that made up the other women's ensemble.

Unlike them, she had an added article to her costume: a long, flowing, dark gray shoulder cape that looked almost like a shroud. The bottom edges were frayed, and the fabric seemed to waver with a life of its own as she stood there, almost as if it had some form of sentience.

After giving her a once over and determining that, out of all the succubi he'd met so far, this one was by far the most dangerous, he addressed her. "Yes. I'm Christian. You must be Heather Locklear. Clarissa told me that I was to report to you and help repel the goblins attacking the southern quadrant of the cavern."

"That's right." Heather smiled, though it was more of a dangerous smirk than an actual smile. Christian shifted from one foot to the other. He did not appreciate the look she gave me. "I love a man who gets right to the point. It makes things so much simpler." She paused, perhaps to give him time to absorb her words before plunging on. "To make a long story short, the goblins have breached our southern perimeter near the entrance to the cavern mouth. We believe they used boats or some other form of transportation to move across the lake to reach the entrance, as that's the only area we were unable to put up sensors. Our job is to eradicate every one of them."

"I understand," Christian said, standing just a little bit straighter. "What would you have me do?"

"You'll be up front and center with me," Heather told him. "I was told by Clarissa that your prowess with those guns and blades of yours are most impressive. You're going to give me the chance to see those skills."

Christian felt a calm settle over him. He found himself falling back into his old habits. The familiarity of being ordered by a powerful woman reminded him of when Samantha had been his commanding officer. This woman had the same presence, the same commanding demeanor as Samantha, so it was easy to fall back into his old persona from before he betrayed the Executioners for Lilith.

"Understood."

At Heather's beckoning, all the women inside of the locker room departed. Christian found himself walking alongside Heather, who gave him a little information regarding the group of women he found himself surrounded by, as they made their way to their destination.

"We're what you would call the Special Forces of this enclave. While all the other girls know how to fight to some extent, the women you see here have been trained extensively for combat. We're literally the best of the best, and we only take on the toughest assignments."

"Is that why your group wasn't there during the last goblin attack?"

"You mean is that why you didn't see us during the attack, right? We were actually there, but we used several hidden passages to sneak around them and attack from behind. Why do you think there were so few goblins coming at you when their numbers were supposed to be in the hundreds?"

Christian's surprise must have been expressed on his face because Heather grinned at him. The grin would have been pleasant, sexy even, but when combined with that scar, it caused a thrill to run down his spine. There was something dangerous about her smile.

Heather was heedless of this, or pretending to be, as she continued speaking. "We're sort of like the black ops of this enclave. We attack in secret. At least when possible. The goblins don't know we exist, and we like to keep it that way in order to add an element of surprise to our attacks. Most of our strikes are surgical and done long before our enemy even realizes we're there."

"Then it looks like this battle is going to blow your cover."

"Not if we play our cards right. There are plenty of ways to attack someone without letting them realize you exist. We just need to come up with the right plan and get our timing right, so they can't see who's attacking them. So long as they suspect they're being attacked by standard forces, we'll be in the clear." Christian nodded his head. that made sense. "We can't use bombs, lest we end up causing the ceiling to collapse on us, but that doesn't mean we're helpless either."

They reached the door leading to the southern passage. Smooth flooring became rough, uneven, and rocky. The walls and ceiling, once looking almost like a regular room, turned craggy and cylindrical, with stalagmites and stalactites spaced around the jutting from the ground or hanging above their heads. Their footsteps echoed along the passage, sounding out several decibels louder than they should have.

"Then you plan on using hit and run tactics?" asked Christian, his voice a whisper so as to ensure it didn't echo far. "Will those be effective in a cavern?"

"Not quite." Heather looked at him, a strange, deadly gleam in her eye that spoke of nothing good for her enemies. Christian would have probably felt some form of pity for the goblins, but considering they were his enemies and had nearly killed him last time, he couldn't find it in himself to care. "Don't think on it too much. You'll see exactly what I mean once the battle gets going. Here, take this."

As the woman, Heather, handed him what appeared to be a set of ear plugs, Christian decided not to ask any more questions. There wasn't much point if they were just going to be deflected by cryptic answers anyway. Instead, he gave Heather a nod and followed her.

Observing his surroundings as they moved, Christian made note of several aspects to this area that he thought would help him in the coming battle.

The tunnel located within the southern quadrant was not much different from the one where the previous battle had taken place. The ground was a little flatter. There were a few less stalagmites. Unlike the other tunnel passage, this one offered a good deal of light. It was a bit dim, but certainly nothing compared to the northern passage. Christian theorized that the reason for the extra illumination was due to this passage being closer to the exit/entrance.

As the group continued to move through the cave, feet padding against the rock floor, the sound of pounding feet and the gurgled, ghoulish voices of goblins could be heard up ahead.

Heather called her party to a stop by raising her hand in the air and making a fist. Everyone halted in their tracks. Christian gently eased the tension in his muscles as he stopped alongside Heather. His black, long-sleeved shirt rustled with subdued gentleness against his skin as he adjusted the angle of his swords. The straps that held his holsters to his thighs groaned and creaked, leather against cotton, as he leaned from one leg to the other.

"Are you ready?" Heather asked, looking at him.

Christian closed his eyes and took in a deep breath. He opened them again, feeling his gaze sharpen a bit as he allowed his mind to open. Everything that his mind had once shut out as inconsequential background noise became glaringly obvious to him, pounding in his ears with reckless abandon. He could hear the breathing of those around him, light and airy, almost silent. The dull drip of water hit his senses, echoing inside of his head. Even the soft draft that blew through the cavern was heard. Its haunting melody drifted through his ears like a gentle lullaby. His ears pricked at the sound of creaking leather and the scratching of metal guns as they scraped against the holsters keeping them in place. Up ahead, he picked out the reverberating sound of hundreds of feet pounding toward them, causing the ground beneath them to vibrate. Those were the goblins, he presumed.

"I'm ready," he murmured in a soft voice.

"Good. Because here they come."

The woman was right. Up ahead, Christian could see the horde of goblins coming their way. Like the last time he'd seen them, there were many of them, and they were all dressed differently. He couldn't spot an ounce of uniformity among them.

He tried to pick out which among the group would be the leaders, but there were far too many goblins this time for him to be able to spot someone who looked like they might be in charge. They were jam packed together in the cavern space, marching shoulder to shoulder, nearly squashing each other, like sardines in a can.

Heather made a gesture, waving her hand above her head in a circular motion, as if she were a cowgirl swinging a lasso. Christian had no clue what the gesticulation was for, but it must have been some kind of premeditated signal. The women around him suddenly reached into a small case attached to their backs.

They all pulled out a long, cylindrical object made of reflective metal that had several holes running along its body. There was a small pin connected to them, which he knew was supposed to be pulled out in order to release the chemical compounds inside to create the effect. The effect, of course, being the production of a blinding flash of light that was emitted from the holes and a loud blast of concussive noise.

So they were going to use flashbangs to blind and confuse the goblins? A sound plan, and at least now he knew why Heather gave him a set of ear plugs.

He put the earplugs in his ears, making sure they were secure and blocked out all sounds. All the women pulled the pin on their flashbangs. They waited one, two, three seconds, and then tossed them into the semi-darkened cavern just several feet shy of the first line of the goblin horde.

Christian closed his eyes. Several seconds later, the deafening boom of nearly a dozen flashbangs going off sounded out. Christian's ears popped as the plugs stuck inside of them expanded to keep the noise out. Even then, he could still hear the blast, muffled thought it was, banging against his eardrums.

Flashbangs, also known as a stun grenade, were a non-lethal explosive device used to temporarily disorient an enemy's senses. Christian had used them to great effect in the past. Werewolves hated them due to their above average sense of sight and hearing.

They appeared to work just as well against the goblins. After waiting for exactly one second, Christian opened his eyes to see that the first six rows of goblins had been completely disoriented. The ones in front were tripping over their own two feet, falling to the ground. Meanwhile, the ones in back were falling over the ones in front.

Heather made some more hand motions, and all of the women around him pulled out their guns. Christian followed suit, unholstering Gabriel and Phaneul, then aiming at the mass of green skin in front of him. Another moment later, all of the women unleashed a barrage of gunfire, a hailstorm that filled the airspace of the cavern with bullets.

The goblins didn't stand a chance.

Dispassionate eyes watched as goblins became perforated with dozens of bullet holes. Blood spurt from the open wounds with constant streams reminiscent of a faucet as they were mowed down. The ground was soon covered in bodies and ichor, which turned into a large pool of expanding crimson.

As the goblins in back proceeded to scramble over their fallen brethren, the succubi holstered their weapons and pulled out more stun grenades. They repeated the process, pulling the pins and lobbing the grenades at their foes, stunning them again.

Christian did not have any flashbangs on him, so he stuck with his guns. Each time he ran out of ammo, he would simply click open the release, let the cartridge fall to the ground, and smoothly slide more ammunition back into his guns, all within a few seconds of each other. After that, he would unleash another barrage of bullets into the horde of scraggly-haired, sharp-toothed creatures. This continued several more times, with more and more goblin corpse piling up on top of each other, before Heather made a gesture that even Christian knew. The sign for them to retreat.

They fell back, moving into the darker regions of the tunnel. It would be a while before the goblins managed to reach this far. Thanks to the tactics that the group of succubi had utilized, there was a large mountain of bodies that needed to be climbed over before the goblins could even think about moving further. Christian had to admit that the idea was rather ingenious, forcing their enemies to climb over the corpses of their dead in order to continue onward. He didn't know if it would leave any psychological trauma on a goblin, but it would have given any human some lasting mental scars. It would also buy them time.

Christian kept a close eye on Heather as he moved, following directly behind her, which was good because he would have missed when the group deviated from the main tunnel, moving into a side passage that was hidden behind a tarp designed and layered to look like the rock walls of the cavern. A clever method of concealment, to be sure.

It did present a bit of a problem, though. Because they were no longer in the main passage, and this tunnel was sealed off by a thick tarp, no light could penetrate the area. Christian found himself surrounded by darkness, unable to see, but more than capable of feeling his body being pressed against by several distinctly feminine bodies. While none of them were Lilith, they were still female, and he was still male. This created an inherent problem, one that he was just barely able to hide by crossing his legs.

Thank God Lilith wasn't present. Christian had no idea how she would react if she could see him now. Not very well, he'd wager.

"Here," Heather's voice whispered in his ear as something was pressed into his left hand. It was too dark to see what it was, but from the general shape, he determined that it was a pair of goggles or something similar.

It was indeed a pair of goggles that he'd been given. Night vision goggles, to be precise. When Christian placed them around his head, adjusting the straps and position of the eye lenses so they fit him, he turned the device on with the flip of a switch. His vision was given back to him, but instead of full range of color offered by a pair of normal eyes, everything was filmed over with a haze of different shades of green.

"Okay, everyone," Christian heard Heather's voice to his immediate left. She must be the one pressing her breasts into his left arm because he could also feel her hot breath on his ear as she spoke. "You all know the plan. Once the goblins move past us, we're going to ambush their flank, hit them hard, and then fade back into the darkness."

So they were now using standard hit and run tactics, then? That was... a pretty good idea, actually. It wasn't something that most people would think up when battling in a cave, but so long as you knew where you were going, then it could prove to be a very effective strategy. This was especially true if your enemy didn't know the area as well as you did.

Christian had never used hit and run tactics before. Most of his strategies relied on hitting the enemy first, running through them fast and hard with a surprise attack, and then taking out the remaining enemies by using his *Fake Opening Style*. It had proven to be a successful stratagem for him thus far. Too bad it only worked when he was fighting alone. It wouldn't work when facing such a large number of enemies.

The sound of tromping feet resounded just a few feet in front of him, not even moderately muffled by the tarp. It was loud and teeth-rattling, which may have also had a little something to do with knowing how close the enemy was. Christian tried to count how many goblins passed, but that proved to be an exercise in futility. He gave up almost as quickly as he started. He instead focused his mind on the coming fight. From the looks of everyone there, they planned on keeping the battle at long-range, likely so they would not find themselves stuck in a close-range battle that they were unable to break away from. Secrecy, as Heather had told him, was their best friend.

He could live with that.

A scream going up from the other side of the tarp had Christian's eyes widening. Even though it was soft, Caspian could hear it, though no one else seemed to notice for some reason. It was feminine and familiar, belonging to a voice that he knew as well as his own.

His breath caught in his throat. Terror caused his heart to hammer against his chest, threatening to break out of his ribcage. What the hell was she doing here?

"Christian wait!"

Christian did not wait, nor did he listen to Heather's continued shouting as he shoved his way out of the mishmash of bodies. He burst out from behind the tarp and charged down the passage where the sound of feet hitting sediment rang out along with the loud, terrified screams.

Behind him, the sound of the tarp being shoved aside alerted him to Heather and the others following him. From the loud and colorful language, Heather was not pleased.

He didn't care.

His guns, already in his hands, unleashed their entire payload into the backs of the goblins the moment he could see them, forewarning his enemies that he was upon them. They turned just as he unloaded and reloaded his guns. He unleashed another barrage of hot iron into their ranks, only stopping when his guns clicked empty.

Out of ammo and now too close to reload in a timely enough manner to be effective, Christian elected to holster his guns and unsheathe his swords. He did so by yanking the weapons out with startling violence and turning the entire movement into a slashing attack that sliced straight through the shoulders of two goblins. The bodies, cleaved from their shoulders down to their hips, fell back in a spray of gore that coated Christian's clothes and made the floor appear as if a mad painter had taken buckets of red paint and blew them up with a shotgun.

Heedless of the thick, viscous carmine liquid coating of clothes, of the horrid scent reminiscent of fifteen-year-old shoes filled with raw meat, Christian threw himself into the horde, slashing and slicing and fighting his way through them. He moved with a sense of reckless desperation. His blades flashed out, the movements graceless and brutal. There was no sense of style to his attacks. His favored style, the one that made him so deadly on the field of battle, was nowhere to be found.

He didn't care. It didn't matter. Nothing mattered to him except reaching the voice that was even now screaming in his ear, the voice that belonged to the person he cherished more than anything else in this world, the voice that was now shrieking in a combination of undiluted fear and pain.

Christian reached the voice, ignoring the stinging pain from several lacerations that ran along his arms and torso, and of the blood flowing from his wounds that mixed with the goblin blood soaking his clothes.

Lilith was lying on the ground, holding her left leg, which had copious amounts of blood pouring from it. She was surrounded by several goblins, one of whom held a knife covered in thick, dark liquid. Lilith's blood.

"They're attacking her..."

Christian saw red, and not just in a figurative sense. Red, red, red, everything was red.

Ripping off the goggles, his vision became sharper, more precise. The green film of the night vision goggles was replaced by a murderous crimson. Everything he perceived was red, shades of blood that dabbled with lighter shades almost but not quite reaching the color orange.

"They're hurting the person you love. You're not going to let that stand, are you?"

Moving with more speed than he ever had before, Christian bulldozed right into the midst of goblins attacking Lilith with a furious roar. Before they even had time to be startled, Christian's first target, the goblin with the knife, found his knife hand removed when Rafael sliced through the flesh of his forearm with so much ease that the skin, bone, and muscle might as well have been made of cardboard. The hand flew off, the knife going a separate direction. The stump spurted, releasing the goblin's lifeblood onto the ground.

"Of course, you're not. These monsters hurt her. You want to kill them. It's only fair. They're trying to kill your woman. They must repent with their lives."

As that goblin squealed, a sound not unlike a dying pig, Christian spun around. He moved his body in an arc, extending Rafael and Michael. Michael's dark blade severed a goblin's head. At the same time, he used Rafael parried a thrust aimed at his side, moved the attacking weapon—a dull and rusty sword—aside, and then he thrust it forward, piercing that goblin's chest, right in between the third and fourth scapula.

"Do not worry. I will grant you the power you need."

A yank of the blade freed Rafael from its place in between the rib cage, dark crimson spraying free. Before the goblin corpse could fall to the ground, Christian pounded the dead creature's chest with a swift and powerful heel kick. There was a concussive noise, like a miniature shock wave, and then the dead body was sent flying into the goblin that was behind Lilith and set to bash her head in with a club. That goblin went down in a heap of limbs and, before it could stand up, Christian whipped out Phaneul, loaded it, and unloaded a bullet right between its eyes.

"Don't let up. Make them suffer."

By that point in time, the succubi that Christian had been with reached the horde and crashed into them with the fury of a raging tempest, a maelstrom of incredible power. The succubi's formation, shaped like an arrow pierced deep into the mass of enemies, and then spread out to push the goblins back. They sliced through their adversaries with swords and daggers and dirks of all kinds. Blood sprayed out of large wounds, enemies found themselves being cut apart, dozens of lacerations appearing all over them.

"That's right. Keep at it. Let them know your fury. Let them feel your rage. Do not allow their attack on your woman to go unpunished."

Christian ignored the arrival of the succubi, for the most part, only taking abstract note of their presence on the battlefield. All his attention was focused entirely on the goblins before him, the foolish, heathenistic beasts who dared to attack his Lilith. He was going to kill them. He was going to slaughter them. He was going to massacre them in such a way that their blood and organs painted the walls, the floor, and the ceiling.

"Kill..."

"Kill them..."

"Slaughter every last one of them!"

And he was going to enjoy it.

Letting out another roar, one that contained all his anger and rage at these monsters, Christian began hacking away. Each brutal slash was unsophisticated and unrefined, containing none of the technique, elegance, and finesse of his normal maneuvers. Not that grace mattered here. When each swing struck something, supple poise and nimbleness meant little. A limb would fall either way.

Christian watched, smiling as Rafael carved a deep, bloody furrow into the chest of a goblin. It screamed its agony to the world before the harsh, guttural noise was abruptly cut off when Michael removed the goblin's head.

He spun, then, lashing out at another enemy, hacking off the creature's arm before sinking the other sword tip first into its torso. With a grunt of effort, his muscles strained, and then he tore the sword through muscle and bone with savage simplicity. The goblins upper torso was cleaved from its lower torso, the two halves flying in opposite directions.

A deep, aching pain spread out from his left arm as it was hit by something hard. He could feel the humerus bone break. He could also feel as the two broken halves were snapped back together less than a second later. An unpleasant feeling that caused lances of agony to jolt up his arm, but one that his anger made easy to ignore.

He turned toward the one that had attacked him, a goblin with a club, wearing nothing but a loin cloth. It had a stupid look on its face, but then, most goblins did so that wasn't surprising. He swung Michael upwards in a diagonal slash from its position near his hip. The blade etched a long, deep trench into the goblin's torso. Dark plasma spouted out of the wound in an almost graceful parabolic arc before painting the ground in splatters of vermillion.

Sharp pain stabbed at his back. Something wet began flowing, blood. His blood. Bellowing in outrage, Christian twirled around and smashed the pommel of Rafael into the nearest goblin's face. His blood sang with joy as he felt bones crunch under the savage assault. He could see the nose shattering, the face caving in as the bones in their skull were crushed. He was sure that attack had also destroyed the beast's brain, as the thing dropped backwards, twitching once before going still.

His teeth bared, Christian's challenging call echoed throughout the tunnel. The nearest goblin turned its head. That same head was split down the center when Christian swung Michael downwards. The ground became coated in carnelian fluids again as the swing continued, cutting through the rest of the monster's body.

Christian, his breathing heavy and his shoulders and chest heaving, glared around for more enemies to butcher. When he realized there were none left, he gritted his teeth. Anger was still coursing through his system, violent and uncontrolled. He wanted more blood. Needed more. Only there wasn't any more enemies that needed to die. Everything he could kill was dead.

But no. That wasn't quite true, was it? He could kill those women, too. They were up for grabs. It would be easy. So easy. All he needed to do was charge them. He could cut them and slice them and rip them apart to his heart's content. He could—

"Ch-Christian...?"

His thoughts were arrested. They came to a screeching halt as a voice echoed in his ears. The voice was scared, maybe even terrified. There was a quiver, a trembling in the tone that denoted fear. But still, even afraid as it was, he knew that voice. Somewhere deep within his mind, past the maelstrom of hatred that had risen to the surface, he recognized it.

The darkness from his mind receded. The desire to slaughter, maim, and relish in the feeling of his enemies' blood staining his hands withdrew, slowly, until it disappeared altogether. And yet, while the hatred and yearning for blood and gore was gone, the anger was not.

He turned around and saw Lilith, still lying on the ground, still holding her bleeding leg. She was staring at him, her eyes wide and round, almost too round to be even remotely human. Her mouth was agape, ruby red lips spread open to create an extensive space of shock and horror. Christian could probably fit his fist in her mouth it was so wide.

The red came back.

Lilith squeaked as Christian stomped up to her. He ignored the sounds of shouting behind him, of Heather calling his name. Without even stopping his march, he grabbed Lilith by the arm, ignoring her yelp as he hauled her to her feet and liberally dragged her through the cave. His ears were deaf to her whimpers, his body ignored her stumbles as he pulled her along behind him.

They reached the entrance to the enclave, a small door made of wood. Christian kicked the door open, a loud bang resounding as it smashed against the wall. He proceeded through. Then he slammed the door shut with his foot.

Lilith's back was then pressed against the wall, his hands on either side of her body, his eyes locking her body in place, save for its leaf-like shaking.

"What the hell were you thinking?" he hissed. Lilith's chest hitched, her eyes grew even wider. She didn't answer, causing Christian's anger to skyrocket. "What the hell was that? Why did you follow me?" Lilith still didn't answer, though her trembling increased in intensity. "Answer me, dammit!"

"Ch-Christian... I—"

"Don't realize how dangerous that was? How stupid? You could have been killed! Did you even stop to think about that? If I hadn't heard you and arrived when I did, you would have been dead, just another statistic. Those goblins would have murdered you."

"I just wanted to help." Lilith looked down. Several droplets of clear, crystalline liquid ran down her fair cheeks, dripping off her chin and onto the floor.

For some reason, her words made Christian even more enraged. "Oh, you wanted to help? I see? So you thought you would render some aid? That you could actually do something to help us fight against those goblins? What a great idea. You really helped us out there. Truly, you were such spectacular help. I don't know what we'd have done without you."

Maybe it was his tone of voice, or maybe something in Lilith just snapped at his thickly layered sarcasm, but when she looked up at him, her eyes, despite the tears flowing down them, were narrowed into a glare.

"Don't you dare talk to me like that, Christian. It might not have been the greatest idea, but—"

"It wasn't a good idea at all! It was the furthest thing from a good idea!!" Christian all but roared as he smashed his hands into the rock wall, cracking it and causing Lilith to flinch. "It was the dumbest, most asinine idea I have ever seen. You're not stupid, Lilith. I know this. How you could make such an unintelligent and brainless decision is beyond me."

The words, once again, caused whatever fear Lilith had at Christian's actions to be driven back. "Then maybe you should try standing in my shoes for a change," Lilith snarled at him. Christian felt surprised as the blond woman glowered, her eyes narrowed into a look that was fierce and determined, her teeth gnashed together in anger. "I sit around all day while you go out and fight, constantly putting yourself in danger. Do you know how worried I get? I'm always wondering if you're going to make it back to me. Do you know how that feels? How much it hurts to sit there, twiddling my thumbs, waiting and worrying for you to return to me? It's agonizing. Every time you go out, my chest aches! It hurts! Don't you dare tell me that my decision was wrong when you haven't lived a day in my shoes!"

In other circumstances, Lilith's words would have touched Christian's heart, would have made his feelings for her soar. Not today. All they did in that moment was increase the rage he was feeling.

"And you think that makes what you did any more intelligent? Lilith, you can't fire a gun, you don't know how to use a sword or even a knife, and you don't know the first thing about combat. You have no talent when it comes to fighting. You're absolutely useless in a battle. All you do is get in the way."

Christian knew the moment he said those words that they were the wrong thing to say. The second they left his lips, his eyes widened. He opened his mouth, but a part of him already knew that it was too late.

"Lilith, I..."

Lilith's eyes were already filled with frustrated and angry tears welled up. Her lips quivered, while small, sniffling sounds started escaping her. "So that's what you really think of me?" Lilith's voice, tainted with sorrow and something else, something that Christian could not identify but caused his heart to feel an acute sting all the same, filled her voice. "You think I'm useless? That all I do is get in the way? That I can't do anything right?" Her shoulders, already shaking, began to tremble with greater magnitude. "I guess you're right. Every time we've been in trouble, I haven't been able to do anything. You're always the one protecting me, always putting yourself on the line for my sake. All I do is stand there and watch as you get yourself hurt for me."

"Lilith, that's not..."

"I mean, it's not like I did anything to help when you fought Damien."

Christian felt like a sledgehammer had slammed into his gut, all the air leaving his lungs.

"And I was practically helpless against Asmodeus."

His knees began trembling, shaking as they weakened from her sharp, biting words, stained with the anguish of someone who's love had just hurt her.

"I suppose all I'm good for is sex, huh?"

Lilith looked up at him, crying, small trails of liquid streaming from her eyes, creating a glistening trail across her cheeks. Her tears were like a blow to the face. They hurt far worse than any physical pain ever could.

Christian tried to speak. He wanted to say something, to apologize. But he couldn't. Something was lodged inside his throat. Maybe it was the guilt, or maybe it was just the last remnants of a fool's stubborn pride. Whatever it was, it kept him from speaking.

"This isn't going to work, is it?" She smiled at him, and every negative emotion, all the anger, his wrathful displeasure brought about by a deep-seated fear for Lilith's safety, evaporated faster than a winters breeze in the summer heat, leaving him feeling empty, save for a single emotion: regret. "You and I, we're not working out. I thought we would, hoped that we would, but the two of us, even if we're genetically compatible, we're just too different. We come from different backgrounds, different walks of life. We can't even begin to understand each other."

Christian's arms were like led. No longer able to bear their weight, he let them drop to hang limply at his side.

"I'm sorry," she whispered. The pain in her voice, an almost physical anguish that made Christian feel like his entire body had been split wide open, was too much for him to bear. "We should have never been involved with each other. All of this was a mistake."

Christian's eyes opened wide. He opened his mouth to say something, to tell her that they were not a mistake, that even now, they could make things work out, but the words would not come. They wouldn't emerge because he was a coward. Because facing death was nothing compared to owning up to your own mistakes.

Instead of speaking, he tried to raise his hand, hoping to stop Lilith, but his arms would not move. He stood there and watched, silently, as the woman he had fallen in love with, betrayed his colleagues for, dedicated his life too, and cherished more than anything else in the world ran out on him.

For a second, he stared at the door as it slammed shut. His mind shut down, incapable of remaining cognizant for even a second longer. He couldn't endure the thought of what he had done, couldn't withstand the guilt that threatened to consume him, nor could he begin to stomach the self-loathing that overwhelmed him like a deluge of sin.

Rage overtook him after that. Anger, not at Lilith, but at himself. Choleric guilt overpowered his mind. Self-loathing overwhelmed his every sense. With an enraged scream, Christian slammed his fist against the wall, leaving a deep imprint in the stone.

Not enough. The pain wasn't enough. He slammed his fist against the stone wall again. And again. And again. The wall dented and cracked, and his fist bled and broke, and still he continued to crash his fist against natural stone. He ignored the carnelian liquid splattering against the wall. He couldn't feel the pain as the knuckles as his fist broke, healed, then broke again. He could feel nothing. Nothing but the agony that was wrenching his heart, the suffering that came from the knowledge that it was his words that had driven Lilith away from him. He had let his anger get the better of him, let the worry that had been so hard to deal turn into the fury that had lashed out at the woman he loved, and now it was coming to bite him in the worst way possible.

Everything but his guilt and regret soon left him. Tired, spent, and feeling like the biggest jerk in the entire world, Christian slumped to his knees, his knuckles leaving a bloody trail along the wall. Tears sprang to his eyes, unbidden and unwanted, yet unable to be stopped. His shoulders heaved. He gritted his teeth hard enough to make his gums bleed. His body began to shake as the adrenaline rushing through him faded, leaving him with nothing but his overpowering culpability and deep-seated regret.

Lilith had left. She might not have gone far, she might not be able to leave this enclave, but she was no longer with him.

And he had no one to blame but himself.

Chapter 13

Samantha and Tristin returned to their hidden base to discover that Leon and Sif were also back from their mission. That was good news. What was not good news was that their comrades were not successful in their mission, though it was through no fault of their own.

"Commissioner Flatcher has no clue where the SIU Sargent Catherine Siegal has gone to," Leon said, running large fingers through his hair. "She never returned from Las Vegas and hasn't called in. It's like she's disappeared."

"Las Vegas," Samantha murmured, her eyes closed. "It seems a lot happened in Las Vegas that none of us were aware of."

The group was sitting around in Samantha's office. Only Samantha was sitting down. Leon was leaning against the wall, arms crossed, his face marred by a large, off-putting frown. Sif stood next to him, not leaning but rather standing with her back straight and her arms behind her back. She looked like a solider whose uniform was about to be inspected by a drill Sargent.

"I suspect she was involved in that fuel truck explosion," Tristin said. Unlike Leon and Sif, he was leaning against Samantha's desk. She would have thrown him a glare for that, but she was too tired to even think of doing such. The journey back home had been long, and she was exhausted. Only sheer force of will kept her from collapsing. "I'm also beginning to think that Christian might have been there as well."

Samantha perked up at the mention of Christian. Just a little. "Why do you say that?"

"Um, because this is Christian we're talking about." Tristin possessed that kind of "duh" voice that made it sound like the reasons should have been obvious. And maybe it was, and she was just too tired to see reason. She still didn't appreciate the sarcasm. "If there is one thing I know about Christian, it's that whenever there is trouble, he is always in the thick of things. Aside from that, our last sighting of him before Vertrou pulled off his trail was San Francisco. We know he wanted to get out of the state, possibly out of the country. From San Francisco, there are only two places he could have gone that would have aided in this endeavor: Nevada or Oregon."

A long pause ensued as Tristin let this sink in.

"Nothing of consequence happened in Oregon during this time. Nevada, on the other hand, had that explosion that destroyed an entire city block." Tristin cast a meaningful glance around the room. It was surprising to see him look so serious. "And while some people might be stupid enough to gobble up the shit the media presents them, I like to think that all of us are intelligent enough to recognize that nothing short of a bomb, or an explosion of demonic energy, could do that much damage."

"Language," Samantha muttered, rubbing her face. She thought about what Tristin said. It made sense. It was also keeping in line with everything they had learned thus far. "So, then, what you're saying is that Christian headed to Las Vegas. At some point while he was there, he possibly met up with Catherine Siegel of the SIU before both of them were intercepted by whoever Vertrou sent after them. Is that about right?"

"That's the gist of it."

"Do we know who Vertrou sent after Christian?" asked Sif. Samantha looked over at the woman, noting her expressionless face. She then glanced at Tristin, a single eyebrow raised.

"Vertrou sent Nicholas Cruor after Christian and his lady friend." Samantha scowled at the mention of Lilith. The scowl deepened when Tristin chuckled. It sounded far too perverse for her taste. "However," he continued, calming down, "I found out while searching through the information I downloaded that Nicholas Cruor isn't his actual name."

"And what is his actual name?" asked Leon.

"Asmodeus."

There was a deep sucking of breath from everyone there. Samantha felt like a bolt of lightning had struck her in the face. It felt like her entire world had ground to a screeching halt.

"Christian faced off against one of the Seven Demon Kings?" she asked. And he was still alive, if Kokabiel was to be believed. "I don't believe it."

"I don't either," Leon added. "That kid was good, don't get me wrong. I've never met another person who was as skilled with a blade as he is, but fighting against a Demon King? Even one stuck in a human body, there's no way he could have survived that."

"And yet he did. I only managed to get a bit of information from that terminal before we were attacked, but the information I acquired is completely accurate. Asmodeus was the one sent after Christian. We all know that a battle between Christian and Asmodeus would not be quiet, yet we have not heard of any major catastrophes happening anywhere other than Las Vegas."

Samantha raised an eyebrow at Tristin's darkening countenance, but she dismissed it a moment later. For some reason that was beyond her, the man who should, in theory, only like women, was awfully defensive when people made slights against Christian. She didn't know why, and a part of her felt she was better off not knowing.

"Which makes the explosion in Las Vegas the most likely place of their battle," Samantha concluded, pushing the intelligence agent's annoyance to the side. Leon rubbed his chin, looking thoughtful but not saying anything. Sif remained expressionless, although her eyes did flicker with hidden emotion, respect maybe. "I can see where you're coming from. Mephisto's presence there also lends credence to your thesis." She paused, thinking. "Considering we have nothing else to go on, I think your idea holds the most merit."

"Aw, shucks." Tristin began to act bashful, like a hillbilly who'd just been told by the local farm girl that she liked his truck. "You're making me blush, boss lady."

"Don't get used to it," Samantha muttered darkly. Leon gave a quiet chortle, which was still loud enough for her to hear. She sent him a warning glare, which made the much larger, more imposing figure uncross his arms and raise his hands in a warding gesture.

Throughout all of this, Sif ignored the byplay going on around her. "What should we do, then? Do you have a plan of action, Commander?"

Clicking her tongue at being called commander again, Samantha turned the problem over in her mind, looking at it from different angles. "Regardless of what happens from here on out, we're going to need allies. I would rather not find myself allying with a succubus." Before Tristin even had a chance to open his mouth, she tossed him a look that could burn through steel, causing his mouth to close with a snap. She held the gaze for a second more, then continued. "That being said, Christian is still one of the best fighters I know and the only person who has defeated a high-class demon in combat." Possibly even two now. "It is imperative that we somehow bring him back into the fold."

"Should we use coercion?" asked Sif. "Take the succubus hostage and force him to work for us?"

"Are you stupid?" asked Tristin. The blunt question actually caught Sif off guard, causing her to look at him, wide eyed. The expression of perplexity might have also been caused by the irritated, humorless look on the blond man's face. Samantha understood. It just wasn't an expression people saw on Tristin often, or ever, actually.

"E-excuse me?" Sif stuttered.

"I was asking if you're some kind of idiot," Tristin said. Leon bristled, though he didn't get a chance to speak his mind before the younger man continued. "You would never even get close to Lilith before Christian ran you through. But let's say, hypothetically speaking, that you actually managed to somehow capture Lilith before Christian killed you. What do you think he would do?"

Sif hesitated, her stance suddenly unsure. She looked at Leon, then Samantha, then back at Tristin. Finally, she said, "I imagine he would do what we told him to..."

Tristin cut her off, laughing in her face. "Do what we told him to?" he mimicked, his voice mocking and derisive. "You clearly don't know Christian very well. On the off chance that you actually captured Lilith and tried to coerce him into doing your bidding, the first thing he would do is shove two feet of cold, hard steel down your throat." Tristin paused, his expression thoughtful. "Or he would just shoot you in the face, depending on whether Lilith was present. The second thing he would do, if Lilith wasn't present, is find her and break her out. No." He shook his head. "Trying to force Christian into doing what you want is just about the dumbest thing I've ever heard."

Samantha, despite the sense of dislike his words invoked, found herself nodding. "Christian has always been protective of people he believes are innocent of wrongdoings. If he left with the succubus, then it is because he believes her to be innocent. If you were to attack her, he would take that as a grave injustice and sin on your part and attack you with extreme prejudice."

Leon looked confused. "But she's a succubus," he pointed out.

Tristin opened his mouth, but Samantha raised a hand, silencing him. "Christian, despite his devout beliefs, has never once held any form of hatred toward abominations. I remember him once telling me that he pitied them because they were born in sin and needed to be cleansed. During his earlier years as an Executioner, he often expressed sadness over the loss of life. I am positive the only reason he continued working with us is because he honestly believed he was doing the right thing."

"And that's not the case now?" asked Sif.

"Obviously not." This time, Samantha was not fast enough to stop Tristin's tongue. "Did you not hear when we said he ran off with a succubus?"

"He could be under the influence of her Aura of Allure," Sif suggested.

"Doubtful," Tristin said. "Christian had been in contact with Lilith for over a week during his mission to kill her and did not exhibit the signs found in a man under a succubus's Aura of Allure once. His mind was perfectly aware. The guy was in perfect control of his mental faculties, which would not be possible if he was under the effects of a succubus's Aura of Allure. We even had Doctor Anastasia Pierce check him over for any signs of his mind being affect and he came up clean."

Leon and Sif frown. Samantha understood what they were thinking. A man being unaffected by a succubus was unheard of. That Christian was presented a series perplexing queries that had no real answer. Was it a matter of intense mental discipline that most lacked? Or was there something special about Christian? If that was the case, then what made him so special? More importantly, was it possible for others to replicate this feat?

"There will be no coercing Christian into the fold," Samantha announced. They had gone off on a tangent, and it was time to get back on track. "We will head over to Yellowstone National Park, where his last known location was. We will talk to him peacefully and ask if he would be willing to work with us. If he says no, then we'll have no choice but to leave empty handed. I don't know about either of you, but I have no desire to fight him."

Sif and Leon looked at Samantha, then at each other. A shudder passed through them, one that started from their feet and moved up to the crown of their heads. They turned back to Samantha and gave a stiff nod.

"Agreed."

***

Clarissa knocked on the door to Lilith's bedroom. She received no response. That was disappointing but expected. Ever since her argument with Christian, the young woman had locked herself in her room. She didn't talk, she refused to come out, and all the women in the enclave were nearing their wits end, as they found themselves unable to figure out how to get the innocent and pure woman to leave her room.

The only person who Clarissa was sure could get the girl to return to her normally vibrant self was Christian, and he was too busy sulking and feeling sorry for himself to help her.

Really, Clarissa thought with a disenchanted sigh, *this entire situation was one big mess.*

"Lilith." Clarissa knocked on the door again and called out the woman's name. Still no response. Frowning, she adjusted the tray in her left hand and used her right to pull a set of keys from the pocket of her jeans. "Lilith, I'm coming in." Once again, no response.

Clarissa stuck one of the keys into the lock and turned it. A soft click emitted from the door. She then opened the door and let herself in.

The room did not look much different from how it usually did. It was messier, with panties and clothes of all kinds strewn about the floor, but the mess was the only real difference.

Lying on the bed was a lump. The general shape was female, all sensual contours that bespoke of a shapely body that most women would commit genocide for. Several strands of blond hair, long, luscious, and shimmering against the white background of the sheets, stuck out from underneath the covers.

"Come on, Lilith," Clarissa said, stopping on the left side of the bed and using her free hand to pull the covers down. The fabric slid down. It moved over a set of slender shoulders, across a lovely torso covered by a pink spaghetti strap top, and then slithered over exquisitely crafted hips and legs.

Clarissa stopped pulling on the fabric before she could uncover Lilith's feet. The young woman in question was still lying on the bed, on her side, not looking at her, but rather, staring off into something distant that only she could see. Her eyes, red and puffy from crying and a lack of sleep, looked unblinkingly at nothing.

"You can't stay in here forever," Clarissa said as she set the tray she'd been carrying down on a nightstand. She proceeded to sit on the bed, her eyes taking in Lilith's form, from her frazzled hair and unblinking red eyes, to her body, which hardly moved save for rise and fall of her chest and shoulders. "Here, I brought you breakfast. Come, eat."

"No thanks," Lilith whispered, her voice grating, harsh, as if she had not used it in several days. "I'm not hungry."

"Lilith," Clarissa sighed. "I know this is hard. Arguing with your mate is never easy, and they always hurt, but you can't let something like this get the best of you. You have to push through this and keep going. What would Christian think if he saw you like this?"

Knowing Christian as she did now, Clarissa was sure the young man would become even more ridden with guilt and sink deeper into depression.

"It doesn't matter," Lilith muttered, her eyes tearing up at the mention of Christian. "He hates me. He called me a burden, told me that I'm useless, said that all I do is get in the way. He hates me, and it's all because I had to follow him when I knew he was going off to fight. It's all my fault."

"It's not entirely your fault," Clarissa said, trying to assuage some of Lilith's guilt. It probably wouldn't work, but she had to do something. "Christian is as much to blame as you are. True, you should not have followed him into such a dangerous situation, as you do not have the training necessary to get out of a predicament like that, but you can hardly be blamed for expressing worry."

Lilith shifted a bit, but she didn't say anything, causing Clarissa to sigh.

"And Christian does not hate you," she continued. "Far from it. He loves you very much. That is why he was so angry when you followed him. When people worry about the ones they love, they tend to act out with more emotions than intended. It wasn't anger that caused Christian to act like that. It was fear. He was so afraid of losing you that he allowed his emotions to get the better of him, making him lash out at you in a way he never would have done had he been thinking straight."

Lilith sniffled, hiccupped, then shifted her eyes from where they were looking at the wall to her. "Do you really think so?"

"I know so. Now, please eat up."

Lilith sat up, the left strap to her top sliding down her shoulders. She absently slid it back up as Clarissa set the plate of scrambled eggs, toast, and orange juice onto her lap. The young woman slowly picked at her food, taking small bites on occasion, but mostly just sitting there, listless and lacking life.

"Listen, Lilith," Clarissa started again, "I was wondering if you would like to get out of the enclave for a while, maybe get some fresh hair?"

Lilith stopped eating her food. Her head tilted to look at Clarissa. Green eyes fixated on her, not blinking, not moving. Clarissa felt a bit unnerved by the dull-eyed stare. It wasn't like the Lilith she'd known for the last several days, but she didn't let the other woman onto that fact. She simply kept talking.

"There's a small hotel called the Grant Village Lodge. I worked out a deal with the family that owns it a while ago in order to get the necessary supplies for my enclave. At the end of each month, a shipment of food and other essentials for us arrives there. As it's the last day of July, I was planning sending Heather out to get some supplies." She gave the destitute blonde a kind look. "Would you like to go with her?"

After another moment, Lilith gave a slow nod. "I guess."

Relief swept through Clarissa. She had been overwrought by Lilith's shut-in attitude. The pretty blonde had been so vibrant when she first arrived, always smiling, her eyes glittering in delight. Most of that, she knew, had been due to the woman's mate. Succubus were always like that around their mate. It was partly because of the life force the one they chose to be with gave to them, but mostly it was because finding love was important for their kind. It was, quite literally, hardwired into their genetics.

"Clarissa," Lilith said, her voice quiet. "Can you tell me about my mother?"

"I had almost thought you'd forgotten about that," Clarissa said after several seconds of surprise.

Lilith shook her head. "There's just been too many other things to think about."

"I understand. Very well, I don't plan on having Heather leave for another few hours, so I believe I can tell you a bit about your mother." Clarissa paused to gather her thoughts. Then she began. "Nevan was a very vivacious woman. Very lively. She was one of the few succubi who absolutely hated it in the enclave. Ever since we were little, she would sneak out to go on some hair-brained adventure, and she would often drag me along with her. We would always get caught, and the elders would scold us harshly."

Clarissa sat back, her hands going behind her, palms pushing down on the bed. She looked up at the ceiling but did not see it. Instead, images flashed before her eyes. Visions that showed a time long passed. Nostalgia rushed through her, surging like an inescapable wave. She really did miss her best friend.

"This didn't stop Nevan, though, and her adventurous spirit soon turned into a rebellious attitude. I remember when we were in our teens, she would always sneak out, and we wouldn't find her for days. No one knew what she did during that time, not even me. As we got older, the elders tried to convince her to calm down, but her attitude refused to change."

"Who are the elders?" asked Lilith.

"They were the original ruling succubi of the enclave," Clarissa answered. "They're gone now, dead. Most died shortly after their mates did. Very few succubi choose to remain living after the death of their mate. I think I am one of the few who has decided to remain."

Clarissa thought of her current mate, a man whose wife had died several years ago and left him with two daughters. They didn't see each other often. Duties kept them apart, but at least six or seven times a year they would get together. For one as old as her, that was enough to give her the energy required to live.

"By that point in time, Nevan and I had a falling out. I had become the leader of the enclave, doing what was best for the whole, to ensure that everyone was safe. I kept telling her that she couldn't go out anymore, kept scolding her, punishing her." Clarissa's smile was self-depreciating as she looked at Lilith. "I think your mother saw that as a personal betrayal. She refused to talk to me after that."

Clarissa kept her face composed, steady and calm, but despite her serene expression, her heart ached.

"It was about nineteen years ago that Nevan decided to leave the enclave for good. We all knew she had been sneaking out at night, even if most of us could never catch her. I found out several months later that she had found a mate when we discovered that she was pregnant. She refused to tell me who, saying it was none of my business and that she wanted to keep his identity a secret, though I do not know why. About a week or so after your birth, she left, with no word and no warning. One night, she was there, and the next morning, Nevan and all her belongings were gone. I never saw her again."

Lilith was silent for a moment. Clarissa watched her, pleased to see a bit of color return to her face, a bit of life flicker behind her eyes.

Sky blue irises looked at her from behind shimmering curtains of silken hair.

"Thank you for telling me about my birth mother. I know it couldn't have been easy," Lilith said softly.

"You're welcome." Clarissa stood up. "Now then, you should go take a shower and get ready. I'm going to speak with Heather and have her meet you at the entrance to the southern exit."

As Lilith stood up and made her way into the restroom, Clarissa took her leave and made her way down to the training hall. She found Heather there. The woman was sparring against Christian. Clarissa stood back for a moment, studying the young man as he battled against her best warrior.

Christian's two blades sang shrill cries as he hacked away at the woman's twin daggers, pounding against the steel blades with harsh, staggering blows. Sparks flew and steel ground together, the blades emitting a loud, pained squeal.

Unlike the first time she had seen him fight, there was no grace to Christian's movements. That unusual ability to predict an opponent's attack and respond with swift surety and finesse was gone. Beastly staggers and savage swings were all that remained of the once awe-inspiring style of combat.

As the fight continued, Heather disarmed Christian of one of his swords, the black one, by catching its crossguard with her blade and using the leverage to yank it from his grip. The sword landed several feet back. Christian was undeterred and merely switched to a one-handed style.

He was summarily disarmed again when Heather blocked his downward slash by crossing both blades over her head, allowing her to take the greater swing's force. Her knees bent, absorbing the kinetic energy. She then lashed out with a kick. The foot was planted into Christian's stomach, causing him to stagger. It was in that moment that Heather maneuvered her blades and hit the sword out of his loosened grip.

"I think we're done here," Heather said, frowning. "You know, I'm pretty disappointed. Clarissa told me your style of fighting was breathtaking, but I just don't see it." Christian didn't respond, causing her to shake her head in disgust before turning to Clarissa. "Something you needed, Clarissa?"

Clarissa did not let her sympathy toward Christian show as she nodded. "Our shipment should be in by now. I want you to bring them back. Lilith will be going with you."

Christian twitched at the mention of Lilith. Heather, on the other hand, frowned. "Are you sure I should take her? I mean, she--"

"Has agreed to go with you," Clarissa cut in. "And I think some fresh air would do her good."

"Alright. I guess I can take the girl. I doubt we'll run into any goblins after our last battle, so we should be fine."

"Good. Go to the southern exit. Lilith should be waiting there."

"Right."

Heather exited the room, leaving Clarissa and Christian alone.

"How long do you plan on continuing to sulk?" asked Clarissa. Christian didn't respond, instead continuing to look at the ground. He was just as lifeless and dull as Lilith had been. She shook her head. These two really were two sides of the same coin. "I'm disappointed in you, Christian. You never struck me as the type to let something like this keep you from doing the right thing, especially when the right thing involves making up with the woman you claim to love."

"How could I possibly atone for what I've done?" asked Christian. He shook his head, messy black hair swaying with the movement. "You weren't there, Clarissa. You didn't hear the horrible things I said to her. I told Lilith that she was worthless. That all she did was get in the way."

"I may not have been there, but I am well aware of the things you said."

Christian hadn't known it at the time, but all the succubus he'd been fighting alongside had arrived in time to hear him say those words. A lot of the respect the women at this enclave had for him because of his status as Lilith's mate had evaporated due to word spreading. She wondered if he was even aware of the glares he received when he walked around these days.

"Right now, your inaction is hurting Lilith. She's wasting away because of you." The words were not harsh. They were stated more as a fact, but Christian flinched all the same. "And if you are not man enough to apologize for what you've done, then perhaps Lilith is better off without you."

Not really feeling the desire to remain in Christian's presence any longer, Clarissa turned around and left the way she came. While she did not dislike him for what he had done and even understood his feelings (she was older than the others and understood a thing or two about relationships that none of the love-driven succubi of her enclave were able to comprehend) that did not mean she approved of what he was doing, to both him and Lilith. Of course, she didn't approve of what Lilith was doing either.

She hoped, for both of their sakes, that Christian made up with Lilith soon. If not, the damage that could be done to their bond might very well become irrevocably destroyed, and the one who would suffer the most would be Lilith.

***

Lilith sat in the passenger seat of a large, forest green pick-up truck. They were not driving down any dirt road, or even a trail. The enclave did not have a trail leading to it. This was done to help ensure the location of the succubus safe haven remained a secret. Passing by the window was all kinds of greenery, trees and plants and shrubs, a limited variety of flora that could be found within Yellowstone National Park.

Sitting in the driver's seat, her mouth set in a frown, was Heather. She was looking out of the corner of her right eye to peer at Lilith, who was doing her best to ignore the woman. There was a lot on her mind that she needed to think about.

As had been the case in recent days, her mind was stuck on the last conversation she and Christian had, of the argument that even now kept them apart. Even now, just thinking about the things that had been said caused white-hot lances of an almost physical pain to stab her heart.

Some part of Lilith was aware that Christian had only been acting out in fear. She understood, logically, the words he'd said had been due to his fear of losing her. Even so, the words remained embedded in her mind and heart. They kept her from seeking him out despite how exhausted she was from not being regularly intimate with him.

"Still hung up on that argument you and your boyfriend had?"

Lilith blinked, then looked over at Heather. "I'm sorry. Did you say something?"

"I asked if you're still hung up on that argument you and Sir Sulks-a-Lot had?" Lilith hesitated, unsure how to respond the woman's blunt words. Heather sighed. "Look, I understand that you two got into a fight, and I know it was pretty bad." Of course she would, Lilith thought. She had been there when the altercation between her and Christian took place. "But you two need to just get the fuck over it."

Lilith had trouble picking her jaw up from the seat, she was so shocked. "W-what?"

"People argue, okay? Couples argue. It's a part of fucking life. You're never going to have a perfect relationship where arguing is something that never happens. You're just not. And for you two to sit around, sulking like it's the end of the fucking world... God, that just pisses me off."

"I-I'm sorry," Lilith stuttered. "I didn't mean to upset you or anything. I—"

"I'm not upset at you, or even at Christian. I'm pissed that neither of you are taking any steps to fix your issues. You sit in your room all day, acting depressed, like the world's coming to an end because you got into a single argument with your mate. And don't even get me started on Christian. That prick's been acting like one of those bitchy little girls from an angsty vampire novel. All he does is mope. You two need to seriously get your acts together."

"But what should I do?" asked Lilith. It wasn't like she wanted things to remain as they were. She hated not spending time with Christian, not waking up to him by her side, and yes, she missed having sex with him, but she wasn't sure how to fix things. She didn't know how to make things right again.

Heather rolled her eyes. "Are you two really that stupid?" Lilith's eyes widened. "It's not rocket science, girl. Just get over yourself and apologize." She blinked. Could it really be that easy? Just walk up to him and apologize? Would that really make everything better? "Then go to your bedroom and have hot, raunchy, and incredibly passionate make up sex."

Lilith flushed at Heather's last idea. It had appeal, to be sure, but she had never heard anyone speak of sex so bluntly before.

She turned her attention elsewhere, back to the problem at hand and the solution Heather offered. Maybe she should start off with an apology. Lilith had her doubts. An apology couldn't make up for everything that had happened between them, could it? Probably not. But at least it was a start. She could tell him that she was sorry for rushing into a dangerous situation without thinking. Maybe Christian would even apologize for shouting at her and saying those harsh words. At the very least, it would get them talking to each other again.

"Maybe I'll do that," Lilith said to Heather. "Thank you."

"Yeah, sure." Heather shrugged. "Just make sure it's done soon. I'm getting sick of looking at that bastard's mopey face."

Lilith giggled but didn't say anything. The rest of the trip was made in silence.

***

Grant Village Lodge wasn't a single building, but rather, multiple buildings that dotted the landscape, placed seemingly at random, with no sense of aesthetics. Although the placement of each structure may have had something to do with the changes in elevation and the density of the ground itself. The area around Yellowstone National Park not only possessed many hills, but the make up of the ground also shifted, changing from stone to mud to dirt in an erratic manner.

The buildings themselves, while looking brand new, were made to appear like old log cabins. They sort of failed at that, however, as while the cabins did look like they were made of logs, the wood was too new, too polished, and seemed almost fake. Lilith was sure that if she went up to one and knocked on them, it would sound like knocking on plastic instead of wood.

Among the constructs was the main building, which held the lobby and various offices for those who worked there. Possessing a palatial interior with a hard wood, varnished floor and an amalgamation of wood and brick walls, it looked very modern. In the center of the sloped ceiling hung a chandelier, its thousands of gems sparkling as the light seeping in through a window on the roof coruscated off their multi-faceted surfaces. This place might not have the old and worn look they seemed to be going for. However, it was definitely a ritzy-looking place—for a lodge near a national park filled with geysers.

Heather led Lilith to the front desk, where a young woman was sitting. She looked up, her blond hair pulled into a neat bun and rimless glasses hovering over green eyes. She glared at the pair. Lilith shifted from one foot to the other at the jealous glance she was sent. Heather remained unaffected.

"Can I help you two?" she asked at last.

"I hope so. We wanted to speak with Jane Hudson. She should be expecting us."

"Hold on just one moment." The hostess picked up a nearby phone, put it to her ear, and pressed a button. "Ms. Hudson, you have two people here to see you. They say they have an appointment." A pause. "Yes, they're both women. Yes. I see. Very well." She hung the phone up and looked at the two succubi again. "If you'll wait right here, she'll come out in just a minute."

"Thank you."

While they waited for Jane Hudson to meet with them, the doors to the lodge opened and in walked four people; two men and two women. One them, the one in the lead, walked into the lobby with confident strides, her long, midnight black hair trailing behind her. Following in her wake was a man, golden hair bouncing with each step and blue eyes crinkling from the mile-wide smile on his face. The other two looked even more out of sync. One was a massive bear of a man, while the other was a petite woman with breasts almost the same size as her head.

"Are you sure Christian is somewhere around here?" asked the woman, scowling at the man with the Cheshire cat grin.

"Of course. Christian's last known location was somewhere around Yellowstone National Park. Kokabiel told us that, didn't he? Given what happened, I doubt he moved far. He should be somewhere in this general vicinity."

Lilith spun around, keeping her back to the newcomers, her heart hammering in her chest. These people were looking for Christian? Why?

"Lilith?" asked a curious Heather.

"Shh!" Lilith shushed Heather, something she normally would never dream of doing. Fear had a strange way of overriding common sense.

Heather looked at her oddly for a moment, then glanced at the group that was now speaking with the hostess. Her eyes narrowed, then she looked back at Lilith.

"Friends of yours?"

Lilith shook her head. "I've never met them before in my life."

The group continued talking for maybe two minutes, their voices muffled. Lilith resisted the temptation to move closer and listen to what they were saying. She didn't know what to do. They were after Christian, and she was almost one-hundred percent positive that it was her Christian. She wanted to know why. At the same time, it wouldn't matter if she knew why if they found her and captured her. So she remained where she was, standing there, her back to them, waiting for the group to leave.

They did, eventually. However, before they could get too far, the man who'd been speaking, the blue-eyed one, glanced at her. Lilith felt a strange, overwhelming need to claw the man's face out. The desire rose when he winked at her, but she restrained herself.

And then he was gone, the feeling evaporated like a puddle of water on a blazing summer day, and the squeaking of shoes on wood directed her attention to the figure walking into the lobby from a door near the front desk.

Jan Hudson was old. Lilith didn't want to sound harsh, but there was no better way to put it. The woman was old. She had wrinkles on her wrinkles. Her hair was shock white, stringy, and appeared to be missing in some places. While she had no eyebrows, the skin sagged so low that it hovered over her eyes, blocking much of her irises from view.

Despite her startling appearance, the warm, friendly smile on her face was enough to ease even the greatest of tension. Maybe it was because she was old. Lilith believed she'd heard something once, about how babies and old people could put people at ease with just a smile.

It was something to think about anyway.

"Heather," Ms. Hudson greeted, her smile growing. "You really haven't changed at all since the last time I saw you. Just as pretty now as you were five years ago."

Heather smiled, too, though it looked just as surely as her normal expression. She accepted the hug and kiss on the cheek from the old woman, which startled Lilith. This Hudson lady must be really familiar with her.

"Five years isn't a long time. And I'm still young."

"Indeed." Ms. Hudson then noticed Lilith, standing just a little behind Heather. She blinked. Or at least Lilith thought she did. It was hard to tell because of the hanging skin on her brow. "And it seems there's someone new with you."

"Yes." Heather gestured towards her. "This is Lilith Vie. She's sort of a temporary resident along with her boyfriend."

"Boyfriend?" Ms. Hudson looked surprised. "I had not realized you allowed men to reside with you?"

"We're making a special exception for the moment," Heather hedged.

Either Ms. Hudson sensed the woman's desire to change the subject, or she had decided to get down to business because her next words were, "I suppose there are exceptions for everything. Now, you'll be pleased to know that the shipment has arrived. The truck is waiting in the usual spot. The manifest will be in the back of the truck, just like always."

"And the person making the delivery?"

"Off enjoying some of the delights Yellowstone National Park has to offer."

Heather smiled, then hugged the woman again. "Thank you."

"Don't mention it, dear."

"The usual spot" was actually just several minutes' drive from the main building, in an abandoned road hidden behind a copse of trees. The truck wasn't a large semi-truck with sixteen wheels and a big rectangle hanging from its hind end, which was what Lilith had expected. It was a regular truck, a pickup like the one they had driven it, except red and not a Ford. Attached to the back was a trailer that was vaguely shaped like a rectangle with rounded edges.

When Heather went over to the back, unlocking it with a key Ms. Hudson had to have given her, and opened it up, she revealed that the inside was filled to the brim with boxes. They were large. Some were made of cardboard, while others were made of plastic. A couple of them actually looked like a cooler of sorts, all metal and reflective.

Lilith could not begin to even count how many boxes there were, or if they would even fit in the pick-up truck they had driven in. Fortunately for her, she would not have to count. Heather held a manifest in her hand, having picked it up from where it was hanging on the left near the trailer's entrance.

"It looks like everything's here," she said, nodding. "Yep. They've delivered it all. Good. Now all we need to do is head back home."

"Will this all fit in the truck?" Lilith asked. She didn't mean to sound skeptical, but there were a lot of boxes inside. And the interior of this semi was more spacious than the back of the truck.

"Fit in the truck?" Heather looked at her, and then started laughing. Lilith frowned. She didn't see what was so funny. "I... I'm sorry," the woman snickered, "but what makes you think we're putting all this in the truck?"

"We're not?" The frown deepened. "But then, where are we going to put it?"

"We're not putting it anywhere," Heather said. "This trailer is ours. All we're doing is uncoupling it from their truck and attaching it to our truck. It's much easier that way."

"Oh." Lilith was embarrassed. Why hadn't she thought of that?

Heather got in a few more chuckles, much to Lilith's increasing consternation. She then hung up the manifest, got out, and pulled the enclosure down. She pulled a wad of cash from her back pocket, at least several thousand dollars' worth of money—Lilith could only see hundreds—which was then set in the driver's seat of the truck through the open window.

"Come on," Heather said, clapping her hands in preparation. "Let's hurry and attach this thing. The sooner we get this done, the sooner I can get to practicing my marksmanship."

"Right."

Lilith nodded and followed Heather. The sun beat down over their heads as they went to work.

Chapter 14

After finding himself without a sparring partner, Christian somehow ended up in the library. Maybe it had something to do with the smell. He always loved the scent of books, that pervading fragrance of ink and vellum, the feel of the paper, both fresh and old as it caressed his fingers. A part of him had always regretted buying that KLReader, regardless of the fact that it could store thousands of books and was incredibly convenient.

Maybe it was a good thing the tablet was gone.

If it were any other time, Christian would have gone over to one of the many book shelves, pulled out a book, and found himself a nice place to sit and read. Such was not the case this time. Too distracted to read and not really in the mood anyway, the young man, his raven rustling with his hurried movements, strode over to the nearest couch, plopped himself down, and began to think.

His thoughts were on the same subject they had been for the last few days: his argument with Lilith. Though calling it an argument was misleading. They didn't argue much. Rather, Christian had irrationally lashed out at Lilith in anger, hurting her with his words.

It has often been said that words can hurt more than any form of physical attack. Bruises eventually go away, and cuts can heal with time, but words stay with you. They can never be taken back. People can't just say sorry and expect that to make it all better. There's no way to kiss this injury either. It's a scar that runs beneath the skin, lurking in the darkest reaches of a person's heart.

He had done that. He had hurt Lilith's heart. That wasn't a wound so easily healed. He didn't know how to make things right again. How do you make up for attacking the person you love in such a manner? Was it even possible to make things right? Saying sorry wouldn't work. An apology could only get a person so far, and a simple "I'm sorry, forgive me" didn't really make the cut. He had to show not only that he was sincere, but that he was truly, honestly remorseful for the biting words that had been discharged from his mouth.

"Why should you have to apologize?"

Christian stiffened as the sound of a voice, one that sounded so much like his own, reverberated through his mind.

"She's the one who's in the wrong here. She shouldn't have followed you, shouldn't have put herself in danger. She almost got killed, and you ended up getting hurt."

But that voice was not his. It sounded wrong, distorted. It was dark and scratchy, and it spoke with an arrogance that he did not have, an arcane and incomprehensible sense of malice that caused a shiver to race up his spine, jolting his brain like he'd stuck his finger in an electric socket.

"You don't have to apologize to her. She should be the one apologizing to you."

You're wrong.

"Am I? Why? Is what you did wrong?"

I hurt her. Of course it was wrong.

"Is it really? The way I see it, she hurt you first. You were only paying her back. She deserved your contention."

No, she didn't. No one deserves to be treated the way I treated Lilith, least of all her.

"So noble. So soft. So weak. You see, this is why you're practically useless without me."

"Shut up," Christian whispered, speaking out loud for the first time.

"Every time you run into trouble, I'm always the one saving you. I did it when Abaddon was getting ready to slaughter you like cattle. I

did it when you were fighting Damien. I aided you on the battle in the train, and again during your last fight with Asmodeus."

"Shut up!" Christian hissed. "Be quiet!"

"Do you know why? It's because you're weak. It's because you're helpless. New born kittens are stronger than you. You lack the desire, the will, everything needed to do what is necessary. You're pathetic. A useless excuse for a warrior. But don't worry. That's why I'm here. Unlike you, I'll do what's needed to get things done, and unlike you, I'll enjoy it."

"Be silent!"

"Eventually, yes, eventually there will come a time when your strength fails you completely. Then I'll step in. I'll do what you could not, what you would not. I'll be the one on top then, King, and what a glorious day that will be. I think I'll have a celebration. I'll take that succubus you love so much, bind her, beat her, tie her to the bed and plunge my—"

"I said shut up!" Christian roared, launching himself from his seat, the sound of his voice echoing through the room. He stood there, breathing in heavy pants, his shoulders and chest heaving. Sweat formed along his brow, trailing down the side of his face, and his heart beat in tune with his rage.

It was only after several seconds, time that he used to calm down, that Christian noticed he was not alone. Several other people, women that he vaguely recognized but could not name, were staring at him with shocked expressions of revulsion. He might have felt embarrassed by his outburst, or humiliated to know that people had seen it, but his mind was too unfocused, too hazy. His rage and fear clouded his rational thought processes, leaving him unable to contemplate what those in his presence might be thinking of him.

He sat back down, shuddering from head to toe. His hands found their way to his head, elbows propped up on his knees. The slow, quivering inhale and exhale pf breath did little to settle his nerves.

That was the first time what he had dubbed "The Voice" had ever spoken to him directly. His first time hearing it was many years ago, during his battle against Abaddon the Destroyer. The Voice had come to him then, whispering sweet words filled with promises. It had offered him power, and he had taken it.

He had not heard The Voice again for a while after that. During his battle with Damien, the voice had not spoken to him, but it had answered his call and given him power. And it had done so again during the train battle against Asmodeus's human form, Nicholas Cruor.

After that, he had not heard the voice again until his second battle with Asmodeus, the one where he and Lilith had almost died. The Voice had come to him once more. It had played on his worries and fears. Then it gave him power, his vision shifted, and he'd been able to find Asmodeus's weakness and send the demon back to hell.

It seemed to Christian that The Voice was getting stronger each time he accepted its offer of power. Perhaps the reason for this had something to do with how it seemed to have a hold over him. Maybe by accepting The Voice's offer, he unknowingly allowed it a foothold into his mind.

That almost seemed like a form of possession. There were many malevolent beings out there in the world who were capable of possessing humans. The Seven Demon Kings did that. To escape from hell, their only option was to possess the body of a human that could contain their soul and a fraction of their power. Poltergeists could also possess humans.

However, the amount of supernatural entities that were capable of possessing a human were few and far between. Most people wouldn't think so, assuming that possessing someone was easy, but it wasn't. The act of either enslaving the mind or inhabiting the body was incomprehensibly difficult.

There were two different types of possession. The first was the act of dominating the mind, subjugating human will and supplanting it with your own. This was difficult, as a human's mind was surprisingly hard to subdue. Influence? Yes. Enslave? No. Vampires, succubi, incubus, mermaids, sirens, all these creatures were capable of influencing a human's mind, but none of them were able to actually dominate them. Of the more regular supernatural creatures, only the No Life Kings and Ancestors were capable of truly forcing their will onto the human mind, and that wasn't possession, but rather, the act of turning a human into a slave to do their bidding. It was different.

The second type of possession was much more invasive. It didn't just involve dominating the mind and enslaving it. This type of possession called for the being in question to delve into the body of the human they were possessing. Their soul was forced into the mortal shell, consuming the original soul that resided within and supplanting the human's conscience with their own. This kind of possession was only available to poltergeists and the Seven Demon Kings. If there were any other beings capable of doing this, then Christian did not know of them.

Was that what was happening to him? Was something trying to possess him? The thought made him sick to his stomach. There were few things he feared; losing Lilith held the top place, but just below that was losing himself. Possession was an act of losing the self. When you were possessed, you were no longer the person you once were but someone else. And that notion terrified him.

The sound of an alarm blaring snapped Christian out of his musings. He rushed to his feet and ran out of the library. His destination was the command room.

Clarissa was already there when he arrived. She was standing behind an aid, leaning over a console, and speaking harshly into a headset. "What do you mean the sensors were destroyed? Goblins aren't smart enough to find those, and we hid them extremely well!" She paused, listening to the other line. "Shit! Alert the Valkyries. Tell them I want them ready to move out at a moment's notice! What's the status of Lilith and Heather?"

Upon hearing mention of Lilith, Christian forgot about everything else.

He stomped up to Clarissa, his expression stormy and worried. "What happened to Lilith?"

Clarissa looked up, then looked back at the monitor, which was rotating through several cameras that appeared to be hidden in Yellowstone National Park. "We don't know. They went out to get supplies and haven't returned. They should have been back half an hour ago. It doesn't take that long to do a supply run."

"Where did they go?"

"...Grant Village Lodge."

Christian turned, marching towards the door.

"Where do you think you're going?" asked Clarissa. Christian didn't stop. He reached the door and gripped the handle. "You don't even know where Grant Lodge is!" He stopped. "How do you expect to find them when you don't even know how to reach their last known location? Much less know where they are now?"

"I'll think of something," Christian said, even though his words lacked confidence. Clarissa was right. How could he find someone when he didn't know their location? Yellowstone National Park was a big place, and he would be running blind. What's more, he didn't have a car. He would be hoofing it.

"Don't be stupid," Clarissa shot back. "There's no way you'll be able to find them. You don't know where they are, and you have no means of transportation. It'll take days for you to cover all of Yellowstone on foot."

"Then what do you want me to do?" Christian whirled around and glared at Clarissa, his face set in a snarl. "I can't just sit here doing nothing! I need to find Lilith! I... I..." Christian trailed off, his eyes widening as a revelation struck him with the fury of tempest. Was this what Lilith felt when he went off to fight those goblins? Had she felt this same fear that he did?

He really needed to apologize to her.

After he rescued her, of course.

"I'm not saying that you should do nothing," Clarissa admonished him, her voice tight. "I am simply asking for patience. We're currently trying to triangulate their location. If you wait for a minute, we'll find them, and you can go with the Valkyries and bring them back."

Named after the Norse mythological female figures who are charged with determining who will die in battle and who will live, the Valkyries were Heather Locklear's personal unit. The ones that wore the black leather clothing. Specially selected by Clarissa and Heather, members of the Valkyries underwent extensive combat training and were tasked with protecting the enclave. They were nothing at all like the group Clarissa had led, which were just regular succubus who were sometimes forced to fight due to various circumstances.

Christian stood there in indecision. Two options were presented to him. On the one hand, he could ignore Clarissa, go off on his own, and search for Lilith himself. The problem came with the fact that he had no clue how long it would take to find Lilith, or if he even could find her. Then there was the other side of the coin toss, which involved him sticking around, waiting and worrying and fretting, while Clarissa tried to ascertain Lilith's location.

In the end, it came down to which option would take less time.

It really wasn't much of a choice.

"Alright," he sighed, forcing himself to calm down, or at least trying to. Keeping composed at that moment was harder than attempting to scrub gore off a thick shag carpet with a toothbrush. "Okay. I'll... I'll wait here."

Clarissa decided to take pity on him. "Why don't you wait with the Valkyries? They'll be the ones to mobilize. You'll find them in the changing rooms by the southern quadrant."

Christian barely gave Clarissa what would be a respectful nod as he left the room. His long strides took him across the chasm of steaming water, his mind a whirl. Agitation blared across his mind, uneasiness thrummed in his veins. Saying that Christian felt perturbed did not do his feelings justice. He felt sick. His entire body rebelled against the notion that Lilith might be in danger, or hurt, or even worse.

When he entered the changing room, it was to see that all of the girls were already there. They were also already dressed. As he walked in, they stared at him. Christian did his best to ignore the stares, choosing to take a seat far from them. He plopped down and inspected his guns.

Both Gabriel and Phaneul had been put through the ringer in recent months. He'd used them to fight both Damien and Asmodeus. They'd been knocked around, beaten, and battered, yet despite this, they were still just as pristine as when he first got them.

The material they were made of was called Oricalchum, and it was the most durable substance known to man. They never stained and never rusted. They were unbreakable, too.

Oricalchum had been made by the alchemist, Robert Boyle, near the end of the sixteenth century, who had been attempting to create a Philosopher's Stone by sacrificing humans. Boyle had been arrested, his journals confiscated, and much of his work destroyed. The means to create Oricalchum had been discovered in Boyle's journals, and the Catholic Church proceeded to use that knowledge to forge weapons.

Of course, creating Oricalchum was difficult, or so Christian had heard. The alloys necessary to create the metal were also difficult to find. That was why only the elite members of the Executioners, those who had earned great distinction, gained the right to wield a weapon forged from the unbreakable alloy. Christian, as the youngest member of the XIII, had been given four weapons made of the stuff: his guns and his swords.

Scuffing feet thudding across the floor alerted Christian to someone approaching him before a set of heeled leather boots entered his vision. He looked up to find a young woman staring at him, her dark eyes, hidden behind satiny black hair, were unreadable. Full bodied lips set upon a face of stunning femininity were turned downwards in a small frown. She did not look pleased by his presence, a fact that became enhanced when he noticed her crossed arms and cocked hips.

"What are *you* doing here?"

Her words may have helped as well.

"Clarissa told me to come here," Christian answered.

"We do not appreciate your presence, Executioner."

What a diplomatic response, Christian thought with frown. And they knew he was a former Executioner. That didn't surprise him overly much. He'd never told anybody, but it had never been made a secret either. Though, since they hadn't said anything until now, he was going under the assumption that they either hadn't known or hadn't cared until recently.

Christian decided not to be as tactful as this woman was. "I don't really care. Lilith is out there, missing. She might be hurt, or worse, and if you think you're going to stop me from finding her, then you're sorely mistaken."

The succubus, Kaylee, he thought her name was, hissed. "Do not take that tone with me, pig! You might think Clarissa's acceptance of you grants some form of immunity, but none of us care for you. I'd suggest you be careful from now on, Executioner. This is a dangerous place for men."

"Is that a threat?" asked Christian, standing up to his full height. He was a lot taller than this woman, standing over her by at least two heads. She didn't seem to be intimidated, however, and tilted her head to glare right back at him.

Out of the corner of his eyes, Christian noticed that they were being surrounded. The other Succubus were standing around and behind the one hissing at him. They looked just as displeased by his presence as she was. The thought came a bit late, but he realized that this could get very ugly very quickly if he continued letting his emotions play him.

Fortunately for him, the door chose that moment to swing open. Andrew walked in, looking as big and bad as ever. His towering mass hunched under the door so he could get inside, then he stood to his full height, his head nearly cracking against the ceiling. Bright orbs of luminescent yellow peered out from underneath a messy fringe of untamable hair.

A second of silence elapsed.

"Clarissa asked me to take part in this mission." His eyes locked on the group crowding around Christian. "I hope this isn't a bad time."

"Tch!" The confrontational succubus cast one last glare at Christian, said, "you got lucky," and then swept herself away with long, slinking strides.

Christian sighed. "Thank you for that," he said quietly as Andrew walked up. "That might have turned ugly if you hadn't intervened."

"You're welcome."

Christian eyed the other man. "I haven't seen much of you lately."

"That's because you've been sulking," Andrew said. Christian flinched. "And I'm not very welcome here, like you, so I mostly stick to my room or the hospital."

"Catherine still hasn't woken up yet?"

"No, she hasn't," he said, his head shaking, sending long, shaggy hair flying out in all directions. "According to Lean, the nurse taking care of her, Catherine suffered some serious trauma to the head. It knocked her cold. Combine that with her injuries and, well, you've got a ton of problems."

"I suppose."

Quiet descended for a second before Andrew brought up something Christian wished he would have left alone. "I heard what happened between you and Lilith. A few of the women in the hospital were talking about it."

"Word gets around here fast," Christian grunted.

"Look, try not to let it get you down too much. Couples argue. God knows my wife and I used to argue a lot."

"Maybe," Christian said softly, "but I don't think most arguments end up quite like ours did. I said something really hurtful things, words that should never be uttered. If you'd have seen the look on her face..." He trailed off, ran a hand through his hair, and sighed. "I wouldn't be surprised if she hated me for it."

"You think you're the only person who's said shit they wished they could take back?" Andrew snorted with what sounded like amusement. "Kid, listen to me right now when I tell you that there are plenty of people in your shoes. Love hurts. It's not all cotton candy and unicorns. It can be painful. You and your woman are going to argue, and it's going to hurt. All you can do is realize you've done something wrong, apologize, and make it up to them."

"I suppose you're right."

Unspoken by Christian was the silent "here's to hoping I get the chance."

***

Yellowstone National Park wasn't just a big place. It contained constantly shifting terrain, sometimes rocky and mountainous, other times filled with forests and glades. There were several paths to follow, dozens, maybe even hundreds, but unless the trails were constantly maintained, travel became increasingly difficult.

Lilith was not using any path or trail as she ran through the woods, stumbling and tripping as her feet caught themselves on rocks and branches. Her left arm dangled uselessly at her side, blood pouring from a wound she had received when the pickup truck she had been in was crushed like a tin can by the creature now chasing her.

She didn't know where Heather was. The last thing she had seen of the woman was her body getting thrown through the front windshield and disappearing down a rolling hill. She would have tried to find the woman, but not only did she not know where to start looking, she also didn't know where she was.

And she was being chased.

A roar from behind her alerted Lilith to the beast closing in, the sound, a vicious, ear-splitting howl that made her bones rattle. Feet pounding behind her, shaking the earth and almost making her lose her balance let her know that the monster was getting closer. A cry escaped her lips as she tried to put on more speed.

Breathing was becoming a problem. Her lungs heaved but very little air was coming in. She just couldn't breathe for some reason. And her vision was blurring. Something salty was stinging her eyes.

She ducked around a large tree twice as thick as she was tall. Her hope that it would buy her some time were shattered when the beast just plowed right through it. Splinters and wood chips were flung in all directions. Lilith could feel them hit her back, several of them sharp enough to penetrate her jacket and stab into her skin.

She cried out but continued to run. She didn't know where she was going, and she didn't care. She just had to get away from that monster. She needed to get away from it.

Her run took her all the way to a large body of water; Yellowstone Lake. She looked around frantically, searching for cover, for somewhere she could hide, but there was none to be had. Unless she wanted to get in the water, which would probably end with her drowning, she was trapped.

Another roar. The beast burst into the clearing. Lilith's eyes, already wide, widened further. The monster before her was a massive creature that dominated her vision. It towered over her by at least a yard. It had a flat face, wide nostrils, and small eyes overshadowed by heavy brow ridges. Two tree trunk-like legs kept it standing, and its arms, like a gorilla, almost reached down to its knees. Thick muscles combined with a wave of rolling fat moved and shook. This thing had no modesty. It wasn't even bothering to cover its dangly bits with something like a loin cloth.

Its eyes zoned in on her. Another ear-splitting howl caused Lilith's teeth to rattle as it bounded towards her with gigantic, lumbering footsteps. The earth shook and so did Lilith. Time seemed to slow down as the beast loomed closer. Lilith closed her eyes, tears streaming down her face.

"Lilith!"

***

Thanks to the massive network of security cameras populating Yellowstone National Park, finding the wreckage of the pick-up truck became a task in simplicity. Finding the people who were driving that truck was another matter entirely.

After being given the signal to move out, the Valkyries made their way out of the cave and to a garage built underneath a massive boulder. The boulder was fake, merely there to serve as a disguise for the storage shed that it truly was.

They rode on four wheelers and dirt bikes as opposed to the other off-road vehicles located there. Christian ended up having to share with Andrew, but that hardly mattered to him. They rode through the trees and around large rocky outcroppings, eventually finding their way to the crash site.

The car, a Ford puck-up, had seen better days. The entire left side was smashed in. Not just busted up, but literally crushed, the metal dented inwards like it had been hit by another car traveling at well over 75 miles per hour. It was also tipped over on its side. The trailer behind it had spilled over, its contents strewn about the ground.

The Valkyrie were all there, spread out, searching the area. They moved with tactical precision, eyes peeled and sharp. Somewhere in the distance, a howl went up.

"We found Heather!"

Christian followed the others. They passed trees and boulders and ran down a large hill, eventually making their way to where Heather lay.

The woman was in bad shape. She lay on her side, her body and limbs twisted, as if she had been tossed and just fallen that way. Blood pooled underneath her, a thickening vermilion puddle. Her hair was matted down with more ichor, showing that she had smacked her head rather hard on something, probably a rock.

All the members of the Valkyries rushed over to their leader, their faces etched with worry. They crowded around Heather, checking her pulse, making sure none of her limbs were broken, and then straightening her out and preparing her for transportation. Everything they did was methodical, efficient.

"Where's Lilith?" Christian did not see her anywhere.

"Shut up, Executioner! Let us work," the woman from before snarled at him.

"Screw you!" Christian snapped. "Andrew?"

Andrew, fur sprouting from his bipedal figure sniffed the air. His long muzzle took in several large inhalations of breath, twitching periodically. The muscles in his neck, covered in thick fur strained, and he twisted his torso several times, the muscles rippling underneath his shag carpet chest.

"I've got her scent," he growled. Yellow eyes flickered toward him. **"Follow me."**

Christian raced off, chasing after Andrew, who moved with surprising silence for someone so large. It was clear to him that the werewolf was not going anywhere near as fast as he could. He would have lost Christian in short order if he had. He traveled on swift feet, dashing between trees, ferns, and boulders, moving over hills and leaping across chasms. Christian followed as best he could, his swords clinking behind his back, ammunition clips clicking together.

It soon became clear that something had traveled this way. Trees were destroyed, literally shattered into splinters. Boulders were turned into nothing but rubble. There were large footprints on the ground, bigger than most what creatures could produce be they super natural or otherwise.

They burst into a clearing, Yellowstone Lake in front of them. Several yards away was Lilith, her back turned to them, and in front of her, charging forward like a raging bull, was a massive monster of lumbering meat and fat.

Shit! That's a troll!

"Lilith!"

Christian dashed past Andrew, Gabriel and Phaneul in his hands. He took aim as he moved, fired as he ran. Sixteen bullets tore through the air, whizzing by the petrified Lilith. Most bounced harmlessly off the troll's leathery skin. Very little could penetrate a troll's skin. That stuff was like armor. However, one of Christian's bullets found a target.

Blood spurted out of the creature's left eye socket, causing it to let out a pained and angry roar. It stumbled, its left hand moving to its eye to stem the flow of blood.

Christian reached Lilith.

"Lilith! Lilith!"

The young woman's head whipped toward him, hair flying about her, wild and chaotic. "C-Christian?" she stuttered in disbelief. Her eyes, wide with fright, stared at him, uncomprehending, like she couldn't believe he was there.

"Get back!"

He moved to stand in front, protecting her from the towering mass of muscle and fat. His two guns began to chug, loud and thunderous in his ears. Christian aimed for the troll's other eye, but while trolls are stupid, that didn't mean they couldn't learn. It used its hand to block the only eye it had left, grunting as the sharp metal balls hit its skin, but didn't penetrate.

Christian clicked his tongue in frustration. Without Oricalchum bullets, he might as well be shooting the thing with paper projectiles. Troll hide might look like leather, but it was harder than brick. Only explosives, certain corrosive acids, and Oricalchum could penetrate that skin.

Close range combat it was.

With a hiss of steel, Christian's blades were unsheathed. Michael, its black surface gleamed as the sun hit it. Rafael, the silver blade's smooth and polished surface reflected everything around it, showing a distorted facsimile of their surroundings. He readied his blades.

Christian charged forward, blades in hand, rushing straight at the troll. The massive, lumbering beast saw him out of its good. It roared a challenge, one that Christian was more than willing to answer.

A large fist came down. Christian threw himself to the left, avoiding the hammer blow, which descended upon the earth with enough force to leave a crater. His world shook, and he stumbled, but he managed to turn his momentum into a roll, skipping back to his feet and charging at the fist before the troll could retract it from the ground.

A long line of blood was drawn from its forearm, dark, blackish blood that oozed, hissed, and steamed. Troll blood was highly corrosive. Just a drop was enough to burn a whole through a human skull. Christian watched as the blood ran into the ground, eating it apart like Pacman ate dots.

The troll roared, though whether in anger or agony Christian didn't know. Probably both. His ears popped as its left hand swung out horizontally, a sweeping gesture with enough power behind it that Christian would have been sent dozens of yards back if it hit.

If it hit.

Christian dropped down to the ground, flat on his belly. A loud "whoosh" sounded overhead. He could feel his hair whipping around him. Then the fist was gone, passing over him, and Christian rose to his feet.

He dashed forward, his body low. He swung Michael forward, striking the troll in its fat belly. Its skin burst open like an overripe fruit. Black liquid, sizzling and viscous, poured from the wound in copious amounts. Christian hadn't struck deep enough to cause the beast's organs to spill, but the attack was still painful. The troll stumbled back, its roar strangled, its face twisted.

If Christian's mind had been in better shape than it was now, perhaps what happened next wouldn't have happened. One moment, he was charging in, pressing his attack and moving to open another deep furrow in the monster's bellow, maybe even strike the killing blow. The next moment all the air in his lungs became compressed as something large and heavy smashed into his chest.

The sound of bones snapping was overpowered by the loud thud of a fist hitting his body and his anguished yelp. Seconds later, Christian was sent flying backwards, where he smacked against the ground and rolled along, hitting rocks and twigs in his wake.

He came to a stop, lying on his back, his mind in a daze and his chest feeling like a professional sumo wrestler had just landed on him from fifteen stories up. Each breath wracked his body, causing sharp pains to pierce him like burning needles. He could feel fluids seeping into his lungs, sending him into a fit of coughing that hurt even more.

"Christian! Christian! Dammit! Let me go! I have to go to Christian!"

Someone was shouting. Lilith. Why was she still there?

"And what are you gonna do? Huh?" Andrew's voice. Why hadn't he taken her back to the enclave? It wouldn't take much effort to toss her over his shoulder and haul it out of there. "Face it! You can't do anything to help him."

"Then you do something! You're a werewolf, aren't you? Help him!"

"I would if I could." There was a grimace in his voice. "But I'm not strong. We werewolves are known for our speed, not our power. My claws would hardly leave a scratch on that thing. Maybe if I had a weapon, but..."

Words became garbled after that. His head was ringing. Christian realized he must have smacked his head against something when he'd taken that spill.

A face appeared at the edge of his vision. Large and flat and ugly. Thick green skin, like leather, did nothing to compliment the hideous visage. Wide nostrils flared, and ugly, rotted teeth were revealed over peeled back lips. It stared down at him, mouth opening in a loud roar that, for some reason, he could not hear. His hearing was vanishing, and his vision turning monochrome.

The beast raised its hands, and Christian knew that it would kill him. He wanted to struggle. He wanted to get up and fight, and yet, he just couldn't find the energy within him to rise.

The troll brought its hands down.

And everything stopped.

Christian blinked. The hands, which had been clasped together to form a fleshy club, had ceased to move several feet above him. The troll's face, its snarling visage, had likewise ceased to move.

What the hell was going on?

"Ah, Christian. You have once again proven your incompetence to me."

Another head appeared in his vision, to his left. It looked like him. It had his face, and his hair, yet there was something different. Its face was pale, pasty, chalk-white in a way that would make vampires envious. Its eyes also frightened him. They were not the one red and one green irises that he had. Both were red, bloody carnelian orbs that glowed with repressed malice. The pupils, slitted like a cat, seemed to seep with amusement at his predicament.

"Y-you're..."

"Ah, ah, ah." The Thing with his face raised a finger, wagging it back and forth. *"There is no need for you to speak. All that you need to do is listen."* Christian would have contended those words, but he was too tired to argue, and speaking hurt. *"This is quite the situation you've found yourself in."* The Thing with his face grinned at him. *"But then, I should have expected as much. You're always rushing off into danger, heedless of what it could cost you."* The Thing's face darkened. *"This is a bit of a problem for me. I dislike risking myself for others. It is fortunate for you that I have no choice in this matter, for the moment. But rest assured, sometime in the future, I will rectify that. Now,"* the Thing reached out to him, *"Take my hand, and I shall give you the power needed to slaughter this thing that has raised its hand against you."*

Christian looked at the hand. The temptation to take it was strong. Very strong. He knew that with the power this... Thing could offer him, he could easily slay the troll. It would be so easy, so simple. All he had to do was take the hand and power would be his.

Christian raised his left hand.

And used it to bat The Thing's hand away from him.

The Thing hissed, an angry, spitting sound. *"So you're going to spurn my aid, then? After all the times you've already accepted it? Do you really want to die? Just take my hand and unimaginable power will be yours!"*

The Thing extended its hand again.

Christian didn't take it.

"Fine then!" A snarl, an expression of rage, was unleashed from between pointed teeth. *"I hope you enjoy being turned into a pancake!"*

The Thing disappeared. Color returned to the world, along with his hearing. The troll also began moving again, its hand swinging down faster than he would have believed possible. It was so close now. Just a few more seconds and it would smash him like a tomato being run over by the semi-truck.

The attack never came.

Christian blinked.

A strange sense of calm enveloped him as the troll, its hands now flailing at nothing, batting aside things only it could see, stumbled backwards. He kept the monster in his sights, watching and wondering.

It was a good thing he kept his eyes open, too, because he also managed to see when a pink blur crashed into it. Another roar emitted from the things mouth before the creature stumbled out of sight. Seconds ticked by. Christian wondered what was going on. He wished he could lift his head, but all the energy he had was gone. He couldn't even feel any more pain, which was actually a bad thing because it meant he might be going into shock.

"Christian!"

Seconds later something, or someone, came into view. This person... thing? Whatever it was sat down next to him, and his wounds flared up when he felt slender hands with sharp claws slide underneath his back and pull him up. It took a moment to realize he was being cradled. The girl, person, thing, had pulled him onto her lap.

He stared at the creature with a sense of wonder. Her skin was pink, and not just rosy, but actually pink. Soft and lovely, the tone of her flesh complimented her full, dark ruby lips. Baby blue eyes peered down at him in concern, framed by silken strands of blond hair. Even more bizarre than that were the two curved horns that poked out from her hair and curved around her head like a crown. He recognized that hair, those eyes, those lips, and that face. He knew who she was.

Even if her skin was now pink and she had horns.

"L-Lilith?"

"Shh." Lilith hushed him before he could hurt himself further. "You're hurt. Just hold on for a second. Let me heal you."

Without any prompting, Lilith pressed her lips to his. Having gone for so long without those wonderful lips, without their silken elegance and soft, velvety feel, Christian felt his mind cloud over with a strange, pleasant tingle.

It was only after a few seconds had passed that Christian realized something. His body was being healed. He could feel his bones crackling and popping as they snapped back into place, could feel the hole in his lungs closing up, and the blood that had welled inside of it being drained. His skin, which felt like one giant bruise, was soothed as well.

Mere moments later all his wounds were healed. Rather than let go of the kiss, Lilith proceeded to deepen it. Her tongue probed his mouth, brushing against his teeth. Christian allowed her entrance, letting the pink appendage slithered inside. Her tongue was longer now. It also had a point. He let her explore his mouth, enjoyed the feel of her now long tongue coiling around his like a snake, his hand going to the back of her head, fingers threading through locks of hair.

By the Almighty did he miss this. The feel of her lips pushed against his, her tongue caressing and touching and exploring, the heat generated between their mouths as they exchanged saliva. He hadn't truly realized how much he missed being with Lilith until now.

"Lilith," Christian gasped as he pulled his mouth back. His hand was still on the back of her head. He pulled her to him, pressing their foreheads together. He stared into Lilith's eyes, those blue orbs that were so deep and soulful. They were most beautiful eyes he had ever seen. "I'm sorry," he said. "I'm so sorry. I should have never said those things to you. I don't know what I can do to make things right, but I want you to know that I'll do anything I can to make things up to you."

"Anything?"

"Anything."

Lilith, her cheeks a little more colorful than the rest of her pink skin, seemed to think on his words. There was a strange noise behind her, like the beating of wings. She regarded him with a steady gaze, as if searching to see whether he meant what he said.

"Alright. If you want to make things up to me, you can start by giving me another kiss."

Christian couldn't help himself. He laughed. Lilith looked ready to pout, but he quickly pulled her back into a kiss, which she melted against, a slow, sensuous moan escaping her muffled lips.

They would have continued, but a cough from somewhere to Christian's left caused them to stop.

They turned their heads to see Andrew standing there, looking awkward, his head turned the other way.

"I don't mind you guys doing that sort of thing on your own time, but could you at least wait until you're in your room?" he asked.

Lilith and Christian looked at each other.

"Yeah, I guess."

With a sigh, they both stood up. Now that he was no longer focused on her pretty features, Christian was able to notice that more changes had taken place on Lilith than just her skin color and horns. The back of her blue jean jacket was ripped and jutting out from what he thought were her shoulder blades were a pair of wings, long, black wings that looked both soft and tough. They vaguely reminded him of bat wings.

"Lilith," Christian said unsurely. "Did you know that you have wings?"

"I do?"

"Yes."

Lilith turned to look behind her to see that, yes, she did indeed have wings. Those same wings gave a short flap, as if trying to emphasize this fact. She then looked back at Christian.

"I didn't know that. Thanks for telling me."

"Um, anytime, I guess." His shock wearing off, Christian studied the changes that had been wrought upon Lilith with a critical gaze. "So, I'm guessing this is that transformation Clarissa was talking about a while back."

"Seems that way." Lilith looked at herself, frowning. "I just wish I knew how I had transformed. All I remember was praying to God for a way to protect you. The next thing I knew, this strange feeling enveloped me, and then I had all this knowledge in my head, telling me what I could do..." She shook her head. "It's weird."

"I can imagine." Christian held a hand to his chin. "Do you know how to turn back?"

"I don't—wait!"

Lilith closed her eyes. Her brows creased, and she worried her lower lip. A small trickle of sweat trailed the left side of her face as she seemed to concentrate really hard. One seconds passed. Then two.

Finally, her features began to morph. Her skin paled back to its original fair color, the horns jutting from her head disappeared back into her hair, and the wings retracted into her back.

"There." She smiled at Christian. "Looks like I... like I..."

Lilith's eyelids grew heavy. She swayed on her feet. Christian had just enough time to let out a startled yelp before the girl fell into his arms. He panicked for a moment, but he soon realized that she was just unconscious. He theorized that first time transformations used up a lot of energy, and she had healed him on top of that. What's more, they hadn't slept together for several days. She must have been exhausted.

He scooped her into a bridal carry. He then looked over at the troll to see that it was lying on its back, mouth hanging open and its eyes ripped out. He couldn't see any sign of how Lilith killed it but supposed she had done something to its brain when tearing out its eye.

A shudder ran through him. Lilith had just killed a full-grown troll. They weren't the strongest or smartest entities in the world, and Christian had killed more than a handful of those by himself, but they were still pretty tough. That she had killed one so easily was astonishing.

He shook his head, dispelling those thoughts, and turned to look at Andrew. "Let's go. I want to be back at the enclave before sundown. I'm beat."

"You and me both," Andrew said, grunting. "Come on. We'll meet back up with the Valkyries and then head back."

Chapter 15

When Christian arrived back at the crash site, he had been expecting most of the Valkyries to have left for the enclave, maybe leaving a small token force behind to gather the supplies from the destroyed trailer.

What he had not been expecting was to find four familiar faces being surrounded by the Valkyries in what looked like a standoff, the kind people saw just before the situation escalated into an epic battle. He froze as shock rushed through him. For one second, he could do nothing but gape at the individuals as they glared at the Valkyries.

"Samantha? Tristin? Sif? Leon?" Christian was having trouble picking his metaphorical jaw off the ground as he stared at the four. Despite having an idea as to why they were here, he couldn't help but ask, "What are you guys doing here?"

Samantha, who had been eyeing the succubi surrounding her and pointing various types of guns in their faces, turned her head to eye Christian. There was a flicker of emotion within her dark blue eyes, something akin to relief or maybe even joy. The expression darkened when she saw Lilith being cradled in his arms.

"Christian!"

While Samantha was the first to notice his presence, it was Tristin who showed the most expressive reaction. A smile, larger and wider than anything Christian had ever seen to date, plastered itself on Tristin's face. The man's eyes lit up, brilliant and sparkling like two sapphires underneath the midday sun.

He began to run toward Christian, his arms held out as if to engulf his friend in a manly bro hug.

"Christian! It's been so long! I've—eeek!"

Stillness. Tristin found himself frozen worse than a caveman who had been trapped in a block of ice.

"Ha... ha..."

Light blue eyes stared warily at the twin daggers that were almost lovingly caressing his jugular. He let his gaze travel away from the daggers to the delicate, feminine hands that held them, up the forearms and biceps, past lovely shoulders and a slender neck, before reaching the pretty face of the succubus standing before him. Dark, hooded eyes were glaring at him from underneath a fringe of brown hair.

"Do not even think of moving, *swine!* You're lucky enough that we decided not to kill you on the spot, but if you give me one good reason to, I will make sure you never leave this clearing."

While Tristin gave a serious gulp, his fear so palpable that Christian could feel it pouring off the man like water leaking from a broken sieve, the other Executioners quickly moved into action. Samantha bent down, lowering her center of gravity as her dominant hand caressed Zaphkiel's hilt, looking ready to put it to good use on all the succubi surrounding her. Sif appeared in the same boat, except rather than wielding a weapon, she was simply crouched in a low stance, her forearms crossed in front of her, the two clawed gauntlets attached to her hands and ready for action.

The only one among them who was not ready for action was Leon, and that was because the large, imposing man seemed to have trouble focusing. His eyes were glazed over. Meanwhile, his body had gone slack, tilting from side to side. He looked like he might pitch over any second.

Not really interested in having to fight another battle so soon after fighting against that troll—especially because he had a person in his arms—Christian opted to use some diplomacy in the hopes of avoiding a fight.

He moved passed most of the succubus, until he was standing almost in front of Samantha and the others. Andrew was trailing behind him, his large feet hitting the ground. Samantha and Sif must have noticed his presence because they looked over his shoulder, their eyes growing wide.

"Samantha." Christian stole the woman's attention again. Her eyes flicked from his face, to Lilith, then back to his face. She was frowning. "What are you doing here?"

Samantha shifted on her feet, looking for all the world like she didn't want to answer him, though she spoke seconds later. "We were looking for you."

"For me? Why?"

"For reasons that I would rather not discuss here."

Christian frowned. He flicked his gaze about the clearing, taking in all of the women standing around them, pointing guns and sharp implements at Samantha, Sif, Tristin, and Leon.

He then looked over at the succubus with raven hair, the one he'd gotten into a spat with earlier. She was standing slightly separate from the others, watching the proceedings with her hip cocked and her eyes narrowed.

"Would it be possible to take these four with us?" he asked.

"You want us to take them to the enclave?" She looked at him like he was crazy. "Are you an idiot? There is no way we can allow a couple of humans into our enclave, especially Executioner humans, and definitely not when they're hanging around *that*." She gestured over to Tristin, still acting like a statue as the twin daggers were held close to his throat.

"Hey! That's not a very nice thing to say!" Tristin shouted.

"Be quiet, fiend!"

"I'm not sure I understand," Christian admitted, looking between Tristin and Heather's second in command. "I get that Tristin is something of an idiot."

"Not you too!"

"And he's a complete lech."

"Why you always gotta be dissing me?"

"But even though he's a chauvinistic pig, he's not that bad."

"You're such a good friend, truly. What would I do without you?"

"You mean you don't know?" The woman's dark eyes furrowed at him. She looked over at Tristin, scowling, then turned back to peer at Christian. "That *man* isn't human. He's an incubus."

Silence entered the already still clearing. Christian felt like someone had just zapped him with a taser.

"I'm sorry," he said, shaking his head. "But could you repeat that? I could have sworn you just said that Tristin was an incubus."

"That's because I did just say that. That thing you are calling Tristin isn't human. He's an incubus."

Christian felt his mind blank. He almost lost his grip on Lilith, but he thankfully managed to reboot the organ responsible for logical thinking and decision making and strengthened his hold on her. Despite his brain working again, he still felt confused, his mind jumbled and in disarray. Tristin was an incubus? Since when? And how come he'd never known about this in all the time they had been working together?

Two eyes, one green and one red, turned to Tristin, who looked like he wanted to be anywhere but there. The man froze with a "rabbit staring down the barrel of a shotgun" expression on his face. He stared at Christian, who stared back, waiting for a response.

"Um, surprise," he said somewhat lamely, the tone of his voice making it sound more like a question than a statement.

Christian stared at him. "You're an incubus?"

"Yes."

"An incubus?"

"Uh huh."

Sif leaned over to Samantha, her expression stormy. "Did you know about this, Commander?"

Samantha grimaced. "Not until a few days after we rescued him."

"And you didn't think to tell us this... why?"

"Because I knew neither you or Leon would take his presence well, and I needed his talents."

Sif looked irritated, or as irritated as someone who didn't express her emotions very often could be. "I suppose I can understand that, but I would have liked to know. I don't think it's appropriate to keep something like this from your subordinates."

Samantha didn't have anything to say to that. Maybe she thought Sif was right, or maybe she just wanted to avoid an argument. Either way, she didn't respond to the much shorter woman's words.

Christian felt like pressing his palm into his face to stem the coming headache. Only Lilith's presence in his arms stopped him from doing so.

"You are so lucky that Lilith is in my arms right now or I would hit you." Tristin looked affronted. He opened his mouth, perhaps to give a reason for why he had never told Christian that he wasn't human, but the young man's eyes had already turned to Heater's second in command again. "Regardless of your dislike of Tristin—which I don't really understand, by the way—I do think we should take them to the enclave with us."

"And why should we do that?" asked the succubus, Kaylee, he was sure that was her name. Hmm... he really should try to remember this woman's name. "Why should I even listen to you, Executioner? You're an outsider."

"Former Executioner," Christian corrected, only taking absent note of the way Samantha flinched. "And we should take them with us because they are obviously here for a reason."

"Yeah. You. This has nothing to do with us."

It seemed this woman was going to be stubborn, which was fine. Christian could deal with stubborn people. He was also quite stubborn.

"You don't know that. Whatever they have to say could very well affect you just as much as it affects me. Besides," Christian's lips twitched into a grin, "I doubt they would take no for an answer, and if you get into a fight, I won't be able to help." He lifted his arms, Lilith's legs and arms swinging limply, her head lolling against his shoulder. "And while Tristin might be useless in a fight and Leon is, uh, not really there at the moment, Samantha and Sif are both members of the XIII."

Several of the succubi shifted uncomfortably at the mention of the XIII. They clearly knew what it meant to be one, which didn't surprise Christian. The XIII was a title synonymous with some of the best Executioners in the world. Even a single member had the capability of taking out hordes of monsters on their own.

And three of them were standing right there, even if only two were fully cognizant.

Kaylee stood in indecision for a moment before, with a snarl, she said, "fine. But, we'll only let the women come with us. The man and the incubus must return from whence they came."

Christian studied Samantha, who eyed him with wary eyes, as if she was no longer sure she could trust him. It was a prudent choice since she probably couldn't right now. Not when he was still unsure of her intention.

"Is that acceptable?" he asked.

Samantha bit her lip. Meanwhile, Sif leaned in to whisper into the woman's ear, though Christian was able to pick up what they were saying easily enough.

"I don't like this."

"Neither do I, but I don't think we have much of a choice. We came all the way out here, so we might as well see this through to the end." The raven-haired commander paused. "And I doubt they'll let us leave here alive if we don't agree."

"We could probably take them. Without Christian, they won't stand a chance. We could probably even take him out right now."

Christian twitched at the comment, but he didn't respond otherwise. That was just Sif being Sif. She had always been the practical sort.

"But can we take them out while protecting Leon and Tristin?"

Sif's eyes flickered toward Leon. The man still looked brain dead. His eyes were the only thing that moved, and all they did was flicker from one girl to the next, as if he did not know who to look at.

Being around this many succubi was clearly affecting him.

Christian noticed that he only looked at certain succubus. Given what he now knew, he took that to mean those succubi were ones who hadn't found a mate. That also meant they weren't 21 years old yet, which was the age a succubus died if they didn't find a mate.

Sif hesitated for a moment before her shoulders slumped in noticeable defeat. "Very well. I suppose we don't have much choice."

After Samantha had agreed upon the terms, the group moved out. Tristin was left with a practically brain-dead Leon. He complained loudly when Samantha informed him that he and Leon would be going back to Grant Lodge to wait. A glare from Samantha herself shut him up good.

There was only one real point of contention. Kaylee had categorically refused to let either of the Executioners into the enclave carrying weapons and demanded they be confiscated. This had almost led to another fight that, fortunately, never happened. Samantha had probably reasoned that if they were going to be killed, it would have already happened.

Weapons now confiscated and the two female Executioners no doubt feeling as naked as Christian did without his weapons, everyone began moving out.

Christian ended up getting his own four-wheeler this time, because he had to carry Lilith with him. He sat down on the seat, positioning Lilith so that she was sitting what amounted to side saddle across his lap. Her head rested in the crook of his neck, and he could feel her hot breath on his skin. It made concentrating hard, especially because her small, tight little bottom was rubbing against him. A slight sweat broke out on his forehead, and his mind hazed over slightly, vision blurring as he realized driving with his beautiful mate on his lap was much harder than it looked.

Fortunately for all things that were good and holy, the bouncing, shaking, and jostling of the quad as it drove over rough, uneven terrain had the effect of waking Lilith. The girl moaned, low and deep, her body shifting against him. Christian sucked in a breath, which invariably drew Lilith's attention to him. She looked up, sleepy eyes, unfocused and blinking, stared at him from underneath blond strands of hair.

"Christian."

Her smile was all dazzling white teeth and gorgeous, full lips. He returned her smile but was soon forced to concentrate on the road, metaphorically speaking because there wasn't actually a road to concentrate on, which was more reason to focus on his driving He had no desire to run into a tree.

Lilith, thank God, seemed to realize that he couldn't afford to be distracted. She remained side saddle, or what amount to side saddle when riding on a quad and not a horse. She set her head onto his shoulder, and slender arms wrapped around his waist.

"I really missed this," she said, her voice quiet enough that the only reason Christian picked it up over the roar of the many vehicles around them was because her mouth was so close to his ear.

Christian felt a strong urge to hug her. He refrained from doing so, barely, by reminding himself that he couldn't hug someone and drive at the same time.

"Me too."

The rest of the trip was done in silence. They arrived at the southern entrance to the enclave shortly, easily distinguishable by the large cave mouth that reared up just a yard or two from the lake.

Everyone immediately knew that something was wrong. The once pristine cave entrance had become a war zone. Gouges and craters in the ground were easily visible in the midday sun. Supplies lay everywhere, a number of weapons were strewn about on the ground. Several dozen trees lay on their sides, looking like they'd been ripped out straight from the roots, the bark splintered.

A dune buggy, the vehicle that had been responsible for taking the injured Heather back to the enclave, lay on its side. The slim bars of its all metal skeleton were twisted and contorted, broken in some areas and just bent out of place in others. Engine parts lay scattered around the clearing, and two dead Valkyrie lay on the ground, their throats ripped open.

"Shit!"

The curse came from Kaylee, who hopped off her quad before it even finished stopping. She rushed toward her downed comrades, kneeling and looking at them. Christian stopped several feet away, disembarking along with the rest of the Valkyries who ran forward as well. Andrew, Sif, and Samantha all stopped just several feet shy of the group.

"Christian," Lilith said, tugging at his sleeve. "Christian, look." She pointed at the ground, indicating something that everyone else, in their haste and panic, seemed to have missed. "Footprints."

There were indeed footprints. Indented into the dirt, slightly clawed, four toes. Goblin footprints. A lot of goblin footprints.

"Kaylee," Christian called out.

The woman looked up, glaring at him with a frustrated expression and teary eyes. "What?!"

"Look at this." He indicated the footprints.

Kaylee's eyes widened. "Are these what I think they are?"

"I imagine so."

"Then that would mean...!"

"That we need to hurry and get to the enclave," Christian concluded. Those footprints had not been there before, which meant they were new, brand new, as in the goblins had arrived at the enclave entrance sometime after they left.

And that meant nothing good.

Before they could move too far, however, a low, pained, rasping moan sounded out from behind the buggy. Everyone rushed over to the other side to see Heather, lying on her back, her eyes partway open and blinking.

She wasn't in the best of shape, and that became abundantly clear to everyone there as they closed in on her prone form. Starting from the bicep and moving into her sleeve, her left arm was bruised, a deep, ugly purple mark that also crawled up her neck. Dark crimson liquid, illuminated by the sun, dribbled down her lips.

"Heather!" Kaylee cried in shock. She knelt, lifting Heather's torso up and letting it rest against her. "Are you okay?"

Heather blinked. Her eyes, slightly dazed, looked at the dark-eyed woman. "Kaylee? Where am I?"

"Outside the enclave."

"Oh? What happened? Where'd the troll go?"

Kaylee looked up at Christian, who slid a finger across his throat. "Dead." She turned back to Heather. "We were taking you back to the enclave when I guess you got attacked."

"You're lucky you were unconscious," Christian added. "Goblins aren't that smart. They probably assumed you were dead and just left you."

"Yes, I suppose I am," Heather whispered.

"We can't get you medical aid like this. Not while the enclave might be under attack." Kaylee bit her lip, then turned to two of the Valkyries with her. "You two, take Heather and hide yourselves in the supply depot. There should be some basic medical supplies there that you can use to patch her up. The rest of us will go to the enclave and help drive the goblins out."

The planned formed, everyone began breaking off to do as ordered. Kaylee turned to Samantha and Sif, hesitating for a moment before plunging on. "I will give you both two options. You can help us drive off the goblins, or you can go back to wherever it is you came from."

Sif looked over at Samantha, who bit her lip as she contemplated the two offers, trying to decide which one was better. Her eyes flickered over to Christian, who paid careful attention to her, then to Lilith standing right next to him. She frowned, sighed, and then looked back at Kaylee.

"We'll help."

While Sif made a distinctly unpleasant sound, Kaylee nodded and had the two Valkyries carrying their weapons come over and return them. Samantha smiled as she held Zaphkiel again, and Christian understood her relief. To an Executioner, especially a member of the XIII, their weapons were a part of them, much like an arm or a leg.

While Sif put her clawed gauntlets on and began adjusting them and Samantha mentally prepared herself for the coming fight, Christian turned to the young woman beside him. Her blond hair looked a tad frazzled from the ride, her eyes, once dreary with exhaustion were, while still tired, now wide open. She looked dead on her feet, yet at the same time too restless from fear to sleep.

"Lilith," Christian started, then stopped. Lilith tilted her head toward him. Blue eyes, lighter than the sky and more brilliant than a pair of sapphires, peered up at him. His speech became momentarily halted by her beauty, but also by his own ambivalence. Still, he plundered on, getting the words out, no matter how much the idea he presented made him ill with worry. "Do you want to go with Heather and the two Valkyrie, or do you want to come with me?"

He didn't want her to come with him. He didn't want to put her in danger. There were few things in this world that Christian despised. Of those things, the idea of Lilith getting hurt because of him stood at the top of that list. If she went with him, the chances of her getting injured increased.

Yet he asked her anyway because he had been in her shoes. He now understood what she went through when he'd gone off without her to fight those goblins. He knew why she had followed him back then, regardless of the danger she had endured because of it.

Christian never wanted to feel the worry he'd felt after finding out that Lilith had gone missing. And he didn't want her to feel the same way when he went off to fight.

Lilith regarded him with a steady gaze, and then pearly white teeth revealed themselves in a full smile, dazzling in their brilliance. "Do you really have to ask that question?"

"No." He shook his head. "I suppose not. Alright." He sighed. The leather of his gloves creaking as he tightened his hands into fists, Christian penetrated Lilith with his gaze, hoping to convey how serious the next words he was about to speak were. "In that case, promise me that you will stay by my side, and that no matter what, you will do exactly as I tell you."

Lilith nodded. "I promise."

Christian tried to rid himself of the nerves he felt, the unpleasant squiggling in his stomach, the shaking of his arms and legs, the fear. It wasn't fear for himself but for Lilith. He didn't mind death. Having walked alongside it for so long, the concept didn't scare him, but the idea of Lilith possibly dying did. It terrified him. It scared him so much that he feared indecision and hesitation would set in when the situation became dangerous.

He couldn't afford that. Hesitation led to death. Indecision led to death. Anything that could stop him from thinking, stop him from acting, would lead to death. And this time, it might not be his.

There was no room for indecision and fear here.

"Okay." He breathed in, then out. "Stick behind me then."

"Right." Lilith nodded with a serious look on her face.

The pair were joined up by Andrew, who had returned to being a werewolf. Samantha and Sif were also near, though not too near. They probably didn't want to come to close to a werewolf.

Christian found himself strangely alright with that. He no longer knew how to act around them anyways, especially Samantha.

While the tunnels had not undergone any massive changes, the difference between Christian's departure with the Valkyries and now was like night and day. Bodies lay strewn about the ground. They were mostly goblin bodies, but a few succubi could be seen lying amongst the corpses. Each one they saw brought anger to the women walking alongside him.

The scent of blood hung heavily in the air, metallic, sweet, and repugnant. It pervaded the nose, all coppery, clinging and cloying, like how that old mildew scent found on worn fabric sometimes refused to come out no matter how many times it got washed.

Vermilion covered the walls and floor, glistening as light from glow sticks and flashlights swept across the passage. The floor was so wet that finding a dry path to walk through became mission impossible. Puddles had formed everywhere, pooling together and expanding from underneath the bodies of those who died.

Lilith shivered as they walked, causing Christian to place his hand in hers. The girl squeezed his hand tightly, almost painfully, as they walked through the sea of corpses.

Upon getting closer to the enclave entrance, the sounds of battle became apparent. Gunfire sang. Screams rang out. Shouts and cries and roars and the clap of thunder all combined into a single massive orgy, an amalgamation of sounds that created a symphony of death, which rolled through the passage louder than any war drum.

Christian was forced to let go of Lilith's hand. He grabbed his swords, unsheathing the blades with a hiss. Beside him, Andrew howled and rushed forward alongside Kaylee and the other Valkyries. Samantha and Sif hung back, neither in any hurry to assist.

"Follow me," Christian shouted to Lilith. She nodded, and together, they picked up the pace into a light jog.

By the time he and Lilith arrived at the entrance, the Valkyries had already joined the battle. Andrew had gotten in on the action, too, using his werewolf given speed to rush from goblin to goblin, swinging his claws with blinding speed and tearing into green flesh with ease.

Christian moved in front of Lilith and attacked. His first victim never saw him coming. The goblin was turned away from him, its left hand raised to swing a pick ax. It would never get the chance as Christian, moving like quick silver, sliced apart its back with an upwards swing of Michael. The goblin yowled, stumbling, its weapon dropping to the floor. Christian took another step forward, then swung Rafael downwards and in the opposite direction. A large "X" formed on the goblin's back as blood spurt from the gashes. It stumbled some more before crumpling to the ground, where it lay still.

Moving with slow, careful, meticulous intent, Christian waded into the battle. Unlike the previous time battle was upon him, he did not lose himself to anger, did not let worry and fear cloud his judgment. He instead dropped into an almost meditative state and expanded his spatial awareness.

Spatial awareness. It was simply the name he had given the ability to "detect" what was happening around him within a limited frame of space, sort of like a bubble in which he could sense everything. Some people also called it the sphere of influence.

There was another name for it, however: Sixth Sense. Many stories had been perpetuated about warriors of such legendary skill and battle prowess that they had developed a Sixth Sense that allowed them to feel out when someone was attacking them. Tales of these warriors, who were so capable, so talented, that they could literally feel out any attack coming their way and counter it in such a way that it almost seemed like they were predicting the moves of their enemies before it even happened. Most people who told these stories, these tall tales, often likened the Sixth Sense to some kind of magical or mystical ability that these legendary warriors had.

These tales were, generally speaking, a lie. However, they also had a grain of truth to them.

When a person has been through more battles than they can count, when they have experienced the flow of life and death struggles in which two or more forces clash, they gain a heightened awareness of the world around them. They perceive the world with more than just their eyes. Hearing. Smell. Touch. The more familiar a person becomes with combat, the more the body begins to unconsciously recognize these other senses and responds accordingly. Eventually, after a certain amount of time has passed, after a certain amount of experienced has been gained, the body will react to these senses on nothing more than impulse.

The sound of shuffling feet behind Christian alerted him to someone's presence. They were small feet, dainty even, the person not weighing more than maybe one-hundred pounds. That was Lilith. If the movement of her feet didn't tell him this, then the scent of vanilla and strawberries did. Not a threat.

The person moving behind her, with a repugnant scent and large, clomping feet, was another matter entirely.

Christian spun around. A current of air, sharp and swift, alerted him to an attack on his left. He raised Michael, blocking the attack and swatting the rusty iron sword away. Then he lashed out with Rafael, slicing through pliant flesh, muscle, and bone, causing a head to go flying off a goblin's body. At the same time that Rafael was taking off a goblin's head, Christian sheathed Michael and pulled out Gabriel. He pointed the gun over Lilith's left shoulder and fired exactly one shot. A gout of blood erupted from the goblin's forehead. Its body jerked back, and it fell to the ground, dead.

Wide blue eyes were seen for only a fraction of a second, long enough for him to holster his gun, unsheathe his blade, and spin around again. A grunt from his left caused him to bring Michael up at an angle. The weapon, an ax, ground against the polished Oricalchum surface and slid off in a hiss of sparks. Christian spun the blade around before thrusting the weapon into a thick green chest, while at the same time bringing up Rafael and using it to divest an attacking goblin of its dagger, along with the hand that came with it.

While a loud, blood-curdling scream erupted from the goblin now missing its hand, Christian yanked Michael from his slain foe, allowing the beast's body to topple onto its back. He spun, then, 360 degrees. White silver flashed as he swung his blade, cleaving through the screaming goblin's chest like it was a stick of butter. Low, pained gurgling emitted from its mouth, but it was already dying, choking on the blood welling up in its lungs.

More sounds occurred. The clanging of metal. The thunderclaps of gunfire. Screams and squeals and yells, battle cries that rang out only to be silenced the next moment.

The air around him shifted. Sharp whistling made his left ear twitch.

He moved to the left, his feet shuffling as he glided across the blood slicked floor. The attack missed and Christian consequently also ended up moving Lilith out of the way of an attack aimed at her from their right. As the weapon to the left, a club, rushed through the now empty airspace to crack against the floor, Christian stomped on the heavy wooden object. The goblin grunted, and tried to pull the weapon back, but goblins were not all that strong physically speaking. The club didn't budge and inch.

Not wanting to let this goblin attack again, Christian removed the hand holding the club with a quick swipe of a black blade. Before the monster who was now missing a hand even had time to scream, Christian struck it in the throat with the pommel of Rafael, causing it to choke. He then shifted to the left, stepping into the goblin's guard. It didn't do anything to stop him, busy as it was freaking out, and Christian was more than able to move behind it and, almost gently, guide it into the piercing thrust of a goblin that had been attacking him and Lilith on their left.

As the goblin died, its eyes wide as it released one last shuddering breath, Christian kicked it in the back, sending it flying straight into the goblin that had killed it. The two went down in a heap of limbs

Christian didn't pay attention.

He was already moving on.

Not much time had passed, relatively speaking, before Christian began to realize how difficult fighting and protecting someone at the same time truly was. His mind had become split two-ways. One part was forced to actively keep track of Lilith, the rustle of her movement, the sound of her footsteps, the scent of her natural aroma. The other was trying to work on autopilot, cataloging the sights, sounds, and feel of battle. However, with Christian primarily focusing on Lilith and her safety, it was only natural that he would screw up eventually.

The screw up came when Christian was forced to step backwards to avoid having his face carved in by a large, jagged looking knife. He only took a single step back, but that minuscule maneuver caused him to bump into the corpse of a goblin, one that he had coincidentally slain just moments ago. The back of his left heel hit the body, causing Christian to lose his balance and take a nasty spill to the ground.

Someone shouted his name, a long, loud, drawn out scream. Feminine. Lilith. Christian looked up, just in time to see an ax descending for his head.

There were certain points in a person's life when they looked back on all the things they had done, all they had accomplished, and they asked themselves, have I done anything worthwhile? What have I accomplished?

Christian did not do that. He did not think about his accomplishments, nor ask himself if he had done anything worthwhile with his life. No. All of his thoughts were on Lilith.

Will she be alright?

The axe was closing in on him.

She's out here, on a battlefield, with only me to protect her...

A shrill whistle pierced the air.

Who will protect her if I die?

A solid question. One he couldn't answer.

It was a good thing he wouldn't have to.

Just as the weapon neared his head, about to cleave his skull open, a loud, concussive gunshot rang out, somehow loud enough to be heard over the din of battle. The ax that had been set to embed itself in his head was sent sailing through the air before it somehow ended up stabbing another goblin in the back. The hand that had been holding the ax was no more, just a stump that looked like someone had stuck it in a blender. All the skin around its wrist was in tatters. Blood squirted out intermittently before splashing against the floor. The goblin looked confused for a moment, staring at its hand with undeniable bemusement.

Another shot rang out. The bullet tore right through the goblin's torso, blood spraying out of its back like a carnelian waterfall. A large hole the size of a fist opened on the creature's chest, showing that whatever had just punched through it packed a lot of power. The creature looked up, gurgled, took a single step forward, and then crumble to the floor.

Christian stood there, staring blankly at the dead goblin. The beast lay there, face down, in a growing pool of blood that was beginning to spread out from underneath its body. He could see the hole in its back where the bullet had exited. The wound wasn't a clean one. The edges of the skin were ragged and frayed. Chunky strands of muscle fibers had flown out of the wound and lay sprawled against leathery green skin. Christian even thought he saw what appeared to be white bone fragments sticking out its back.

A second later, Christian was being hauled to his feet by a small hand with a strong grip.

"Christian, what in the blazes is going on here!?"

Christian felt like his head was on a swivel as he looked at the voice, his eyes widening as surprise slammed into him. Brown eyes glared at him, surrounded by a head of messy brown I-just-woke-up-and-didn't-have-time-to-use-a-comb hair. Sharp features appeared even sharper as the harsh light from the bulbs overhead created dark contrasting shadows on her pale face.

"Catherine?" Christian blinked. Once. "You're awake!"

"Obviously," Catherine snapped, clearly irritated by something. That something became clear as she continued. "Now maybe you could tell me what the hell is going on? I wake up on a strange bed, in a hospital I've never seen, guns are firing off, strange creatures are storming the place, and I can't even find my clothes!"

It was in that moment that Christian noticed that Catherine was indeed not wearing anything decent, just a white hospital gown that went down to her knees. He also noticed that she wasn't wearing a bra. Her nipples were poking at the fabric.

He shook his head.

"I really don't think this is the best time. In case you haven't noticed, we're under attack."

"Yes, but this place has been cleaned out for the most part." Indeed, Catherine's words rang true. There were only a few goblins left, maybe two or three, and they were in the process of being killed by Samantha and Sif.

"That doesn't mean we're in the clear yet," Christian said, shaking his head at her. "I'll tell you everything you want to know, but only after this enclave is safe."

"Fine," Catherine sighed. "I guess I can wait a while longer."

"Thank you."

At that instant, a scream tore through the air. Christian and Catherine both whipped their heads to Lilith, who had moved further from Christian during the battle. A goblin was attacking her. They both aimed their guns at the same time, Christian firing a round with Gabriel and Catherine did the same with her gun. The smaller bullet hit first, putting a hole in a goblin's shoulder. The larger bullet hit second, tearing a large chunk out of the creature's torso and causing its organs to spill to the floor.

Christian gaped at the weapon in her hand, a gleaming silver Desert Eagle Mk XIX Hand-Canon. Desert Eagles were what many people considered the pinnacle of high-powered handguns. They weren't *just* a large pistol, but a hand howitzer. Powerful didn't begin to cover it. A single shot from a Desert Eagle could punch a hole in an engine block, never mind shooting a living thing.

"So you can find your handgun, but you can't find a pair of clothes to wear?"

"Bite me," Catherine snapped. "I woke up just as something big, green, and ugly barged into the hospital and tried to kill the nurse. My gun was more important."

"Point."

They swiftly moved over to Lilith, who was taking deep, calming breaths.

"Are you alright?" asked Christian.

"Yes," she said, shaking just a bit. "I'm fine." The shaking stopped. She looked at him with a smile. "I think I'm beginning to get used to this."

"I don't think that's a good thing." Christian's voice was laced with sorrow. When Lilith just frowned at him, he gave her a sad smile. "I wanted to protect you from all this," he admitted. "I never wanted you to be forced to witness this kind of violence."

Lilith's eyes conveyed to him a sense of gratitude. She took his hand, the one that was now empty of gun or sword and pressed it to her mouth. Her lips were warm, soft, and a little dry, but the contact caused Christian's body to hum with a pleasant tingle.

"I know you did," she said, her voice soft, gentle, and loving. "But Christian, what you're trying to do is impossible." When he just frowned at her, Lilith sighed and looked away. "Damien took away much of my innocence when I was younger. I might not have seen a lot of violence, but I did have to watch as my foster mother was killed."

"I guess it is kind of a moot point now, especially with everything we've already been through."

An image of train car after train car filled with blood and chunky pieces of raw meat and liquefied organs filled his mind, of a man ripping off Lilith's clothes and trying to violate her in ways only the worst kind of rapists would do. Christian had already failed to keep Lilith's innocence intact. Trying to do so now was futile.

Was it wrong that he still wanted to protect her? To shield her from the horrors this world had to offer?

"Christian."

Something soft, smooth, and warm touched his cheek. It was a delicate hand, far softer than his own. There were no rough callouses from constantly handling weapons.

Christian refocused to find Lilith looking at him, her face exhibiting affection.

"I know you want to protect me," she told him. "I know that, and I'm happy that you do. It makes me feel special, important. But I also don't want to be treated like a glass figurine or some porcelain doll. You said it yourself; I'm not a weak little girl."

He did indeed say that, back in that police station in Las Vegas. And he meant it. Lilith was strong. Most people would have broken after witnessing the horrors that she had. That she had not stood as a testament to how strong she really was.

"That doesn't make me feel any better."

"I know. You're a protector. It's what you do." Lilith's smile became slightly amused. "And stop pouting. It might look cute, but it doesn't suit you."

Christian frowned. "I do not pout." Lilith just continued smiling. "Don't look at me like that. I don't pout. I don't." When Lilith just continued smiling, Christian began to feel self-conscious. "Do I?"

"Yes." Lilith, still smiling, nodded. "Yes, you do."

Chapter 16

Samantha Gale watched Christian and Lilith, her fists clenched, her emotions boiling. It hurt. Watching the man she had spent more time with than anyone else in the Executioners act so intimate with another woman hurt a lot.

She had no idea that seeing how these two acted together would cause her so much pain. Christian acted so differently around Lilith than he had with her, or anyone else, for that matter. The look in his eyes, the expression on his face, the way he touched her and let himself be touched. This was not the Christian she had known so well.

Did that mean the Christian she knew had just been a shell? Had the real Christian been hiding all this time? Or was this just a new side to him that she had never seen before?

Or maybe... maybe this new Christian had been created by Lilith. Yes. Perhaps Lilith had used her succubus powers to create this new Christian, one who was subservient to her.

She would have to be wary around that girl.

Wanting to distract herself from the two lovebirds as they made eyes at each other, Samantha looked at the woman who had stormed into the room and began blasting goblins apart with her Desert Eagle.

Brown hair, brown eyes, sharp features. She was wearing a hospital gown, but that was not what Samantha found herself focusing on.

She walked over to the woman, the soft footsteps of Sif following behind her.

"Catherine Siegal, I presume?" Samantha asked, stopping just a few feet from the woman.

Catherine turned to her, a single eyebrow raised. "Do I know you?"

"We've never met in person. I'm Samantha Gale, former commander of the Executioners western hemisphere in the United States."

"I see." Catherine narrowed her eyes. "You and I will have a lot to talk about when this is over."

Samantha frowned but nodded. She didn't like the look on the other woman's face. It was reproachful, and it made her feel like this woman had a bone to pick with her.

"Yes, I imagine so."

"We'll have to do that later, however. Much later, as I'm still waiting for Christian to explain some things to me. And speaking of..."

Catherine glared over at the Christian and Lilith, who were lost in each other's eyes, completely ignoring everyone in the room. It was a very good thing that all the goblins in this area had been disposed of, or they would have been gutted before they could say "succubus."

"Hey! You two! Lovebirds! Stop making googly eyes and each other! We've got to move!"

Christian and Lilith snapped their gaze away from each other and turned their heads. They blinked, then looked around, finally seeming to remember where they were and what was going on. Catherine sighed. At least they had the decency to look ashamed.

"Come on, you two! We need to head out! Andy and the others are already moving on!"

Despite not wanting to, Samantha found herself admiring Catherine's ability to make herself heard and listened to. As a leader, she knew very well how hard it was to make others listen to her, so she could respect those who had that leadership quality.

The group made their way out of the entrance room and into the enclave proper. There, the group began to realize just how bad the situation truly was. Goblins were everywhere, crawling along the walkways, bursting into and out of buildings, destroying and killing and shouting. There had to be thousands of them. Up ahead, Samantha could make out the hairy form of the werewolf charging several goblins, that rude succubus who'd tried to kill them earlier, and the other Valkyrie members running behind them.

"We need to get to Clarissa," Christian said. "That should be our first priority."

Samantha had no clue who this Clarissa was, but she assumed her to be the leader of this group of succubi.

"Shouldn't our first priority be saving as many people as we can?" asked Lilith.

"We'll be able to do that on our way to Clarissa but getting to her is imperative." While Samantha had no real care whether any of these creatures lived or died, she found herself nodding. If Clarissa was indeed the leader, then her safety would take top priority. "Besides that, we can't be everywhere at once."

Catherine grunted as she held her mini-canon in both hands. "Let's not waste any more time. Come on."

They ran forward, catching up with Andrew, Kaylee, and the other Valkyries. The first building they entered was the cafeteria. The expansive room had seen better days. Most of the tables and chairs had been smashed to pieces, the metal that composed their legs twisted in a sick imitation of organic life. The buffet tables were also broken beyond repair, the frames that made them crushed, as if a giant had stepped on them. A fire had started up near the baking area, where the women in charge of making the cuisine cooked.

The entire room was also host to one massive brawl. The place was littered with bodies. Succubi and goblins were fighting everywhere. Samantha could see the werewolf tearing goblins apart with large slashes of his claws.

She frowned. She really needed to ask someone why there was a werewolf in an enclave of succubus.

Shaking her head, Samantha placed her hand on the hilt of her blade and rushed forward. She reached her first enemy, zipping up to the ugly creature, closing the distance between them at an impressive rate. Her sword was discharged from her sheath, nothing more than a flash of light. She slashed at the creature as she passed, flicked her blade clean of blood, then slid it back into the sheath.

A gurgle came from behind her. She didn't turn to see the creature die and instead threw herself headlong in the fray.

Maybe killing some goblins would help ease the anger she felt toward Lilith.

***

Lilith watched from behind Christian as her mate mowed through goblins faster than a scythe cut through wheat. This wasn't the first time she had watched him fight, but she felt no less impressed. While not a fan of violence—unless it was fictional violence—she could not help but admire his grace. Christian was beautiful when he fought. He somehow combined the grace and elegance of a dancer with the speed and precision of a bullet, somehow turning a life and death battle into something, not beautiful, but at least not ugly. No one else she knew could do that.

She would admit to being biased.

As she followed Christian while he carved through the goblins, Lilith took in a bit more of the scene. Over to her left, those two new women (what were their names again?) were cutting through the ranks of green skinned monsters almost as fast as Christian was. The raven-haired one used an odd fighting style. She would pull her blade from its sheath, then put it back in again right afterward. Goblins fell in her wake. The other woman, the short one with big breasts, was using a set of gauntlets with sharp-looking claws on them to tear through goblins like they were wet toilet paper.

So they were also members of the Executioners? Was every person who came from that group a monster in battle?

To her right, Lilith could see Catherine standing almost right next to her, taking shots at any goblin that was not in Christian's path. It was loud. Booming. Lilith flinched, her face turning green, as she saw the damage done by the gun. There was so much blood. Lilith had to turn away, and it was all she could do not to vomit.

She thought she would be used to this by now. She had told Christian that she was used to it, but the truth was that even after everything she had seen, everything she had gone through, the sight of so much blood made her sick. Worse, it made her remember that train ride, the one where Asmodeus, disguised within the body of a human called Nicholas Cruor, had brutally slaughtered everyone on board and tried to rape her.

While much of that memory felt like a distant dream thanks to Christian, it had not disappeared. It remained in her mind, lurking within the depths of her subconscious, restrained by Christian's love for her, but not wholly gone. Part of the reason why she didn't want Christian protecting her was simply because she wanted to overcome the leftover fear she felt from that experience.

Up ahead, Andrew had grabbed two goblins by the head and smashed them together, crushing the skulls and causing blood and some kind of pink ooze to leak out. He howled, tossing the dead bodies away and bounded up to another enemy, which he began mauling with sharp, blooded claws.

Lilith turned her head again, her teeth grit, her mind struggling not to let the repulsive scene get to her, her body fighting against its natural inclination to run. She didn't want to be weak anymore. If she wanted to have any hope of being useful to Christian, then she had to overcome this, her fear of battle, the sickness that came from the sight of blood, from its scent invading her nose, the repulsive aroma of death.

The goblins within the room were soon disposed of. Lilith found herself surveying the cafeteria, the dead bodies lying strewn about the ground, like dolls that had been tossed aside by an angry child. A majority of the dead were goblins, but she saw at least three succubi. Her heart clenched. She had not known these girls very long, but they had been supportive of her. Seeing them like this, their bodies lying still, their eyes wide and sightless, filmed over and dull, made her eyes water and her heart tremble.

"Lilith," Christian said, making her look away from the bodies and turn toward her mate. His eyes held compassion and love. They drove the desolation seeping at the edge of her mind, making the terrible sights, sounds, and smells around her a little bit more bearable. "Come on. We need to keep moving."

Lilith nodded and followed the group as they made their way out of the cafeteria. The walkway on the other side had more goblins on it than she could count. Their forces extended all the way to the end, where walkway turned into buildings, their bodies crowding the one-meter wide path.

Andrew, Kaylee, Samantha, and Sif led the charge, plowing into the horde with the force of a terrifying and powerful storm. They proceeded to rip through the forces arrayed against them, slaughtering the goblins with ease. Limbs were removed in sprays of gore, and bodies were sent flying off the walkway. Andrew's howl went up as he leapt several dozen feet into the air, over the heads of several goblins, and then landed on one of them with bone breaking force.

Christian stayed behind. Lilith knew that he wanted to go and help, but he was not willing to leave her. Her heart warmed up.

"Excuse me," she said to the nearest Valkyrie, a woman not much older than her, or so she thought. This female looked around the same age, but her stormy gray eyes told a different story. "Do you have a weapon I could use... like a pistol or something?"

"Lilith?" Christian turned questioning eyes on her, but Lilith only smiled.

"I want to help out."

"Lilith..."

"Please," she said, "let me do this."

Christian sighed. "I'm not trying to stop you because I don't want you to help." Lilith didn't think he was being honest, but she didn't get a chance to say anything about his desire to shelter her before he continued. "I'm stopping you because you don't even know how to use a gun yet."

Lilith felt her cheeks turn red. She also felt her face puffing up, just a bit, as she pouted. "I know how to fire a gun. You showed me."

"No," he corrected, "you know only the basics of gun handling. You know how to load and unload, and you know how to shoot. But there is a big difference from knowing how to pull a trigger to being a capable marksman. Right now, you're just as likely to shoot an ally as you are an enemy."

Lilith looked down at her feet, embarrassed. She had not thought about that. A part of her was already berating herself for her lack of forethought. She wanted to help, but without being a good shot, there was little she could do.

Well, she might be able to use her succubus powers, but she still didn't know how to use them to any great extent. So far, she had only managed to wield them during times of great duress, like when Asmodeus had been going to kill Christian, or when that troll had been about to kill Christian. Basically, the only times she'd been able to use them were times when Christian was in danger.

"I guess you're right," she mumbled, her voice soft.

Christian put a hand on her shoulder. "I promise, when we get out of this, I'll teach you how to shoot. I'll make sure you become a capable marksman."

Lilith looked up and smiled at him, her heart soaring. "Thank you."

"You're welcome."

***

Catherine walked behind Christian and Lilith, taking up the rear. Her Desert Eagle had been tied to her gown with a belt she'd found on one of the dead succubus. She didn't like raiding dead bodies, but her gun was out of ammo. She didn't want to leave it, but she also couldn't hold it if she wanted to have use of both her hands.

In her hands was a new gun—or new to her. It was a standard 9mm pistol. The weapon was small, too small for her tastes. While she would never admit it to anyone, she had a taste for larger, powerful guns. They were more effective at killing things that went bump in the night. She also loved the sound they made when fired.

The only 9mm she had seen that had proven capable of killing powerful supernatural creatures were Christian two handguns, but there was nothing standard about those weapons. She knew they were special somehow, even if she had no idea what made them such exceptional weapons.

She looked up ahead. Andy and those two women had really torn through those goblins handily. They were almost at the end of the walkway now and were mopping up the last few enemies in their way. Even as she watched them, she saw Andy run into the building, which she realized from its design must be the command structure.

Catherine found herself shaking her head. She couldn't believe she was actually fighting goblins. While Andy had told her they existed, she had never really taken him seriously. Goblins? Really? They were supposed to be fictional beings, creatures created by nerds who played Dungeons and Dragons. They weren't supposed to be real.

Times like these made her almost regret agreeing to become the head of the SIU.

To distract herself from those thoughts, Catherine let her gaze wander over the women they were surrounded by. Each woman was beautiful. Catherine thought herself rather attractive, but these women made her feel hideous.

They must be succubus, she reasoned. There were no other creatures on this God given earth who could be so insanely ravishing.

Great. So she was surrounded by succubus. She didn't have a problem with that, not really, but these women were just killing her self-esteem. It was a good thing she had never been one to care for her looks as much as other females.

Christian and Lilith entered the building ahead of her. As she stepped into what appeared to be a hallway, a loud roar, several of them, in fact, shook the building.

"What was that!?" she asked of no one in particular.

Christian answered her anyway, his eyes wide. "Trolls."

Catherine felt her own eyes widen. "You're kidding me?"

"I wish I was. The goblins must have brought them here."

That was just fantastic, Catherine thought to herself in sarcasm. Not only were there goblins, but there were trolls, too. How many more mystical, magical fantasy creatures was she going to run into today?

In spite of her feelings, and her trepidation about coming face to face with a troll—or trolls, as Christian had used the plural term—she ran alongside the young man and Lilith. Her hair swished around her, getting in her eyes and making her wish she'd had time to at least pull her hair into a bun. She really didn't need this kind of distraction, and she would feel humiliated if she died because her hair was blocking her view.

They entered what looked like a command room. Perhaps it would be more accurate to say that it *had* looked like a command room at one point. Now it was just a mess. The table in the center was broken, its frame shattered, the metal that made it up was warped, crushed, and dented. Several craters littered the ground, cracks spreading from them to form intricate patterns. A part of the wall farthest from her had been destroyed, like someone had taken CO_2 and blasted it apart.

She could see outside, the endless expanse of steaming water, several walkways where a number of succubi were being pushed back by the overwhelming forces. Catherine still didn't have the foggiest idea as to what was going on here, but she knew one thing for certain.

This place, base, enclave, whatever, was lost. All they could do was save as many of the women—succubi—as they could and make their escape.

Though Catherine was beginning to wonder if they even could escape.

The reason for this was because of the three large trolls standing in the room with them. They were massive things, gigantic even. Each one towered over everyone in the room. The smallest one of them stood at least two times larger than Andy in his werewolf form, and he was pretty damn big. Green skin, thick arms the size of tree-trunks, oddly small legs, a distended gut, and a tiny head made them one of the most hideous creatures she had ever laid eyes on.

Why were most supernatural creatures so ugly?

The giant beings were fighting against several succubi, along with Andy and those two human women. Andy seemed to be having some trouble. His speed allowed him to get in range of them easily enough, but his claws were unable to penetrate the troll's thick hide.

The two women were having much more luck. They wove around the monster they were facing with impressive dexterity. Their weapons flashed out, and each swing of sword or claw caused blood to arc out of a newly made wound. The troll would roar and attack them more furiously, but it seemed to do little good against the nimble women.

The last of the trolls appeared to be having the most success. It was roaring and flailing its arms, keeping the women surrounding it from getting too close. Guns didn't affect it. The bullets just bounced off its hide.

Already, the woman who had been fighting alongside Andy was several feet away, her limp body lying on the ground. Dust and debris from the wall she had crashed against covered her like spray paint. Catherine hoped the woman wasn't dead.

"Stay back," Christian demanded of Lilith. The girl looked ready to snap at him, but he sent her a look. "I mean it. These things are strong, and unless you can do that transformation thing again, I doubt you'll be able to help out much." That made the girl stop in her tracks. She sighed but nodded. Christian then looked at Catherine. "Protect Lilith for me, alright?"

"Okay." Catherine knew she wouldn't be much help against those trolls—not with her dinky little handgun. The least she could do now was defend Lilith. "I'll keep her safe for you."

"Thank you."

Standing there, the two women watched as Christian dashed forward, his two swords in hand, traveling toward the troll giving the succubi a handful of trouble in a full-blown sprint.

Catherine turned to Lilith. The young woman, her eyes staring longingly at Christian's back, looked like she wanted nothing more than to go after him. The way she stood, the look in her eyes, the pursing of her lips, all of it conveyed her desire to remain by the side of the dark-haired young man with the dual-colored eyes.

She found herself envying Lilith, just a little. Catherine had never had any luck with men. Most were afraid of her. Those who weren't couldn't deal with her because they gained an inferiority complex around her. Even her marriage years before, when she had been just a simple officer with the LAPD, had dissolved when the man had proven incapable of dealing with her independent streak.

Yes. Her love life truly had sucked ever since her husband died.

A shake of her head brought her back to the present.

"Lilith," she called, getting the blond woman's attention. "Let's move off to the side. I don't much care for standing in the doorway where we could get run over."

Lilith nodded. "That's probably a good idea."

Together, they moved over to a corner, the one farthest from the action. Catherine then turned back to the battle. Samantha and Sif had already managed to kill their troll. Somehow, the shorter woman had made it onto the large creature's back, and then driven her clawed gauntlets right into its skull. The troll had died instantly, its body belly-flopping to the ground with a loud rumble, Sif flipping off its back before well before it smashed against the stone floor.

The two split off. Samantha went to assist Andy, while Sif rushed toward the troll Christian and the succubi were fighting.

That particular one already looked to be on its last leg, literally. Christian had taken to weaving around the much larger creature, flaying its skin with quick slices of his swords. The troll was covered in cuts, dark blood oozing from the multitude of slash marks. It was also missing a leg, which Catherine found lying nearly a few yards from its body.

A roar erupted from its mouth. One of the women was sent flying when it swatted at her. It didn't have as much power as it used to. Because of its missing leg it couldn't generate much force. She was surprised it was still standing. The succubus got back to her feet, albeit, she was shaking from the pain of the hit.

Christian darted forward. The troll spotted him. With another roar, it attempted to smash him flat, but the young man sidestepped the attack. He then closed the rest of the distance and thrust the sword in his left hand upward.

The blade went straight through the creature's chin. Blood spurted out of the wound, dark black, looking more like ooze than blood. It hissed and steamed. Christian pulled back before it could touch him, his blade going with him, pulling out of the newly made hole, which gushed blood the moment his sword left. The troll hunched there, its body wavering left and sight, back and forth. Its eyes rolled up in its head. It gave one last gurgling, like a desperate moan, then pitched forward, smashing into the ground with earth-rumbling force.

Andy and Samantha managed to finish off the other one in short order as well. Even now, Catherine could see the woman with midnight hair standing on the monster's back, pulling her sword out the back of its neck. She flicked the blade, sending blood arcing out to splatter against the ground, then resheathed the weapon and jumped back to the floor.

Catherine looked over at Lilith. "Let's—" she started, then stopped when she saw that Lilith was no longer standing next to her. She looked around before spotting the woman in question, already running over to Christian. She sighed. "What an impatient girl," she said, then started off after her.

***

Christian, flicking Rafael clean of blood, sighed, resheathing the blade and bringing his now free hand up to wipe the sweat from his forehead. This day had been long and difficult, and he already knew it would be longer still. Even now, upon looking out the window, he could see the battle taking place outside. His swords and guns would be getting another work out soon, it seemed.

"Christian?" someone asked.

But there was a conversation that needed to be had first.

"Clarissa." Turning to the woman speaking to him, Christian decided that Clarissa had obviously seen better days. Her hair was a mess, covered in blood both her own and not. Lacerations littered her body, and though most were tiny and inconsequential, they added up. She looked tired. He imagined that she had been fighting for a long time now. "What do you want us to do?"

"Right to the point, I see." The woman chuckled, though it was without mirth.

"We don't really have any more time for discussion." Christian shrugged. "Your people are still in danger."

By now, Lilith had reached them and was standing by his side. He glanced at her but focused most of his attention on the olive-skinned woman.

"Yes." Clarissa grimaced. "You are correct, of course." Her slumped body straightened as she fixed him with a look. "Is the southern passage safe?"

"It should be. We cleared out all the goblins there."

"Good." Her eyes swept across the women, piercing each and every person there with the kind of hard expression that only a leader could have. "All of you are to follow me. We will rescue everyone we can, and then make our escape."

No cheer went up. This was not a situation where they rally themselves like barbarians going to war. In silence, the group moved out.

There was work to be done.

Chapter 17

In the end, they had managed to rescue, at most, half of the succubi population. Each time Clarissa had seen the body of one of the young women she'd sworn to protect, it had caused her to almost age before their eyes. Christian had only ever seen someone appear so despondent once before, and that had been a time he wished he could forget, even if he knew he'd never be able to.

After rescuing everyone they could, the group had made their escape. The enclave that had been built by Clarissa's grandmother several hundred years ago had become lost to them.

They had made their way to Grant Lodge. It had been fortunate for them that goblins, greedy little things that they were, weren't all that smart. They had not even bothered searching for the storage shed that hid the enclave's vehicles, or if they had searched, they had not done so thoroughly enough.

Jan Hudson, the owner of Grant Lodge, had allowed the group to stay in one of the unused hotel buildings for "as long as you need to." Christian didn't know why the human woman was so accommodating, but he assumed Clarissa, or maybe the olive-skinned woman's mother, had done some great service for her in the past.

The room they were situated in now was of moderate size, spacious, but it wouldn't be able to hold more than fifty people before it became uncomfortable. It wasn't a bedroom, but rather, a lobby that connected all the rooms together. It contained only one exit at the northern end of the room. The other doors, on the opposite side of the exit, lined up in evenly spaced rows of about four feet, led into the bedrooms.

Christian sat on one of six couches located within the lobby. Tucked neatly into his side was Lilith. The young woman was asleep, her head resting against his shoulder, warm breath from each of her exhales tickling his neck in a way that was definitely not unpleasant. He could feel her body, the swell of her breasts, the curve of her hips, pressing into his side. Her legs were stretched across his lap, her bare feet resting against the other end of the couch.

Lilith had not wanted to leave his side. When he had suggested that she go with the young succubi to get some rest, she had grabbed him by the back of the head, kissed him so firmly his lips were still bruised, and then glared at him and told him, in no uncertain terms, that she would not be leaving him.

He decided not to argue with her.

Even though a part of him was thoroughly tempted to, just to see if something good would come of it.

He hoped he wasn't turning into some kind of pervert.

Also sitting on the couch with him were Andrew and Catherine. Catherine was on Lilith's side. While Christian had nothing against Andrew, he didn't want the other man getting too physically close to Lilith. Call him jealous, call him paranoid, call him whatever you wanted, but until Lilith displayed more than just basic acceptance toward the werewolf, he would not be letting the other man get too close.

Which would explain why Andrew was sitting on the armchair of the couch and not Christian's other side. Even if it was just her cute little feet, Christian did not want Andrew, or any other man, really, to be near her.

"I guess it would be in the best interest of everybody if I introduced the newcomers," Christian said into the stillness of the group. It had been silent and tense ever since they first arrived. No one seemed to know what to say, so it looked like it would be up to him to break the ice, so to speak.

"Yes," Clarissa said, not even bothering to hide her glare. "You probably should. I would very much like to know why there is an incubus in our presence."

Said incubus gave a nervous smile. Tristin was well-aware of the many glares being sent his way. His presence was not welcome by the opposite gender of his species, though Christian wasn't sure why.

"That's just Tristin." Christian made a dismissive gesture toward the man in question. "He's an intelligence agent for the Executioners."

"Oi! I'm not just an intelligence agent!" Tristin shouted forcefully, faux anger allowing him to ignore the glares. "I'm also your best friend. Come on, tell them."

Every turned to stare at Christian. He looked back at them and presented his best smile.

"I've never been friends with him in my life."

"You're so cruel!"

"Shut up, Tristin," Samantha said. "We have neither the time nor the inclination to deal with your stupidity right now."

"Mu~" Tristin slumped from his place between Samantha and Leon, who was now wearing a medallion very similar to the one around Andrew's neck. "No one appreciates me." His comment earned several snorts from those who knew him.

"I'm curious, though." Christian looked at Clarissa, who returned his gaze evenly. "Why do you all seem to hate Tristin so much?"

"Because he is an incubus." When everyone who was not a succubus, meaning at least half of the people present, just looked at her in confusion, she sighed. "Incubus and succubus have a vastly different set of ideals and beliefs. Succubi believe in monogamy. Those of us who are fortunate enough not to become corrupted by the sins of man only ever have one mate at any given time. That one mate is the sole center of their universe until the time of his death. Then we either choose to move on and find another mate or allow ourselves to wither away."

Christian and Tristin gave a nod while everyone else just looked confused. None of them were in the know.

"Incubus, on the other hand, are polyamorous." Clarissa cut Tristin a scathing glare. The man "eeped!" at the look at tried to hide behind Samantha. He got a smack to the back of his head for his troubles. "They sleep with multiple women, uncaring of who the woman in question is, or whether or not they are already in a serious and committed relationship. They care little for the thoughts and feelings of those they fuck, as long as those women give them the energy they need."

"That is a blatant lie!"

Everyone stared at Tristin, who actually looked kind of annoyed.

"Are you telling me that you do not have sex with multiple women, incubus?" asked Clarissa, a single eyebrow raised.

"No, he does," said Christian.

"He's a complete man whore," added Samantha.

"You guys are mean." Tristin puffed out his cheeks in childish anger. It seemed that not even the hatred of half a dozen angry succubi could make him lose his immature demeanor. "It's true that I'm not monogamous, but that's because our physiology is different. Incubus do not have the luxury of genetic compatibility. A succubus has a few select individuals with whom they can gain energy from without the risk of killing their partner or making themselves go insane. An incubus is compatible with every female, but we run the risk of killing them if we drain too much of their energy."

Christian furrowed his brow. "So that's why you sleep with a bunch of women?"

Tristin nodded. "Contrary to what you people think, I haven't slept with half the female population of Los Angeles. I have a select group of women, seven, who I share my bed with. Each one of them is already aware of my species, along with why I can't be with more than one of them, and why I need to rotate between them each day." He paused. "I did try adding another woman because all the women in my harem are currently in California, but Samantha put a stop to that."

"Damn right I did," Samantha grunted.

"You mean you've actually set up a rotation schedule?" the question came from Andrew, but everyone else clearly wanted to know as well.

"Yep!" Tristin looked quite proud of himself. "Amanda sleeps with me on Monday. Susan on Tuesday. Madeline on Wednesday. Christina on Thursday. Brittney on Friday. Kelly on Saturday. And Justine on Sunday. I also let them know what they're getting into before they agree to be my partner. I tell them that any time they want out of our relationship, all they have to do is tell me. So far, only one woman has ever wanted out, and I erased her memory so that I wouldn't ruin her for other men." It was only after completing his monologue that he realized everyone was staring at him, their jaws hanging off the floor. "What?"

"I can't believe you set up a rotation schedule," Andrew's voice was a mix between shock and awe. "What the fuck?"

"Language," Christian, Leon, Samantha, and Sif all said at the same time. Andrew looked more amused by their Catholic synchronicity than angry.

Christian sighed. "I guess if that's how it is, and each woman knows what they're getting into beforehand, then it's alright."

"Christian!" Samantha looked at him, aghast. Leon and Sif did as well, but they were silent.

"What?" he asked.

"I can't believe you would think it's alright for a man to be in a relationship with multiple women! Especially one who's not even human!"

"I resent that!" Tristin yelled some more. "I might not be human, but I treat my women right!"

"Shut up, incubus! The only thing you treat right is your dick!" one of the succubus yelled back.

"Now that's just rude!"

The discussion soon devolved into a massive argument. A threnody of voices rang out, each one trying to overpower the others.

"You think that just because you only stick with a single person that it makes you better than me! Get real!"

"I don't think! I know I'm better than you, Scum!"

"How could you betray your ideals like this, Christian?! Have you allowed your love for that succubus to destroy your integrity?!"

The loud noise caused by the increasingly vehement argument not only caused the younger succubi and those who were not involved with this discussion to peek out of their rooms in order to see what all the racket was about, it also woke up Lilith. She rubbed tired eyes, blinking slowly as they adjusted to the low lighting of the room.

"Christian," she muttered, her voice only heard because her mouth was right next to his ear. "Why is it so loud?"

"Because people are being stupid," Christian growled.

"Could you get them to stop?"

Don't worry. I intend to."

Having had more than enough of everyone trying to outshout each other, Christian pulled Phaneul from its holster, pointed straight up into the air, and fired off several rounds. The loud thunderclap of his gun going off, of the bullets blowing a hole through the roof, caused everyone to cease speaking and stare at him with wide, shocked eyes.

"I think we should all get some rest," Christian suggested in a mild voice, as if he had not just blown several holes in the roof. "We've all had a long day, everyone is tired, and emotions are running hot right now. Let's go to bed, and tomorrow, when everyone is well rested, we can restart this discussion like civilized people."

"Says the guy who just fired off his gun," Leon murmured. Unlike the others, he had not been arguing, mainly because he still appeared somewhat confused about the whole thing. Christian didn't blame him. While a nice enough fellow, the big man had only ever really cared about following orders. He wasn't much of a thinker.

"We're far enough away that I doubt anyone else will have heard the gunshots," Christian defended. He then stood up, a tired Lilith in his arms, and looked at everyone there. "Good night."

In the silence of Christian's departure, only Tristin had something to say.

"Now that's how you end an argument. I've always liked his style."

***

Christian entered the room that was to be his and Lilith's... and whoever else they needed to share it with. There were only six rooms, and each one only had enough space for about ten people if they crowded around each other. There were about fifty succubus all told, plus the four Executioners, himself, Lilith, Catherine, and Andrew made for a grand total of 58 people, which meant that at least a few of those people would be sharing this room with them, especially since he doubted Tristin and the other Executioners would feel comfortable sharing a room with a group of succubi.

He moved over to one of the two beds (just because the room was large enough for ten people did not mean it had ten beds), and carefully set Lilith's feet on the ground, holding her up with one hand, so he could pull the covers back. When he did, he laid her down on the bed. He thought about taking her clothes off, but he decided not to. He divested himself of his own clothing instead. Unlike Lilith, who had been given a set of sweat pants and a large shirt, Christian only had the clothes on his back, and they were covered in blood.

He was just about to start removing his pants when the door opened.

Christian looked up to see Samantha entering the room. Her locks of raven hair trailed behind her like small tendrils. Like his own hair, hers was covered in blood and clumped together. With everything that had happened, none of them had been given the chance to take a shower.

She stopped moving when she saw him standing there, shirtless. Her eyes widened a bit and, despite the darkness of the room, Christian thought he saw her cheek turning red.

"Christian," she muttered, staring.

"Samantha," he greeted, hesitating for a second before zipping his pants back up. "Something I can help you with?"

"Yes, I wanted to talk to you, in private," she added at the end, her eyes straying toward the bed.

Christian's eyes narrowed. He glanced back at Lilith, still sleeping, then turned to Samantha.

"Alright." He gave a nod.

"Great."

They walked out of the room. Christian looked around the lobby for a moment, to see who was still there. Clarissa had not moved from her spot yet, and neither had Kaylee, who was acting in her capacity as second in command of the Valkyries since Heather was still out of commission. They were sitting on one of the couches and discussing something.

"Clarissa," he called. The woman in question looked at him. "Would you mind keeping an eye on Lilith for me?"

"Of course." Clarissa rose from her seat, graceful despite her evident exhaustion. "I'll make sure Lilith is kept safe." She eyed Samantha, Sif, Leon, and Tristin, who put his hands up, as if to say, "I won't touch her." Snorting, she looked back at him. "Myself, Kaylee, and Catherine shall be spending the night in your room anyway."

"But my lady," Kaylee argued, "you can't expect me to spend the night with a man like this."

"It's either that or spend the night with the Executioners."

"Tch!" Kaylee looked away, causing Clarissa to nod.

"Come."

The two made their way into the room with Lilith, Christian stepping aside to allow them entrance. When the door closed behind them, he began moving toward the upstairs, which contained a second lobby that had a television and several comfortable chairs. It was one of the chairs that Christian went to.

"You really don't trust me anymore, do you?" asked Samantha, sitting down on the chair opposite of Christian.

"It's not you I don't trust. It's Sif. While I believe you are capable of thinking beyond the immediate problem and looking at the bigger issue, Sif does not have that capacity. She is an excellent Warrior; she is fierce, dedicated, an able fighter, and a devout believer. However, she is not much for thinking beyond the now. It's why even after ten years as a member of the XIII, she has not been given a position of authority."

Samantha looked surprised, then tried to mask it by nodding. "I see. Thank you, then—for the trust, I mean."

"You were my commander at one point. I would like to think I know you well enough to trust you." Christian paused, gathering his thoughts. "What it is you wanted to talk to me about?"

"I wanted to ask..." Samantha stopped, swallowed the saliva that had gathered in her mouth, then continued. "I want to ask why you left the Executioners for that... that..."

"You mean for Lilith?"

"Yes."

Christian sat there for a moment, studying the woman before him. She squirmed, just a bit, but remained mostly unmoved.

After another moment, he spoke slowly, choosing each word with care. "There really isn't much to it. There's no great reason as to why I decided to leave the Executioners. I simply—" he shrugged, a helpless gesture "—fell in love."

"Fell in love." Samantha's expression betrayed her. "And what about us?"

"Us?" Confused, Christian looked at the woman a little more closely, noting the clenched fists gripping her jeans, the flat line of lips, and the storm brewing in her eyes. There was clearly something to her words that he was missing. "You mean like us, the Executioners?"

"No. I mean 'us' as in you and me."

"You and me?"

Something clicked into place. A piece to a puzzle that he'd always had but never focused on for long. He recalled all the looks Samantha gave him, the warm eyes, the soft voice, the times he would catch her staring when he took his shirt off during their spars back when they had both just been trainees.

"You like me."

It wasn't a question, but it was not really a statement either.

Samantha froze, then slumped her shoulders. "Yes. I like you. Maybe even love you."

Christian scratched the back of his head. "I didn't know."

"That's becoming increasingly obvious," Samantha said, sounding disappointed.

"You know it wouldn't have worked out anyways." Christian looked away, running a hand over his messy, blood flecked hair. "Executioners are not allowed to love. Even if the laws among our kind have changed to allow for sex, meaningful relationships between a man and a woman are technically forbidden."

"And yet you fell in love with Lilith."

"Lilith and I just sort of happened," Christian defended. "We have a lot in common, and without the laws being shoved into my face, I was able to get closer to her than I was to any other woman I know."

"And what would have happened had your mission to Seal Beach not turned out as it did?"

"You mean what would have happened if Lilith turned out to be human?"

"Yes."

"I would have asked for an honorable discharge." In the face of Samantha's wide eyes, Christian could only offer an uncomfortable shrug. "Before Tristin told me that Lilith was a succubus, I had already been planning to ask for a discharge. I had been sure you would have allowed it, provided I turn in my weapons and allow a minder to watch me."

When Samantha flinched, Christian frowned.

"You would have allowed me to leave, right?"

"I... maybe."

"Samantha..."

"You were important to the Executioners," Samantha muttered. "Important to me. I wouldn't... I didn't want you to leave. Even after we learned that you had run away with the—with Lilith, my intention was always to bring you back alive."

"Why?"

"Because you're one of the best we have. No one else in the entire force can do what you do, fight like you do. Not even the other members of the XIII have your talent."

Christian studied the woman for a moment as she stared at him, her eyes earnest. She really did believe what she said.

He shrugged. "You would have been better off trying to kill me. Even if you had managed to capture me alive, I would have never served as an Executioner again."

Samantha reared back as if struck. "Why?"

"You mean aside from the fact that you obviously had no intention of letting Lilith live?" asked Christian, his voice tinged with bitter sarcasm. "Because I can no longer believe in the Executioners cause."

"I... I don't understand," Samantha said, her voice small. The way she shrank her shoulders was something he'd never seen from her before. It made her look like a child being scolded by her parents.

Christian sighed. "The Executioners mandate is the slaying of monsters in order to protect humanity from the supernatural beings that inhabit this world."

"We carry out God's will," Samantha added.

"Do we?" Christian shook his head. "I'm not so sure of that anymore. The Executioners kill monsters because the Catholic Church believes them to be evil, because they are supposedly the personification of sin. Yet the Bible tells us that humans are born sinners. Wouldn't that make us just as evil as the creatures we slay?"

Samantha didn't say anything. He waited to see if she would, but when she remained silent, he leaned back in his chair.

"We don't slay supernatural creature's because they are evil. We do so because we are afraid, because they have powers that humans don't, because they are different. It's like how white people used to hate and fear black people for having different colored skin, only on a much larger scale because these people aren't human."

"Take succubi for instance. They are a monogamous species. They find one mate, or at least one mate at a time, who they more or less pledge their life to. They remain loyal to that single person for the rest of their mate's natural life, and when their mate dies, they can choose to find another mate or die alongside them. They are far more loyal to their partners than most humans."

"But they drain men of their life force through sex!"

"They only do that if their bodies have been defiled by a man who is not genetically compatible with them. Succubi only become monsters after being raped by humans." When Samantha sat back onto her couch in shock, Christian plunged on. "The Catholic Church and the Executioners have always just assumed they were evil because a few ended up going mad after being sexually assaulted by humans. They were never evil; we just misunderstood their situation."

"But what about their Aura of Allure."

"It's a part of their physiology. A man who is genetically compatible will be immune. That's how they find their mates."

"I... I see..." Samantha placed her hands on her forehead and closed her eyes. He didn't think he'd ever seen her look more tired.

"It's the same with many other species," Christian continued, deciding to press his point home. "Andrew is a werewolf, but he's already saved my life several times." Samantha looked at him, and he added, "he also works for the LAPD, and I am told that the Special Investigations Unit has several other non-human police officers in their force."

Samantha remained silent. Christian waited, knowing that he had just bombarded the poor woman with a lot of information. Eventually, however, she spoke up. "So you're saying that we've been wrong all this time? That we have never been doing God's will?"

Knowing that he needed to tread carefully, Christian tried to put this as delicately as possible. "In a way, though I do not think it's entirely the fault of the Executioners and the Catholic Church. There have been many creatures that have harmed humans. Vampires and werewolves who do actually pose a threat, succubi who have gotten drunk off feeding on the life force of men, mermaids who lure sailors to their doom. They exist, and they are a threat. But, just because a few of them are dangerous and should be put down before they can harm humans, that doesn't mean all of them should."

Despite the seriousness of the conversation, or perhaps because of it, Samantha gave Christian a smile. "I'm not surprised it was you who came to this conclusion. You've always been the philosophical type."

Christian shrugged. "This is just something I've been thinking about since learning that Lilith is a succubus." With a heavy sigh, he stood up. "Now then, I'm really tired, so I think I'll be going to bed."

"I suppose I should get some sleep, too." Samantha stood as well. "Though I don't know if I'll be able to. You've given me a lot to think about."

"I'd imagine so. Good night, Samantha."

"Good night... Christian."

***

Faust walked through the succubi enclave, feeling disappointed. Over to the side, about several dozen yards away, his goblin minions were piling up the bodies of the succubi who had been killed during their assault. Even now, he could see two of his minions carrying a succubus between them, a pretty little thing of maybe eighteen. Her arms dangled limply, swinging back and forth like a pair of pendulums, her head lolling around as her half-lidded eyes stared at nothing. They held her, one by the armpits and the other by the feet, moving over to the growing pile, where they proceeded to toss her on top like she was trash.

He shook his head. What a waste. He hadn't even gotten to bed one of them.

Faust was no Asmodeus, but he still craved the feel of a woman's flesh against his, and unlike Asmodeus, he was not willing to fuck a corpse.

In some ways, he thought it was good that the demon was once again residing in Hell. Asmodeus was a sick man, even by the standards of other demons.

He took in the simple architecture of the buildings, paying more attention to the goblins moving in and out of them than the actual constructs themselves. They were looting the place. He could see them carrying all kinds of objects: lamps, clothes, pillows, tableware, anything and everything that could be expected of an enclave of women to have.

He frowned in disgust. Bunch of vultures. Still, they had their uses, and he would use them until they had fulfilled their purpose.

After some searching, he eventually found the goblin he was looking for. This one was taller than most, standing almost a head shorter than Faust himself. His silver armor held a dull gleam, the intricate patterns that ran along the breastplate, gauntlets, and grieves had long faded. The helmet on his head was chipped and pitted in some places, signs that it was a well-used piece of equipment. Resting at his hip, attached by a belt, was a basic falchion.

Faust walked over to him. "Have you found the succubus and Executioner?"

The goblin glared at him and garbled out a reply, which sounded more like a series of snarls, grunts, and groans than an actual language.

Faust returned to glare. Useful these creatures might be, but they were very disrespectful.

"I do not care," Faust said. "I want those two found. Send out a search party and have them scour the area. They can't have gone very far."

The goblin "spoke" some more, and as he did, Faust's expression began to darken.

"Very well then. If you shall not send out a search party, I will merely relieve you of your duties and find someone else who is more... pliant."

Faust swung his hand faster than the goblin could blink. The swing, a horizontal one that moved level with the goblin's throat, passed by with nothing more than a whisper. His cape moved along with the action, billowing about behind him.

Faust then turned spun around on his heels and began walking away. As his booted feet descended to the floor at an even pace, thudding with the sounds of hard leather on granite, the head of the goblin he walked away from slid off with nary a sound.

The head hit the floor with a dull thunk. The body dropped onto its knees, standing still for several seconds, swaying from one side to the other. A second later, it pitched forward.

Faust did not look back. He had to find a goblin that was willing to do his bidding.

It was so hard to find good help these days.

Chapter 18

"Everyone not holding a weapon, move to the second floor!" Samantha, ever the pragmatic leader, was quick to take charge. "Christian! Cut a path to the stairway! Leon! Sif! Drive them back! Werewolf! Help Christian!"

"I have a name, you know!" There werewolf howled. He still ended up rushing to Christian's side, because really, what else was he going to do?

Christian paid little attention to the now furry Andrew standing at his side. Instead, he charged forward and plowed into the goblins trying to go up the stairs.

There were five goblins in his path. The first one was killed instantly when Christian swerved around the monster's incoming blow and carved through its stomach. He paid no heed to the blood spilling on the ground, nor the organs falling out of the creature's now disemboweled body as it keeled over. He simply moved onto the next target.

Andrew howled as he reached rushed in front of Christian due to his superior speed. The goblin in front of him raised the sword in its hand, but before it could actually do anything, the werewolf smashed a clawed paw into its face, tearing the flesh to ribbons and causing dark ichor to fly from the wound. The goblin spun around, shrieking in pain. It was silenced when Christian finished the creature off by plunging Rafael into its back as he passed.

Another goblin lost its head as Christian spun around, blades flashing. The fourth one came in to bash his face in with a club. Christian parried the attack, then bisected it from left hip to right shoulder. He pushed the dying goblin into its only remaining brethren as a distraction. Then he impaled them both on Rafael. They died, soaking his weapon in their blood.

They made it to the stairs, Christian guarding the staircase itself, his twin blades flashing, creating arcs of brilliant luminescence as the lights played off their polished surface while he cut down any foe foolish enough to come near him. Unlike the young Executioner, Andrew created a sort of passage using his werewolf speed and sharp claws to rend apart any goblin trying to get by.

Lilith, along with Clarissa, Kaylee, the young redhead, and Tristin moved quickly toward the staircase, following in the wake of the two. None of them had their weapons on them—Lilith couldn't even use a weapon—which rendered them useless in battle. The other succubus, the defenseless women who were not inured to fighting, also went up the stairs.

They ran up the stairs quickly, the adrenaline in their veins no doubt granting them a boost in speed. Christian created a wider path for them to follow, killing two more goblins that tried to attack them, one with a masterful stroke to the back of its neck, the other by impaling it through the heart when he spun about in a clockwise motion and thrust Michael through its chest.

Up ahead, near the door, Leon was laughing.

"Come on, foolish goblins! Give me a fight!"

The large, muscular man swung his warhammer, Sandalphon, onto the nearest goblin with great force, crushing it beneath the immense weight. Gore splattered out in a manner that looked eerily reminiscent of a child jumping into a puddle. Vermilion decked the floor, walls, and other goblins filling the room. Several goblins screeched as it happened, though whether from horror or anger was unknown.

Darting around Leon was Sif. The surprisingly buxom young woman, her hair whipping about her in a fierce hurricane of motion and energy, spun around one of the goblins that began screeching. She moved behind it, her feet sliding along the carpet in smooth and economic locomotion. She thrust out her left gauntlet-covered hand, penetrating the base of the creature's skull, killing it instantly. As she removed the claws from its cranium, she slid back, spun around, and shoved the other claw right into an approaching goblin's eye. It, too, died instantly, falling to the ground when the claw was removed.

Unlike those four, Samantha had taken to defending the back. Several goblins had gotten the bright idea to break in through the windows of the bedrooms—a surprisingly brilliant maneuver on their part. They had broken down the doors with ax, club, and sword, and they were now streaming in through the small entrances.

None of them got very far.

Samantha stood in the center of the central point between all the doors, knees bent, dominate leg forward, her center of gravity low. She breathed in slowly, gripping Zaphkiel's hilt. The goblins rushed her, seeing her as the first of many kills.

They would be disappointed.

An arc of light was all anyone saw. Samantha spun about in a half-circle, then stopped, her back to the goblins she killed. Her blade, already being sheathed, closed with a light "click."

Blood sprayed out of several deep wounds. The goblins reared back, stumbling, their hands going to the wide split in their flesh. They died, tumbling backwards, scrabbling for life, twitching and spasming as they slowly weakened, eyes glazing over and mouths hanging open in a facsimile of human emotion.

More came and more died. Samantha spun around again, her blade flashing out, going back into its sheath, flashing out, going back into its sheath. Several times this repeated and several times no one got past her.

"Damn," Andrew muttered upon seeing the woman work. **"She's frightening."**

"There is a reason she was selected to the commander of the entire western hemisphere," Christian said. There were no more enemies for them to slay yet. Leon and Sif had a handle on the front doors, and Samantha was dominating the entrances to the bedrooms, even though she was constantly outnumbered six-to-one. "In all the years I've known her, I never once won any of our spars."

"I thought you were supposed to be the best."

"I am. But Samantha is also one of the best. She just happens to be better than me."

"What a terrifying woman."

A loud roar rumbled in the distance. Another soon went up. Then another, and another. Christian paled as he whipped toward the direction they were coming from.

"Andrew! I need you to guard the stairs!"

"What? Why?"

The wall on the opposite side exploded inwards. Splinters ranging from the size of a thumbnail to bigger than a person's forearm rained upon the room. A troll lumbered through the newly made entrance, roaring with more ferocity than a lion.

There were several more trolls behind the first.

"That's why!"

"Shit!"

Christian rushed forward, away from the stairs, Andrew taking his place.

Being the first to react, he also ended up being the first to reach the trolls. His blades were sheathed as he pulled his guns from their holsters. The first two shots he fired blinded the troll by taking out its eyes. The creature roared, staggering and swinging its large fists. Christian avoided them, moving swiftly left, then right, swerving around the lumbering blows, allowing them to create large dents and cracks in the floor.

He holstered his guns and pulled out his swords. He swung Rafael, slicing through leathery flesh along a tree-trunk arm. Another roar. The arm jerked back as the pain shocked it. Christian used the troll's distracted state to move in, past its arm's guard.

Lashing out with Michael, he soon carved a trench into the creature's belly, slicing through skin, fat, and muscle with impunity. The acrid smell of sizzling blood filled the air, burning his senses as it invaded his nostrils. Few things smelled more horrible than troll blood.

Taking several steps back allowed Christian to avoid getting his skull crushed when the troll fell forward onto its hands and knees. He moved again, in front of its face. The troll looked at him, its face a snarling mass of putrid teeth and hairless gray skin. It opened its mouth to roar but ended up choking on blood as Christian opened up its throat with Rafael. Black, sludge-like liquid oozed out, pouring down its chest and legs, falling to the floor where it spat and sizzled, eating through the wooden tile. It then fell forward, landing face first on the ground.

Dead.

Christian coughed, choking as the smoke from the acidic liquid caused fumes to rise from the floor as it ate the wooden tiles. His eyes watered, tears stinging and blurring his vision. Hoping to avoid inhaling anymore of the crud filling his lungs, he moved back several feet.

It wasn't far enough.

The entire wall before him exploded.

Christian's style, otherwise known as the *Fake Opening Style*, was based upon the concept of creating holes in one's guard that enemies would not hesitate to exploit, thereby allowing the *fake opening* user to predict where attacks would come before they actually came. The entire style had been created by Christian, under the belief that so long as he knew where someone would attack, he could take control of the flow of battle by directing the actions of those he was fighting against. It was a suicidal style, and one that had been conceived to allow Christian to fight beings whose strength, speed, and power dwarfed his by a large margin.

Samantha, despite her dislike of the danger it put the one using it in, had applauded it as one of the most ingenious fighting styles ever created.

Yet despite how amazing it was, it had several weaknesses.

Wide area assaults, such as an entire wall exploding, sending thousands of sharp, deadly projectiles in the form of wooden splinters, was one of them.

Unable to do anything more than cover his face and what vitals he could with his arms, Christian found himself being relentlessly pelted by wood splinters. Several of them managed to pierce his body. One of the larger ones stabbed into the left side of his torso. A dozen small splinters pierced his left arm. One large piece of wood smashed into his right arm, breaking it at the elbow. Christian just barely bit back a scream of pain, even as two more several inch-long splinters stabbed his thighs, sending him to his knees.

His swords clattered to the ground. Christian winced as he moved his right hand over his body, grasping the large wooden splinter and yanking it out. He clenched his teeth, biting back a cry. The splinter dropped from his hand, which moved back to the wound, already pouring with blood, staining his shirt and pants.

It hurt. By the Almighty did it hurt. No matter how many times he got stabbed, that intense flare of pain that came with it never got any easier to bear. Even now, despite feeling the wound slowly close, agony still lanced out from the wound, causing his brain to jolt as its receptors received the pain.

The rumbling of feet pounding the ground caused Christian to look up. Another troll towered over him, a large shadow that blotted out all the lights. Its eyes, dark and filled with a primitive rage, glared down at him. Troll's were basic creatures, violent and stupid. They didn't have the ability for complex thought, and the only things they seemed capable of understanding was their need for food, sleep, and killing.

He could see the desire in those eyes, the need to kill.

It raised one gigantic hand nearly twice the size of Christian's head, the club it carried held high. His legs were pierced by several shards of wood. He didn't have enough time to pull them out and let the wounds heal.

Christian tried to move. He really did. He didn't want to die there, kneeling on the floor, completely helpless. But trying was completely different from doing. The fact was he couldn't move. The bones in his legs lanced with white hot anguish at even the slightest twitch. His muscles spasmed and shook more fiercely than a leaf caught in a tornado. He could do nothing but look up and glare defiantly into the troll that was about to kill him.

He thought he heard screaming. Someone calling his name. Maybe even multiple someone's. He couldn't be sure. He could hear nothing. Nothing but the harsh, guttural growls of the foul-smelling creature before him.

The club came down—

—and was then inexplicably yanked to the side. It crashed into the ground. The troll blinked. Christian blinked. Then the club was lifted again, and the troll's arm was swung wide. It struck the side of one of its brethren, bashing the other troll's face in and sending it stumbling back. Bloodied with what appeared to be a broken nose and several missing teeth, that troll roared, a bellow of outrage, before it returned the blow that had been dealt with a crushing hammer swing upon the other troll's head.

Gravity works in its favor. No matter how hard the head of a troll was, it couldn't withstand the forceful downward swing of another troll.

The head was crushed like a three-hundred-pound body builder stepping on a grape.

There was no contest.

"Come on!" A voice shouted in Christian's ear. An arm grabbed him by the armpit and began pulling him back. Christian just barely managed to pick up his swords as he was forcefully pulled along, dragged across the ground, to the stairs, where Lilith stood at the bottom, staring at him with wide, horrified eyes.

He was dropped to the ground in front of her. She knelt, her hands making frantic movements, like she wanted to do something but didn't quite know what. "Oh, God. You're injured."

"Yeah."

Christian almost felt like rolling his eyes. Those words actually deserved a sarcastic response, but this was Lilith, and she was worried for him. He couldn't find it in himself to respond with sarcasm.

"W-what should I do?"

"Help me pull these out. Start with the ones in my arm."

Lilith did as asked. Heedless of the blood that became caked to her hands, she pulled the wooden shards embedded into his flesh out. Christian gasped, pain lancing along his nerves as one of the dozen splinters in his arm was removed. Lilith's hand jerked back at the sound, dropping the splinter to the floor.

"A-are you okay?"

"No." Christian gritted his teeth. "And I probably won't be until all of those are pulled out. Keep going, please."

Lilith quivered but nodded. She reached out, grabbing the next one, then yanking. Christian sucked in a deep breath, hissing. Another was soon removed. Then another. And another. One by one they were yanked from his arm, which began to hiss and steam as the cells were fused together.

Christian did what he could to numb the pain, or at least distract himself. He looked at the lobby that had become a battleground. Leon had taken his place and was taking great joy in swinging Sandalphon around, bashing it against the body parts and faces of trolls with the kind of barbarianism you'd expect to see from a caveman. His joyful laughter rang out clearly over the roar of combat.

Christian shook his head.

"I can't believe you would do this," Lilith said as she continued pulling splinters from his arm. There were only a few left now, six, no five.

"Do what?"

"Keep throwing yourself into danger like that," she hissed, prying another shard from his flesh. Christian winced. That one had hurt more than the others. "Every time we're facing some kind of danger, you just rush in without thinking. Don't you ever give any thoughts to your own safety?"

"Of course, I do." Christian frowned, then winced again when another brutal yank caused his arm to jolt in pain. "But my safety is secondary to the safety of others."

"You should try thinking about yourself for once."

Christian shook his head. Lilith didn't understand. He was a protector. His purpose was to protect. Humanity. The weak and defenseless. And now Lilith. He had to protect her. Any danger to her had to be exterminated with extreme prejudice. That had become his task and duty, his purpose in life.

"Don't bother trying to talk sense into him," Tristin said, coming down the stairs. "He's an idiot who doesn't listen to anyone unless it suits his purpose."

Christian grunted. Lilith had finished with the splinters in his arm, and now had both hands wrapped around one of the larger fragments in his thigh. Gritting her teeth, muscles straining, she yanked, prying the shard out in a spurt of crimson gore.

"I resent that," Christian said, shuddering, his breathing heavy as he tried to stifle his urge to scream in pain. That shard must have hit a bundle of nerves or something because that really hurt.

"Resent it all you want, my friend. It doesn't change the fact that you have no sense of self-preservation."

Christian didn't say anything. Partly because he had nothing to say, but also because Lilith was pulling out the second of the large shards. He bit his lips, muffled groans escaping his mouth. It was all he could do not to shout in anguish.

The shard was soon pulled free. Christian released a slow, hissing breath, the pain spreading out, then numbing as the wound began to heal, the flesh knitting together at a steady, if ponderous, pace.

Tristin saw this and whistled. "That's interesting."

Christian gave a noncommittal grunt as he and Lilith pressed their hands onto the wounds in his legs, trying to stem the flow of blood while they healed. He didn't want to pass out from blood loss. His head was already beginning to feel light and dizzy.

Their allies were beginning to get overwhelmed. Without Christian to help stem the tide of enemies, Andrew, Leon, Samantha, and Sif were forced to retreat, losing ground with each second. It wasn't long before the only space they were left defending was the staircase.

The fighting then stopped, startling the defenders.

A surging pressure filled the room. It was choking. Stifling. None of the defenders dared breath for fear of breaking this silence.

Footsteps approached from outside. Unhurried and unconcerned, the sound reverberated around the room.

The sea of goblins and trolls parted, allowing the person in question to walk forward. It was a man. He wasn't very tall, but neither was he short. Dark, neatly combed hair with a part down the middle sat atop a pale face. His sideburns had turned gray, which, when combined with his salt and pepper goatee, made him look distinguished. Eyes the color of granite peered out from sunken in sockets, complimenting the gauntness of his cheeks.

A cape flowed behind him as he walked, dark purple lined with silver, billowing out as if it had a life of its own. His clothes looked like they belonged in a Renaissance fair: a short-sleeved brown leather jerkin worn over a padded, lace-up cotton gambeson of an off-white color, the sleeves of which were laced with Nordic designs; a pair of fitting black cotton velvet pants adorned his legs; he wore dark leather boots and equally dark gloves. Strapped to his waist was a double wrap belt, attached to which was a Celtic sword sheathed in hardened leather.

The man's eyes, cold and emotionless in ways Christian could scarcely comprehend, glanced at the group, pausing on him and Lilith.

"You two," he said, eloquent and articulate, his tone like velvet. He sounded almost as smooth as Tristin when the incubus was hitting up a member of the opposite sex. "You are the ones who have been giving my master so much trouble."

"Don't look at me," Christian said when everyone stared at the two of them. "I have no clue what he's talking about."

"It matters not if you know of that which I am speaking of," the man said. "My master will be very pleased with me when I bring him your heads."

Chapter 19

"Leon!" Samantha barked.

"Aye!"

Leon laughed as he swung Sandalphon around like it weighed less than a feather. Every goblin within five feet were subsequently blown off their feet when the overpowered swing smacked them. The crunching of bones as they were broken was overpowered by the shrieks emitted by each goblin struck as they were sent flying off, some hitting the walls, while other simply soared through the air until they struck the ground.

Most did not get back up.

Her path now clear, Samantha darted forward, Zaphkiel sliding out of its sheath at lightning speeds as she swung it. The blade, soaring straight for the man's throat, was abruptly halted by the Celtic sword that had appeared in his hand so quickly Samantha swore he used magic.

Sparks flew. The two ground weapons against each other before Samantha was pushed back by the gaunt male's greater strength. For someone who was so pathetically thin and bony, he had an awful amount of power.

The man swung his Celtic sword. Samantha raised her sword, sheath and all, blocking the blade with two hands, one on Zaphkiel's hilt, and the other near the edge of her sheath.

Using the advantage granted to her via her grip, she spun sheath and sword in a clockwise circle, disentangling the two weapons and causing the Celtic blade to strike the wooden ground, which became embedded deep within the surface.

She then struck out with her blade again, using her Iado technique to pull her sword from its sheath at speeds that would normally be impossible for most humans. The man clicked his tongue as he was forced to jump back, pulling his sword out of the ground and soaring across the room.

Samantha took off in hot pursuit.

***

Most people who knew her tended to fall under the belief that Sif was cold and uncaring, and they would be right, to an extent.

Sif was an unusual woman in that she believed emotions hampered a person's judgment. It was only when looking at things from a cold, logical perspective that people could truly perceive the world around them as it was meant to be perceived and make the correct decisions. Some people called that cold, but Sif preferred to think of it practical.

As she looked at the situation she found herself in, the chaos around her, the roar of battle, and Leon's laughter, Sif felt the part of herself that was cold, logical, and unfeeling warm up. While not as enthusiastic as her partner, Sif did enjoy battle. It was what made her such a good Executioner.

Her body moved before she became consciously aware of it, feet gliding along the surface floor. The first goblin in her path, one that thought to stick a sword in Leon's back, was felled when she pushed Daniel, the gauntlet on her left hand, into its lower vertebrae. The creature cried out, its body falling limp as the weapon was pulled from its spine.

She moved onto her next enemy, gliding toward Leon's right as her giant partner smashed a goblin like a tomato, crushing it into the floor. Gladreel, her right gauntlet, found purchase in the pliant flesh under a goblin's chin. It sank through the skin, into the mouth, through the roof, piercing the brain, killing it instantly.

Another success.

Gunshots began going off. Sif, after killing another goblin by severing the tendons in its neck, saw Christian sitting on the staircase, firing rounds into as many goblins as he could. The rate of his fire was insane. All twelve bullets from each gun were discharged in less than a split second. Not only were all the bullets fired in about .002 seconds, but every shot was a headshot. Christian then reloaded the guns in less than a second and fired again.

So, that was the famous quick load ability? It was one of the two skills that had earned Christian his place among the XIII. How terrifying.

Turning back to the battle, Sif leapt into the air, catching a goblin with a heel kick to the face. It reared back as struck, stumbling into one of its brethren. Sif spun, Daniel slicing a into the throat of a goblin on her left. She then thrust Gadreel forward, impaling the goblin that recovered from her spin kick through the chest.

The roar of a troll filled the air, followed swiftly by Leon's laughter. The roar, a loud bellow, was abruptly cut off. After Sif finished tearing five long gashes in a goblin's stomach, she turned her head to see one of the trolls already dead, its face crushed inwards, various fluids leaking from its mouth and eyes.

Leon's laughter permeated the air, joyful, like a kid who'd just been told Christmas had come early.

"Come, troll! Let us see if your strength is a match for mine."

The answering roar was met by a bellowing laugh. Sif shook her head. At least someone was enjoying themselves.

***

Samantha and the gaunt man traded strikes at unparalleled speeds. Flashes of light emitted between them as he used his Celtic sword to try and slay the former Executioner commander. Using her unique two-handed grip, the young woman, her raven hair flowing with her movements, maneuvered both sword and sheath to intercept the blows coming her way.

A strike from below was blocked and diverted to the side. Another came from above but merely glided off the sheath as Samantha held it at an angle above her head. Two thrusts came back to back in quick succession, each one avoided when Samantha stepped back and to the left.

A pause appeared in the battle as both combatants took a step back to reassess the situation. Samantha used that time to also catch her breath, something that her opponent did not seem to need.

"Faust," he said.

Samantha paused. "Excuse me?"

"My name is Faust." He smiled. "I thought you'd like to know the name of the man who killed you."

She twitched. "Do not speak of killing someone when you have yet to actually kill them."

"Hmph!"

The two engaged again, dashing forward and meeting in the middle. Sparks and flashes emitted from between them as sword met sheath. The sound of metal grinding against metal, of clanging weapons, resounded through the air.

Samantha moved left, shuffling to avoid a blow to her face, bringing up her sheath at the same time. She thought she had avoided his attack, but a sharp sting and the feeling of blood trailing down her cheek let her know she was a second too late to react.

"First blood goes to me." Faust smiled again.

Samantha narrowed her eyes.

Deciding to go on the offensive after deflecting another series of strikes, the young woman knelt, shifted her grip on Zaphkiel, then dashed at Faust with speed. She slid her blade out of its sheath and was upon Faust in a flash.

A flurry of strikes were defended against by the faultlessly swift movements of impeccable swordsmanship. Faust managed to block most of the lightning quick strikes. Those he could not block were dodged by swaying his body from one side to the other. His feet shuffled, moving him backwards as Samantha pressed her attack. After exactly five seconds, he struck back.

The first blow crashed against Samantha's sword, causing her arms to move wide. The second attack would have impaled her through the chest, but she proved quick in turning her body sideways and leaning back. She still ended up receiving a cut across her bosoms, but it was a light wound compared to what she could have received.

"Second blood goes to me, too. It looks like you Executioners are not as strong as I thought."

Her lips pursing, Samantha rushed forward and attacked using a more methodical and basic stance. She watched as the man arrogantly batted aside her sword strikes. He looked like he wasn't even paying attention anymore.

Frown deepening, she began paying more attention to Faust's style. There was no doubt in her mind that this man was a master at sword fighting. His way of fighting, the economy of his movements, his ability to adapt to on the fly changes in a person's stance and attack pattern were all flawless.

If this man was indeed Faust, his talent would make sense.

However, while his abilities were undoubtedly exceptional, maybe even superior to her own, his belief in his own inherent superiority were a weakness she could exploit, provided she could give him the right kind of bait.

I can't believe I'm going to be taking a page from Christian's book.

Samantha had no talent at using the *Fake Opening Style* that her former Executioner so coveted. It took a certain mindset, an alien way of thinking, that she just couldn't do. The style itself was a twisted one, designed to knowingly give someone several openings to direct their attacks. Only someone who lacked a sense of self-preservation could ever use a style like that to its full efficiency.

That did not mean she could not at least do something similar.

And so, Samantha presented an opening, one that she could live with getting struck. Faust, as she suspected, took the bait. It was not in his nature to leave an opening like this. He moved forward, batting her sheath aside, then thrusting his Celtic sword forward. It moved fast— too fast for Samantha, who could not use the *Fake Opening Style*—to respond. The blade went through her shoulder, sinking all the way up to the hilt and extending out of her back.

Samantha gasped as she felt the cold chill of the blade contrast with the sharp, white hot agony of skin, muscles, and bone being pierced. A large stain on both her front and back began soaking her shirt red. She could feel blood trailing across her skin, pouring down her back and chest.

Faust was no longer smiling. He was frowning.

"You were more than capable of dodging that."

"True."

"Then why didn't you?"

"Because I needed to do something that would leave you open."

At those words, Faust seemed to finally realize something that he had missed.

He looked down at the elegant guard of Samantha's sword, a series of interweaving black and silver "strings" made of Oricalchum that wrapped around Samantha's hand in a protective embrace. It was the guard of the same sword that had pierced his chest, exactly where his heart should have been. No blood emerged from his chest, no growing stain of vermilion ichor expanded from the wound. However, if one were to look closely into the rip, they would see the skin around the sword dissolving.

"So I see." Faust looked back up at Samantha, who was surprised to see the man smiling at her. "Thank you. Perhaps now I will finally be able to see her again."

As Samantha watched Faust's body dissolve until nothing remained except ashes that were soon blown away by the wind, she found herself wondering who the gaunt man was speaking of. After a moment of consideration, she decided that it really didn't matter. She had defeated him, sending him back to wherever he'd come from. Now she had to help the others push back the force of goblins and trolls.

***

Leon had often been described as simple. Most people who met him thought he lacked intelligence because of his straight-forward personality. His uncomplicated and nearly childish joy for violent combat didn't help.

"Hahaha! What are you all doing? Don't disappoint me now!"

It really didn't help.

While a very devout follower of Christ, Leon had one large problem, and it had nothing to do with his size. He loved combat. The thrill of being caught in a life and death struggle, the adrenaline that raced through his veins when he found himself involved in vicious conflict, when each breath he took could very well be his last. The only time Leon ever felt alive, truly alive, was during battle.

Named after one of the archangels and who was often depicted as being exceedingly tall (During Moses's visit to the Third Heaven, he was said to have glimpsed Sandalphon and called him the "tall angel"), his weapon truly fit him better than anything else could.

He swung his warhammer, Sandalphon, at a goblin, laughing out in a joyous symphony as the creature's bones were turned into mulch from the force of his attack. The goblin went careening into a wall, where it struck so hard and with so much power behind it that the wooden structure splinter, and the goblin, already broken, flew through it and out of sight.

Weaving around him, darting in and out from between her enemies, he could just barely pick out Sif as she methodically killed each goblin in her path. Wherever her speedy form appeared, at least one goblin died, either from their neck or stomach being split open like an overripe fruit, or from their back or skull being penetrated by her clawed weapons. Either way, regardless of the attack used, there could be no denying that Sif was as effective a killer as him.

What an amazing woman, he marveled. Truly, there didn't existed a better person on this good green earth to be his partner.

Something sharp stung the left side of his back. Reaching out with his free hand and grabbing the offending object, Leon tossed what he guessed to be a knife away. He could feel the blood dribbling down his back, warm and wet. Unlike most people, who would have been at least hurt by that point, he simply ignored the wound like it didn't exist and went right back to smashing his enemies.

The sound of gunshots continued to sound out from the stairwell. Leon knew that to mean that Christian still had some fight left in him. Even as he smashed his hammer against another goblin, knocking them for a loop so hard their heads popped off with a splatter of blood, he could see several enemies that were felled from precise shots to the head.

For such a little guy, he sure had a lot of spirit.

A howling to his left sounded out seconds before the werewolf leapt onto one of the goblin's in the rear, tearing out beastie's throat with its sharp teeth. The werewolf howled again, startling those around it, before spitting out the nearly black fluid in its mouth. It probably didn't like the taste of blood.

Leon wasn't quite sure what to think of fighting alongside a werewolf. Wasn't he supposed to kill monsters? Still, Samantha had said they were working together for now, so he guessed it was okay. The werewolf was a good fighter anyway. It'd be a shame to kill him right now.

Another troll lumbered up to Leon, who grinned as the gigantic beast roared at him in challenge. Several of its brethren had already been killed by him. Killing trolls was something of a specialty. His incredible strength and constitution made him ideal for taking down larger monsters like trolls and cyclops.

A pair of fisted hands tried to smash Leon into the ground. Unlike Sif and Christian, who would have dodged the attack, he made no such effort, and instead lifted his warhammer, grunting as the two giant fists struck.

His knees buckled, and the wooden tiles underneath him cracked from the powerful blow. Yet even though his body shook with exertion, Leon held true, and then used his own immense strength to push back.

The troll didn't seem to have expected that kind of resistance because it stumbled backwards when he shoved at it. It also didn't seem to expect an attack from him so soon, because the thing didn't even try to block when Leon thrust the hammer into its face, knocking it for a loop. As the creature stumbled about, dizzy and confused, it's now broken nose bleeding, Leon let out his own challenging shout.

He leapt into the air, raising Sandalphon over his head. He soon brought his weapon down, smashing straight onto the cranium of his foe. He could see the way the skull caved in, bending and crunching where he struck. The troll, its brain crushed under the assault to its noggin, impacted hard enough with the ground to crack it. The thing twitched several times where it lay, but then it stilled.

A glance around the room revealed that to be the last of the trolls. Too bad. He wanted to fight some more. Sif could still be seen darting about, and the werewolf was doing a rather good job of pincering the goblins between him and Leon's partner. Several goblins were felled by bullets, blood shooting out, sort of reminding him of what happens when a rock is thrown into a body of water, or when a kid stomps on a puddle. They fell to the ground, crumbling faster than Jenga blocks when there's only one block on the left to keep the balance and it's on the far-left side. That meant Christian still had some ammo.

The battle began winding down soon. Leon noticed that there weren't many goblins left. Most of them were now corpses. He could see Samantha running in through the exit made by the trolls. Since that gaunt man wasn't with her, he decided to assume she had won. No surprise there. The woman had earned her title of Queen for a reason.

With nothing left to kill and no more enemies to be fought, Leon took a gander around the room. It was littered with bodies and body parts, and blood, what looked like several other fluids, brain matter, and organs.

This place would definitely need to be cleaned before it could be used by anyone else again.

***

A good several hours after the battle was spent disposing of goblin and troll corpses. The goblins were easy. Just find a place well away from any of the lodges, dig a pit, place the bodies in the pit, and then light them on fire before burying the ashes. That was the standard procedure when destroying goblin bodies.

The trolls? Not so much.

Trolls were very large creatures. Even the smallest towered over the largest human by at least three feet. Not to mention their skin was fire retardant. Andrew and Leon had to deal with them, dragging the large carcasses through the woods and toward West Thumb, a smaller inlet that made up a part of Yellowstone Lake. There, they rolled the bodies into the lake, far enough out that the waters became deep and the heavy corpses sank to the bottom.

This entire process took the two of them six hours. They were exhausted by the time they had finished.

Even after the corpses had all be taken care of, they still found that more had to be done. There was the matter of the damage that the lodge had incurred. Jan Hudson needed to be informed of what happened and restitution had to be paid. For that task, Clarissa had chosen herself, as it had been because of her that they were allowed to stay.

Another issue that needed to be resolved was what they should all do now. Each one of them were officially enemies of the Church. This battle had merely reinforced that point.

Faust was a human that had been turned into a demon by Mephisto, becoming the greater demon's right-hand man. Faust had also been in charge of the goblins, or had gained control of them at some point, which meant he'd been going specifically after the succubi, and Lilith and Christian being there had just been a happy coincidence. Samantha and her ilk were enemies of the Church for obvious reasons, and Lilith and Christian were as well. It was therefore agreed upon by all parties, however reluctantly, that they should stick together. At least for now.

"Lilith and I will be going to Old Faithful Snow Lodge and Cabins," Christian determined. "We don't have very much options left to us. Even if Samantha and her people were inclined to protect us, they have neither the strength nor the resources to do so."

Maybe it was an act of selfishness on his part, but Lilith's safety was his top priority.

"And I'll be going with them," Tristin added. When Christian looked at the man with a raised eyebrow, the incubus grinned. "Sorry, but you're not getting rid of me so easily. It was always my intention to hook back up with you when we met again." He pouted, cheeks puffed out in childish anger, arms crossed over his chest. "It took a lot longer than I anticipated, but that's hardly my fault. There was a lot more going on in the background that I didn't know about."

"Fine. You can follow us." Christian was too tired to care. "Just don't slow us down."

"Aye!" Tristin gave his friend a sloppy salute.

"There's really no stopping you, is there?" asked Samantha.

Christian shook his head. "No. Sorry. If there's even the slightest chance that Azazel can offer us protection from the Church, I'm going to take it."

"What if he wants to lure you into a trap? Sell you out to the Church?"

"It's well-known that fallen angels do not get along with demons. The animosity the Grigori feel toward demons from the time they were angels of Heaven is well documented. I think there are even more stories about demons and fallen angels fighting each other than there are angels and demons fighting each other."

"That is true enough." Samantha grimaced before her face hardened. "If you really are going to go through with this, then I suppose we should go with you."

"But I thought you didn't want to have anything to do with that Zazel guy," said Lilith.

"It's Azazel," Christian corrected, making Lilith blush. He looked at Samantha. "I'm curious to know why you've changed your mind so suddenly as well. You're not the type to give in like this."

Samantha's shoulders slumped, a tired sigh escaping her parted lips. "Just like you, we might not have much choice. The Executioners are only fifty strong now, and only ten of those are actually Executioners. The rest worked in either the Science Division or the Intelligence Division."

"Though I'm still the best of the Intelligence Division."

"Can it, Tristin."

"So cruel..."

"We simply don't have the manpower to make a difference anymore. And if the Church ever decided to eradicate us, well, that would be it." Tugging on a lock of raven hair, Samantha suddenly looked more insecure than Christian had ever seen her. "Truth be told, we've been backed into a corner. I don't want to admit it, but everything that's happened so far proves this. We're out of our depth and out of our league. Even if I *had* managed to convince you to join, I think it would have only prolonged the inevitable."

"It may have shortened it," Lilith said. When Samantha frowned, she waved a hand through the air and elucidated. "Christian and I aren't just enemies of the Church. They seem to be hunting us specifically for some reason. If we went back with you, and the Church found out, they would have come in force to kill us and destroy you."

Samantha thought that over, and then slowly nodded. "You may be right."

Christian smiled at Lilith. "You're really good at analyzing a situation, you know that?"

"You think so?" Lilith asked, flushing in exultation at his praise.

"Yes."

"So," Samantha got things back on track. "It looks like we'll be going with you two."

Standing several feet away, Sif shifted, looking uncomfortable. No one really paid her any mind, but Christian did take note of it. That woman really didn't seem to enjoy the idea of being with them. Was it because Lilith was a succubus?

"And what about all of you?" Christian asked Clarissa. "What are your plans?"

"We shall be going with you as well."

Behind the olive-skinned woman, the fifty or so succubi all nodded—at least those that were not still numbed from the day's events did. A lot of the younger ones were standing around with deadened eyes. They must have been in shock.

"Alright then." Christian ran a hand through his hair, parting his bangs. "I guess we'll be sticking together for a while longer."

Lilith turned to look at Catherine and Andrew. "What about you two?"

Catherine and Andrew looked at each other.

"I don't think we can," Catherine spoke for them both. "Andrew and I need to return to the LAPD and let them know what happened. Also, I'm worried about my daughter. She should be at a friend's house, but with everything that's happened, I want to make sure she is safe."

"You two will keep in touch, right?" asked Christian.

"Of course we will," Andrew answered before Catherine could. "With all the crazy stuff going down, demons and hostile take overs of the Catholic Church and whatnot, you can bet we're going to keep in touch."

"I would suggest not telling the LAPD about what's going on," once again, the suggestion came from Lilith. "Or at least, only informing whoever is at the top."

Samantha was the one who asked the question on everyone's mind. "Care to explain your reasons?"

"Because the Catholic Church is huge," Lilith said, shrugging. "They are the largest religious community in the world, and with the Church possibly being taken over by demons. Well..." she shook her head. "Christian told me that they have eyes and ears everywhere, including police forces and the military. If Catherine and Andrew let the LAPD know what happened here, the Church would probably find out as well."

"You make a good point." Catherine blew out a low breath and rubbed her jaw. "Very well. We'll only tell commissioner Flacher. He's an atheist through and through, so I doubt he has any ties to the Church."

"Good." Lilith nodded, satisfied.

"Do you have a way for us to reach you?" asked Clarissa.

Catherine cocked her head to the side, then nodded. "Yes. I'll give you my cell and home number, since it'll reach me personally and not someone else. Call my cell first. If I don't answer, call my home number."

She searched around for a sheet of paper and something to write on, and then quickly scribbled down her contact information before handing it to Christian.

"Well, I guess this is it, then." Christian looked at the mass of faces gathered around him. There were a lot of them. Most of them young women in their teens. He felt a slight pang as he realized these girls were alive thanks to the sacrifice of the older succubus. "We'll travel to Old Faithful Snow Lodge and Cabins and meet with Azazel to see what he wants."

"Hey, do you think we should come up with a name for our group?" asked Lilith.

Christian gave her a look. "Why would we do that?"

Lilith shrugged, not deigning to look him in the eyes, her face flushed. "All the groups in books and light novels name their group."

Christian palmed his face, but that was more to hide his smile. "I suppose we could."

"Not another one." Samantha scowled. "We're not some kind of anime fellowship here. This is real life, you know."

"I know that." Lilith, though embarrassed, still managed to give a rather cute pout. "I just think it would be appropriate."

"And what would we call ourselves?" asked Christian.

Tristin, unable to contained himself, said, "how about the Jiggling Jugs and Dangling Dicks?"

"NO!"

That day, everyone learned a valuable lesson. Never ever let Tristin name anything. He sucked at it.

Afterword

Hey, everyone. It's Brandon, and I've finally been able to release the third book of The Executioner Series… which ends on another cliffhanger.

Fuck.

I think it is safe to say that I'm not a very good urban fantasy novelist. The Executioner Series was inspired by Jim Butcher's series, the Dresden Files. I know. I know. Brandon, this series is nothing like the Dresden Files! Where is your snarky wizard PI living in Chicago?! Where's your cheerleader police officer? Where your sexy investigative reporer?! Where's that perverted creature living inside a skull?! Yeah, I don't have any of those.

When I say this series was inspired by the Dresden Files, what I mean is that after reading the entire Dresden Files series (as in all the books that were available at the time I began writing The Executioner Series), I was inspired to try my hand at writing something that was purely western urban fantasy. Not western as in "wild west" western, but western as in "not littered with anime tropes" western. Again, I don't think I succeeded in this regard. I mean, let's be honest: even though I tried my best not to make this story seem like an anime in book format, it is still littered with anime tropes. About the only thing that isn't anime is my protagonist who, unlike those poor losers in harem anime, isn't getting cockblocked or cockblocking himself.

There were a lot of problems I stumbled across when writing this series. The first was, of course, trying to stay away from anime tropes. I found so many littering my page that I think I just gave up on getting rid of them at some point. However, the other problem came in the form of a monetary one.

I am pretty sure I've mentioned it in other Afterwords, but it costs money to publish a book. Granted, I could write a book, make my own cover, not hire a copy editor, and publish this on Amazon Kindle and it won't cost a dime, but that is the recipe for a crappy book. If you want to make a high-quality book, something that is actually worth publishing, then you need to hire an artist (or book cover designer), a copy editor, and at least one proofreader. The general cost to publish a book that is worth publishing is about $3,000 to $5,000.

As a self-published author, I don't make much money. Right now I'm making enough to pay my bills, buy food, and have my next book published, but I'm not making enough that I could afford to publish more than 7 books a year. I currently have four different series that I'm publishing: A Most Unlikely Hero, American Kitsune, Arcadia's Ignoble Knight, and The Executioner Series. Of the four, The Executioner Series is not only the least popular (which also means it makes the least amount of money), it is also the one I have the hardest time writing. Because of this, I decided to forego publishing this one twice a year in favor of my other series.

It's sad, but as much as I don't want to, I have to treat my writing like a business… because that's basically what this is. My livelihood comes from my writing. Unfortunately, things like people illegally downloading copies of my books, my books not being mass marketable (I write for a niche market), and a lot of other issues means I'm just not making enough to cover the cost of another book.

Fortunately, that was last year.

At the moment, I'm actually doing pretty decently, which is why despite this crappy cliffhanger ending, I do have some good news.

The Executioner IV will be published early next year. I'm not sure when, but I'm hoping to publish it either in February or March 2019, so you all won't have to wait that long for the final book of this series to come out.

Anyway, that is all for this afterword. I apologize for making it so heavy. I think this was something I've been keeping in for quite a while. I hope I didn't scare you all too much. Before I go, I would like to thank my artist, Lawrence Mann, for making my cover art. I'm a little sad that my writing can't hold up to his awesome covers. I also want to thank my editor, Dominique Goodall, for fixing the little mistakes that I just can't seem to catch during my self-edits. Finally, I would like to thank you readers for buying my books, putting up with my cliff hangers, and reading my depressing ass afterwords. It means a lot to me.

I hope to see you all in the final volume of The Executioners Series!

~Brandon Varnell

P.S. if anyone would like to support me more than you do now, I officially have a Patreon that I'm using to try and hopefully fund some of my publishing expenses. https://www.patreon.com/BrandonVarnell

All Alex wanted was to
become a hero…

Instead, he picked up a harem
of beautiful women!

Follow Caspian's Journey to become a Sorceress's Knight in Arcadia's Ignoble Knight vol. 1-3!

He was their best Executioner